About the Author

Teresa F. Morgan lives in sunny Weston-super-Mare, trying to hold onto her Surrey accent where she originates from. For years she persevered with boring jobs, until her two boys (and a budgie called Rio) joined her nest. In an attempt to find something that would work around them, and to ensure she never endured full time boredom again, Teresa found writing.

Family holidays in Cornwall, the scenic Cornish coastline and the city of Bristol have influenced Teresa's novels.

She's at her happiest baking cakes, putting proper home cooked dinners on the table (whether the kids eat them or not), reading a good romance, and sitting at her PC emptying her thoughts onto the screen.

Teresa loves writing contemporary romance, stories with a touch of escapism and creating heroes readers will fall in love with.

🐦 @Teresa_Morgan10
📘 https://www.facebook.com/teresafmorgan12/
http://www.teresamorgan.co.uk/

Also by Teresa F. Morgan

Plus One is a Lucky Number
One Fine Day

TERESA F. MORGAN

Meet Me at Wisteria Cottage

A division of HarperCollins *Publishers*
www.harpercollins.co.uk

Harper*Impulse* an imprint of
HarperCollins*Publishers*
The News Building
1 London Bridge Street
London SE1 9GF

www.harpercollins.co.uk

A Paperback Original 2017
2

A catalogue record for this book
is available from the British Library

ISBN: 9780008225346

Typeset in Birka by Palimpsest Book Production Ltd, Falkirk, Stirlingshire

Printed and bound in Great Britain by
Clays Ltd, St Ives plc

MIX
Paper from
responsible sources
FSC˚ C007454

For my dad, my real life hero

Chapter 1

Maddison Hart threw her bag on the passenger seat, turned the key in the ignition and, checking the pavement was clear, reversed off the driveway. A bad memory reminded her to glance in her wing mirror just in time. She was about to hit her neighbour's pickup truck on the opposite side of the road – again. She slammed the brakes and cursed. She'd only just had her damn brake light fixed.

'Bloody idiot,' she said, screwing up her face.

Why did he park it there, on the road, and not on his driveway? It was big enough!

He always seemed to be parked there when she wanted to reverse off her drive, too! *Damn the man.*

Her neighbour, wearing only a pair of knee-length khaki shorts, and busy putting some tools into the back of the black pickup, smirked.

Oh, crap, he'd heard her too, with her window partially down. Sod it, he'd been living here three months, and now it was getting annoying. She pressed the button, and lowered her window further. She would not be intimidated by his bare chest and muscles.

'Mr . . .' she glanced at the stickers reading 'Tudor Landscapes' along the truck's side, 'Mr Tudor,' she said more assertively, 'could you not park your truck right there?'

'It's Harry.'

'Okay, *Harry*,' she sniped, 'could you please not park your truck right there.' Everything about him, his whole demeanour, infuriated Maddy.

'Why?'

'I nearly hit it – again!'

'What do you mean *again*?' He glanced at the truck, rubbing his hand along the paintwork.

'I said nearly.' She lied. Last time she had clonked it, but it had done more damage to her car than his.

'It's easy, look in your mirrors as you reverse off your drive, lady.'

Maddy took a deep breath, her teeth clamped together and she dramatically swished her strawberry blonde hair off her shoulders before choosing her next words. 'It's awkward whether I look in my mirrors or not.'

'Drive slower then.'

Maddy refrained from growling with frustration, instead she gripped the steering wheel tighter. The man was obviously too arrogant to listen. 'It doesn't matter how fast I go. I'm used to reversing off my drive, hassle free. The people

2

who lived in the house before you never parked on the road. They used their *driveway*.'

'Then reverse onto your drive, so you can see what you're doing when you leave, if it's so difficult.'

'It's not easy to reverse onto my drive either, with your monstrosity of a truck in the road.' The road was too narrow, as it only led to a handful of houses.

'Maybe you should own a smaller car if you can't handle it.'

Deep breath, Maddy. One, two, three . . . She did not like his smug expression, and wished he wasn't six feet tall and built like a marine, standing there baring his tanned torso, because she wanted to wipe that smirk off his face. *Bastard.* She hated smug bastards.

'Are you implying I can't drive?' Her eyes narrowed. She drove an estate car so that her paintings fitted in the back. A smaller vehicle was not suitable – she'd tried it. However much she'd loved her Mini Cooper S in racing green, it had not been practical.

'I can't see why it's so hard, but I'll tell you what, I'll stop leaving my truck here when you stop your damn cat from crapping in my front garden.'

'My cat has a litter tray.'

'Well, the thing isn't using it!' He slammed the remainder of the tools he held into the flatbed, and headed back up to his garage, cursing about cats.

How had this conversation gone from cars to cats? *Idiot.*

'You're such an arsehole!'

'I'll take that as a compliment!' he called over his back, without turning round.

Maddy swore again, and forced the car into gear, crunching it with anger. 'There is more than one cat in this close, you know!' she shouted and sped off. Well, tried to. Her wheels spun with her quick release of the clutch and a bit too much throttle. And then her front tyre hit the kerb with the lack of turning space, making a rubber-scraping-concrete sound, angering Maddy further.

She loved her cat. Sookie was very affectionate, and Maddy liked how her little companion purred and greeted her when she got home. Her cat's love was the only sort she got lately.

And it was enough. All she needed.

Harry was obnoxious and fancied himself. It seemed to her there wasn't an affectionate bone in his body. If there was, it was probably buried under his bulk of muscle. Too cocksure, the way he flaunted himself – shirtless or with too tight a T-shirt. She hated men like that.

Bastard.

Look what the man did to her. She hadn't stopped cursing since leaving her house. She felt red with rage, and probably looked it too. She feared it wouldn't be the last time she'd have heated words with Harry.

Her thoughts whirred, mainly about the old man from across the road dying a few months after she'd moved in, and his elderly wife being put in a home by their children, and selling up. The house had been empty for nearly six months. She'd got into the habit of not really having to concentrate while manoeuvring her car off her own driveway. The old couple opposite had owned a vehicle but it had remained in the garage, the man being too ill to drive it.

She'd liked them as neighbours.

Now she had to put up with Harry and his monstrosity.

***

Harry slammed down his garage door. *What was it about that woman?*

Returning to his truck, he checked it over carefully, sure his neighbour, in her complete incompetence, had probably hit it before. He'd seen the lie in her eyes, the way she'd been unable to look at him, and more obviously, avoiding glancing at his chrome bumper.

He couldn't see any marks, so maybe her car had come off worse. Well, serve her right. He paid his road tax, his pickup had as much right to be on this street as did her Ford estate.

A few deep breaths and he got into the cab of the truck. He was quoting for a new landscaping job today, and he didn't want to be late. It was a big contract in Tinners Bay, an ex-holiday home in disrepair and the garden in similar state. With rain due later this afternoon the sooner he got started the better, but that woman had him so rattled he wondered if he needed to go back to the docs to check his meds.

Actually, let's face it, he hadn't got angry, more like sarcastic. Maybe his meds were working. Although frustrated, he felt positive – his whole world wasn't closing in on him anymore. Even the nightmares had lessened. Karin played less on his mind. He'd get to work and feel better. Gardening was his new vice. You couldn't stress about gardening really, unless you had a lawn to cut and rain was imminent, and even then it wasn't a matter of life or death. Unlike his old job.

To turn the truck, he reversed up his drive. As he was about to pull out, he noticed his neighbour's front lawn needed cutting, and the bushes pruning . . . *Even her blasted garden infuriates me*. And there sat her black cat in the front window. Ha! His neighbour was probably a witch. Did she have green eyes? She certainly had the red hair . . . well, strawberry blonde his mother would call it. He narrowed his eyes at the cat. The thing was probably twiddling a whisker like some Doctor Evil, waiting for him to leave, so it could crap all over his front garden.

Being a landscape gardener, Harry took pride in his own garden – obviously. How else could he prove he was good at what he did? His own garden may be small but he made sure it showcased that he was good at his job. His intention was to build his business, then he could buy a larger property.

That was the good thing about places like Padstow and Tinners Bay: there were plenty of holiday homes and second homes needing regular garden maintenance. Perfect for a landscape gardener starting up – he'd picked up quite a few contracts, and hopefully he'd pick up this one he was attending today.

Damn cats were the bane of his life. Even in the fire service, the amount of stupid cats he'd had to rescue stuck up a tree, or in some tight gap. He understood the saying curiosity killed the cat more than ever now. He would have been more than happy to release a well-aimed jet of water to get cats out of trees, but with an adoring owner watching you had to handle these matters with a lot more care.

Though, rescuing cats were the easy jobs . . . a calm before a storm. Others were much harder . . .

Harry gave himself a mental shake, bringing himself back to the present, and drove out of Annadale Close. His new home. His fresh start.

His neighbour would have to put up with his truck, if he was to put up with her annoying cat.

***

Maddy huffed and puffed, slamming the gallery door shut. Leaving her house in such an anxious state, she'd nearly had an accident at a roundabout, then followed a bloody camper van going at what felt like two miles an hour for most of the journey down the narrow country lanes to Tinners Bay, flaring her temper and impatience further. *Sometimes, there was a downside to living in rural Cornwall.*

'What has got you in such a tizz?' Valerie said, appearing from the back of the gallery with a steaming mug of coffee. 'This is not a good start to your Wednesday.' Valerie was Maddy's colleague and surrogate aunt. She was always smartly dressed, today wearing a powder blue trouser-suit and cream blouse, smelled of Chanel No 5 perfume and wore her light-blonde hair in a fashionably short bob. Valerie had always been a friend of the family. Growing up, Maddy had known her as Auntie Val, and she could tell her things in confidence she couldn't tell her own mother. When Valerie had moved to Tinners Bay with her new husband some years ago now, it had meant family holidays in Cornwall, which had developed Maddy's love for the area.

Maddy gratefully took the cup and hugged it for comfort. 'Oh, my bloody neighbour again. I nearly hit his truck. He's got the sheer nerve to question my driving.'

'Ah, yes, men.' Valerie chuckled. 'I assume you're talking about the one built like a brick—'

'Yes! That's him.' Maddy scowled.

'How dare he strut about showing off his tanned, taut body,' Valerie said, sarcastically, mischief and an air of envy in her eye. 'I assume that's what he's been doing again?'

'Yes, he had his shirt off! And at this time of the morning, too.'

'It is the summer. It's not a crime, Maddy,' Valerie said, chuckling. 'I wish I had a young hot neighbour I could drool over.'

'Not funny, Val.' Any other time, Maddy would have joined in and laughed with Valerie, but nothing could snap her out of her mood. Once Maddy got riled, it took a while for her rational thinking to return. 'He's vain and arrogant. He's the worst bloody type. He's been annoying the shit out of me for nearly three months, and today I had it out with him.' She regretted she hadn't said more now, and got the whole lot off her chest.

'Okay, calm down.' Valerie rested a reassuring hand on Maddy's shoulder. 'Talking about arrogance and vanity, have you heard any more from that ex of yours?'

Valerie's grimace showed she couldn't even bring herself to say his name. She never failed to express her disgust at how Connor had treated Maddy. Valerie had given Maddy the strength to leave him, too.

Maddy gently shook her head. 'No, I think he's got the message I don't want him back in my life.'

For a couple of weeks now her phone had remained silent. No texts, no calls – not that she'd reply if he did. He'd said he was returning to Bristol. *Thank goodness.*

'Good. The rage you're in I thought it was him who'd caused it, but the less we hear about that man, the better. It's about time he got the message and left you alone.' Valerie's expression softened. 'Now, go and set yourself up at your easel for a couple of hours. That always puts you in a better frame of mind.'

Maddy nodded, then twisted up her hair into a messy bun. She'd come in her not so posh clothes today, opting for old three-quarter length jeans and a short-sleeved floral shirt already with acrylic paint marking it. The clothes were clean on, but you could never get the paint out once dried. Some days she sat at her easel working on a commission, or something just for her. She'd set up an area in her gallery so that people could come in and watch her paint. Funnily enough, this had been one of Connor's good ideas. She found it helped sell paintings and got more commissions because it made her approachable to the customers.

Maddy loved painting landscapes and seascapes, and would often disappear to different parts of Cornwall, and sometimes even North Devon, for inspiration. But most of her commissions were houses, something she'd started specialising in when living in Bristol and working from her mother's gallery in Clifton. She painted for those with cute cottages or beautiful thatched houses, wanting their homes transferred eternally on to canvas. Luckily, gorgeous houses were in abundance in Cornwall. She also did pets. However, she was at her happiest painting landscapes because she could add her own imaginative touches to those. It didn't matter if she omitted a tree or added some flowers, whereas houses and pets you had to get right. Currently, she was working on a seascape which she'd started a few weeks ago, trying to escape her thoughts of Connor. She loved creating the energy of crashing waves, of white surf and its swirling movement – a great mood improver.

'While it's quiet, I might go upstairs for a bit,' Valerie said. She couldn't work in public like Maddy did. She liked to tuck herself away somewhere quiet, so she usually worked upstairs above the gallery. The space was smaller, but there was a window that gave enough natural light. She worked in the room where they stored all the extra paintings, ready to go up when another sold, or commissions to be collected. Valerie and Maddy worked so well together, able to give each other advice. They knew each other well enough not to get offended by any constructive criticism. 'When is Josie in next?' Valerie called down the stairs.

'Tomorrow morning,' Maddy replied. She'd employed Josie part-time, so Maddy and Valerie weren't always stuck at the gallery – they needed a life too. But with the holiday season rapidly approaching, the gallery had to be open seven days a week. Josie worked her shifts around her college work and covered the weekends. In the summer holidays, she upped her hours further.

Maddy's gallery exhibited a mixture of paintings from local artists – Josie being one of them. She did the same deal for them all; they were responsible for framing their work if necessary and she took thirty percent commission on anything sold. Some worked in pastel, some watercolours, oils, and like Maddy, acrylics. She even had a local photographer who sold his photographs in her gallery too. Maddy usually relied on Valerie's expertise to help price the work. Tinners Bay attracted a mix of holidaymakers – some from wealthy areas of London, and some average families – so it was about setting the price right. Or having a good selection of affordable pieces and some more exclusive work.

This was to be her first full summer in Cornwall, and she needed to make it work. Setting up the gallery last year, coupled with the purchase of her new house, had eaten up all the funds she'd inherited from her grandfather, so now she really needed to pull in the money to survive. She did not want to return to her mother in Clifton with her tail between her legs.

Plus, Connor had returned to Bristol. And the further she stayed away from him, the better.

***

Maddy turned the key in the lock to the gallery, checked the handle to make sure she had actually locked the door, then slipped the key into her handbag. She looked up at the signage 'Captured by Hart' with a heart diagonally resting at the end and smiled. Her gallery.

Being holiday season, they tended to shut the gallery around seven p.m. but the rain that had come in a couple of hours ago had cleared the beach, so they were shutting slightly earlier tonight. The kids hadn't broken up from school yet so the tourists were families with very young children, making the most of a cheaper holiday. She looked out over the horizon. Now the clouds had dispersed, the clear blue sky showed the sun descending over the Atlantic. With the tide right out, it revealed a vast expanse of golden sand and she could just make out black dots of hardcore surfers amongst the white horses of the waves. Being late June, the weather was being very kind and hot. She could see there were even a couple of bathers still in the water. *Mad buggers. It's still bloody cold. Wouldn't catch me in there without a wetsuit.*

'Same time tomorrow,' Valerie said, kissing Maddy on the cheek.

'I'll be in a bit later, but Josie will be here. I want to work on my painting, the one for a commission. Might even make the most of the light evening and do some tonight.'

'Well, I'd best let you get off then, dear.'

'Would you like a lift?'

'No, no the walk always does me good.' Valerie lived locally. 'I'll probably be expected to cook for the rabble when I get home.' Valerie had three sons, who had all moved out, but would still call in for their mum's cooking. She waved and headed up the hill towards her home, in the direction of where Tinners Bay Hotel was visible in the distance, resembling a five-star cruise liner shipwrecked in the landscape. The prestigious hotel even had some of Maddy's paintings on display. She got the odd sale from there, which helped her cash flow.

Maddy strolled round to the back of the gallery to where she'd parked her car, feeling much happier than when she'd arrived this morning, her thoughts swirling about how well the gallery had done today, with a couple more commissions taken. Valerie always helped put her head straight too. Washing away the negatives and replacing them with positives. 'Everything has a positive, if you look hard enough,' was Valerie's catchphrase. Maddy smiled to herself, thinking about Valerie. She was a woman of experience: never judged, always cared, and they always had a very good laugh about things, even the serious stuff.

Maddy had managed a couple of hours painting today, taking away her stress. She found every brush stroke therapeutic. Although the rent was high, she felt so lucky to have a gallery opposite the beach where she could watch the ocean come in and out, surfers riding the waves, and families pitching camp on the beach for the day. Sand castles, ice cream and Cornish pasties, all added to her inspiration for her pictures.

Yes, she was blessed, and she would make this work. Although things had been messy with Connor, her life was finally back on track. Being single again wasn't all bad.

Maddy lived inland; a twenty-five minute drive through narrow country lanes if she didn't come across any tractors or cars towing caravans – *or slow moving camper vans*. As

14

she pulled into Annadale Close, she imagined what she needed to pull from the fridge to make her dinner. *Chicken, salad . . . a bit of Caesar dressing . . . oh, with a glass of Pinot Grigio.* Turning the corner, she noticed blue flashing lights, reflecting off neighbouring houses. Then she became aware of the smell of something burning. The kind of smell that clung to the hairs in your nose and made your eyes water.

Carrying on, as she turned around the corner towards her home, two red fire engines, monstrous in size up close, blocked the road. It was sheer chaos with yellow hose pipes, firefighters and neighbours standing back to watch. Black smoke bellowed against the clear pink-blue sky ruining a good summer evening's sunset.

Cold fear entered her belly. *It's not . . . It can't be . . .*

Maddy screamed, and in seconds, her car door flung open, she was out of her car and running towards her burning house.

'Oh my God, oh my God,' Maddy cried hysterically. 'Put it out! Put it out!' She accosted a firefighter. 'Do something. That's my house!'

Chapter 2

As if a switch had been flicked inside her, Maddy lost all control. Anger, fear and hysteria replaced her usually composed personality. Rationality had gone up in smoke, like her house.

HER HOUSE.

Maddy swore every expletive under the sun. Where had she put her paintings? Were they in the house, or garage? Would she have any possessions left? As thoughts whirred around her head erratically, she fought to get past the firefighters, because none of them were working fast enough to put the fire out. NONE OF THEM. Black smoke billowed out of the back of her house and from her kitchen window.

'Will someone get her out of here!' a firefighter called.

'Miss, you need to get back,' another shouted. 'We've got it under control.'

'But that's my house!' Tears streamed down her face. Her voice was sore from shouting, but still she screamed. This could not be happening. *Why her house? Why?*

'Roses, old friend, give us a hand, mate. Get her out of here.'

Despite her vision being blurred by tears, Maddy went to make another run towards her burning home, filled with an indescribable fury. Suddenly, her feet no longer touched the ground as she was lifted up and flung over the shoulder of a tall, muscular man.

Being thrown into this firefighter's carry enraged her further. She kicked and punched. 'Put me down. Put me down, you bastard.' But he was strong, holding her in such a way she couldn't break free. Her hip dug into his shoulder, but her fury relished the pain.

'I'll put you down when you stop fighting,' the man said sternly.

She tried lifting her head, but all she could see was the carnage of her house surrounded by firefighters and red trucks. She cried and cried helplessly.

The door closed behind her and the man put her down on her feet. She glared up into bright blue eyes. He folded his arms and stared back. She recognised the burly man with his black hair and his stern unforgiving expression.

Harry.

The sight of him stoked Maddy's fury further.

'Let me back out there!' As she wiped her tears, she tried to barge Harry out of the way, but he stopped her firmly, both palms pushing on her shoulders.

'You're not helping the situation. Let the fire brigade do

their job. They'll get it done quicker without a hysterical woman getting in their way.' Harry stood his ground, placing his hands on his hips. 'In all my days, I've never seen anything like it.'

Maddy glared fiercely at Harry. He glared back, blue eyes like ice.

'Calm down,' he said sternly, still not budging from his post.

Maddy sucked in gulps of air, her chest heaving as slowly she calmed down. What with everything that had happened lately, this was the final straw. And she'd had such a good day at the gallery too. She should have known it wouldn't last. Why couldn't she be happy and stay happy?

'I'm sorry,' she said hoarsely, a thirst for water hitting her throat. She tried generating some moisture in her mouth by swallowing.

'They were here within ten minutes, so hopefully there won't be much damage.'

'How long have they been here?'

'Not long, they'd just arrived and gone through your back door by the time you arrived. Now do you want some tea? Or something stronger?'

Maddy shook her head. She was standing in her neighbour's house. The arrogant man she'd only this morning had a row with about his pickup truck. She didn't know what she wanted.

'Oh, hell, I left my car in the middle of the road. My

handbag is in it too.' She started shaking, another form of panic racing through her. All she needed was her car and handbag to be stolen. These things came in threes. Her handbag contained her phone, Tablet and her purse.

'I'll go and move it, and get your bag,' Harry said, then instructed more sternly, 'Stay here, please.' Blue eyes narrowed on her, and she nodded.

Maddy watched him leave, locking his front door and taking the key. He *so* didn't trust her. She tested it too, and found she couldn't get out. *Bastard*. She was using that word a lot today. *And about him.* Helpless, she stared out of the window watching the firefighters put out the fire. It looked like they had it contained now. As Harry had said, they were round the back of the house. They'd entered via the back door, into the kitchen. What would the damage be like? Would everything smell of smoke? What had caught fire?

She tried hard to think back to the morning. Had she left something on in the kitchen? Could a kettle catch fire? She'd heard of washing machines and tumble dryers being the cause of fires, but hers were in the garage. And had she moved her paintings to the garage? She felt certain she had, but couldn't remember actually doing it. Her memory was coming up blank. She was supposed to be delivering the paintings this weekend. And tomorrow she'd wanted to start on a new commission – fat chance of that happening now.

Five minutes later, Harry returned with the keys to her car and her handbag.

'Do you want to make a phone call to someone?'

She shook her head. She needed to calm down first. Valerie was her first thought. She'd need her to man the gallery tomorrow. Maddy couldn't even contemplate the mess she would need to deal with tomorrow morning. Phoning her mother was not an option either. She didn't need her racing here.

There wasn't anyone else she knew to call. Since moving to Cornwall a year ago, she had only made few friends and she didn't know them well enough to impose. Her time had been spent building her art business. Unsociable hours painting or manning the gallery. Her closest friend here was Valerie.

She checked her handbag for its contents – *all present and correct, phew!* How stupid to leave them in the car unlocked. Cornwall didn't exactly have a high crime rate, however there was always the chance of an opportunist.

'I've just realised I don't even know your name.' Harry stood facing Maddy, hands on his hips. Large hands too, totally in proportion with the rest of him. She'd never stood this close to him and appreciated his full size. If he wanted to be intimidating, he could be, but at the moment, she could see he was trying to help her. A small voice whispered inside her head. *You're safe.*

'It's Maddison, but everyone calls me Maddy,' she said, her breath hitching occasionally, like a small child who'd been crying too much.

'Harry.' He held out his hand, so formally, Maddy shook it.

'Yes, I know, you told me this morning.'

'Ah, yes, I did, didn't I?' A hint of a smile softened his expression. 'Right, I think you need a drink. Will vodka do, or whiskey? I don't have any wine. And I avoid gin like the plague.' Maddy followed Harry into his small kitchen. His house layout was identical to hers. But his kitchen was old pine units, whereas she'd had white melamine. There would be three bedrooms above and a bathroom. 'Or I may have some rum.' he said, opening an overhead cupboard.

'Vodka, please. Do you have anything to mix with it?' However much she wanted to numb her brain, she'd need to be able to concentrate tomorrow morning.

'I have orange juice,' Harry said, pulling a carton from the fridge.

'Perfect.'

'And don't worry; you can kip here for the night.'

'Thank you.' Her voice was softer now, almost a whisper. Her throat hurt and she didn't have the energy to speak. A numbing shock was taking over her now. She didn't care where she slept tonight. She doubted she'd actually sleep. Should she stay here though, or call Valerie? She didn't know the man who stood before her, only this morning they'd been at loggerheads with each other. His truck, her cat.

'Oh, God.' Maddy's drink sloshed in the glass as she moved suddenly. 'Sookie.'

'Who's Sookie?' Harry was sipping a darker liquid, whiskey she presumed. She hadn't noticed him pour himself one.

'My cat!'

Harry rolled his eyes. 'It'll be all right.'

'What if she didn't get out of the house? What if she tries to get back in? She must be hungry now.' Anxiety crept up Maddy's back, stiffening her shoulders, but she tried to keep her hysterics in check. Did she have any more tears left to cry? 'I should go and find her.' She placed her glass on the counter, and as she moved, Harry held out his hand to stop her, blocking her way.

'Wait!' He clearly didn't want her leaving the house. 'Do you have a cat flap?'

'Yes.'

'Well, hopefully she got out.'

'But it's in the kitchen! Oh, god, what will she do now? I usually keep her in at night.'

'Shouldn't cats be out at night?'

This time Maddy rolled her eyes. 'Everyone assumes this, but actually they're more likely to get run over at night.'

'Annadale Close is hardly the A30.'

'And they do more damage to wildlife. Maybe I should go and look for her. She'll be hungry.'

'You are staying right here.' His eyes glared, matching his

firm tone. 'I'll go and look for her. And while I'm there I'll have a chat to the fire brigade, to assess the damage to your house.'

'She's completely black, with one white paw.'

'I know what she looks like.' Harry sounded irked. He didn't need to keep Maddy locked in his house, she was calmer now. The hysteria had ebbed away. Though she wanted to cry she was now holding it in around Harry. And the vodka was helping; he'd poured a very large measure.

***

Harry locked Maddy in his house again, and went in search of her cat. He scratched his head, and rolled his shoulders, trying to relieve some of the tension out of his body. How had he managed to get involved with her problems?

When he'd swept his neighbour off her feet, into a fireman's carry, he really hadn't thought things through. Maddy, now he knew her name, was not what he needed in his life. He wanted simplicity, quiet, solitude. Not a hysterical woman. Or house fires! Now he'd offered her a room for the night. *It only has to be one night.* What had he been thinking? For a start, he didn't have a spare bed. *Looks like you're on the sofa tonight, mate.*

The look in his former colleague's eyes, telling Harry to get the crazed woman out of the area and to let them work, had kicked his old firefighter instinct in. To help and protect, and calm the situation, that's what led Harry to react the way he did – the only way he knew how. Grabbing her arms, and hoisting her, full firefighter carry, over his shoulder and into his house. It was almost prehistoric. It would have been if he'd hit her over the head with his club first. If he'd had one of course.

Probably would have helped actually. She'd turned even more enraged by his actions. Kicking, screaming. Luckily he had the strength to hold her small frame though he probably was going to have a few bruises for his trouble. Fierce green eyes had glared at him when he'd set her down. *Yep, definitely a witch.*

Now he was looking for her damn cat. Could his evening get any worse? *Oh, the irony.* The thing is, he'd seen the cat in the house when he'd left this morning. He hadn't wanted to tell Maddy that piece of information. Had the thing had the sense to leave the house before the blaze caught? Cats had a sixth sense, didn't they? Or was it just nine lives? However much he disliked cats, he hoped it was alive, and he would find it, because Maddy had been through enough tonight.

With the smell of smoke still in the air, and firemen clearing up, reeling in the hoses, Harry could see the black scar of fire around Maddy's kitchen window where the smoke had escaped. Some neighbours still milled around watching what was going on. Luckily, the small window at the top must have been left fractionally open on the safety latch. It had allowed the smoke to escape which had meant the fire was quickly detected, otherwise it might have gone on for longer without anyone realising. Guilt ate away at him. This was shit for Maddy. He'd seen the devastation over the years of people's livelihoods and family possessions destroyed, never to be replaced. You couldn't replace photos and memorabilia. He'd been the one to spot the fire and had called the emergency services. It looked like the kitchen had taken the worst of it, yet he feared her whole house would stink of smoke, and there would be a black layer of soot in places you wouldn't dream of. Despite their differences, he knew he couldn't have watched what was happening to Maddy from the sidelines and done nothing. What were neighbours for?

And at least nobody had got hurt . . . unlike Karin . . .

Don't think about her now. He shook his head, unclenching his fists, shrugging off his dark thoughts.

'Hey, Collins, what's the damage?' Harry called out to the fire officer in charge, jogging over to him. He wore a white helmet, while his colleagues wore yellow ones. His first name was Phil, but the guys of blue watch had nicknamed him Collins after the singer. He'd been caught singing in the kitchen while cooking for the watch one time and it had stuck.

'Roses, good fellow.' The two shook hands. 'How are you doing? It's good to see you.'

'I'm good, thanks. Enjoying the landscape gardening.'

'We were all sorry to see you go,' Collins said. 'But hey, you've got to do what's right for you, huh?' Harry smiled his agreement. 'Did you get the damsel out of distress?'

'Yeah, she's a bit shook up but she's safe in my house.'

Collins chuckled. 'It's not like we haven't seen it before. Anyway, the boys are surveying the damage and securing her back door and kitchen window. Tomorrow a team will be back to put our report together – you know the routine.' Harry nodded. 'But it looks like one for the police.'

'Okay,' Harry replied, frowning. Did he tell Collins what he'd seen? Would it get Maddy into trouble?

'Did you see anything suspicious?' Collins asked, as if reading Harry's mind.

'How do you mean?' *See what Collins had to say first.*

'I'm not supposed to say anything,' Collins lowered his voice, 'but it looks like it could have been arson. We could smell the mild scent of an accelerant. Do you think she . . .?'

Harry shook his head. 'No, no, she didn't do this. She's stressed about her paintings and her cat and all sorts. You saw how hysterical she was. Did you manage to contain the fire?'

'Yes, most of the damage is in the kitchen. Good job we got the call as early as we did,' Collins said. 'Otherwise it might have been a different story.'

'I made the call. I saw the smoke coming out of the gap in her kitchen window. In fact, I smelled it first.' As quick as a Beagle could pick up a scent, Harry would always smell smoke at the slightest whiff. 'Unfortunately I couldn't get in, otherwise I'd have tried to stop it from spreading.'

Collins nodded. 'You did good calling when you did. Please don't enter the house until the fire investigation officer has been. I suspect the police will leave someone outside all night to guard it as CSI won't come till the morning now.' Harry nodded back; he knew the procedure. 'We'll secure the back door for now the best we can, and tomorrow we'll get it boarded up, so the house is secure. Has she got somewhere to stay the night?'

'Yeah, I've offered to let her stay at mine.'

'Always the hero.' Collins slapped Harry on the back.

Harry gave a fake laugh. *What had he got himself into?* 'By the way, you haven't seen a cat have you – dead or alive?'

Collins chuckled. 'A black one?'

'Well it will look black if it's burnt to death.'

'Oh, it's not dead.' Collins pointed to a tree in Maddy's neighbouring garden to the right. A small tree, but big enough to provide refuge for a cat. Sookie's eyes reflected the light from the fire engines, making it easier for her to be spotted in the dimming light.

'Ah, yes, thanks.' Harry shook hands with Collins then walked over to the tree. Tiptoeing, Harry reached up and grabbed the cat out of the tree while it hissed at him.

'Hey, I'm not happy about this either, girl.' She stank of smoke, reminding him of the smell of soot. 'Sweep would be a good name for you right now . . . or as you're a girl, maybe Sue.' She hissed and struggled, and when Harry held her more firmly, dug her claws into his arm. Resisting the urge to release the cat – or drop her – he rushed back to his house, one-handedly unlocking his front door, and as soon as he closed it, released the cat as she gave another hiss. Frowning, he rubbed the scratches along his forearms.

'Sookie!' Maddy picked up the cat, stroking her between the ears. The cat purred and rubbed its head against Maddy, its mood changing immediately. 'Where have you been, young lady? You smell like an old pub ashtray.'

Harry noticed Maddy brighten too, stroking her cat, so it purred and meowed more. He'd rescued many animals in his time, handing them over to relieved owners. Even the times when needing rescuing had been the stupid animal's fault, to see the happiness and relief of pet and owner being reunited always softened Harry's heart – he just never let his colleagues know it. Setting aside his dislike for cats as a landscape gardener, the cat being alive was a positive thing for Maddy. 'I'll get her some food.'

Back in his kitchen, he searched his cupboards. What did he have that a cat would eat? He found a can of tuna and opened it, draining the brine down the sink. He forked out a little on a saucer and placed it on the kitchen floor. In another saucer, he placed water. He put the rest of the can in the fridge. It could be the cat's breakfast.

The cat ate hungrily, purring loudly.

'I've got some sand in the garage. I'll sort out a litter tray for tonight as she can't go back outside until it's safe.'

'Thank you,' Maddy said, smiling at Harry for the first time. Her eyes were still red and puffy where she'd been crying, and sadness shadowed them, but she certainly appeared calmer now he'd found her cat alive and well.

'Hey, this is what neighbours are for, right?'

Harry found a seed tray, lined it with a carrier bag, and filled it with some sand. He placed this too in the kitchen. He really was doing his good deeds for the day, allowing a feline pest into his house. *It had better not scratch his furniture.*

Karin had liked cats. Maybe that was another reason why he hated them.

Don't think about Karin.

He rubbed the back of his neck, taking in a deep breath, then breathed out slowly.

'Right, time for a top up on your drink,' he said, reaching for the two spirit bottles and grabbing the orange juice out of the fridge. He gestured for Maddy to sit in the lounge. She held out her glass while he poured her another large measure of vodka, then poured himself another Jack Daniels. Harry needed to think of a way to break it to Maddy about her house, so she was prepared for tomorrow.

Maddy sat rigidly on the edge of the sofa, obviously in a stranger's house and unable to relax. Harry found himself doing the same in the opposite armchair.

'You can relax, Maddy. I don't bite, you know,' Harry said, sitting back in the seat. 'And I don't mind you staying the night – unless you have somewhere else you'd prefer to go?'

She shook her head. 'No, I haven't. While you were fetching Sookie, I phoned my friend Valerie, and there was no answer. I didn't want to leave her a distressed message either. Also, I think I've had too much vodka to drive myself anywhere even if I did.'

He would have offered to drive her, however, he was likely over the limit as well now. 'It's probably easier if you stay here. You can't go back in the house until the fire brigade have finished assessing the damage.' A fire investigation usually meant there could be something suspicious, and Collins had pretty much confirmed it, too – but maybe Harry shouldn't worry Maddy with that detail yet? She was going to find it hard to sleep as it was. 'But at least you're on site so you can talk to them tomorrow.'

'I hope I don't get burgled now. That would be just my luck.'

'There's a police car parked outside. They'll watch the house all night.' Did he confess to her tonight that they were treating it like a crime scene?

'Really, they do that?'

'Yeah, sometimes.' Harry's guilt increased. But Maddy would need to try and sleep. She'd been through enough this evening.

Maddy took another gulp of her drink. 'Thank you, you've

been really kind. I'm sorry I was such a mess earlier. I'm not usually violent.'

'I might have a few bruises to show for my heroic actions.'

'I am so sorry.' Maddy wouldn't meet his eye, and silence fell between them. As if on cue, Sookie emerged from the kitchen licking her lips. Tail raised, she trotted over to Maddy, who timidly smiled and stroked the top of her head.

'Do you feel better now, girl?' Maddy cooed. The cat jumped into her lap, and whilst purring, licked her paws and then set about routinely cleaning herself. Maddy sat back a little deeper into Harry's sofa and looked almost comfortable.

'Well, at least you know your cat is safe,' Harry said, finding it hard to know what to say. The woman's house had been set on fire – possibly deliberately. He started thinking about how much damage smoke could do. He wouldn't worry Maddy unnecessarily. No point until they knew what they were facing. No one had died, so that was always a positive in his line of work — when it had been his line of work, that is. Now he only had to worry about plants dying. But lifting Maddy into that carry had given him a buzz. Seeing the action unfold as the fire engines had arrived, sirens blaring, blue lights flashing; a part of him missed his firefighting days, missed the adrenalin rush. However, he knew he was no good to his colleagues in the field. One bad day, and he'd freeze, flashbacks would paralyse him, and he'd be no good to anyone. In fact, he'd be a danger to himself and others.

Karin's death would always haunt him.

Chapter 3

Maddy glanced at her watch. It was nearly eleven. The night's events were closing in on her, fogging her brain and making her eyes heavy. She yawned, and sipped her third large vodka. The heat from the spirit sent warmth from the back of her throat down to her stomach. Harry had insisted on another drink.

'It'll help you sleep,' he'd said as he'd poured it out for her.

It probably would, that's why she was feeling tired, because she felt drunk. Not hammered and out of control drunk but the giggly, light boned-feeling drunk — *if only she felt giggly. Far from it.* In fact, if she weren't careful she would burst into tears. She wouldn't stop worrying until she knew the extent of the damage to her house, and to her paintings. The house could be redecorated — although the thought of the task plagued her with worry — but the paintings were her income. It was a large commission and she didn't want to screw it up by delivering it late. She wouldn't have time to repaint the two pieces she was supplying – they'd taken a month to complete. They were ready and framed, due to be delivered this weekend, in time for the opening of a new restaurant in Padstow. The owner had asked for a couple of pieces and was happy to pay generously. She hadn't refused. If they were damaged, there would be no way she'd have them ready by the weekend.

'I'm sorry, Harry, my head is a mess.'

'Hey, it's totally understandable. Only this morning you were cursing me, so it probably feels a bit strange to be sitting in my house right now.'

'Well, you still have a monstrous truck.' Maddy looked at him, smiling to show she was teasing and he gave a hearty chuckle. Then Maddy yawned again, just about getting her hand to her mouth remembering her manners. *Not attractive.*

'I think it's time we went to bed,' Harry said, standing up.

Maddy's heart raced. Did he think she was going to sleep with him? He must have caught her worried expression because he took her empty glass out of her hand and laughed. 'Don't panic, you can have my bed, and I'll kip on the sofa tonight.'

'You don't have a spare room?'

'No, not yet.'

'Oh, I thought when you said I could stay I assumed you had a spare bedroom.' He did have a three-bedroom house exactly like hers.

'One's a gym and the other is the dumping ground for all my crap. I'll eventually get around to clearing it out. You know what it's like when you move house, takes a while to empty all the boxes.'

Maddy smiled wanly at him. 'Yes, I remember. I still have boxes in my garage I haven't opened yet,' she said, her voice still hoarse from her hysterics earlier. 'I've been in my house barely over a year.' She started to cry, silent tears.

'Don't cry,' Harry approached Maddy, 'it'll be all right, you'll see. I think most of the damage was in the kitchen.' His strong hand squeezed her shoulder, sending an unexpected ripple of delight through her body. She felt safe. She caught his scent; a mixture of a day's work and a spicy Lynx deodorant. It wasn't unpleasant. 'Maybe we should hit the sack. It's been a long day.'

Maddy nodded at him.

'Come upstairs, and I'll show you where everything is.'

Exhausted emotionally and physically, Maddy was relieved to follow Harry up the stairs. Whether she would sleep would be another thing, but she knew she needed to lie down. He gestured towards the bathroom which was the first door on the right, at the top of the stairs. Of course she knew this, it was her house, only decorated differently.

'I haven't had a chance to decorate yet,' Harry said, as if reading her mind. The bathroom was very pink and floral, reminding her of the old couple who had lived in the house previously.

Maybe the tiredness made her smirk. 'At least the suite is white, so it's a case of just a lick of paint.'

'And changing those hideous tiles,' Harry said, shuddering.

Maddy giggled briefly. 'Oh, I thought the flowers were so you.'

'What with being a landscape gardener?'

'Absolutely.'

Harry gave her a speculative look, as if appreciating her teasing, and opened the bathroom cabinet above the sink. 'I think I have a new toothbrush in here. Hope you can cope with it being blue.'

'Blue's fine. Might have been a different story if I was eight.' Maddy's eyes widened as she stared inside the cabinet. 'Wow. There's enough drugs in there to open a pharmacy.' Too late – she'd opened her mouth and said the first thing that had entered her head.

Harry slammed the door shut. 'Here you go.' He handed Maddy the new toothbrush still in its packaging.

She gulped and started fiddling with the toothbrush packaging. It was none of her business why he had so many tablets hoarded away, although if he was a complete psychopath, and she was staying under his roof for one night, maybe she needed to know. Was she safe? *Now you are being overdramatic. He probably has a very good reason for the tablets.* Maddy struggled with the packaging trying to take out the toothbrush, which was an impossible task even when sober. The perforated card would never tear.

Ignoring Maddy's comment about the prescribed drugs in his cabinet, Harry took the toothbrush and ripped it out from the plastic wrapper with ease.

'Sorry, I've had too much vodka.' She hoped this sounded like a good excuse for her blurting out rubbish, and the fact she couldn't open toothbrush packaging without scissors.

'Do you want to shower?'

Maddy shook her head. She'd have one in the morning. Now she needed sleep.

'Clean towels are in the airing cupboard, help yourself.'

'Okay.'

Harry led her to the master bedroom. A king-size metal framed bed took centre stage, with navy blue bed linen clashing with the pastel green chintzy wallpaper. 'Like I said, I haven't decorated yet. Wanted to move in and get settled first.'

'Of course.' Maddy became tongue-tied, the meds in the cabinet eating at her curiosity.

'I need to pinch a couple of pillows, if that's okay, and I'll be downstairs. I'll let you use the bathroom first.'

'Oh, Harry, could I borrow a T-shirt or something, please . . . to sleep in?' She didn't fancy sleeping naked. But she'd been wearing these clothes all day, and probably would need to wear them all day again tomorrow if she wasn't going to be allowed back in her house.

'Yes, of course, sorry.' He rummaged in a chest of drawers opposite the bed and pulled out a white pinstriped shirt. 'This is too small for me now. Use this.'

'Thank you,' she said, taking the shirt. 'And thank you, Harry, for everything. You didn't need to take me in.'

'What are neighbours for?'

Sookie padded into the room, and jumped onto Harry's bed, and immediately started washing and purring, as if Maddy and Harry didn't exist.

'Do you mind if she sleeps in here?'

'No, it's fine,' Harry replied, but his expression didn't match the words he spoke. 'Right, I'll let you sleep.' Harry gave a gentle wave, and as he walked downstairs, Maddy entered the bathroom and locked the door.

She cleaned her teeth, and assessed the dark circles under her eyes, hoping some sleep would reduce their dullness tomorrow. Splashing her face with cold water helped remove some of the puffiness. She stared at her reflection in the mirrors of the bathroom cabinet. Behind those mirrors contained Harry's drugs. She thought of taking a better look, but resisted, fearing he would hear the clicking of the magnets on the cabinet as she opened and shut the doors. And anyway it wasn't any of her business.

Her mother had brought her up properly not to be a snoop. Or was it Dad?

'I'm finished in the bathroom,' Maddy called down the stairs, then closed the bedroom door behind her.

Under the watchful eye of Sookie curled up on the bed, Maddy stripped off her clothes, neatly piling them up and buttoned up the shirt Harry had given her. It may have been too small for Harry, but luckily on Maddy's petite form, although long in the arms, it covered her bottom nicely making a good night shirt. If caught out in the middle of the night using the bathroom, at least she'd still keep some of her dignity.

She slid underneath the duvet, and once comfortable turned off the lamp by the bed. She was in darkness until her eyes adjusted to the street lighting that bled between the curtains.

She closed her eyes and listened, hearing Harry leave the bathroom, pulling the cord to turn the light off, and the sound of the toilet cistern refilling. All normal sounds, and not dissimilar to her own home's, yet she tensed, feeling alien and uncomfortable. She was sleeping in a stranger's bed. A man she'd hated this morning. Sookie didn't seem bothered, so maybe Maddy needed to take a leaf out of her cat's book and try to sleep. Things would look better in the morning, wouldn't they?

***

With the taste of the pills he'd just swallowed still on his tongue, Harry closed the bathroom door as quietly as he could. He winced, pulling a face. *Would he ever get used to those things?* Usually he swallowed them, then cleaned his teeth to disguise their chalky, rancid taste. But with everything running around his brain, aware he had a house guest and wondering whether she was comfortable and settled, he'd forgotten to take his medication until he was about to leave the bathroom.

Harry found the spare duvet in the junk room of bedroom three. It really was the 'box room', the amount of boxes he still had stacked up. Too small for a bedroom, one day it would be his study. One day. He needed to find the strength to sort through the boxes. He knew there would be some memorabilia, photos that would remind him of Karin. He wasn't ready for to face them yet.

Having grabbed some bed linen from the airing cupboard, he made up his bed on the larger of his sofas. In the past, he'd slept well on this sofa, as a fireman and working shifts and not wanting to wake Karin. Only in a different house ... their house ... Nowadays, his medication made him drowsy, so he'd sleep better than Maddy's cat on this sofa tonight.

Damn cat on his bed. Whatever next? The rows he'd had with Karin over that.

Feeling the tension creep up his back, he pushed his thoughts of Karin aside. Harry puffed pillows and wriggled to get comfortable. Usually, he preferred to sleep naked, but because of his houseguest, he decided to keep his boxers on. He didn't need Maddy coming down the stairs and being greeted by his bare arse – or worse!

Hoping tonight's events and the lingering smell of smoke wouldn't bring on a flashback – he'd not been near a fire in months – he closed his eyes and thought of the next gardening project he had lined up, trying to map out the garden, plan the plants he'd use. It worked better than counting sheep. And if that didn't work, his medication would soon kick in.

Chapter 4

The next thing Harry knew, daylight was streaming through the gap in the curtains, and a cat was purring on his chest, pawing and kneading at him. He pushed her off and the cat gave a hiss. It took him a minute to gather why he was sleeping on the sofa, and why he had a black cat on top of him. For one very brief moment, he had thought he was back, with Karin, still working as a fireman.

'I guess you're hungry are you, Socks?' He thought that was a better name for the cat, having one white paw.

As Harry sat up, the cat persisted trying to jump back on top of him. He swung the duvet off, burying Sookie, and strolled into the kitchen, the cat trotting by his feet, tail pointed. Squinting, his eyes not yet ready to fully open, he looked at the clock on his microwave. Stupid cat, it was only five thirty-two a.m.

He pulled the tuna out of the fridge, and like last night, forked it onto a saucer. Sookie sniffed it and looked up at him in disgust.

'What? You ate it last night.' Harry held his hands up at the cat.

'Last night it was at room temperature. It's probably too cold for her at the moment.' Maddy had appeared in the kitchen doorway, wearing only his shirt, unaware how sexy she looked, with her hair tousled and barelegged. *Wow!*

'Good morning,' Harry said, quickly turning and busying himself. *Why hadn't he slipped a T-shirt on himself?* He flicked the switch on the kettle and pulled two mugs from the cupboard.

'Morning.' Maddy sounded grumpy, splashing cold water over his hot thoughts.

'You sure your name's not Moody, rather than Maddy?' He teased over his shoulder. Maddy scowled.

'I'm not a great morning person at the best of times,' Maddy said, curtly. 'But if you haven't forgotten, my house was on fire last night. Not exactly something to wake up to and put you in a good mood.'

Maybe she had a point. 'Did you sleep okay?'

'Not bad. It was broken sleep, but the bed was comfortable, thank you.'

'Maybe you should take a shower while I get us some breakfast on.' Harry focussed on her green eyes, and tried not to let his own stray lower, to how her amber-blonde hair fell softly over her shoulders, and onto her breasts, curling at the ends. *Stop it.*

'Yes, I will, but I'm worried my face will feel dry and itchy as I don't have any moisturiser.'

'Ah, I might be able to help you out there. I'll put it on my bed. Go get in the shower.'

'Oh, that would be great. It's amazing how much you take for granted when you can't get into your own home.'

He let Maddy return upstairs before he followed, throwing on a T-shirt and his shorts from yesterday. He waited until he could hear the shower running then darted into his box room, opening up some cardboard boxes. 'Now where is it,' he mumbled. In his attempt to tidy the room he'd stumbled across some of Karin's cosmetics and skincare bottles. It had stopped him from opening any more boxes.

Karin had been a hoarder of beauty products, and all of these tiny bottles were samples or freebies which hadn't even been opened. At the time, when he'd found them, he hadn't the heart to throw them away, so they'd been thrown back in a box instead. In fact, he wondered if his mother had packed them into his boxes by mistake, because until moving here, he hadn't been aware he had any of Karin's belongings. In his grieving state, his mother had helped clear out Karin's things, taking them to her parents. But he knew there would be some things left to remind him of her.

And he shouldn't forget the good things.

The scents of some of the moisturisers and perfumes reminded him of Karin, and he clung to them from time to time, worried he was forgetting the good stuff about her. He wanted to remember her alive, not how she died. Now, nearly two years after her death, he should be healing – his intention was to see if a charity shop would want the items so had set them aside – but he still couldn't face the other boxes. Harry found the carrier bag on the top of a box. It contained make-up and skin care samples, full pots Karin hadn't started. With the shower still running, he placed it on his bed ready for Maddy to find.

Maddy returned to the kitchen in the clothes she was wearing last night – a flowery short-sleeved blouse and three-quarter length jeans, both items covered with splodges of dried paint. 'Thanks for the toiletries,' she said, towelling her hair dry.

'Not a problem. You can keep them if you like. I was only going to give them to a charity shop.'

'Whose are they?'

An unease churned inside his stomach as he frowned, not wanting to answer. He'd turned his back on Maddy so she couldn't see the discomfort her question had caused in his face. He wasn't ready to talk about Karin. Not to a stranger. He popped two slices of bread into the toaster. 'No one's. Like I said, you can have them.'

'Sorry, I'm doing it again. Only this time I no longer have the vodka to blame.'

Harry smiled, trying to relax. It wasn't Maddy's fault. 'It's okay, just a very long story.'

'I could really do with some clean underwear, but I suppose you don't have any?'

Harry chuckled, shaking his head. 'No sorry, I can't help there.'

***

After a small breakfast – Maddy couldn't stomach eating much – she took her coffee into the lounge. From here she had a better view of her house and wanted to wait for the fire brigade to show up and go through the charred remains of her kitchen. Dread filled her at the amount of work ahead of her, because even if only the kitchen were damaged, the rest of the house would probably need redecorating to get rid of the smoke stains and stench.

And then there were her paintings . . .

The first thing she'd do when allowed back into her house was check the paintings, and then dig out her insurance details.

Last night she hadn't taken much notice of Harry's lounge. His dark leather sofas clashed with the pastel chintz borders around the top of the wall and the floral curtains. Maddy's house wasn't the only one in need of decorating.

Harry, after showering and changing, joined Maddy in the lounge with a mug of coffee, cupping it with both hands.

Last night she hadn't taken much notice of Harry either. He created quite a presence. She tried not to stare at his bum as he walked around his lounge, his small, tight buttocks accentuated by his khaki cargo pants. Her eyes roamed upwards – *because staring at his bum was totally unacceptable* – to appreciate his narrow waist spreading to broad, muscular shoulders, which his black T-shirt stretched across. His clothing didn't leave much to the imagination. *He would make a fantastic life model.* She gave herself a mental shake. She shouldn't be ogling him. What was she thinking? *He fancied himself, remember? This is the same guy you were rowing with, only yesterday morning.* Although, he was being very nice currently, and he didn't have to be. Last night he could have left her on the pavement outside screaming at the firefighters.

'Do you need to go to work?' she said.

'I'll call them to say I'll be over later.' Harry turned to face her. 'I'll wait with you to see the fire brigade.'

Maddy nodded. She'd already made the call to Valerie this morning while Harry was showering, who had been sympathetic. 'Oh my dear girl,' Valerie had said. Her casual tone had immediately sharpened to more alert when Maddy had said there had been a fire. 'I'm so sorry I was out last night. You should have left a message.' Last night Maddy hadn't wanted to leave a distressed message on Valerie's phone, though. 'Don't you worry about a thing with the gallery. Get yourself sorted and keep me posted.'

Maddy wished the fire brigade would hurry up. 'I'm dreading what it's going to look like inside,' she said, feeling her lip quiver uncontrollably. Tears began to well in her eyes, and so she glanced away from Harry's gaze, not wanting him to see her falter. The damage that would need to be fixed worried her. And she'd been doing so well this morning, too.

'Hey.' Harry sat himself down beside her, placing a hand on hers. It was warm from holding his mug of coffee. 'This is what insurance is for. The fire brigade arrived quickly; the fire was contained in the kitchen.'

However reassuring Harry was trying to be, Maddy couldn't help worrying. Anxiety crept up her spine and weighted itself on her shoulders. This year she needed to make the gallery successful – her business. Would the house fire destroy everything she'd tried to achieve in this past year?

Chapter 5

Maddy heard the truck before she saw it, the morning song of the birds drowned out. One large fire truck pulled up, impressive and intimidating as it parked in the narrow street of Annadale Close. It was just after eight-thirty a.m. *What must the neighbours think?* With the arrival of the fire service, the police car stationed outside her house moved off, turning around at the end of the close.

'They're prompt,' Harry said, heading out of the front door. Maddy put her coffee mug down and followed.

Four men jumped out of the fire truck, and each shook Harry's hand and greeted him. It suddenly dawned on Maddy — he used to be a fireman. How else would he know this stuff, and the crew all know him? It explained his build, too. And the way he'd carried her into the house last night. It couldn't all be down to landscape gardening. She'd noticed the impressive equipment in his second bedroom – his gym.

'All right, Roses,' one said, patting Harry on the back.

'You're looking good, my man. Collins said he'd bumped into you last night. All that weeding must be doing you good.'

Maddy's thoughts exactly.

'Thanks, Dixons.' Harry laughed with the fireman.

'We should go out for a drink sometime.'

'I'd like that,' Harry replied, but Maddy saw the flash of anxiety in his expression as if he wasn't sure about socialising with these men.

A red car pulled up behind the fire engine, and the driver approached them, carrying a clipboard. He too wore a fire brigade uniform, but there was something much more formal about him.

'Right, Miss . . .?' Dixons turned his attention to Maddy after acknowledging the other man.

'Hart,' Maddy said, blushing with embarrassment, remembering her hysterical actions the night before. 'And I'm so sorry for being a pain last night.'

'Think nothing of it. Your house was on fire. Most people don't react too well to that, miss. Our boys take it all in a day's work.' When he smiled, creases around his eyes gathered. It was hard to tell his hair colouring under his white helmet, but his clean-shaven face was attractive enough. Age-wise, he had to be mid-forties, Maddy guessed. 'This is Gary. He's our fire investigation officer. He's here to put a report together.' Gary said a hello, tucking the clipboard under his arm and headed towards the back of Maddy's house with a couple of the fire crew.

'Can I see the damage?' Maddy asked, wringing her hands and glancing over Dixons' shoulder, watching the men enter her house.

'Yes, but I need to let Gary take a look first with CSI – Crime Scene Investigation.'

Maddy knew what it stood for. Sounded like the American TV show . . . was her house fire turning into a TV show? It all felt very surreal. And why were they treating it like a crime scene?

To add to the dream – or Maddy's worst nightmare –three vehicles pulled up, a dark Ford Focus and two vans with detailing down the side 'Scientific Investigations' and more men and women got out. The people who got out of the car were smartly dressed in suits. The people who emerged from the vans were dressed as police officers with black combat trousers and blue polo shirts with epaulettes and 'FORENSICS' printed on their back. They started to don red protective overalls and hard hats from the back of the vans. The narrow, quiet, and usually sleepy Annadale Close was full of people again. The small close felt even smaller crammed with vehicles. Neighbours twitched curtains or opened their front doors pretending to put their cat out. Maddy wanted to be whisked off by the wind, Mary Poppins' style, and returned firmly back on her feet, once this was all over.

Harry came out of his house with a tray of mugs, steam rising from them. He'd done the tea run. He handed Maddy the first mug. 'I made you a fresh cup of coffee.' His smile was so gentle and caring for a man she didn't really know. Then, clearly noticing she needed some reassurance, he said, 'Don't worry, this is usual procedure when the fire looks suspect.'

'Thank you,' she said, taking the mug from him. 'But why is it suspicious?'

Harry shrugged and continued to give out the mugs of tea and coffee. *Did he know more than he was letting on?*

Maddy remained static, frozen on the spot, whilst the world continued to spin, and she observed everything going on around her. As the team in red overalls dusted her front door for fingerprints, another took photos. Fire officers worked around the back of her house, securing her back door and kitchen window. Some of the plain clothed officers were knocking on doors, with notepads in hand. It looked like they were taking statements from neighbours.

What will they all think? At least Harry was one of them. He could calm the neighbourhood gossip.

'Hi, I'm Rachel,' a woman in red overalls approached Maddy, shaking her out of her reverie as she stood motion-less letting the earth rotate. 'Are you the house owner?'

'Y-yes.'

'I need to take your fingerprints for elimination.' Rachel waved a kit at Maddy. 'Is there somewhere we can go?'

'Yes, sure.' Maddy gestured towards Harry's house.

In Harry's dining room table, Rachel unrolled an A4 piece of paper and took Maddy's prints using pre-inked flimsy plastic strips. Rolling each finger and thumb into its designated space, then turning the page over, she took a print of Maddy's palms, too.

I feel like a convict.

Rachel left Maddy to scrub the inky mess off her hands. It was stubborn and took three attempts with washing-up liquid leaving her hands red and her skin feeling dry. She kept telling herself this was all procedure and she had nothing to worry about. However, she couldn't help feeling confused by the whole situation. She'd expected to just be let into her house to assess the damage with the crew. *Not be fingerprinted by forensics!*

Maddy shut Harry's front door and joined the throng in the close once more, not exactly sure what she could do to help. She'd never felt so useless. She was met by two smartly dressed, plain-clothed officers, one female and the other male.

'Miss Hart?' said the male officer, flashing his badge – *God, it really was like something out of* Life On Mars, *only without the flares. Would a gold Ford Granada appear and wake her from this nightmare?* She'd only been watching some old episodes a couple of nights ago . . . was this *her* subconscious?

If only she could wake and find out this was all a dream.

'Yes. That's me.' Maddy's heart chilled, goosebumps travelling down her arms. *No, this was real.* The sun was already warm; there was still the smell of old bonfires in the air.

'I'm DC Adams, this is DC Stone, we've been asked to investigate the fire at your property. Is there somewhere we could go to ask you some questions?' Both officers looked a similar age to Maddy, in their late twenties, yet their presence intimidated her, whether intentional or not. She hadn't done anything wrong, yet guilt, dread and anxiety washed through her.

I haven't done anything wrong.

'Officers, you can use my house.' Harry had come along yet again to Maddy's rescue.

'Yes, yes, I'll lead the way,' Maddy said.

She crossed the road, and welcomed them into Harry's house offering teas and coffees. The three of them sat in Harry's lounge, one making notes while the other officer talked. They asked what time she'd left the house, where she'd been all day, did she have a witness? Why did Maddy feel like a criminal? She had nothing to hide.

'I didn't do this!' she blurted, unable to hold in her tears. Her chest had tightened, rising to her throat. 'Why would anyone want to burn down their own home?' The female DC pulled a packet of tissues from her jacket pocket and handed one to Maddy.

'It's okay to be upset,' she said, smiling tenderly.

'Miss, we have to ask these questions as a matter of

procedure. To rule you out as a suspect,' said DC Adams. His expression was sympathetic towards Maddy, putting her at ease. 'Our team are making enquiries with the neighbours to see if anyone saw anything. And we'll speak to,' he flicked through his notes, 'Mr Tudor, too.'

'Yes,' Maddy nodded, wiping her tears and then her nose with the tissue, 'Harry.'

'Miss Hart, do you know of anyone who would wish you harm?'

Maddy shook her head. 'No.' She tried hard to hold in her tears, taking a deep breath to steady her fear.

'Does anyone else have a key to your property?'

She shook her head again. 'No.'

'Have you always lived at the property on your own?' DC Adams asked, always keeping eye contact with Maddy while DC Stone continued scribbling notes.

'No, I used to live there with my boyfriend, Connor.'

'Did he used to have a key?' DC Stone looked up from her notepad. Both officers suddenly focussed intently on Maddy.

'Yes . . . of course, but he gave it back.' Maddy frowned. Would Connor do something like this to her? And if so, why?

'Even so, we'll need to follow this up.'

More notes were made as the officers took more information from Maddy, everything she could give them on Connor, and also Valerie's contact details, so she could verify

Maddy had been at the gallery all day, and then they let her go.

Maddy left Harry's house with her brain in a whirl. CID had asked so many questions; she couldn't believe how long she'd been sitting with them. She prayed she'd repeated strongly enough that she wouldn't want to set fire to her own home. The officers had been nice, not condescending. So hopefully they believed her.

She found Harry outside talking to a couple of the fire crew while wiping his hands on an old rag. As soon as she drew near, he turned his attention to her, so she smiled meekly. 'The police would like to speak to you, as you discovered the fire,' she said, hoping her eyes weren't swollen and her face too blotchy from crying.

'Of course, I'll go talk to them now.' Harry nodded thoughtfully. 'I need to go wash my hands, too.' He showed his large, ink-stained hands to her – the black ink ingrained into the creases of his palms and fingers. CSI had taken his fingerprints too.

'See you in a bit.'

***

Maddy found herself watching everything going on around her again. What she desperately wanted was some clean clothes.

A lady wearing red overalls and a hard hat stepped out

of Maddy's front door. Maddy recognised her as the same woman who'd taken her fingerprints earlier.

'Excuse me . . . Uh, Rachel, isn't it?' Maddy asked.

'Yes.'

'Is it possible for me to go in and get some clothes? And I need to get my insurance details.'

'Yes, of course,' the woman replied, smiling. 'Hang on a minute, though, and I'll check it's okay to bring you through.' Rachel came back five minutes later and ushered Maddy through her front door. 'It's safe to come in, but please don't touch anything downstairs.'

Straight away, the stench of smoke, so much stronger than outside, hit her. The burnt, blackened smell turned her stomach, making her hesitate in the small hallway. Usually, her habit would be to kick off her shoes here. *Little point today*. She shrugged off her fear, needing to face the devastation, and followed the crime scene investigator into the house. Walking through the lounge, it seemed untouched, although there was some black soot in places around the ceiling. A small wave of relief flashed over her – Maddy couldn't see the two canvases she'd wrapped up for a commission. The fact that her paintings weren't in the lounge meant she had moved them into the garage. She still wanted to check on them to put her mind at rest. Currently, her brain was doing cartwheels with all the thoughts and worries buzzing around.

'You're lucky you'd shut the door to your lounge, otherwise

59

there may have been a lot more damage in here,' Rachel said, leading Maddy through her own house, her overalls making a swishing noise as she walked.

Weird, I don't remember closing it. Maddy always left the door between her dining room and her lounge open so Sookie could go out of the cat-flap in the back door. *Should she mention this? If she did, would they think she'd set fire to her house? Maybe she'd discuss it with Harry first.* The lounge had minimal smoke damage because the smoke had travelled up the stairs instead.

They entered the small dining room, and Maddy felt transported into a film set where a crime scene investigation was taking place; people working, wearing overalls, photos being taken. Only it was real. She could smell it. The reek was even stronger here. The door between the dining room door and the kitchen was charred, hanging off its hinges, and the carpet was black and sodden near the kitchen entrance. Her dining room was blackened by the soot and the smoke, stinking worse than a working men's club in the days when you could smoke inside a pub. The smell clung to her nose. The dining table was grey and dirty with the soot. On the wall closest to the kitchen, hung a frame, the family photos of her niece and nephew inside ruined. A tear trickled down Maddy's cheek. The devastation fire could do overwhelmed her. But she had to look at this more logically and less materialistically. Importantly, no one was hurt; she and Sookie were alive. The kitchen could be replaced. Everything could be replaced. But not a life. Even in this day and age, so could the photos. She'd printed them off, taken from her own phone. And as the disaster had happened in the kitchen, her old family photo albums and other irreplaceable items stored in the loft hadn't been lost either. *This situation could have been a whole lot worse.*

'Can I . . . can I . . . take a look at the kitchen?' Maddy asked Rachel, who nodded.

Maddy approached the door leading to the kitchen, hands in her pockets so she wouldn't be tempted to touch anything, wanting to make herself as small as possible, and surveyed the wreckage before her. The uPVC back door was distorted and was being boarded up on the outside by two burly firemen. The fire investigation officer – Gary she'd heard him called – and another member of the CSI in red overalls were in the small kitchen, taking photos and analysing the ash around the hob. Maddy stood silently observing the horrific scene. Not only was there fire damage to contend with, there was water damage too from the fire hoses. There was a black puddle of water on the kitchen floor.

'As you can see, the fire came from the hob,' Rachel said, still accompanying Maddy. This was where the fire had attacked her kitchen the worst. Maddy assessed the damage. The cupboards either side above the hob were burnt out, the only contents remaining were those that could take the heat, like tins, but even they were misshapen, the paper labels burned clean off. What had been white cupboard doors, were now blackened and scorched. Other units had bubbled due to the heat. Grey and white ash lay everywhere. Bits of plaster were missing from the ceiling. Maddy hoped the fire hadn't reached the room above.

Amongst the charred remains were what looked like her recipe books. She glanced at the top of the fridge where she kept them. All her books had been removed. Had they been used to feed the fire? Should she raise this, or again, would they assume she'd done it?

No wonder it looked suspicious. Someone had set fire to her kitchen.

'It looks like you left your hob on,' Dixons said, appearing beside Maddy, Rachel making room for him.

Maddy frowned at him. 'That's impossible. I was out all day. And I didn't even use it in the morning.'

'A lot of people forget. Anyway, with the white spirit on the rags and oil paints so close by—'

'Oil paints?' It was hard to tell, but there were some remains of metal tubes on the floor which could have contained oil paints.

'Yes, they didn't help matters. I suggest you store those in your garage in future.'

'But I don't use oil paints!' Her favourites were acrylics, far quicker drying, or she dabbled in pastels or watercolours. She liked working with acrylics because they were water based, so there was no need for white spirit to clean the brushes. The white spirit she did own was in her garage, left over from the last time she'd done some decorating – when she'd first moved in.

Dixons explained the damage, indicating where the worst of it was.

'I didn't do this by the way. I was at work all day. It's not like I needed a brand new kitchen or anything stupid like that.'

'Bit of a drastic way to get a new kitchen,' another fireman piped up. 'But you'll be surprised what some will do.'

'I swear, I didn't leave the hob on,' she insisted.

'I know, Miss Hart, but it does look deliberate,' Dixons said, his tone noncommittal.

'I didn't do it!'

'Well someone did.' Dixons' wore a grim expression. Anger bubbled inside Maddy. She didn't know which made her angrier: being tacitly accused of arson, or the idea that someone had entered her house with the intention of burning it down. 'All I can say is, it's a good job Harry noticed the fire when he did, otherwise your house would be looking a lot worse.'

'Harry?' Maddy's breath caught.

'Yeah, he made the call.'

Gosh, she had a lot to thank Harry for.

'We're making the back door secure and boarding up the kitchen window too, so your house will be safe. We suggest, to access your home, you only come through your front door for the time being.' *Didn't most people usually access their home through the front door?*

Maddy bit down her sarcasm – the firemen were only trying to help her – and nodded in agreement. It all made sense, yet it didn't. How had a hob she hadn't left on caught fire? Someone had to have done it. These things didn't turn on by themselves. Her recipe books didn't just move. But who would do that? And why?

'But we'd rather you didn't access the house at all until we've finished our investigations,' Rachel said. She looked at Maddy with sympathy. Maybe she believed her? After a moment of silence, Rachel continued, 'Would you like to go upstairs and get some things?'

'Yes, yes, that would be great.' Maddy nodded, her heart heavy, remembering the reason why she was in her house and walked up her blackened staircase, refraining from touching the bannister as she climbed. Rachel followed.

'Everything is clear upstairs,' Rachel said, as if trying to reassure Maddy. It wasn't working. Downstairs looked like a bomb had hit the kitchen. 'It smells a bit smoky up here, where there's a little smoke damage, but nothing that can't be fixed with a lick of paint. Up the stairs is the worst of it. Luckily all the bedroom doors were shut, so they haven't got any smoke damage.'

'I always shut them to stop the cat going in there,' Maddy said, reaching her bedroom door.

Rachel stood outside while Maddy grabbed her everyday essentials from her bedroom, putting them into a woven cloth bag, including her phone charger – a crucial piece of equipment, as how else could she make all her calls if her phone was dead?

She rummaged for some fresh clothes but everything reeked of smoke despite the bedroom door being shut. They would have to do for today. Fortunately, having a small kitchen, her washing machine was in the garage, so she'd be able to access it. She thought of the mammoth amount of washing she would have to do. The bed would need changing, the duvet and pillows would have to go to the laundrette and then there were the towels in the bathroom. For now, she needed a change of clean underwear, whether they stank of smoke or not. With everything going on downstairs and knowing Rachel was standing outside, Maddy opted for changing at Harry's, so stuffed a couple of pairs of clean knickers into her bag. Then, she bundled some clothes together to wash, throwing them into a plastic wash basket.

Laundry basket balanced on her hip, bag over her shoulder, Maddy closed her bedroom door behind her, as if it would keep the room from being contaminated further by smoke and soot, and went into the bathroom to grab her toothbrush and her other indispensable toiletries. Then, closing that door too, she walked past Rachel and entered her third bedroom – the box room like Harry's. Only hers was a study. In her small filing cabinet under her old oak desk, she found her house insurance details.

She closed the bedroom door behind her as she exited. Rachel smiled. 'Got everything?'

Maddy paused, thinking of everything she'd grabbed. *Had she forgotten anything?* Satisfied she hadn't, she nodded, hugging the basket full of clothes, the heavy bag full of her essentials weighing on her shoulder as she followed Rachel back down the stairs.

Rachel escorted Maddy out of the front door and left her on her driveway. Maddy made her way through her decrepit back gate, dodging firemen and planks of wood, as they boarded her kitchen window and back door. The back gate had taken a beating more from the firemen to gain access to the kitchen, than actual fire damage, as it hung off its hinges lopsidedly. The gate would have been locked from the inside. It had had a fight with an axe. The axe had won.

Maddy would need a notepad and pen to list everything that needed repairing.

While juggling the laundry basket between hands and hip, she pulled the key out of her pocket and unlocked her garage door. She closed her eyes, taking a deep breath. *Please let her paintings be safe.*

As she opened the door, she switched on the light, and relief flooded over her. A weight of worry lifted. There, nice and safe, were her paintings for the Trewyn commission. All wrapped and sealed, ready for delivery. Another painting stood on an easel, started, but by no means completed. This was another big commission she'd received, and she didn't want to let the buyer down. She would move the paintings to the gallery as soon as she could, but for now, the summer warmth kept the damp out of the garage, so it made the perfect storage place. In the winter it would be a different story.

With the clothes bundled into the drum, she switched the washing machine to a quick wash setting. Dread filled her at the amount of washing she now faced. Hopefully, if it stayed sunny over the next couple of days, she would get most of her clothes dry. The rain usually arrived just as the school holidays started, so she had time yet.

Then she'd have to iron it all. *I might consider paying someone to do that bit. Or just wear creased clothes.*

Maddy locked up her garage and headed over to Harry's house with her bag. The front door was open, which she was grateful for. She found Harry still talking to the police in his lounge as she entered.

'Oh, sorry, is it okay if I use the bathroom? It's a bit busy over at mine.' *Understatement of the year.*

'We were just finishing up, Miss Hart,' said DC Adams, standing up. Harry and the other officer, DC Stone, also rose from their seats.

Awkwardly, Maddy smiled, fearing at any moment the police might arrest her – even though she was innocent – and headed up the stairs to the bathroom. Locking the door, she used the bathroom, changed her underwear, giving herself a spray with her bodyspray afterwards – almost emptying the can. *There, no one will smell smoky knickers.* Entering her house had left a whiff of smoke lingering around her. She checked her face in the mirror sensing her eyes were puffy. She splashed her face with water and slapped on some of her own tinted moisturiser, hoping this would give her some colour and reduce any redness in her cheeks.

When she came back downstairs, the house was empty. Outside, Harry stood on her drive shaking hands with the fire crew. He fitted in with them; big, muscular, burly men. He waved them off, then turned to face her, putting his hands in his pockets. He smiled as she crossed the road towards him. For someone so powerfully built and who could appear intimidating, he had a kind, gentle expression and his blue eyes emanated trustworthiness. She'd never noticed this before. *Usually too busy being angry with him and seeing red.*

'The fire brigade have finished. They've boarded up the back door and the window until you can get them replaced,' he said. 'And CID have gone, but they've left their card with contact details for you to give to your insurers. I've left it on my mantelpiece. The crime scene investigators are still working, though, so you can't enter your house yet.'

'I need my back gate repaired too.' She hated the thought

of someone having access to the back of her house –
especially with the back door damaged. They could attempt
to get into the garage, if not the house.

'I can do it.' They walked around to the back where Harry
examined the gate, assessing how it could be repaired. 'I've
got to go to Truro at some point anyway; I can pick up the
materials I need there.'

'Oh, no, you don't have to,' Maddy said.

'It's what neighbours are for. I mend a lot of fencing and
stuff. I've probably got something knocking around in my
garage that will do the job. Some of the wood is salvageable,'
Harry said. 'And you'll sleep easier if you know your house
is safe.'

'Thank you.' Maddy's chest heaved as she tried to hold
in her tears. He was being so considerate. After the past few
months of badmouthing Harry, and cursing him behind his
back, did she deserve him being so good to her now?

She wanted to call her insurance company, which the
police said she could do as they would be forwarding on
their report. Was she insured for arson? Why would someone
want to set fire to her house? And would her insurance
company believe it wasn't her? Insurance companies were
good at finding some small print that meant they didn't
need to pay out money.

Everything appeared very black and bleak for Maddy
right now. A bit like her kitchen.

Chapter 6

'I'm popping over to Truro today,' Harry said, placing a toasted cinnamon bagel dripping with melted butter and honey in front of Maddy. 'Why don't you come with me?'

After a sleepless night, worrying about who would want to set fire to her house, Maddy wondered if the distraction would be a good idea. 'Yeah, might do.' She licked the sweet honey on her fingers.

'It's not like you're allowed back in your house yet.' Harry sipped a coffee, having had his breakfast earlier. Apparently, Sookie had woken him up – again.

'True.' CSI wanted to come back this morning and finish off and had told Maddy she still couldn't enter her house.

'Come with me, and you can get some items you need to tide you over. A bit of retail therapy may do you good.'

'I need to call my insurance company first. Get the ball rolling there.' She'd held off yesterday, fearing she'd burst into tears down the telephone to some poor agent. Today she was stronger. Or at least she hoped she was.

'Of course. I'm in no rush.'

'And I'd better call Valerie, to update her.'

'OK, I've got to pop out for a bit to see a customer I missed yesterday. I'll be back in an hour.' Harry grabbed his truck's keys hanging off a hook in the kitchen by his back door.

After finishing her breakfast, Maddy made a call to Valerie who reassured her the gallery would be fine. It didn't stop Maddy pacing around the living room while she spoke.

'I've organized for Josie to be in all day today, and over the weekend,' Valerie said. 'You must have so much to do, so don't worry about the gallery, I will manage it. The summer holidays don't start for a couple of weeks yet. You get yourself sorted.'

'Thanks, Val.'

'Are you sure you don't want to stay here?'

'I'll see what Harry says. Thank you so much for the offer.'

'I'm here if you need me, Maddy. Please don't forget that,' Valerie said. The sincerity in her voice choked Maddy. She really didn't want to blub down the phone, though, otherwise Valerie really would worry. 'But you can do this, my dear. This is only another of those obstacles that life likes to throw in your way.'

'Just when I thought everything was going along smoothly.'

'I'm afraid, as you get older, you soon learn life was never meant to be easy. I'm sure these things are sent to test us. To weed out the weak from the strong.'

'Which am I?' Maddy asked.

'You'll come out the stronger – if you're anything like your mother.' Valerie laughed, and Maddy found it contagious and giggled with her. Valerie always had a positive influence on her. 'Let's face it; life would be dull if it was all plain sailing.'

Next, notepad and pen in hand with her insurance documents in front of her, Maddy took a deep breath and called her home insurance company. She tried not to get frustrated with the automated messages directing her to the right department. 'All I want to do is talk to a human being!' she said to the automated voice, tapping the end of her pen against the pad.

When she finally spoke to someone, some ten minutes later due to the high volume of calls – *how many other people had had house fires, for God's sake?* – she found them extremely helpful, putting her mind at rest. They asked a lot of questions, possibly more because she'd confessed the police were involved, providing their details. They couldn't arrange for a Loss Adjuster to inspect the damage until they'd received the reports from CID. Maddy put the phone down feeling a little less stressed – but it still meant she couldn't really do anything with the house until sometime next week. Today was Friday.

They'd asked her if she had somewhere to stay or if she

would need rented accommodation. However, because of the situation, and the company needing to ensure she wasn't the one who'd caused the house fire, she was made aware they would have to recover payments from the policyholder – i.e. her – if found negligent for starting the fire or allowing someone else to start it.

The insurance company offered to put her up in Bodmin, and although it wasn't far away, Maddy thought it too far for her. 'I think I'm okay, I can stay with a friend, but I'll call back if I need further assistance,' she said. Worst case scenario, she could sleep at the gallery. The insurance company had said they paid a daily accommodation rate, so even if she stayed with a friend, she could give them compensation.

Once the insurance company received the police and fire reports, they would be able to send out a Loss Adjuster, and the ball could get rolling in getting her back into her house. But this all depended on the police reports. Clearly, if they believed she'd set fire to her own house, the insurance company wouldn't pay out.

Harry was still out, so Maddy busied herself with the dishes in his kitchen, clearing away the breakfast things. She was generally a tidy person, and it appeared Harry was meticulous, too – which wasn't a bad trait in a man – so she liked to keep everything straight, as if she wasn't even here. She decided to let Sookie out who had been sitting by the front door and meowing noisily. She'd been looking very unimpressed at being stuck in Harry's house yesterday. Maddy knew she liked to be outside if the sun was shining. She had a favourite place in the garden underneath a rose bush, where she would pretty much sleep all day. With her backdoor firmly sealed, Sookie couldn't get into Maddy's house and she would soon find her by the front or back door of her house when it was feeding time.

***

When he returned, Harry found Maddy in her back garden, her strawberry-blonde hair tied back in a ponytail, swishing as her head moved. She stood in the sunshine, an easel before her, with a metal plate in one hand covered with blobs of different shades of blue paints, staring at a canvas.

'Everything okay?' he said, standing beside her and admiring her preliminary sketch for a new painting – the ocean and waves crashing against rocks. He recognised the beach as Tinners Bay.

Maddy nodded, chewing on the end of the paintbrush. Once she'd removed it, she said, 'As I wasn't allowed in the house this morning, I thought I'd come out here and start on this painting. I don't feel so bad not being at the gallery and at least I feel like I'm doing some work.'

'It looks like they've gone now.' There were no more vehicles parked in Annadale Close outside Maddy's house.

'Yes, yes, they handed my keys back about half an hour

ago and said I'm allowed back in now. The first thing I did was grab some more washing.' Maddy laughed. 'Sad, aren't I?'

'Not at all, more like practical. What did the insurance company say?'

'They can't send a Loss Adjuster out until they've received the reports, but they can put me up in rented accommodation in Bodmin.'

'Nonsense, you can still stay at mine,' Harry said, before thinking through the implications. It would mean a few more nights on the sofa. But he knew it made sense. Maddy could keep an eye on her house this way. The sofa wouldn't kill him.

And he could keep an eye on Maddy.

Where did that thought come from?

'Are you sure?' She looked up at him, squinting as the sun shone behind him. She raised her hand holding the brush to block the sun, but it didn't stop the light brightening her green eyes, drawing Harry to her gaze. Their eyes locked briefly until suddenly, a scratching sound came from the fence and they both looked in the direction of the scrambling noise. Sookie's head appeared, then she swiftly jumped over the garden fence and trotted over, weaving around their legs, purring. Maddy stroked her. 'It would make it easier for Sookie, too. Less of an upheaval.'

Harry hadn't thought about the cat. But however much he didn't like cats, it did make sense. This was about making life easier for his neighbour – who he'd developed a soft spot for. *Nonsense*. He was even, ever so slightly, becoming fond of the cat, too. *I'll never admit that*. 'Yes, I'm sure. This way you can pop back and forth, and when the insurance guy comes you can tell him to call for you at my house.'

'The insurance company said something about paying for my accommodation, so I could always pay you.'

'I don't need paying.'

While Harry waited for Maddy to finish up and put her easel back in the garage, he took a closer look at her back gate to see if he would need any extra materials to repair it. Maddy stepped out of her garage laden down with a laundry basket piled high with damp clothes and a peg bag. He went to her aid, taking the basket off her, and helped peg out her washing. He grabbed the larger items like T-shirts and let Maddy hang out her underwear. *Because that would just be weird.*

'I'll fix the back gate tomorrow for you,' he said, focussing back on the job. He would pick up some hinges and better locks in Truro.

'Thank you. I can definitely pay you for replacing the back gate. It will come out of the insurance payment, so tell me what I owe you. I don't expect you to do it for free.'

'I'll keep the receipts.' *Anything to keep the woman happy.*

***

While Harry drove, Maddy enjoyed the views of the Cornish countryside and tried to forget about her scorched kitchen. Once the police had left her house, and she'd gone in to retrieve some washing, she couldn't help taking another look at her devastated kitchen. Tears had fallen but, giving herself a pep talk, she'd wiped her eyes and ran upstairs. Valerie was right, she couldn't change the situation, she couldn't go back in time – time machines hadn't been invented! – so she needed to get on with life and everything it threw at her. She could do nothing about her kitchen until her insurance company contacted her, but she could at least tidy and clean the upstairs.

Sitting up higher than she was used to in the cab of Harry's pickup truck, and not having to concentrate on the road as a driver, Maddy was able to see so much more of the lush Cornish landscape. She watched the wind farms on the horizon, how some turned faster than others – what was all the fuss about those things? Surely people would prefer a windmill outside their house rather than a nuclear power station.

'Your phone's ringing,' Harry said, pointing towards Maddy's handbag where a muffled Bruno Mars' *Uptown Funk* could be heard.

'Oh, yes.' Maddy scrabbled for her phone. Would she get to it in time? When she saw the caller, she wished she'd let the call go to voicemail. *I must designate her a different ring tone.*

'Hi, Mum,' she said as cheerily as she could. Maddy had avoided calling her mother until she had everything organized her end. Plus, she didn't need Harry seeing her turn into another blubbering mess. She'd hoped to call her mother as soon as she believed she wouldn't break down.

'Are you all right? Gosh, I phoned the gallery, and Val told me everything . . . why didn't you call me?' Sandra Hart said with exasperation. She'd spoken so fast she sounded out of breath. Her mother was possibly more put out that Val knew more than she did. Although Valerie and Sandra were the best of friends, Maddy always wondered if there was a hint of jealousy in her mum over Maddy and Valerie's closeness.

'Mum, calm down. I'm fine. I haven't had a chance to call you.'

'Not a chance to call your own mother!' Sandra shrieked. Maddy winced, taking the phone away from her ear briefly. 'Where are you now?'

'I'm heading into Truro.'

'Are you driving? Should I call you back? You know you shouldn't answer the phone while you're driving.'

'No, I'm not driving.'

'Who is then?'

'Oh, Mum, enough with the questions.' She stared at the roof lining of the cab, biting her tongue and trying to remain cool, especially with Harry right beside her. He glanced at her but then returned his attention to the road.

'Maddison, dear, why don't you come home for a bit?'
This was another of the reasons why Maddy had postponed
calling her mother. She knew her dad would worry unnecessarily and Sandra would urge her to come home. 'It must
be awfully scary there. And with so much work needing to
be done to the house.'

'Mum, it's not scary, and there's not that much work,' *lie
mode cancelled,* 'but what work there is will need to be
overseen.'

'The insurance company will sort that—'

'And then there's the gallery.'

'Valerie can manage there—'

'And besides,' Maddy wasn't going to let her mother bully
her into anything if she could help it, 'Harry has said I can
stay with him.'

'Who's Harry?'

'My neighbour.'

'Not the one you moan about all the time?'

Maddy gulped. She hoped Harry couldn't hear her mother
on the other end of the phone. She switched the phone to
her left ear, just in case.

'Yes, him,' she hissed.

'Pardon? I can't hear you . . . You said you disliked the
man.' *Is it me or is she shouting down the phone?*

Maddy's cheeks flushed. The cab was getting hotter. Had
Harry turned off the air-con? 'Mum, I can't talk about this
right now,' she glanced at Harry, who appeared to be

concentrating on driving and not listening to Maddy's conversation – *Thank God* – 'but Harry has been a tremendous help.'

'Nothing any neighbour wouldn't do.' Harry winked at Maddy. The creases around his eyes, the dimple in his cheek sent heat rushing to Maddy's inner thighs. What with Sandra's embarrassing nagging combined with Harry's good looks — Maddy's body was suddenly on fire!

'Connor would take you back.' As Sandra blurted out the words, a chill coursed through Maddy, as if she'd had a bucket of icy water thrown over her. Her hackles rose.

'Mum!'

'Don't bite my head off,' Sandra said. 'Only I saw him this morning, and he asked how you were, and said how sorry he was it hadn't worked out with you, how much you meant to him. So I called the gallery, and here we are talking about him.'

'I would *not* go back to Connor if my life depended on it,' Maddy muttered, cupping her mouth over the mouthpiece as if it would help keep her conversation private. *Fat chance.* She knew Harry had heard what she'd said, but her mother needed putting straight. Connor did not bring out the best in Maddy, and now, having realised this, the better off she was without him. Until her kitchen fire, her single lifestyle had been treating her well. Yes, deep down she really wished she had someone to share this burden with, give her a hug, but she had to deal with it – on her own. Harry was helping, actually, keeping her strong, but she had to stand on her own two feet.

'Okay, okay, I'm sorry I mentioned Connor. I thought he was a nice enough chap.' Maddy bit her tongue. *He was a control freak. And was her mother forgetting how he called her Sandy and she hated being called Sandy?* 'Please be careful, though, darling, you don't know this Harry. He's only a neighbour and you hear terrible things in the news. You don't know what your neighbours get up to behind closed doors. You said you two didn't see eye to eye, so for all you know he could have started the fire.'

'Don't be silly.' Maddy glanced at Harry as a momentary coldness ran down her spine. He was an ex-fireman. He would know how to make a fire look like an accident. Even the firemen had hinted it was suspicious.

It was suspicious! The police were looking into it as arson.
Maddy had seen the evidence with her own eyes – it had to be arson.

But then he was the one who had alerted the fire service. He could have started it and then felt guilty.

And why would he let you stay at his house?
Maddy's mother continued to warble on while Maddy had this ridiculous internal argument.

'Well, I'd best let you go. You know where I am. Let me know how you get on, and if you need to escape, then there is still plenty of room for you here. Maybe Dad and I will pop down to see you.'

'No. Don't.' Maddy snapped back to the reality of the conversation.

'Why not? We're worried about you.'

'I can't put you up.'

'We can stay in a hotel.'

'It'll be very expensive this time of year.' Maddy tried to think of a million excuses why her mum shouldn't visit.

'Nonsense, that doesn't matter—'

'And probably everywhere will be booked up already.'

'I'm sure somewhere will have availability. Think about it, dear.'

'I will.' Maddy winced. 'Bye, Mum.'

'Love you, dear.'

'Love you, too.' Maddy returned her phone to her handbag and looked at Harry, who smiled. Did she look flushed scarlet, riled by her mother? *Probably*. Oh, the joys of having a pale complexion that gives you away immediately. She could never play poker.

'All okay?' he asked.

Maddy sighed. 'What do you think?'

He chuckled, emitting such a calming warmth. The side she'd never seen because she'd been too busy arguing with him about his monstrosity of a truck – which she was currently comfortably sitting in. *Oh, the irony* . . .

Of course Harry hadn't started the fire. Had he?

Chapter 7

Maddy waited for Harry at the place where they'd agreed, on a bench in the cobbled area at the front of the cathedral. Sunglasses perched over her eyes, she relaxed in the sunshine, soaking up the warmth and the busy atmosphere, listening and watching. They'd arrived in Truro soon after midday, and although she'd only been shopping for a couple of hours, her feet were sore and her legs ached. Knowing there were seats, she'd decided to head to their meeting place early. To fill the time, she took a photo of the cathedral, the cloudless blue sky as a backdrop and posted it to her Instagram account.

Truro reminded Maddy a little of Bath, only smaller, with the Georgian architecture and mellow stone buildings. Cobbled streets ran through most of the original parts of the city. The cathedral, grand and impressive, stood tall, prominent on Truro's skyline. The cathedral could be seen from most of the streets, and heard as well when the bells chimed, as if to ensure you hadn't forgotten its presence.

The seagulls gave occasional cries, a reminder you were in Cornwall, albeit inland, and the coast wasn't too far away. She wondered if they were as cheeky and aggressive here as in Padstow or Tinners Bay, and would have the audacity to steal a pasty right out of your hand. *Probably.* Maddy wasn't prepared to find out.

She spotted Harry approaching before he saw her – over six foot and with broad shoulders, the man stood out from the crowd. She gathered up her shopping and walked towards him.

'Get everything you need?' he asked.

'I think so, I lost interest after a while,' Maddy said, shrugging her shoulders. 'I'm not really in the mood.'

She wasn't a huge shopper at the best of times. It was always when you fancied a spending spree you could never find anything, and when you didn't have the money, all sorts of lovely things jumped off the rails at you. This apparently was true for everyone, not just Maddy, so her friends assured her.

Today, she'd strolled around her usual favourites, Next, Topshop, and even TK Maxx hoping for some inspiration. She'd bought some essentials, like underwear and toiletries, to tide her over and a couple of pairs of shorts and some summery vest tops on offer – good job the weather was holding. But to be honest, her heart wasn't in it. She was stressed at the mound of things to sort out at home, and although it had taken her mind off it for a while, she now needed to return and get things in motion. At least do the chores she could be getting on with before the Loss Adjuster arrived, like stripping the beds. *Oh, the high life.* Whether the insurance paid out or not, these things would need doing.

What was she going to do if the insurance didn't pay out?

Maddy pushed the chilling thought aside. She had no more savings. They'd been used up buying the house and setting up the gallery.

Thoughtfully, Harry had left her to her own devices, realising she needed privacy to shop. He was only her neighbour after all. The poor man didn't want to traipse around a load of women's stores. He was hardly her boyfriend. Even Connor had hated shopping with her.

'Shall we find somewhere to have a coffee? Then I'll drive us home.' Catching Maddy off guard, Harry took her shopping bags from her, adding them to his own, like the perfect gentleman. Connor never offered to hold her bags; she'd always had to ask him to carry them. She certainly hadn't expected Harry to insist on it.

'Yes, that sounds like a good idea.'

Harry led the way and found a quaint coffee shop down one of the narrow lanes. As it was so warm, Maddy opted for an iced skinny latte feeling the need for caffeine but not fancying something hot, while Harry asked for a normal latte.

'Do you want anything else? Cake or a sandwich?' he asked.

Even though the cakes did look delicious, Maddy shook her head. She'd lost her appetite, which usually happened when she was stressed. 'No thanks. Better not.'

The woman behind the counter patiently held her hand out for payment as Harry opened his wallet. 'I'll pay,' Maddy said, purse in hand, taking a five-pound note out.

'No, I'll get these.'

'No, it's the least I can do. I insist. You've done so much for me since Wednesday evening.' Harry frowned as Maddy handed over the money. With a playful nudge, she said, 'I'll let you carry the tray.'

With the sun shining, Maddy and Harry opted to sit outside at one of the small bistro tables. Maddy stared in horror while Harry emptied four sachets of sugar into his coffee.

'You'll never stay fit if you keep putting sugar in like that.'

'I burn it off,' Harry said, grinning. 'I have a high metabolism.'

'Can you actually taste the coffee?' Maddy sipped her iced latte, not having to wait for it to cool down.

'I like sweet coffee.'

'It'll catch up with you one day. You'll wake up and wonder where all your muscle went.'

'I don't take sugar in my tea, though – and I drink that mainly when I'm at work.'

'I drink too much coffee. I'd be the size of a house if I put four sugars in every cup. I barely make time for the gym as it is.' Just looking at Harry's tanned arms, his biceps bulging under the light blue T-shirt he was wearing made Maddy feel flabby. Now the weather was getting warmer, she'd have to make sure she took more dips in the sea after work. She enjoyed body-boarding and the exhilaration of catching a wave, even though she wasn't as good as those who did it regularly, those who had been born surfing, living in Cornwall all their lives.

A silence fell between them. The cathedral bells chimed three o'clock. Shoppers and holidaymakers passed them by, seagulls squawked from rooftops, and for a while, they people-watched and drank their coffee without talking. Two people who barely knew one another and thrown together under unusual circumstances, Maddy thought to herself. If this were a date, they'd be trying to get to know one another better rather than sit in silence. It was an odd situation. Would there be any harm in finding out more about her neighbour?

'So . . . you know the fire crew then?' Maddy asked, wanting to break the now awkward silence developing between them.

'Yes,' Harry said, nodding. 'I used to be a fireman. I transferred from Exeter, but I was only with them six months.'

'Oh, why did you leave?'

Harry grimaced for a split second, and he looked at his half-full latte glass. Without meeting Maddy's gaze, he said, 'I'd rather not talk about it.'

'Oh, okay, sorry . . .' Maddy found herself fumbling with the straw in her iced latte. *Change the subject. Quick.* 'So, can you tell me why one is called Shep?' She'd heard one of the firemen call another by this name, and had thought it unusual.

Harry's expression softened. 'His real name is Shaun.' Maddy frowned at him in confusion. 'As in Shaun the Sheep? At first he was Sheepy, but it got shortened to Shep.'

'Oh, I get it, as in a sheepdog.' She smiled her understanding. 'And Barrows?'

'That's his surname.' Harry chuckled.

'That's not very exciting. Why do they call you Roses?'

'Tudor . . . War of the Roses . . .'

Maddy laughed. 'I get it! Firemen are odd. Why don't you all call each other by your real names?'

'Where's the fun in that?'

'And Dixons . . . because he likes spicy curries? Get it – Curry's – Dixons?'

Harry chuckled. 'Not quite, but I like your line of thinking. It is actually because he has to have every latest top of the range gadget going. 3D HD TVs whatever they are . . . surround sound, you name it the man's got it. He was named Dixons before they merged with Carphone Warehouse – obviously.'

'Obviously.' Maddy nodded, finishing her drink and feeling more relaxed in Harry's company. Harry emptied his glass.

'Shall we head back? Have you got all you need?' Harry crumpled his paper napkin and poked it inside the empty glass so it wouldn't blow away.

'Yes, I have so much to do, it doesn't bear thinking about.' However, she wasn't sure she'd get much done by the time they returned. Maddy stood, gathering her shopping bags. Harry took them off her as if it was the most natural gesture in the world – that a man should carry a woman's bags. To remove the temptation to link her arm through Harry's, like she would have with a close friend or Connor, and cause herself more embarrassment, Maddy pushed her hands into her pockets, unsure what to do with them. They started walking, weaving their way through the crowds, towards Lemon Quay where Harry's truck was parked.

'Oh, cat food!' Maddy said, spying a Tesco supermarket by the car park. All of her food had been destroyed in the kitchen.

'Good idea,' Harry said. 'I only had the one can of tuna.'

'What did you feed her this morning?' Maddy asked. Her brain was all over the place, and she was even forgetting to feed the cat.

'I nipped round to number twenty-two – I know she has a cat, too. She gave me a can.'

'Oh, it's all right that *she* owns a cat,' Maddy said, smirking. 'I bet you haven't fallen out with her over *her* cat.'

'Funnily enough she's never moaned about where I park

my truck.' His eyes narrowed on Maddy, but there was mischief behind them.

'You know, she has two cats, don't you? So there are plenty of cats in the close that could be crapping in your garden.' Maddy pouted. Her ponytail swished as she picked up her step more confidently next to Harry.

'I know, I know, I take it all back – about your cat! She's living with me isn't she?'

'I bet you twinkled those blue eyes of yours and made the poor old woman at number twenty-two weak at the knees. She didn't stand a chance.'

'Nothing wrong with using the charm. If you've got it, flaunt it.'

Maddy gently elbowed him, chuckling. The touch of his hot skin against hers sent a shot of electricity through her. *He had it all right.*

Between them, they picked up some groceries and food for Sookie, Harry pushing the shopping trolley around the store. Then, laden with heavy shopping – Harry carrying most of it – they made their way back towards the car park.

'So why's she called Sookie?' Harry loaded the shopping into the back of the flatbed then closed the tailgate and pinned the cover back down. 'Anything to do with socks?'

Maddy laughed, shaking her head. 'No, at the time I adopted her, I was reading the Sookie Stackhouse series by Charlaine Harris. Because Sooty is a common name to call a black cat, but it's more a name for a tom, I thought, being a girl, Sookie would suit her better.'

'Oh, so it's nothing to do with her having one white paw then. I keep calling her Socks.'

'If you feed her, she'll answer to anything.'

Twenty minutes into their journey, the traffic had come to a standstill on the A39 northbound, while traffic whizzed by on the other side. Unlike the A30, this road was single carriageway for most parts.

'All we need – there's been an accident,' Maddy said, presuming that was the cause of the delay. She huffed out a breath, anxious to get home.

Momentarily, Harry's eyes widened, then he breathed as if trying to calm himself down.

'No, no, it looks like they've just broken down,' he said, pointing out the windscreen.

He sounded relieved. Maddy was pleased too. It might mean the traffic would get moving quicker. She'd been deep in thought, her head heavily clouded with stress, processing the amount of jobs stacking up, from the small menial tasks of the washing coming off the line, to where to start on the house so she could move back into her home. Plus, when she could go back to work at the gallery.

'Let me see if they need a hand.' Harry pushed the button on the dash and his truck's hazard lights flashed. Before opening his car door, he said, 'Stay here, Maddy, please.'

As Maddy watched Harry jog up to the vehicle three cars

ahead, she wondered if she'd imagined his expression of panic when she'd assumed it was an accident in front. It was as if he'd physically relaxed as soon as he'd realised it was only a broken down car.

She waited patiently in the truck as Harry spoke to the driver of the car – a distressed looking man in his forties, who had his young family out on the side of the road, up on the bank for safety. The mother carried a crying toddler, while an older child held her hand. Maddy watched Harry take control of the situation. With the window down, she could hear some of his instructions. He gathered a couple more helpers from the cars in front and sent an older man in his sixties back along the traffic, to keep any cars from passing. The last thing anyone needed was an accident. With the help of the other men, Harry pushed the car along to a safer position on the road. There was a lay-by not far ahead.

***

Panting and sweating from the exertion of pushing the car, Harry jogged back to his truck. Maddy was looking at her phone, with a finger poised, scrolling along the screen. As he opened the driver's door, Maddy jumped.

'Harry, don't do that!'

'Sorry,' he said, his breath still heavy. He could see worry etched on her face. This was a woman with a lot on her mind. 'Are you okay? I didn't mean to make you jump.'

'Yes, sorry, I was away with the fairies, worrying. Thought I'd try to distract myself with Facebook.' She waved her phone at him, then gestured ahead to the cars starting to move. 'We're lucky it was only a breakdown. An accident could have meant us sitting here forever.'

'Yeah, he's called the roadside recovery service. This way the car and his family are safe. I don't like seeing people stranded.' Turning the ignition, Harry started his truck and pulled away as the traffic moved again, turning off his hazard lights.

'What's wrong with the car?'

'He's run out of petrol. Thought he had enough to get to the next station.'

'A holidaymaker?'

'Yes.' The amount of gear on the back seat in between the two child car seats gave it away. 'I usually have a can of petrol for the lawnmower in the back of the truck. But it needs filling up.'

'How very unprepared of you.'

'I know.' His grip tightened around the steering wheel. Even though he could tell by Maddy's tone she was joking, it had frustrated Harry that he was unable to help the family more. He gave a wave to the man and his family as he drove past. Hopefully, they wouldn't have too long to wait until the recovery services arrived.

'Are you always this helpful?' Maddy turned from the window and looked at him.

'Must be the firefighter in me.' *Shouldn't have said that.* But it was true. It was in his blood to help people – however reluctantly recently. It's what had driven him to become a fireman. He glanced at Maddy.

'If you enjoy it so much, why did you give it up?' she asked curiously.

Harry gave another fleeting look at her then turned his attention back to the road. 'I'd really rather not discuss it, Maddy.'

There was a moment of silence, where Harry knew he'd killed the conversation. *Just like at the coffee shop.* But Maddy, in true female style – *they usually know how to break the silence!* – spoke up, 'Well . . . I don't think I'll ever be able to thank you enough for noticing the fire at my house. I mean if it had burned for much longer, who knows how much worse the damage would be? It could even have spread next door.'

'Luckily, due to the rain, I'd returned home early from work.' Harry wasn't sure he believed in fate, not when he thought about Karin, but it had certainly been lucky he'd still been around Annadale Close at the time. He'd had a number of jobs to do, but he'd been in the right place at the right time. 'I was loading my pickup with some tools for another garden job the next day.'

He'd been considering digging over one of his regulars' vegetable patch – a frail lady in her seventies who lived at the end of Annadale Close and who liked to feed him up with tea and biscuits every time he cut her lawn. In the summer sometimes he preferred doing some jobs in the evening, as it was a cooler time to work. The lighter evenings allowed him to do it too.

'Well, my mum thinks you might have started the fire—' Maddy's hands shot to her mouth and her cheeks grew pinker. Her redhead's complexion always gave her away. 'Sorry. I have a way of speaking before engaging my brain.'

'I know. I heard.' Harry smiled, pretending not to notice her embarrassment. If he mentioned it, she'd probably turn even redder. 'I mean about your mum, not about you speaking without thinking.' He'd watched out the corner of his eye how Maddy had blushed while speaking on the phone to her mother on the journey to Truro – like she was doing right now. He'd found it highly amusing, and a good way to read Maddy. She certainly couldn't keep secrets. 'And I definitely didn't do it, okay? I was trained to put out fires, not start them.'

'I know. And helping me so much wouldn't make sense if you'd wanted to burn my house down in the first place.' Looking at her lap, Maddy twisted the gold ring on her middle finger. 'Unless you just wanted me out of the neigh-bourhood . . .'

'I wouldn't have offered for you to stay at mine now, would I?'

'No, true, I didn't think of that. But we have had our differences.'

'Differences aside, Maddy,' Harry glanced at her sternly, his eyes fixed on hers for a moment, 'I didn't want to tell Collins this at first, on the night of the fire, because it could slow the process with the insurance company if it's arson. But the fire brigade were already suspicious and informed the police, so I had to tell the police in the end. I saw someone on your driveway. He just appeared, as if he'd come out of your front door. I didn't see if he had done that because I'd been in my garage. And then not long afterwards smoke was seeping out from your kitchen window.' Because he'd been putting some tools on his truck at the time, he'd a clear view of her window, and her front door was on the side of the house like his. If what Dixons had said was true, whoever had started the fire, had lit it on the hob, and fuelled it with items from Maddy's kitchen. It didn't take long once a fire caught hold, and if accelerants had been used flames would lick at the cupboards and spread quickly.

'Really? I know I didn't leave the hob on . . . but a small part of me hoped it would be an accident, not arson.'

'Smoke was escaping via the kitchen window. Fortunately, you'd left it slightly ajar—'

'Yes, I usually leave it on the latch to let steam out while cooking, and it lets air in. It stops the house smelling stale.'

'It's how I caught the fire early. I could smell it. I'm sort of attuned to the scent you could say.' Remembering the smell of Maddy's house burning had sent the hairs up on the back of his arms and neck, setting off nightmares he hated reliving. He loathed the stench of burning now. It was why he could no longer be a fireman.

'Maddy, does anyone else have a key to your property?' Although evidence of any forced entry might well have been destroyed by the fire, and by the firemen gaining access to the house, it would complicate matters for the insurance company if they believed the fire to be deliberate. Maddy could lose everything if they thought she'd had anything to do with purposely causing the fire. He wouldn't worry her with that bit of news yet, although she was probably well aware of this.

'No.' She frowned at him. 'The police asked me the same thing. Connor used to.'

'Who's Connor?'

'My ex-boyfriend . . .' Maddy said. 'But he gave the key back.'

'Are you sure?'

'Yes. I did tell the police all this.'

'He could have had another key cut without you knowing.'

'No, he wouldn't do such a thing. Why would he?' Maddy frowned.

'I don't know. He's your ex-boyfriend. I've never met him.'

'We split up before you moved into the neighbourhood.'

Harry nodded. He certainly hadn't recognised the man. 'What does Connor look like?'

'A controlling bastard.'

'I need a bit more to go on than that.'

Maddy rolled her eyes. 'Gosh, he's about five-nine, brown hair.'

'The guy I saw was wearing a baseball cap, with his head down so I couldn't see his face.' Harry grimaced but remembered one thing, though. 'Does he smoke?'

'Yes, yes he does. Much to my distaste.'

'I did see the guy throw away a cigarette butt,' Harry said, rubbing his chin. But this really wasn't enough proof the man he'd seen was her ex-boyfriend. Lots of people smoked. Harry wished he'd taken a lot more notice of this guy. At the time it had seemed odd, but not important. He could have been delivering pamphlets, anything, so Harry had forgotten him and carried on with his own business. 'Did he jointly own the house with you?' There was no relevance to that question, only Harry was intrigued. But if he owned the house he could have a set of keys.

'No – luckily. He had no money to invest in the property at the time, and deep down I think I knew our relationship wasn't going anywhere. He lived with me, but it was my house.'

'So . . . do you have anyone else who might wish you harm? Any enemies I should know about?'

'No!' Maddy glared at Harry. 'Not that I can think of. I'm an artist. I run a gallery and take commissions, and sometimes I even exhibit.'

'Oh yeah?' Harry raised his eyebrows at her, still smiling.

'My paintings. I exhibit my paintings! Seriously, Harry, I'm in no mood to joke.'

'Okay, Moody.' Maddy shook her head, sounding more frustrated as she reiterated, 'No, it couldn't have been Connor.'

Chapter 8

Maddy breathed a sigh of relief to see her house still standing as Harry drove into Annadale Close. *Fire couldn't strike twice, could it?* She went to her washing line and removed the clothes, all dry and fresh from the sunshine and the Cornish breeze. Harry had opened up his house, washed his hands, and then come over and helped.

'Can I borrow your ironing board?' Maddy asked as Harry took the basket of washing off her. This man was doing so much for her and he really didn't need to. 'I should have bought a new cover for mine. It probably stinks of smoke.'

'Yes, of course. You can do my ironing while you're there.'

'I have enough of my own, thank you!'

Harry chuckled, holding up his hands. 'I'm joking.'

She worried she was over imposing by staying at Harry's. Maybe she could go back to her house soon. But the smell of the smoke . . . would she even be able to sleep? Maybe she should stay at Valerie's.

'Are you sure you don't mind me staying with you? I could stay with a friend.'

'Maddy, how many more times do I have to tell you, no I don't mind.'

'Even the cat?'

'Well,' Harry pulled a face, making Maddy laugh, 'obviously, I'd have preferred it if you didn't have a cat, but I can't do a lot about it now.'

They walked over to his house, Harry carrying the basket, like he'd carried her shopping. 'Did you want to do some of your ironing while I cook us dinner?' Harry set the basket down in his lounge.

'Oh, good idea, I'll pop across and get my iron.'

'You can use mine.'

'Oh, no.' Maddy shook her head. 'I want my own iron. I'm used to using it.' Harry shrugged, as in disbelief. 'Hey, if someone said you could use their lawnmower, I bet you'd prefer to use your own.'

'Okay, good point.'

Maddy ran across the road to her house, and quickly retrieved her iron. There was a creepy ambience. It wasn't dark, but with the burnt stench still lingering, she didn't like being in the house on her own. Harry had said he'd seen someone around the house. Had they set fire to her house? Could it have been a burglar? She would check her belongings thoroughly tomorrow, but she hadn't noticed any upheaval in her bedroom or in any of the other rooms, which was the usual sign of a burglary. *And surely the police would have said something . . .*

As she locked her front door, Sookie appeared purring.

'Hey, girl,' Maddy said, picking her up. 'We're living at Harry's for a bit. I bet you want your tea.' Iron in one hand, and Sookie under her arm, Maddy returned to Harry's. The door was unlocked so she let herself in. Aware of the strangeness of it all, she wondered if she should have knocked first. Then a very different smell hit her, much more pleasant than that of her house, reminding her she was hungry: food cooking.

'Look who I found.' Maddy set Sookie down, and tail raised high, she trotted into the kitchen, also smelling the food. Harry's expression said it all. He definitely wasn't keen on cats. 'She's hungry, too.'

'I'll sort her out too, you get on with your ironing. You don't want to be standing there doing it all night.'

'I don't think I could if I wanted to. I'll only get some essentials done.'

Harry had already set up the ironing board for Maddy. He did seem to think one step ahead of her at times. *He would be very good husband material . . .* Maddy chided herself over the thought. *He's a neighbour, doing you a favour . . . don't read any more into it than that.*

But then she remembered Truro . . . had he been flirting with her?

He could have a girlfriend . . . although that looked highly unlikely because Maddy was sure if he did, his girlfriend wouldn't be too pleased about a strange woman using his bed. At least they weren't sharing it.

Half an hour later, Harry called her into the dining room. She switched off the iron, admiring her pile of clean, ironed clothes. She'd not been too meticulous about it, only choosing items she was more than likely going to need for working at the gallery and everyday use. It would keep her going for a week. In the dining room, two pasta dishes were on the table, steaming with a creamy mushroom and chicken sauce over fresh penne. Two glasses of white wine stood next to the plates, condensation forming on the glass, and there was a side bowl of baby leaf salad.

'Take a seat,' Harry said, coming out of the kitchen, carrying the condiments.

From the table, Maddy could see Sookie tucking into her food in the kitchen, her bowls sitting on some newspaper on the tiled floor.

'Parmesan?' Harry asked, passing Maddy a small tub of freshly grated cheese.

'Yes, please.' She sprinkled some over her dinner, then ground a little pepper. Blowing the chicken on her fork, she then took a bite. 'Mmmm, lovely.'

'I love pasta,' Harry said after finishing a mouthful. 'I need the carbs.'

'Your high metabolism, yes?'

'Yes.' He raised his glass to Maddy, and they tapped their

glasses together before taking a sip. The wine hit the spot for Maddy more than the food – even though she was hungry. Taking one sip helped to relax her as it slid down her throat. She would need to be careful, she didn't need to drink the whole bottle. But then again it might help her sleep.

'It's a shame we've got to wait until the insurance company have been in because we could have used this weekend to start redecorating your bedrooms,' Harry said.

'Trying to get rid of me already are we?' Maddy waved her fork at him, then put it down realising how rude she looked.

'No, no, no, not at all.' Harry shook his head. 'I thought, well, you'd want to be back in your own house as soon as possible. You could sleep there, and eat here while your kitchen is being fitted.'

'Look, Harry, if you're regretting letting me stay, I won't be offended. I can rent somewhere.' Maybe he had changed his mind about her being there with him.

'Nonsense. It's not that. Honest.' Harry looked both apologetic and sincere. 'Look, we could look at paint, if you like? Good excuse for a change of colour.'

'If feels like a mammoth job at the moment. I don't even want to think about it.' Her legs ached still, from traipsing around Truro, then standing there ironing. The thought of redecorating her house, choosing a new kitchen, just . . . daunted her. Some people would be excited to be getting a new kitchen and their house decorated, but Maddy's had come at a cost, and with the busy summer season looming, and her need to make her gallery work, anxiety overpowered her. Where was she going to find the time to do it all?

'The insurance should pay for decorators if you don't fancy doing it yourself.'

'If they pay out.'

'They will.'

'I hope so because I'm not sure I will have time to redecorate.'

'I can help you, if you need it.'

'Harry, your place needs decorating too. Maybe you should concentrate your efforts on your own home. I can't take up all your time.' Maddy pushed her plate away, still full to the brim, anxiety killing her appetite. The man could certainly cook, and seemed the perfect gent from carrying her bags to providing a roof over her head. So far he had successfully rescued this damsel in distress. Yes, very good husband material indeed.

Stop thinking like that.

'I haven't done anything to the house because I decided establishing my business first was a priority.'

'Clearly.' Maddy gestured to the dated floral wallpaper in the dining room, and snorted. *Dear God, how un-lady-like.* Luckily, Harry, in true gent style, ignored the fact she'd made an embarrassing noise through her nose and finished his glass of wine. She could empathise with Harry's need to build up his business. She'd done the same with her own house. She'd just been lucky a young couple had lived in her house before her, so it hadn't needed much redecoration.

'I quite like the flowers.' He smirked, trying to keep his face straight.

'Yes, well, these kinds of flowers went out in the seventies – didn't they? Those large floral designs in bold colours – now they're in.'

Harry screwed up his face. 'I think I'd prefer plain walls eventually.'

'Yes, much more bloke-ish.'

Harry stood, taking both the dishes. 'Would you like a top up on your wine?'

Maddy had finished her glass – like Harry – and she had a taste for it now. 'It would be rude not to. Think I need the alcohol to help me sleep.'

'Shall we sit in front of the telly, maybe watch a film? It might help you relax.'

'Oh, no, I need to do the washing up first, you cooked.'

'Don't worry about it; I did most of it as I was going along.'

'Well, those dishes need washing. Let me at least do those.'

'There is really no need. Go sit down.'

Maddy's hackles rose. She didn't like being told what to

do at the best of times. She felt useless and didn't want to look as if she was abusing Harry's hospitality. 'Harry, if you're going to let me stay, please let me help with the chores. It will keep my mind busy if nothing else. I can't do anything at my house, and I feel really bad. I don't expect you to wait on me hand and foot.'

'You're a guest.'

'No, I'm not, not really.' Maddy stared at him, determined. 'Please, I don't like to be idle.'

'Okay,' Harry held his hands up in defeat. 'You wash, I'll dry. Deal?'

'Deal.'

***

After they'd finished the washing up, and Maddy had been satisfied she'd helped, Harry suggested again that they watch a film while finishing off the bottle of wine. He kept thinking about how he'd offered to help Maddy with the decorating. What was he thinking? Besides, the insurance company would pay for the decorators. He didn't need to get involved. He'd thought the quicker he helped get her house back to normal, the quicker she could move back into her home. Because that's what she wanted, and so did he. Not that he didn't like having her in his house, but they were strangers, after all, only neighbours. He wasn't sure he wanted her living here too long under his roof. At this moment in his life, he needed some time alone to work things through, to try and forget about Karin. He needed to keep things simple in his life.

Or was Maddy a good distraction?

As Harry switched the television on and navigated through his Sky channels, Maddy sat, poised on the other sofa with her glass in hand, still looking tense, as if unable to relax. It was odd, really, Harry thought. This is what he used to do with Karin, yet she'd be curled up in his arms, as they watched the film. Maddy had chosen an action movie over a romantic comedy and laughed heartily at the one-liners.

Half way through, Harry could hear a phone ringing. It wasn't his; it was in his pocket and not vibrating.

'Is your phone ringing?' Harry asked, pausing the film. It was a different ringtone to the one that had played earlier when her mum had phoned her. It sounded like an alarm bell, a siren type ring tone. The type that warned you the caller was unwanted.

Maddy leaned around the sofa, to where her handbag was sitting on the floor and pulled out her phone. She scowled as she answered it.

'What do you want?' she said abruptly, dragging a hand through her loose hair, scrunching it with her fingers.

Harry tried not to listen to the conversation, but he could see by Maddy's reddening cheeks she wasn't happy. He went out to the kitchen, putting some of the pots and pans away that they'd left to dry on the draining board, trying to busy himself. He could still hear her half of the conversation.

'No, I'm not coming home . . . No, I don't care what my mum thinks, thank you. I'm a big girl; I'm staying with a friend,' she caught Harry's eye as he returned, 'and I'm safe. I need to be here to sort out my house.'

Maddy looked as if she was about to explode as she listened to her caller. When she'd clearly had enough she said, 'I am not listening. Goodbye, Connor.' She hung up the phone, mumbled a 'fuck off' for good measure, and fiddled with her phone for a bit – Harry assumed she was putting it on silent – then threw it into her bag, and tucked the bag around the side of the sofa. Then, she finished her glass of wine in one large gulp.

'Another glass?' Harry said, standing up to take her glass.

'Didn't we finish the bottle?'

'I have another or would you prefer something stronger? I take it that was Connor, your ex?'

'Yes, and he had the audacity to tell me I should come home, that my mother's worried about me and blah blah blah.' Maddy let out a short scream of frustration. 'How dare he?'

Harry hesitated. Did he hug her, comfort her? What should he say? He disliked seeing Maddy distressed, he suddenly realised.

'Does he still see your mother?' he said.

'He's bumped into her. Probably deliberately if I know him. My mother was blind when it came to Connor. Only Valerie saw the controlling nature of the man. His possessiveness. He's seeing this as an opportunity for me to come home, so he can try again to get back in my good books. But I'll tell you now; it is *never* going to happen.'

'Something stronger . . .' Harry nodded, saying it more out loud to himself than Maddy. She was clearly angered, and like her red hair – *sorry, strawberry blonde hair* – hot-headed. 'A vodka?'

'Yes please.'

Harry poured them both something stronger and handed Maddy her drink before sitting back down. He pressed play for the film to continue, and tried to relax back on the sofa but, occasionally glancing at Maddy, he could see she was not relaxing. He fought the urge to sit next to her, hug her, worried it would be inappropriate. Did he talk to her? Or was it none of his business? And how much did he really want to get involved? Was he ready to bear someone else's burdens? He was doing enough by providing a roof over her head and her cat's – and as if he'd summoned her there just by thinking of her, Sookie suddenly jumped up onto his lap and nuzzled him, purring.

Maddy noticed the cat. 'Sookie, stop bothering Harry.' Apologising for her cat, she picked Sookie off his lap and placed her on her own, stroking her until she settled. Maybe the cat did have a sixth sense. She purred making Maddy stroke her more. He noticed Maddy slowly relaxing, looking more comfortable on the sofa, and her expression softening, the frown disappearing as if all thoughts of her ex were ebbing away.

The film ended. It was close to half past ten and finally dark outside. Harry switched off the TV and Skybox as Maddy took the glasses to the kitchen.

'Time to hit the sack,' Harry said, stretching.

'Yes, it's been a long day.'

Harry let Maddy use the bathroom first while he made his bed on the sofa. As she walked into his bedroom, he said, 'Good night, and don't look at your phone.' He'd noticed Maddy had taken her handbag with her. 'Don't let this Connor upset you.'

She returned his gaze with a gentle smile. 'I won't.'

***

Maddy shut the bedroom door and changed into the shirt Harry had lent her two days before. The bedroom was warm, so she opened the window to allow a breeze to come into the room. It was a clear night, and she could see the familiar star constellations. Taking a deep breath, Maddy closed the curtains again and slid between the sheets. Sookie had already jumped onto the end of the bed, washing herself to settle down for sleep, too. Comforted by her cat, Maddy soon relaxed.

Then, remembering her phone needed charging, Maddy retrieved it out of her handbag, and placed it on the bedside cabinet, plugging it in. The screen flashed on and she couldn't help seeing a message from Connor.

Please, Maddy, I'm sorry, come home. I love you.

Chapter 9

Sunlight beamed through the curtains, and the early morning birdsong trilled, waking Maddy. She rubbed her eyes and looked at the end of the bed. Sookie was gone, the bedroom door ajar. Poor Harry. He'd probably got another five a.m. start.

She picked up her phone and looked at the time, which wasn't a good idea. Immediately her bad mood resurfaced. Not because it was five minutes past seven, but she remembered Connor had texted her late last night.

Never go back, always move forward, as Valerie had often quoted to her. And how many chances had she given Connor over the months? Their three-year relationship had been bumpy from about four months in. But he'd always managed to win her back. He knew how. In her heart – if she'd listened properly to it – she'd known he wasn't the one, that's why she'd followed her dream to come to Cornwall. And he'd followed, dutifully, but then the cracks had really started to show.

Cornwall had been a bit too laid back for Connor, too slow. He wanted the busy bustle of the city whereas Maddy wanted sea air and sunshine. She wanted the sand between her toes; he'd wanted tarmac under his feet.

Maddy slipped on her shorts underneath Harry's shirt and made her way down the stairs listening carefully for any noise. If he weren't awake, then she'd go back up to bed for a bit. To her relief, she could hear the kettle boiling and the clatter of mugs.

'Good morning,' Maddy said, secretly admiring the view of Harry's back. His hair all ruffled from sleep. *Not a bad view first thing in the morning.*

'Morning,' Harry said grumpily over his shoulder. He shoved a kitchen drawer shut, and the contents inside it clattered.

Maddy tensed. 'Everything okay?'

'It would be if I didn't get an early wake-up call from your cat.'

'Oh, I'm sorry.'

'I can't see why she can't be outside at night.'

'It's safer, that's why.' Maddy's tone matched Harry's. 'And it's not good for the wildlife, as this time of year the birds are about earlier.'

'Well, she's outside now.' Harry slammed the fridge door, putting the milk away. 'Probably shitting on my garden.' He handed her a cup of coffee, but Maddy hesitated, reluctant to take it. When he was angry, Harry looked intimidating.

Maybe he didn't realise how big he was towering over Maddy's five-feet four-inch petite frame.

What Maddy lacked in height, she made up for in feistiness. 'And you have the cheek to call me moody. Is something the matter? Surely this isn't all about Sookie?' She placed her hands on her hips and pushed out her chest. 'Because if it's a problem, maybe I will go to Val's.'

'No, the damn cat didn't really wake me. I was already awake.' Harry groaned as he leaned against the kitchen worktop and combed a hand through his wavy black hair. 'I didn't get much sleep last night. The accident, the fire . . .' He trailed off as if he'd said too much.

'What about them?' Maddy thought he looked troubled. Every now and then she saw a glimpse of some deep trauma in Harry.

'Nothing. It's nothing.' He grabbed his coffee and left the kitchen. 'Do you mind if I use the bathroom first?'

Maddy shrugged, frowning at him. 'Of course not. It's your bathroom.'

***

Harry ducked his head under the hot water and let it flow over his tired body. He needed to wake up and improve his temper. It wasn't fair to take it out on Maddy. He'd never been a moody person; it wasn't normally in his nature.

Although Karin had had terrible ups and downs, he recalled, which he'd dealt with patiently.

He hadn't slept well at all last night, tossing and turning on the couch. Maddy's ex calling hadn't helped. His tablets had knocked him out for a good four hours, but in the early hours of the morning, he'd awoken, sweating and panicked. He dreamt of fire, of Karin, the horrors all over again. Either Maddy's house fire had triggered it, or helping the family out who had broken down. There on the road, for one brief moment, he'd thought it was a traffic accident, a collision, sparking visions of crumpled cars, trapped bodies, the smell of smoke, petrol and hot tarmac. As he'd started to drift back off, the cat had pounced and in a dreamlike state he'd confused her purring with other terrible noises.

It had been about five thirty. He'd fed the cat, put her out and then he'd lain on the sofa, hands behind his head, wide awake, until it was a reasonable hour to get up.

Dressed and ready for the day, Harry stomped down the stairs, his head full of thoughts. Some thoughts were better than others, in an attempt to crowd the bad thoughts out. If he kept himself busy, the memories would dull again.

'Feeling better?' Maddy was sitting at the dining table nursing a fresh cup of coffee. She had obviously made some breakfast and washed up everything because the kitchen was tidy, with washing up piled on the draining board.

'Yes, sorry, I've got some jobs I must attend to today, but I'll fix your back gate too.'

'I might show my face at the gallery. No point moping about here, so I'm going to stick some washing out then head to Tinners Bay. As it's Saturday, it will be fairly busy. Valerie will need a hand.'

'Sounds like a plan.'

'Are you sure you don't mind me and Sookie staying at yours? I could put her into a cattery – the insurance said they'd pay.'

Harry hesitantly shook his head. Would the dreams cease if Maddy moved out and his life went back to normal? 'No . . . for the last time, Maddy, there's no need.' Realising he still sounded angry, he softened his tone. 'I just had a rough night, that's all.'

'Would you like your bed back? I don't mind sleeping on the sofa.'

'The sofa wasn't the cause of my rough night.'

'What if we took it in turns?'

'Maddy, I said I don't mind.' Harry grabbed his truck's keys. 'Oh, while I think about it, here's a spare key to the front door. Then you can come and go as you please.'

'Are you sure?'

'Yes, as long as you don't burn my house down.'

'Not even funny,' Maddy huffed, snatching the key out of his hand. 'Go, have a good day at work.'

***

'Hello, stranger.' Valerie, open-armed, greeted Maddy as she walked into the gallery, and gave her a squeeze. Then, holding Maddy by her shoulders, taking a good look at her, she said, 'But you don't need to be here, I've got it all under control.'

'To be honest, I've done as much washing as I can bear, and I don't fancy doing the ironing during the day – far too hot. I can't do anything with the house until I see the insurance guy so I might as well make the most of my time and help out here.'

'Okay, if you're sure.'

'I'm better off here, investing time into my business. Let's face it I need the money.'

Valerie smiled her understanding. 'I've put the kettle on. Coffee?'

'Could murder one,' Maddy said, beaming.

While the kettle boiled and Valerie made the coffee, Maddy filled her in about Connor's phone call last night.

'He said I should come home, my mother's worried about me.'

'Your mother always worries about you. She's your mother.' Valerie looked at her sternly. 'Take no notice of him. He's trying to exploit a bad situation, trying to catch you while you're weak.'

'I'm not weak.'

'I know you're not, dear,' Valerie said, patting her arm. 'Connor, however, may believe so.'

'Good point.'

'And you wouldn't though, would you? Go back home?' Valerie said, eyebrows raised, her expression concerned.

'Hell no!' Maddy shuddered, and they both laughed.

'What's it like living with your neighbour?'

Maddy shrugged. 'It's okay, I think. I do worry I'm getting under his feet. And really, we are strangers after all. I don't know much about him.' Maddy thought of the medication in Harry's bathroom cabinet, and Harry's reluctance to talk about it. She wouldn't worry Val about those niggles, though. Val was as bad as her own mother for fretting really.

'You can stay at mine.'

'I don't want to impose on you either, though.'

'You wouldn't be,' Valerie said, squeezing her shoulder.

Once they both had a mug of coffee in their hands, and forgetting Connor, Valerie showed Maddy around the gallery, pointing out some new pieces delivered by a local painter, Declan, and updating her on the ones sold. Maddy remembered she'd spoken to Declan a couple of weeks ago to agree terms for exhibiting paintings in her gallery. He'd said something about popping in with a couple of pieces of his work.

'You had a busy day yesterday, then?'

'Yes, luckily the artist who came in with his paintings hung them for me,' Valerie said. 'Even at my age, I know how to bat my eyelashes.'

'You do know Declan is gay, don't you?'

'No! Never! What a waste! Josie and I were swooning

over him all bloody day.' Valerie looked horrified with her eyes wide. 'He was bloody gorgeous.'

Maddy chuckled. Valerie was a breath of fresh air and the medicine she needed was right here in this gallery. She would paint her worries away.

***

After a couple of hours, Maddy put her paintbrush down, only realising she was hungry by the growling of her stomach. She'd got so lost in her work she hadn't realised the time had flown by incredibly quickly.

She told Valerie she was going to head out for some fresh air. It was a beautiful day outside, and she would make the most of the sunshine. You never knew how long this weather would last. Maddy walked to the cafe on the corner of the high street by the entrance to the beach, and bought a freshly made toasted bacon and brie sandwich, with lashings of cranberry sauce, and a mango and pineapple iced smoothie. She slipped off her flip-flops and walked on the beach, delighting in the warm sand between her toes.

She always admired the houses situated above the beach, looking down on this beautiful view, and out to the ocean. She dreamed of owning one of those houses . . . one day. But they rarely came onto the market, and she'd need to be making a success of her gallery first. There was a cottage looking sorry for itself situated amongst the row of houses.

It had done for a while now, but as far as she could tell, building work was underway, although the overgrown thicket of brambles in the garden made it difficult to see. It would look beautiful once it was finished. Would the owner live in it, let it or sell it? Maybe once it was finished, Maddy could capture it on canvas, painting its new look?

She found a spot to the side of the beach which was sheltered from the chilly sea breeze that took the heat out of the sun, and settled on a rock. She watched the sea and the surfers.

Tonight, to thank Harry, she'd cook dinner. If he were prepared to let her stay, then she would at least help around the house. Only what to cook? His physique told her he ate healthily and looked after himself, but with all that toned muscle, maybe he'd appreciate a good steak? Or oven-baked chops? Or perhaps a nice fillet of grilled salmon?

A seagull cry brought Maddy back to the beach, with the realisation she had a couple of gulls eyeing her sandwich greedily. The little bastards were nifty thieves. On many occasions, she'd watched them steal ice creams from children's hands or burgers straight from the barbeque. She huddled around her sandwich. If she threw out a bit, she'd be bombarded. It was best not to encourage the little critters.

Maddy finished her sandwich and closed her eyes, letting the warmth from the sun soak into her skin. Until Wednesday night, everything had been going to plan. She loved her life by the coast. You couldn't beat lunch on the beach with the sun shining. She'd chosen this part of Cornwall, possibly as a safety net.

She had known Valerie since birth (not that she could remember that bit). Valerie was an 'aunty' but not by blood. Sandra and Valerie had been best friends since their school days. Maddy had moved here knowing Valerie would help with the gallery. It was her dream too. Valerie had moved to Tinners Bay many years ago, and Mum and Dad had brought Maddy and her brother, Edward, here on holidays. Tinners Bay didn't feel alien to her. It had always been her second home. Valerie had been the one to tell Maddy about the shop space becoming available, and this had spurred her to take the plunge, and give it a go. 'Tinners Bay needs a gallery,' Valerie had urged, 'it'll work.' It would mean being surrounded by everything she enjoyed painting: landscapes, seascapes, gorgeous cottages – and no longer having to travel up and down the M5 and A30 for commissions.

And, however much she loved her mother, she was out from under her net. Maddy was able to stand on her own two feet without Sandra breathing down her neck, making her 'recommendations'.

After half an hour, Maddy strolled off the beach, depositing her rubbish in one of the bins. She resolved she would do a couple more hours' work then head back so she was home in plenty of time to cook dinner. She brushed the sand off her legs the best she could and slipped on her flip-flops. She crossed the road and entered the gallery to see a tall, muscular man in shorts and a ripped T-shirt talking to Valerie. He turned and looked at her, smiling. Raising her sunglasses to place on top of her head, she gave herself a mental shake. It was Harry.

'Hi,' she said, realising she sounded surprised. Then she panicked. What if something else was wrong with the house?

'Hi, I thought I'd call in,' Harry said, oblivious that Valerie was giving him the once over. 'I was only up the road. I've got a few contracts here. I just started a new one, plus I do a garden on Sandy Lane and I have a couple of holiday home gardens in Tinners Bay I maintain as well.'

His mood was certainly better than it was this morning.

'Oh right, I was just thinking about you,' Maddy said, trying to get her brain to catch up with her mouth. Harry tilted his head, raising a curious eyebrow at her. 'I mean, uh, I was thinking I'd cook dinner for us tonight. It's the least I can do.'

'You don't have to.'

'No, I do. You're not fussy are you?'

He rubbed his stomach. Not one ounce of fat. 'Do I look like I'm fussy?'

Maddy shut her mouth and shook her head. She went to lick her lips, but pressed them together until she could think of something to say. 'So . . .' she took a deep breath, 'I see you've met Valerie.'

'Yes,' Valerie said, eager to join the conversation. 'I've told him how I've known you since you were in nappies.' Valerie smiled smugly. She was worse than her mother for embarrassing her. Only Valerie knew damn well she was doing it.

Maddy blushed. 'Thanks for that.'

'Actually, she's been showing me your work. I love what you're working on at the moment,' Harry said walking over to the easel set up in the corner. Maddy hadn't moved from the spot all morning until lunch. It was her seascape with the waves crashing. She'd painted streaks of pink in the sky for a sunset. The picture still needed a lot of work.

'Thank you,' Maddy said. 'I think I've ended up making the sea choppier due to recent events.'

'Understandable.'

'Did you want a coffee?'

'No, no, I better head off. I have a big contract I need to put some time into.' Harry pulled his truck keys out of his pocket. 'Just thought I'd say hi as I was in the area.'

'Okay, I'll see you later. Remember, I'm cooking dinner tonight.'

'I know better than to argue.'

'Bye, Harry, lovely to meet you.' Valerie waved coquettishly. Maddy watched her suspiciously. *She's such a flirt.*

Harry waved back and was gone.

'Now I know why you didn't want to stay at mine,' Valerie said, hands on her hips, her tone teasing, giving an all-knowing nod. The sixty-two-year-old had been positively drooling over Harry's backside as he had walked out.

'He insisted!' Maddy blushed.

'I'm sure he did.' Valerie had a twinkle of mischief in her eye. 'It's okay,' Valerie placed a supportive palm on Maddy's shoulder, 'you probably wouldn't want to stay with an old biddy like me anyway.'

'You're not an old biddy.'

'Well, if I had the choice, I'd definitely be sleeping in his bed.'

'Valerie! It's not like that.'

'It should be. He's gorgeous. And he doesn't seem obnoxious. You said he was obnoxious.'

'That's before I got to know him – remember?' Only Maddy still didn't know him well. Why the restless night? Why the drugs in his bathroom cabinet? Why had he left a job he'd loved so much?

'Well, I approve.'

'Approve of what?' Maddy frowned, suspicion etching into her thoughts.

Valerie coughed, clearing her throat. 'Um . . . he is safe to stay with . . .'

Maddy's eyes narrowed. That wasn't what she meant at all.

'He comes across as a perfect gent,' Valerie continued, 'Which is a shame really because sometimes us girls don't want them to be gents . . . well, not in the bedroom.'

'Valerie!'

Maddy probably wasn't his type . . . was she? She ticked

herself off. She shouldn't be thinking along these lines; Harry was simply doing her a platonic, neighbourly favour.

And even if he were interested in her, after Connor, Maddy wasn't sure she was ready to try again.

Chapter 10

Maddy clocked off at the gallery early, leaving Valerie to lock up. She needed no persuading, literally pushing Maddy out the door.

'I have no idea what to cook for dinner,' Maddy said, slinging her bag over her shoulder and hesitating in the open doorway. 'What if he doesn't like my cooking?'

'He will,' Valerie said, still holding the door open, 'I'm sure you'll think of something. Pasta? A man like Harry can do with the carbs.'

'But we had pasta yesterday.'

'What about oysters? They're supposed to be an aphrodisiac.' Valerie tried to keep her face straight, but failed.

Maddy tutted. 'I do not need an aphrodisiac. And even if I did, I wouldn't eat oysters unless you paid me. They are revolting and I can't think of anything less sexy.' Maddy grimaced at the thought. 'And knowing my luck, I'd probably get food poisoning and spend the night with my head down the toilet.' Valerie chuckled. 'You are not helping, Valerie.'

'Oh, go get some inspiration from the supermarket then.'

'I will.'

Maddy pushed the trolley around the Co-Op in Wadebridge, going down each aisle for some *inspiration*, agonising over what to cook. Cooking for someone really proved how well you knew them. She really didn't know Harry very well at all. It had only been a couple of days and before that, they'd usually been at each other's throat.

She used to hate cooking for Connor. She'd be on tenterhooks dishing up dinner. He'd been so fussy about food, and controlling, usually ending up taking over in the kitchen.

As she walked past the fresh fish counter, Maddy decided to stay away from fish, in case Harry was allergic. Or fussy, like Connor. In the end, erring on the side of caution, and deciding it was probably best to keep things simple, she picked up a couple of steaks. It wasn't a date or anything; she was providing dinner as a thank you. Nothing more.

Harry had eaten chicken the night before, so Maddy was confident he wasn't vegetarian. To go with the steaks, she decided to stick with the healthy theme, picking up some new potatoes and a packet of posh veg as she called it – all ready-prepared; baby carrots, mangetout, baby corns and green beans. She would make a peppercorn sauce. She was no Nigella Lawson, but her mother had taught her to cook simple tasty dishes.

Although in case it went wrong, Maddy grabbed a packet sauce off the shelf too.

Because she didn't know what time Harry was due home, she had everything prepared in his kitchen. To complement the steaks, she'd picked up a couple of bottles of red wine, and decided to open one while she waited.

Harry's back garden was north facing, which made sense as hers was south facing – their houses were opposite one another. But it meant his back garden was now mostly in the shade unless she sat at the front, so she sat outside his front door, on the step, facing the sun and sipped her wine, the sun warm on her face. The only problem was it meant she was staring at her house and feeling useless. She would chase the insurance company on Monday.

Sookie trotted over, rubbed her head against Maddy's leg and purred. Maddy had already fed her, which would keep her out of the way. Sookie made herself comfortable on the drive sunbathing and swishing her tail.

Around half past six, Harry reversed his pickup onto the driveway. He got out of the truck and immediately stripped off his T-shirt.

'Hey,' he said, using his T-shirt to wipe the sweat off his face. 'Been waiting long?'

'No.' Maddy stood up, empty wine glass in hand, and tried to keep her eyes focused on his, and not on his tanned, muscular flesh. His skin gleamed with sweat, and his torso was lightly covered with dark swirls of hair; not too much, enough to be manly but not ape-like. She imagined what it would feel like, her fingers combing through the curls and up his solid chest.

'Any wine left for me?'

'Oh, uh, yes of course.' Maddy blinked, shaking out of her reverie. 'I poured myself a glass while preparing dinner. It's nothing complicated. It won't take long to cook so I thought I'd make the most of the evening sunshine until you came home.'

'Do you mind if I shower first?' He showed his hands, palms up. They were ingrained with dirt.

'No, no, I'll start cooking – the potatoes may need twenty minutes.'

'I'll be ten.'

'Wait. Um . . . how do you like your steak cooked?'

'Medium rare.'

'Great, like me. I mean, that's how I like my steak . . .' *Oh shut up and cook the dinner, woman.* The man's half nakedness had gone to her head. Yet, she'd seen it plenty of times. Only now she knew Harry wasn't as obnoxious as she'd always assumed, it obviously affected her differently.

Harry came down the stairs ten minutes later drying his hair with a small towel. He placed the towel over the chair and came into the kitchen, reaching above Maddy's head to get a wine glass.

Wearing a clean T-shirt and a pair of shorts, he smelt fresh with a hint of a spicy aroma. She couldn't remember Connor ever smelling so good. Maddy tried to shift her concentration back to stirring the peppercorn sauce rather than the presence of Harry – with great difficulty. He leaned over her and sniffed the sauce. He wasn't even touching her, but sensing him, inches away from her, made Maddy's body temperature rise.

It's not Harry; it's standing over a hot stove.

'Looks good.' Harry leaned against the counter, pouring himself a glass of wine, then topping Maddy's up.

'Thought I'd keep it simple. Now go sit down, this kitchen isn't big enough for the two of us.' *Literally*. Harry was taking up so much airspace, Maddy couldn't breathe.

Harry did as he was told, and the temperature in the kitchen dropped. With Harry out of the way, Maddy was able to focus on the steaks and the sauce and managed not to burn anything. Satisfied, she placed the plates on the table and sat down.

'This looks fabulous,' Harry said, cutting up his steak. 'Did you see I'd fixed your back gate?'

'Yes, when I came home I got my washing in. When did you do it?'

'This morning, thought I'd get it over and done with, and then we know the back of your house will be more secure.' It sounded like he wanted the reassurance as much as Maddy. 'I've got a lock to put on it.'

'Tell me how much I owe you, won't you? I'll talk to my insurance company on Monday.'

Harry nodded whilst chewing. 'I've kept the receipts.'

After dinner, Harry washed up the plates and cutlery. He studied the bottle of red Maddy had opened. There was enough left for a small glass each.

'Tell you what, shall we go to the pub?' Harry suggested, to Maddy's surprise.

Maddy hesitated. It would beat being stuck in front of the television, and it was a warm Saturday evening. She wouldn't feel so on edge being in a house with a man she hardly knew. 'Yes, all right, why not. But can I get freshened up first? I need a shower, too.'

***

Harry and Maddy walked to the pub on the high street; the Molesworth Arms was only a fifteen-minute stroll downhill. Harry had waited patiently for the half an hour it had taken Maddy to shower, put fresh clothes on and apply some make-up. In his opinion, she didn't need the make-up to make her look more attractive, yet he couldn't deny the dark eyeliner and mascara highlighted her stunning green eyes. She wore her hair loose, the front curling, framing her oval face.

'You grab a table; I'll get the drinks. Shall we share a bottle of red?' Harry said as they entered the pub. Warm, muggy air engulfed them as they entered and he realised he'd placed his hand on her lower back. He quickly took it away, shoving his hand into his pocket. If she'd noticed she said nothing.

'Yes, let's. Shall we sit outside?'

'Yeah, sure, it's still warm. We can come in if it gets chilly.'

Harry brought out the bottle of Australian Shiraz and two large wine glasses, joining Maddy at a picnic table out the front of the pub. The high street was pedestrian-access only so it was a great place to people-watch. The 16th century, white-washed pub was idyllic this time of year with hanging baskets and window boxes bursting with a mix of trailing flowers and cerise petunias tumbled down over the front pillars of the entrance. He poured the wine and opted to sit opposite her, fearing next to her would be too cosy.

'I know what I was going to ask you,' Maddy said. Her tone caught Harry off guard, worrying him.

He eyed her suspiciously. 'What?'

'The other day I noticed some of your post addressed to a Mr Henry Tudor.'

Harry chuckled with relief. 'Yes, that's my name; Henry Arthur Tudor. But I've been called Harry since birth. I'm a month younger than Prince Harry.'

'Oh, yes, I see.'

'My mother couldn't resist, with a surname like Tudor, she wanted to name me after a king.'

'Why do parents do that to their children? And why didn't she just name you Harry? Did you used to get stick about it at school?' Maddy said, setting her glass down. 'Actually, looking at the size of you, I doubt you were ever bullied.'

'Believe it or not, I was one of the smallest in my class

for a while. Luckily, there were at least three Henrys in my year. It did make it easier that I was called Harry. Sometimes my mates teased me about the whole king thing, especially when we were learning about the Tudors and Stewarts, but it was only when I joined the fire brigade they nicknamed me Roses.' Harry sipped his wine, watching Maddy. 'Do you know where Maddison comes from?'

'I have no idea.' Maddy shrugged. 'I'd like to think I was conceived in New York, but I doubt it. I would have been Madison with one D.' They both laughed. 'But knowing my mother, she chose to be different.'

Two bottles of red wine and a bowl of chips to soak up the alcohol later, Maddy and Harry walked – stumbled – home, arm in arm. Mainly because she needed support more than anything. She'd stood up and wobbled, and he'd grabbed her to steady her. He'd been thoughtless to suggest the second bottle, but he'd been enjoying Maddy's company and hadn't wanted it to stop.

Harry had let Maddy do most of the talking through the evening, but they'd laughed and talked about nonsense really. Now, as they staggered into Annadale Close, Maddy gossiped about another neighbour.

'I don't think much of her at the end,' she said, slurring her words a little and waving her arms about. There were about twenty houses in the close. She could have been talking about any one of them. Most of their neighbours were retired. A few families lived on the close, with children ranging from toddlers to teenagers. Sometimes the younger kids were out on their bikes or playing football on the weekends, or after school.

'Who?'

'You know the one who won't even say good morning. Always got her nose in the air. The mad cat lady – she has five cats, you know?'

'Five?' Harry snapped louder than intended. 'What is it with you people and bloody cats?'

'Shhhh . . . you'll wake the neighbours,' Maddy protested, giggling.

'We are the neighbours.' Harry stood facing her as they reached his drive. Maddy had stopped and stared at her house, letting out a heavy sigh.

'Phew, it's still there.'

'Of course it's still there. And before you argue, I'm cutting your front lawn. It's getting out of hand.'

'Will you now?'

'Yes, you're letting the close down.' Harry lifted his head haughtily but couldn't keep a straight face.

'I'm sorry, I've been busy.' Maddy pouted. 'I'll pay you.'

'You'll do no such thing.'

'Harry, you've done too much for me already.' Maddy touched his arm. Then she stumbled, so he supported her by grasping her arm. He released his grip as soon as she'd found her feet.

'I'm not doing it for you. I'm doing it for me,' he said. 'It will mean I can look out my front window and see a pristine garden. Both your neighbours keep their gardens looking so smart with their flowerbeds and roses. You're letting the side down.'

She narrowed her eyes at him. 'Oh, that side,' she pointed to the house to the left of hers, 'they're almost as bad as her down the end, but they're polite enough. Mrs Delphine is lovely, though.' She gestured to the house adjoining hers. 'We're on a close with a load of old dodderys though.'

'A lot of people come to retire in Cornwall.'

'I suppose.' Maddy shrugged, the urge to argue gone from her. Harry unlocked his front door, and let her in first. She went to the kitchen, poured a glass of water and gulped it down. Harry watched, mesmerised, from the moisture on her lips, to her throat as she swallowed, down to the V of her cleavage revealed by her blouse. She wiped her mouth, less conscious of her appearance due to her tipsiness, and said, 'You're just as bad, too. Old fogey.'

'Oh yeah, I'll show you old fogey.' Swiftly, Harry took the glass out of her hand, placing it on the counter and dipped his head, his lips crushing hers.

Maddy's eyes widened, then relaxing into the kiss, her hands wrapped around his neck and she pushed her body up against his. His grip tightened around her slim frame as he gently explored her mouth with his tongue.

Chapter 11

Maddy awoke, her vision blurry, her head pounding and her mouth as dry as if she'd been marooned on a desert island and hadn't tasted water for days. She ran her tongue around her mouth, hoping this would moisturise it. She tried to move. A solid, heavy arm, draped over her chest, weighed her down.

Harry's.

She froze, afraid to budge. Over the sound of her heart pounding in her ears, she could hear him breathing. She prayed he was still asleep while she got her head around this.

What the hell did she do last night? *Think, Maddy.*

Did she sleep with him?

Well, clearly she'd slept with him – they were in the same bed, weren't they? – but had she actually had sex with him?

Lifting the duvet gently, she saw she was wearing his shirt. The one she'd been wearing to bed the last couple of nights. But the top buttons were undone, and if it weren't for Harry's arm, her breast would be bare. As slowly and as subtly as she could, dread filling her, she brushed her free hand against her hip – the other was trapped under Harry. *Oh, hell, no knickers.*

Her memory was lethal when drinking red wine. Two bottles between them, plus what they'd had before heading to the pub. She was such a lightweight when it came to red wine.

You're such an idiot.

But she'd know if she'd had sex, wouldn't she? Usually, her insides throbbed a little or even ached – depending on how good the sex was . . .

Her head throbbed. She knew that much.

Maddy kept her eyes closed to stop the drum thumping in her head and trawled through the evening's events, but she couldn't remember much past leaving the pub and walking home.

Then suddenly, she remembered. Harry had kissed her.

Maddy's eyes shot open and she glanced at the sleeping man next to her. The image replayed over and over in her head like a mini video. She couldn't remember anything else, only that he'd kissed her. And it had been rather good. Butterflies swirled in her lower stomach at the memory. He'd taken her by surprise, his lips rough on hers, and then he'd softened, and become so gentle.

But that was it, all she could remember. How she'd got into bed with him, or got undressed . . . nothing.

Maddy needed to use the bathroom, and needed water

and some painkillers. Whether she could stomach breakfast would be another matter. In as smooth a movement as possible, not wanting to wake the sleeping giant beside her, she ever so slowly lifted his arm and started to slip out from under the duvet.

Harry's limp arm tensed, his eyes opened and he raised his head. Maddy hastily moved back, pulling the duvet around her, staying in the bed.

'Morning,' he said, his eyes barely open.

'Morning,' Maddy replied, clutching the duvet close to her chest.

'Did you sleep okay?'

Maddy frowned – which hurt. He wasn't even surprised they were in bed together.

'Yes . . . but I'm having a bit of a memory lapse . . . did we, you know?' She chewed her lip anxiously.

Harry squinted his eyes then rubbed them. Quite clearly naked on his top half. God, she hoped he had his boxers on but was too afraid to look south as the duvet moved. She blindly buttoned her shirt under the covers.

'Did we what?' Harry said, wearing a confused expression. 'You know?'

'You had too much wine that's what I do know.'

'Oh, for god's sake, did we have sex?' Maddy said, impatience lacing her tone.

'Oh.' Harry rose up onto his elbow, resting his head in his hand, looking more awake. *And gorgeous.*

She was in bed with Adonis. Really, she should not complain, although she was hardly Aphrodite.

'No, of course not,' he said. 'What do you take me for? You were so drunk – as was I – it would have been wrong.'

Relief washed over Maddy. 'Oh, thank God.' But with it so did nausea. 'Oh, I think I'm going to be sick.' She rushed out of the bedroom, caring not whether the shirt covered her naked bum and dashed to the bathroom, making it to the toilet just in time. She hadn't had time to close the bathroom door so Harry would have heard every un-lady-like retch coming from her as she emptied her stomach. And even when it was empty, she still retched.

Finally, feeling like death warmed up, she returned to the bedroom completely embarrassed. But she had to lie back down. This was going to take a while to pass. These hang-overs usually did.

'Better?'

'No. Never let me drink red wine in that volume ever again. I can't handle it.'

'I'd say,' Harry chuckled the words.

'Oh, God, what did I do?' Maddy kept her eyes closed, placing a hand on her forehead.

'Let me tell you over breakfast.'

'No, no, I can't face food . . . water, please, just some water.'

'Okay, I'll get you a glass of water,' Harry said, smoothly evacuating the bed, keeping his back to her. Maddy squinted, to sneak a look if he had boxers on. He did. She caught

144

sight of them, as he hitched his jeans up to his hips. She heard a drawer slide and assumed he was fetching a fresh T-shirt.

With every step Harry took down the stairs, Maddy's head pounded. Minutes later, he'd returned placing a glass of water on the bedside cabinet beside her.

The bed dipped as he sat down on the edge of it. She opened one eye to look at him, but even that hurt. He was smiling at her. 'So, is there anything else I can get you?' Very carefully Maddy shook her head and groaned a no. The back of his hand brushed her forehead. 'Then, I'll leave you to sleep.'

Maddy waited for Harry to leave, then took a sip from the glass. She lay back down, closing her eyes. She kept herself as still as possible in the foetal position and hoped the nausea would pass.

***

Maddy awoke, her head feeling a little better. Not brilliant, but definitely better. Her stomach grumbled. She was ravenous, yet, would anything she put in it stay down?

She fumbled for her phone to check the time. The battery was dying – she'd forgotten to put it on charge the night before, which was hardly surprising all things considered. There was one missed call and a text message to say she had a voicemail message. Well, at least she'd remembered to put her phone on silent for the night.

Through squinted eyes, she rested her head back on the pillow and listened to the voicemail.

'Hi, Miss Hart, this is Roy Trewyn. I know we agreed for you to deliver the paintings on Monday, but I was wondering if we could have them today.'

'Shit!' she said as he rattled off a telephone number for Maddy to call him back on. She couldn't mess this up. Roy Trewyn was a friend of Valerie's and she didn't want to let either of them down. She sat up quickly and instantly regretted it, her rumbling stomach still unsettled.

What time was it? She glanced at her phone. *One o'clock. Double shit.*

She tried to move out of bed. 'Ow, ow, ow.' Her head hated the movement. Would food help or make her feel worse? She had to try.

Maddy plugged her phone in to charge, not liking the five percent battery life status. It triggered an OCD Maddy didn't realise she had. She liked her phone charged; anything below fifty percent battery life made her nervous.

She hoped she'd saved the voicemail message because she hadn't noted the number Roy had given, and it wasn't the same as the number he'd used to call her on. She needed a pen, some paper and some food.

As quick as her throbbing head would allow, she donned last night's clothes, which she found crumpled on the carpet beside the bed, and went downstairs in search of her handbag.

Harry walked through the back door into the kitchen. 'Oh, great, you're up.' Then he must have seen her expression because his smile dropped. 'Everything all right?'

'No, I can't find my handbag.'

'It's over the bannister where you left it.'

'Like I can remember where I left it.' Her head throbbed more. Realising her tone had been inappropriate, she said, 'Sorry, it's not your fault.'

'What's wrong?'

'I'm supposed to be delivering my commission tomorrow, but they've called and asked if I can deliver it today. I need to make a note of the number so I can call him back.' Maddy sighed with frustration. 'And my head hurts. It's one o'clock. He called at ten.' She held her head in her hands and took deep breaths. However much Harry's dining room needed redecorating he wouldn't be overly impressed if she threw up on his carpet. 'And how can I drive in this state?' She hated how desperate she sounded.

Harry placed his hand on her back, and rubbed, slow movements, up and down, soothing her. To Maddy's surprise, her body betrayed her, relishing his touch. 'Right, phone the man back, then get in the shower, and I'll drive you to wherever you need to go.'

'You'd do that?'

'Of course. Do you want me to get you some breakfast first?' Harry glanced at his watch, his hand leaving her spine. 'Well, technically, lunch?'

147

Maddy wanted the warmth of his touch to return but knew she couldn't ask. 'I can maybe stomach some toast and orange juice.'

'Go call the guy back, and I'll fetch you some food.'

Maddy nodded, and headed back upstairs to her phone, praying she wouldn't be sick again.

***

Her heart lighter after the reassuring conversation with Mr Trewyn, Maddy came down the stairs to the mouth-watering smell of bacon cooking. Harry stood with his back to her in the kitchen, buttering thick wholemeal bread. He looked over his shoulder and beamed. *He really had lovely teeth.*

God that was a bit random.

'Any sauce?' he said, placing the bacon onto a slice of bread.

'Brown sauce, please,' Maddy said, snapping out of her thoughts. 'Is this mine?' She pointed towards the tall glass of orange juice.

'Yes.'

She took a sip from the glass, her taste buds welcoming the zingy orange juice. Harry handed her the bacon sandwich. 'I figured a bacon sandwich would sort you out better than a bit of toast. I had some earlier. It should still hit the spot.'

'Thank you.' Maddy gingerly made her way into the

dining room, still feeling delicate. She took a small bite into the sandwich. Although starving hungry, she didn't want to make herself feel sick by eating too fast. The mixture of melted butter, soft wholemeal bread, brown sauce and bacon did the trick. She savoured every bite and with every swallow her stomach seemed to churn less.

'Have you any painkillers?' She'd been too afraid to take them earlier, fearing they wouldn't stay down. But now she could actually eat, she might manage a paracetamol. With the amount of pills in Harry's bathroom cabinet, he must surely have some painkillers among them?

'Yeah, sure.' Harry went back into the kitchen, then returned with a packet of silver foiled tablets with a couple cracked open and empty.

Maddy broke open two tablets, and swallowed them one at a time with a swig of orange juice, pausing momentarily before each swallow. She always had to think before taking tablets, as if to tell her body not to chew them first. She hated if they got stuck in her throat, it made her gag, and she really didn't need to do that today, under the circumstances.

'So what did the guy say?' Harry pulled out a chair opposite Maddy and sat down at the table.

'He was great. I made the excuse that my phone had died. He said to come over when I was ready. Although he'd like them before three this afternoon if possible.' Maddy finished her sandwich.

'Yeah, we'll make it,' Harry said glancing at his watch. 'It's in Padstow. Are you sure you don't mind driving?'

'I said I would, didn't I?' Harry's eyebrows rose, in the not to argue with him type of way. When he said he'd do something, Maddy was beginning to realise he meant it.

***

Feeling better, thanks to the shower and bacon sandwich, but still hung-over and tired, Maddy handed Harry a canvas carefully wrapped in bubble wrap and brown paper. They were in her garage retrieving the paintings for the commission. She picked up the other one and followed Harry, where he loaded them into the flatbed of his truck. She feared it would be muddy and grimy, but Harry had thought of everything. He'd lined his truck with a clean plastic sheet, and secured the paintings so they wouldn't move around too much in the back of the truck. While showering and dressing – she'd chosen a cerise summer dress, smart but casual to meet her client – she tried hard to remember the night before, but nothing was coming back to her.

'Are you going to tell me what happened last night?' Maddy asked as she watched Harry close up the tailgate of his pickup. 'I'm assuming you at least remember.'

Harry chuckled. 'You still can't remember anything?'

'No, I can't,' Maddy said.

'Okay.' Harry leaned on his truck casually, folding his

arms. Everything he did was so damn . . . sexy. 'I'd made some comment about getting my bedding for the sofa out of the spare room, and you insisted I slept in my bed. We were too drunk to mess about and you said it was big enough for the two of us. You wouldn't take no for an answer. Those were your words. When you stripped off my T-shirt and pushed me onto the bed, I decided not to argue with you. You're quite fiery.'

'Seriously? You tower over me, and yet I'm fiery?'

'Trust me, I didn't want to argue with you. Not last night.'

Maddy could feel the heat rushing up her neck and to her cheeks – her skin was probably blending with the colour of her dress right now. *How the hell had she got his T-shirt off? And why couldn't she remember it?* 'And we . . . definitely didn't have sex?' she asked.

'God, no!'

'Gee, thanks, am I that unattractive?' *Shouldn't have blurted that out. Best not to know the truth.*

'No, no, no,' Harry held up his hands, 'I didn't mean it to sound . . . Oh, Maddy, I mean, you're here as a guest, and I wouldn't take advantage of you. Besides, we were both ridiculously drunk.'

'What? You mean . . .?'

'Yes, I probably wouldn't have been able to, you know, perform?' Harry glanced away. 'I didn't even take my meds.'

'Meds?' *All the stuff in his cabinet.*

Harry walked around to the cab of his truck and got in.

Maddy followed and climbed into the passenger seat. This was where he was going to change the subject, she was learning.

'What are the meds for, exactly?' Maddy couldn't help herself. Harry combed his large hand through his hair. She loved looking at his hands. Strong, hard-working, manly hands. The roughness of them stroking her smooth skin. *Stop. Stop. Stop.* 'Harry, you can tell me. I would rather know I'm safe and not staying with a psychopath or schizophrenic.'

Harry laughed. 'I'm neither of those. They help me sleep okay, but clearly the red wine helped me enough last night.'

'So they're sleeping tablets?'

'Not exactly.' Harry started the engine. Reversing the truck off his drive, he said, 'They help me, Maddy, all right?'

Maddy could tell when Harry didn't want to talk about things – especially about this. He concentrated on the road and changed the subject.

Finding his sunglasses, Harry said, 'Okay, where in Padstow are we heading?'

Chapter 12

Maddy shook Mr Trewyn's hand, thanking him for his business. She had a cheque in her handbag for the sum of fifteen hundred pounds and he had two of her finest paintings. One of her best-paid commissions to date. And really she had Valerie to thank for introducing them. Both pieces were large in comparison to the more affordable pieces she sold in the gallery. To justify the price and due to their size she had put countless hours into them over the last couple of months, hence she'd feared them being damaged in the fire. Mr Trewyn had been more than happy with the price, as long as she provided an invoice for tax purposes as it was part of the cost of opening his new restaurant. She was proud of these pieces because they had been her biggest focus after Connor had left; they'd been her therapy.

Mr Trewyn had wanted a couple of paintings to give the flavour of Cornwall and Padstow to be hung in his wife's new restaurant. He'd shown Maddy the two bare walls where he wanted to hang the pictures, large spaces in need of impressive coverage.

'You know, if you'd like to hang a couple of pieces in here to sell, I'd be happy to do that, too,' Mr Trewyn said. 'It's good to support local businesses.' He was a handsome man, even for his age – somewhere in his early sixties – and he looked and acted younger than he probably was. A charmer. Maddy could see why he ran front of house in the restaurant and his wife was the chef. 'I might see if my daughter is interested, too. She and her husband own a restaurant here in Padstow as well – From Under The Sea, it's called.'

'Okay, thank you, Mr Trewyn.' Maddy had seen the restaurant but had never eaten there.

'Roy, please . . .'

'Roy.' Maddy gently nodded and smiled. 'I'll see if I have a couple of pieces in my gallery to fit your restaurant. I'm not sure if you've caught up with Valerie recently, but I've had a bit of disaster with my house.'

'Yes, she did say. You've had a house fire. I'm sorry to hear that.'

'Thank you. My head is all over the place, and I'm not painting as much as I should. So, in the meantime, could I leave some business cards?'

'Of course, because I'm sure these pictures will gather

lots of interest – can't wait to show Anne – but they're a bit of a surprise.'

'Oh gosh, I hope she likes them.'

'She will love them, don't you worry.'

'Well, in return, please give me some of your business cards, and I'll put them in the gallery. I'll keep them by the till. And I'll try to come to dinner one evening. I'm dying to see them hung in place.'

'That would be lovely. I'll give you a discount off the food.' He winked, then glanced at Harry waiting by the front door, keeping an eye on his precariously parked truck. 'Get the boyfriend to treat you. I can tell you're newly—'

'Oh, no, Harry's not my boyfriend. He's my neighbour.'

Roy gave Maddy an unconvinced expression. 'We open Friday evening, but we're full to the brim. Give me a call and we'll fit you in over the next couple of weeks.'

'Fantastic.'

'Thanks again for dropping these over a bit earlier. I realised tomorrow would be too much of a rush with all the final touches.'

'Thank you for giving me the commissions.'

'My pleasure. Tell Val we'll catch up soon.'

'I will.' Maddy smiled and waved, then joined Harry, who nodded and signalled his goodbye to Roy too.

'We have to come here for dinner one evening. It'll be my treat for you driving me around.'

'Great, I was admiring the menu. It's a date, I mean deal,' Harry quickly corrected himself as Maddy's expression must have shown her surprise.

***

'How's your head feeling now?' Harry handed Maddy a cup of coffee. She looked deep in thought, elbows leaning on his dining room table, with the patio doors open and the summer breeze cooling the air. Wisps of her hair fluttered with the moving air, the sunshine highlighting the gold, reds and blondes.

He watched as she came out of her reverie and took the mug. 'Thank you. Head is feeling better, and I also feel better now those paintings are with their new owner.'

'Well, I'm going to make the most of the sunshine and cut your front and back lawns.'

'You really don't have to.' Maddy looked up at him, frowning. Could she remember the conversation they'd had on the drive last night?

'Oh, I do.' It irked him to see her front garden looking scruffy, and now he was on better terms with Maddy he could use it as an excuse to tidy up her garden.

'Why do you say it like that?' Beautiful green eyes stared up at him, questioningly. Now no longer the neighbour from hell, as he was getting to know her more, Harry appreciated her prettiness. In fact, something inside him stirred. *Please do not let it move to my groin.*

He coughed to clear his throat. 'I mean it's the least I can do. You've got enough on your plate.' *Plus, he could do with the therapy.*

'I'll be glad when someone from the insurance company can come, then I can crack on with getting my house back to normal.'

'If I tidy the front up and give the back a mow too, at least we'll be able to see your house and know it's tidy on the outside.'

Maddy shook her head at him and started idly scrolling through her phone, looking through Facebook. Apparently, she'd been left a lot of messages of encouragement from her close friends who had learned of her news about the house fire.

As Harry mowed the grass, using the strimmer around the edges, he pondered over the night before and how drunk they'd got. He had no idea what had made him kiss Maddy other than blind drunkenness. *Surely? But she was pretty.* He hadn't liked how she'd called him an old fogey. The kiss couldn't have been bad, because she'd deepened it, rather than pushed him away. Then blushed sweetly when she'd realised what she was doing and had pulled out of the kiss.

To hold a woman again, and kiss her like that, had ignited something in Harry. He hadn't felt lust like it for a long time now. Maybe he was getting over Karin. Maybe he could finally move on. But he was afraid of lust turning to love . . .

And should he really fool around with his neighbour? What would happen when these things went sour? Because they would. They always did.

But holding Maddy in his arms, aware of her softness pressing against him, had been such a great sensation. He'd used a lot of willpower last night not to seduce her further as he'd known she was too drunk. And so was he.

Because Maddy's gardens, front and back, were small like his, it didn't take him long to cut the lawn. So, enjoying doing what made him feel at his best and trying not to think too much about what it would be like to go to bed with Maddy, Harry grabbed his hedge-trimmer out of the garage, and tidied the hedges and bushes, and even started to dig over some of the beds in the back.

'There you are,' Maddy said, holding out a bottle of Stella in one hand and a can of Coke in the other, clearly having raided his fridge. The skirt of her dress fluttered in the breeze, revealing more of her legs. 'Thought you might want a drink. But with it being hot, I wasn't sure what you'd fancy.'

Harry wiped the sweat off his forehead with the back of his arm and grabbed the bottle of lager, popping the cap off with his hand. 'Thanks,' he said. How long had she been there? Harry had his shirt off now, and was working in nothing but his khaki shorts, his body glistening with sweat. 'Have you been enjoying the view?'

Maddy's lips pouted, trying to hide a smile. Her eyes were definitely giving him the once over. 'Yes, I have, the garden looks fantastic, thank you.' Dropping her gaze, she opened the can of Coke and took a sip from it.

No way was she checking out the garden. More like the gardener. Harry smirked, then took in large gulps of the ice cold Stella, the liquid cooling and refreshing him.

He raised his bottle. 'You're not joining me?'

'Oh, no, I drank way too much last night. Need to give my liver the night off.' Maddy raised her Coke can. 'How long will you be? I think I should repay you for making my garden look so lovely by at least cooking you dinner again.'

Harry shrugged. 'Another half hour at the most.'

'Okay, I'll go rummage through your cupboards.'

Harry watched, mesmerised, as Maddy walked out of the garden, her pink dress accentuating her slim frame.

Maybe if the feeling was mutual, maybe they should get each other out of their systems . . . and then simply stay friends afterwards.

What was he thinking?

She'd only been under the same roof as him for a few nights and he was already thinking about getting into bed with her. He should be ashamed of himself.

And besides, it never ends in a friendly way, Harry.

***

Maddy busied herself in Harry's kitchen, opening cupboards to see what lay inside. It wasn't quite like her kitchen where she had tins and jars of ingredients, herbs and spices to hand so she could pull together her favourite pasta recipes. Harry tended to buy what he needed and use it. His cupboards were not well-stocked like hers were. Although currently he had more in his kitchen than she did, because everything of hers had perished in the fire. She tried not to dwell on that too much. It made her angry.

'Okay, he has a tin of chopped tomatoes,' she said pulling it out of a top cupboard. 'I can make a basic sauce with this.'

Harry liked his pasta. Of that, he did have plenty in stock. It wasn't like he didn't burn off the carbs. And there was still some bacon in the fridge. She rummaged a bit more, finding some other ingredients and vegetables to add flavour to the sauce and started cooking.

She did feel guilty helping herself to Harry's kitchen, but he had said – quite a few times – she was to treat his place like her own. Men were so much more laid back about these things. She used to have a fit – internally, unable to bring herself to say something – when Connor helped himself to stuff out of her fridge without asking. It seemed rude. It was okay when they'd been together for a while, and he moved in with her, but at first, new into the relationship, it had struck her as odd.

She was making Harry dinner, though, as a repayment for tidying her garden, and taking her to Padstow, and basically being the perfect gent. Connor had usually left it to Maddy to mow the lawn, put the bins out . . . *Lazy bastard. What had she seen in that man?*

She poured the pasta and sauce into a Pyrex dish, sprinkling some grated cheese and slices of tomato on top, deciding to cook it in the oven as a pasta bake. This way if Harry took longer, she could leave it in the oven.

'Seriously brainwashed with his sweet talking early on,' Maddy mumbled to herself angrily, thinking about Connor and his faults again. 'I blame myself for being young and naive.'

'Are you talking to yourself?'

Maddy jumped and turned, holding her oven-gloved hand to her chest. 'Don't do that!'

'Sorry, but I thought I'd tell you I'm jumping into the shower.'

He needed it. Sweat beaded on his forehead. His body was covered in flecks of dirt and sweat. Maddy imagined joining him in the shower and helping him scrub all the dirt off his muscular body . . . She moistened her lips.

'Have I got time?' Harry asked, unaware of exactly how hot he looked.

'Oh, uh, yes, yes. Plenty of time. Twenty minutes at least.'

'Good.' Harry disappeared up the stairs. Maddy waved a tea towel to fan herself. It was hot in the kitchen due to the oven being on, and it was warm outside. Nothing at all to do with Harry.

But all the windows were open, and the patio doors. Harry's house was actually quite cool.

Okay, it was definitely Harry. Get a grip.

As Maddy laid the table, opening another bottle of Stella for Harry and placing a glass of iced water on the table for herself, her thoughts strayed once again. She imagined Harry, all fresh from his shower, coming up behind her, brushing her hair aside and placing a kiss on her neck, and giving her a squeeze. She'd had affectionate boyfriends in the past. Even Connor when they'd first started out had always had a way of wheedling her back using a show of affection, and it dawned on her how much she missed the intimacy of someone close by and holding her. It had only been four months since she'd ended the relationship with Connor. Was she ready to start again? Or should she remain single a bit longer? Valerie had advised her to live a little, and find her inner strength. Let her heart and mind heal.

But living under the same roof as Harry, albeit only for a few days, had reminded her how she liked to be in a relationship, to be part of a couple. Did she want to start something with Harry, or was it because she was living under his roof, was that messing with her head?

The timer on the oven beeped and as if on cue, Harry tramped down the stairs his hair still damp. He wore a tight T-shirt which didn't leave much to the imagination when it came to his broad, muscular physique. He grabbed the bottle of Stella and took a swig. Maddy dished up the dinner. It was as normal and relaxed as it could be for two neighbours living under the same roof. Harry was her neighbour, and now a friend. She should forget any romantic intentions. She couldn't think about things like this now — she had enough to contend with in her life.

Chapter 13

Arms folded in front of her, Maddy stared into her coffee. She'd taken the day off. She would give Val the day off tomorrow. They still had time before the busy season started and they'd need to be in the gallery practically every day. The gallery was quiet, and she still felt tired from yesterday's hangover. Or maybe she was just fed up. One thing was for sure she wasn't in the frame of mind to paint. Maybe it was her time of the month due? She usually suffered the 'blues', as her mum called them, a couple of days before. Or became murderous. Whatever, she felt down, and couldn't shift the mood. There was a dark cloud looming over her, stopping her from thinking straight, weighing on her shoulders and pushing on her breastbone. Today, thinking about her fire-damaged house depressed her. Additionally, she worried about living with Harry. She didn't want to abuse his kindness, plus with the mixed feelings she had for him . . . Was it healthy to be under the same roof?

She was afraid.

She needed to think about eating something for lunch soon. She'd done nothing with her day off, still waiting for news from her insurance company, the police . . . What a mess. Life had been running so smoothly before all this.

And what a waste of a day off. But she didn't care.

Maddy heard the front door bang shut, giving her a start. 'Hello!' she heard Harry call. *What was he doing home so early?* Maddy gave her head a shake trying to shift her gloomy reverie and plastered on a fake smile as Harry entered the dining room, where she sat nursing her now cold coffee. He was smiling, his eyes bright and he was giving off a positive vibe in the way he greeted her, which bounced right off Maddy. She was *that* fed up.

'Why are you back so early?' Her forehead creased with a frown, unable to keep her smile in place.

'Done all my jobs this morning. Got a couple I can do later when it's cooler. Thought I'd pop home for lunch. What have you been doing?'

She shrugged her shoulders. 'Nothing.'

He raised an eyebrow, his expression etched with concern, his chirpiness deflating momentarily as if gauging how he should approach her. With caution, Maddy thought she should warn him. 'I know what, why don't we go out for lunch?' he said, resting his hands on the back of a dining chair.

'I don't think I'll be great company today.'

'Nonsense. Come on; I've got the perfect idea in that

case.' Harry gave Maddy the once over where she sat. 'You're wearing shorts. Perfect. Let me get changed and we'll be off.' He was tugging off his gardening polo shirt as he went up the stairs.

Wearing linen shorts and a vest top, with her hair pulled back into a ponytail, Maddy didn't think she looked perfect. Far from it. She dumped the remains of her coffee down the kitchen sink, leaving the cup there to be washed up later. Next minute, she was being ushered out of the house by Harry who had donned a blue Salt Rock T-shirt and a pair of khaki shorts, filling the side pockets with his wallet, phone, keys as they were walking towards the high street. Maddy was practically jogging to keep up with Harry's long, energetic strides. She almost wanted to tell him to leave her behind. A moment of dread filled her, thinking they'd return to the pub and he'd come out with red wine. *No more alcohol. You drank your weekly quota on Saturday night.* But they walked past the Molesworth Arms.

'Where are we going?'

'You'll see. How hungry are you?'

'I'm not.' She folded her arms in front of her, pulling a face.

'You will be when I've finished with you.' He beamed at her. *Why was he so bloody happy?* He strolled off faster than Maddy, heading towards the Lidl store. *Was he going to grab something out of the supermarket? He could have done that and left her at the house.*

With her nose to the ground, gazing at the pavement, she hadn't seen where Harry had gone. She stood around, her thoughts bleak. *Where was he?* There was a new cafe open next to the bike hire shop. Maybe he'd gone in there. She hated the thought of walking in on her own, her face probably looking like thunder.

She was about to enter the cafe when Harry appeared with two bikes from the hire shop next door. One ladies and one gentleman's. He also carried two bike helmets.

'You said lunch, and they're not very edible,' Maddy said, approaching him, folding her arms truculently.

'It's the easiest way to get to Padstow.'

'Padstow!'

'Yes, now hop on. You're not arguing with me.'

Maddy snatched her bike off Harry. She really didn't want to do this, but with everything Harry had done for her lately, she had to play nice and stay polite. What she wanted to do was scream . . . or cry . . . *Yes definitely PMT.*

Harry handed her a helmet. 'It should fit.' He put his own on and fastened it under his chin. Maddy did the same. 'Ready?'

She nodded, then with her right foot she pulled the pedal into place so she could push off and follow Harry along the pavement. They cycled along a stretch of car-free road, then onto the Camel Trail to Padstow. It was once an old railway line, from Bodmin to Padstow, with Wadebridge in the middle and now was a cycle path. If you wanted to cycle the other way, you could ride to Bodmin from Wadebridge, but Padstow tended to be the more popular option with the tourists.

They passed a sign which told them it was five and a half miles to Padstow. Maddy hadn't ridden a bike in years. She hoped she wouldn't fall off. That really would make her day.

'This way you'll be hungry when you get to Padstow.' Harry cycled along easily beside Maddy. With his hands gripping the handlebars, she could see the taut muscles of his caramel-tanned arms. She seemed to be cycling more than Harry, her legs spinning faster. She was already feeling her heart rate and breathing quicken. At this rate, she'd be worn out before they got to Padstow. She adjusted her gears on her bike so that she was doing less work and still keeping up the pace. 'And I get my exercise in for the day,' he said, still smiling, flashing his white straight teeth at her. But his smile wasn't working on her today. He'd need to up the wattage.

'Could you not have done this without me?'

'You looked like you needed cheering up. And exercise is the best way to get you out of your funk.'

'Funk?'

'Well, it helps me keep the mood swings away,' Harry said, though Maddy wondered for a moment if she'd caught a glimpse of the expression that showed he feared he'd said too much. 'Healthy body, healthy mind, isn't that what they say?'

'If you say so.'

They fell silent, and Maddy observed the scenery to her right. The tide was out, so there were sand banks along the Camel Estuary, only a narrow river flowing. It was a beautiful day, the sun warm on her face. She'd never actually done this before and had forgotten the cycle path even existed. The views were beautiful. Another possible scene to paint.

'I thought this would be fun to do before the schools break up. It will be so busy in the holidays, and not so much fun.' They did meet other cyclists, and some walkers, but Maddy could well imagine when the summer season really kicked off, it would be much busier and they wouldn't be able to cycle so fast, which Harry was making her do.

'Wow,' Maddy said, as they approached a metal bridge that trains would once have travelled over, and to the right they could see a miniature Padstow on the horizon. She stopped, setting her feet down so that her bike wouldn't fall and took in the view.

'Beautiful, isn't it? I never tire of it every time I run this track,' Harry said.

'It sure is.'

The blue sky, the whites and reds of the buildings raised against the green hues of the hillside and the cerulean of the river meeting sea — another composition idea she could add to her collection. She loved Cornwall; it was forever giving her inspiration for paintings. She got her phone out and took a picture. Then she snapped one of Harry standing beside her, one foot resting on the ground. Then he insisted they take a selfie with Padstow behind them.

'Race you!' Harry said once she'd put her phone away. As he got going on his bike, he stood on his pedals and pushed, his calves bulging. He raced away from her over the bridge.

Damn him.

'Hey, not fair!' Maddy, too stubborn to let him win, gave everything she had into pedalling the bike. Head low, hunched over the handlebars, she started to catch up. Her calves and thighs burned but she didn't care. Harry was stronger than her, but she wouldn't be too far behind him, she was determined.

Whether he'd deliberately let her catch up or not, they were both laughing by the time they'd come to the end of the trail and reached a bike park. Their brakes screeched and squeaked as they came to a halt.

Harry winked as he locked the bikes up together. 'I knew this would improve your mood.'

Maddy faked a scowl. 'Who said it has?'

'Well, if it hasn't you're paying for lunch, Moody.'

Maddy laughed and punched him lightly on the arm. 'Actually, I do feel better, thank you.'

'You'll feel better with some good food inside you too.' As they walked, Harry wrapped his arm around her shoulder and gave her a quick squeeze, then let go. The brief hug took Maddy by surprise. For a second there, she'd wanted it to be something more, something intimate. She knew he was just being friendly, trying to cheer her up. And he'd succeeded.

It had been breezy along the cycle path, keeping them cool. Now the sun was hot on her skin as Padstow, tucked round away from the ocean, was protected from the sea breeze. They ambled through the town's main street which circled the harbour. Even though it wasn't holiday season, the town was busy with tourists. In a couple of weeks, it would be even busier.

Harry led the way, occasionally touching her elbow, or letting her go first through the crowds. He clearly had somewhere in mind and Maddy was happy to follow. The cafe was up on the hill. It had a crazy golf course, which had a couple of young families playing with children under school age. Harry chose a picnic table with an umbrella, and Maddy slid along so that she was in the shade. She'd forgotten to put sun cream on – not realising Harry's intentions to cycle to Padstow – and at this rate, she'd be burnt redder than the lobsters she'd spotted in some pots they'd walked past. Harry sat opposite. He had some shade, but his back was in the sun. The sun almost created a halo around him. Maddy really was in a strange mood, now thinking of him as some guardian angel. But by God, he was gorgeous.

Stop thinking like that.

But Maddy couldn't help thinking envious eyes were upon

172

her, sat there with this gorgeous specimen of a man. She should add paranoia to her list of moods today.

Harry passed Maddy a menu and then perused his own. 'Hmmm . . . I'm thinking a cream tea,' he said.

Scones, jam and clotted cream. Maddy's mouth watered at the thought. 'I will join you.' When she looked up from the menu, she met his blue-eyed gaze. The way he looked at her, gently smiling, made her nervous. His eyes had a way of penetrating her soul.

'What?' She brushed her top down and made sure her appearance was as good as it was going to get. She should have applied some make-up or at least brushed her hair more neatly into the ponytail. She dreaded what her hair looked like having had a helmet stuck to her head.

Harry shrugged his shoulders. 'Just noticing how different you look without your scowl.'

She pulled a face. 'Go on, say it, I told you so. I know you want to.'

He was right. She was feeling better. The gloom that had shrouded her had lifted.

He grinned. 'I didn't like seeing you down and had to do something about it. This is fun, admit it.'

Before Maddy could, the waitress approached the table, fetching a notepad out of her apron. 'Are you ready to order?'

Harry turned his smile to the young waitress, who started to blush and look flustered by Harry's good looks. 'Yes, I think we're both going to have the cream tea.'

'Would you like tea or coffee?'

Harry looked at Maddy for her answer.

'Coffee please,' she said to the waitress.

'And I'll have a tea, please,' Harry said.

'Anything else?'

'No that's all for now.' Harry handed the menus to the waitress.

A comfortable silence fell between them. Or at least Maddy assumed it was comfortable. It was for her. She looked out over the fence they were seated beside and down into the harbour. She watched people walk through the town, some licking ice-creams or devouring pasties, cars trying to drive along the roads crowded in places by tourists. Harry pointed out a cheeky seagull swooping over an old man eating a Cornish pasty. In amongst the familiar sound of squawks and cries of seagulls, the rigging on the sailboats moored in the harbour rattled and chimed in the breeze. Out on the sea, the sound of a motorboat rumbled and revved, taking passengers on an exhilarating trip around the bay. Maddy soaked it all up.

Harry stretched out his legs underneath the table and brushed Maddy's knee. 'Oh, sorry,' he said, moving them back. His touch hadn't caused discomfort, in fact, it felt very much the opposite. Not that she'd admit it.

Maddy shifted over on her seat. 'It's okay, stretch them out. You've got longer legs than me.'

Soon the waitress arrived with their drinks, followed by

the scones, with pots of homemade strawberry jam and fresh, thick Cornish clotted cream.

'That's sacrilege,' Harry said, eyes wide, as he watched Maddy spoon jam onto her scone first as he spread cream first on his.

'I could say the same about you.'

'That's how we do it in Devon.' Harry bit into his scone and his expression showed delight. 'Cream then jam.'

'I was taught jam then cream.'

Harry screwed up his face, making Maddy laugh. 'That's the Cornish way.'

'I forgot, you're a Devon boy.'

'What's your excuse, you're from Bristol?'

'Val moved to Cornwall when I was a kid, so when we visited we'd always go out for a cream tea. Ed, my brother, and I were guaranteed to eat it.'

They laughed and chuckled, licking sticky fingers as they ate their scones. To keep Harry happy, she spread cream on first then jam, and couldn't really tell the difference. Comfortable and relaxed, they squeezed in a slice of home-made cake, and sank more tea and coffee before walking back through the crowded, quaint streets of Padstow, to where they'd locked up their bikes.

'Oh, can I just pop in here?' Maddy gently tapped on Harry's arm, gesturing to a small gallery slotted between a boutique and a home-made fudge shop. Padstow not only boasted prestigious restaurants, but also some decent galleries. 'Might give me some new ideas for the gallery.' It was always good to check out the competition, and to see what other galleries offered their customers, what Maddy might be missing in her own gallery. The shop was bright with white walls and real oak floors. It had a selection of abstract work from a local artist, to the traditional seascapes, capturing Padstow's essence as a fishing town. The gallery had a more minimalist feel than hers, and she wondered if the average holiday maker might feel too intimidated to enter. She hoped her gallery had a more relaxed atmosphere, for all to enjoy the artwork.

'I think I prefer your paintings,' Harry said softly to Maddy. She smiled. His breath on her neck had sent a strange sensation of pleasure through her, which she hoped she was hiding from him. *No doubt my cheeks have flushed pink.* Why did Harry do this to her? Did she even want these feelings? She'd promised herself she'd concentrate on the gallery, focussing on its success, and not on her love life. The time she'd wasted on Connor she would never get back. She needed to focus on herself.

They visited a couple more galleries on their way, and Maddy made mental notes of the things she liked and didn't like. *I could do with more 3D art, more sculptures.* Not something she specialised in herself, but she could investigate, and she could even (although it grated a little to think this) ask her mother for advice.

As Maddy sat back in the saddle, she was reminded by

the soreness in her bum around the 'bony bits' that she'd already cycled five and a half miles. And now she had to do it all again. Fortunately, Harry took it steady, and they rode back to Wadebridge at a more leisurely pace. The Camel Estuary was now on their left, and they spotted a cormorant sunning itself on a sandbank that was shrinking with the rapidly rising tide.

In Wadebridge, Harry returned the bikes to the bike hire shop and they walked back to Annadale Close. Maddy couldn't help thinking how easy it was to spend time with him. She'd got him so wrong before her house fire. But should she continue to live with him?

Could she handle the different feelings and sensations he produced within her?

It was now late afternoon. Harry changed back into his work clothes and was gone, leaving Maddy. She shook off the slightly bereft feeling as he left, thinking she was being silly. Her heart felt lighter, happier: she needed to make the most of this, and make her day productive, not fall back into the misery she'd felt this morning. There was nothing she could do or change about her past or about her house. Only time would tell how everything would pan out. She fetched a sketchpad and in a shady part of Harry's garden, inspired by her new-found good mood, started to sketch ideas for paintings she'd seen that day and jot down notes for the gallery.

Chapter 14

'Hey, I thought you were having today off, as I took yesterday off,' Maddy said, looking up from her canvas as Valerie entered the gallery. It was blustery outside, and rain looked imminent, typical British summer weather, so her friend wore a light-blue waterproof jacket zipped to her chin, which she undid a little. Maddy didn't know how one day could be so different from the last. Yesterday had been glorious sunshine cycling with Harry to Padstow.

'Yes, yes, I was, but I needed to see you.' There was a mix of excitement and anxiety in Valerie's voice, which left Maddy unsure whether to be excited or worried, too. She frowned at Valerie. 'Well, you know how you aren't sure whether you should be living under Harry's roof?' Maddy had shared her concerns with Valerie every day she saw her. How much she liked living with him, yet it worried her. How their relationship was developing and they were getting closer but was it because they were living together? Was it becoming all too cosy? Could it force something to happen that shouldn't? And then yesterday had been fun. It left Maddy's feelings in turmoil. 'Well, I may have a solution as you don't want to stay at mine either.'

'You have enough going on in your house, without me adding to your worries.' This time of year, Val's three sons and their wives and girlfriends descended on her.

'Yes, well, I bumped into Roy Trewyn yesterday.'

'Oh, yes, how are the paintings, did his wife like them?'

'Yes, she loved them.'

'Great, and did he drop off his business cards?' Maddy dropped her paintbrush into a jar of water on the small table beside her.

'Yes, yes, but don't interrupt me. You know how I lose my train of thought.' Valerie waved her hands about. 'You know that holiday home overlooking the bay, the one that's having all the work done to it?'

'The one that looks rather sorry for itself?' Maddy found a towel to wipe her hands.

'Yes, that's the one. I didn't realise Roy owns it. He bought it as an investment. Thought he'd do it up as it was in such disrepair, and then sell it on making a small fortune.' Valerie sat herself down on a stool beside Maddy.

'All right for some.'

'His intentions were to get it ready slowly and sell next spring. With the opening of the restaurant he's not been able to keep an eye on things – he's got a project manager in place but he's not sure if the builders are doing all they say they do, plus the money has become a little strained for him, the restaurant tying up more than he thought.'

'Oh.' Maddy shrugged, unsure where Valerie was heading with this.

'So I suggested you could live there.' Valerie beamed at Maddy.

'What?'

'Well, you said your insurance company would pay your rent.'

'Yes, they would.' Maddy wasn't sure about this. What would Harry say too?

'Roy doesn't want a lot because he realises the house is a building site, but it's habitable. It's got a kitchen and the bathroom which are pretty much finished. And this way you won't feel you're abusing Harry's hospitality.'

Maddy remained silent, mulling it over. She'd be closer to the gallery too. And the builders wouldn't really disrupt her because she'd be at the gallery most days. It would just be somewhere to sleep.

'I assume it's unfurnished, though, so I would need a bed.'

'I've got a camp bed we could put in there and one of those fabric wardrobes I bought from IKEA years ago.'

'But what about Sookie? If there are builders coming and going, I can hardly take her with me.'

'I could have her or Harry might look after her.'

'He hates cats.'

'She could come to mine, then.' Val patted Maddy's shoulder. 'Say you'll think about it.'

'Oh, I will. Definitely.'

Valerie left the gallery, and it was all Maddy could think about. If she discussed this with Harry, she knew he'd talk her out of it. Or would he? Maybe he was being polite saying she could stay at his, when really, he'd be glad to see the back of her.

But then, yesterday, the bike ride . . . Harry was always keen to please her.

After an hour of mulling it over, Maddy called Valerie to ask if she could go see the house. Valerie made a call to Roy then called her back.

'Roy says of course, the builders should be up there. He'll let them know you're coming. Go take a look around, then let me know. You'd be doing him a huge favour, Maddy.'

The greyness of the weather was keeping people away, so the gallery was quiet. Maddy popped a note on the door to say 'back in half an hour', and took a stroll up the footpath that ran parallel to the beach below. She knew exactly which house Valerie meant. The garden was full of brambles and two-foot high weeds from years of neglect. Who would want to holiday in this sorry looking rundown cottage, Maddy couldn't imagine. It had probably been empty for a couple of years by the looks of things. She couldn't even attempt to open the little wooden gate on the footpath that led up the back garden to the cottage, so had to walk all the way along the footpath to where it met the road, and backtrack along it.

The old cottage had a farmhouse feel to it with its Cornish grey slate roof (albeit with a few tiles missing, which a roofer was currently replacing) and chimney stacks either end. The brickwork had once been painted white, though it was flaking in places and was more a dirty grey now. It looked like new leaded windows had been installed in the rest of the house, however the old wooden front door, which stood wide open, hadn't been replaced judging by its peeling lilac paint, and the decaying porch above it. The front garden looked tidier than the back, in the sense it had been strimmed, but still looked like a work in progress, and with the builders coming and going it looked trampled and muddy in places. A shrub had once climbed the front of the house, and over the little porch, but it appeared dead now. To the right side of the cottage, there was a large weed-ridden driveway with three vans parked, presumably the builders. There was no number on the front door, and the remains of a nameplate hung loosely to the side of the wide open door, which was unreadable. Maddy could make out a W, wondering what it stood for. From inside the house, there was hammering, drilling and a radio blaring.

'Hello,' Maddy called through the bare hallway.

'Hello!' A tall, dark man bellowed back, approaching Maddy. His T-shirt had holes in it, wear and tear from building Maddy assumed. Somewhere in his late twenties to early thirties, he had tanned golden skin from being out in the weather, short dark hair full of dust, and brown eyes which flashed a hint of mischief. He wiped his hands on his shorts before shaking Maddy's hand. 'Are you Maddison?'

'Maddy, yes . . .'

'Pretty name. I'm Simon, the project manager.' *And involved in the building work, by the state of him.* He smiled, enhancing his good looks. 'Let me show you around.'

Maddy followed the tall man admiring his build, and his bum, from which she quickly averted her eyes to the ground and his worn out Timberland boots, ticking herself off for her inappropriate thoughts. *But she was allowed an opinion. As long as she didn't say it out loud, what was the harm?* It was hard not to admire his body. He wasn't as broad as Harry, or as tall, but the guy was solid.

'So, Roy says you need somewhere to live because you've had a fire at yours.'

'Yes, that's right. I had a kitchen fire. I need somewhere more for the evenings, as I'll be at work during the day,' Maddy said. She didn't want to add about it possibly being arson and that she'd been a potential suspect.

'Oh, where do you work?'

'I own a gallery in Tinners Bay.'

Simon nodded. 'I know the one. There's some really great stuff in there.'

'Thank you.'

Making idle chat, and saying hello to the other workmen

in the house, Simon started on the ground floor, showing Maddy around. He turned the radio down in the hallway, opened a door to a downstairs toilet and cloakroom which needed tiling and the plaster painting, but was otherwise useable. There was also another room on the same side which seemed to have tools, paint, wood and all sorts stored in it. He then walked her past the stairs, along a passage to a lounge with beamed ceilings and a huge fireplace to the right. The room was bright with natural light from the large windows and patio doors, looking out towards the beach. An interior wall must have been removed to create this open plan space, Maddy thought. With the tide out, she could see the expanse of golden sand. If the sun had been shining, the view would have been spectacular, however the clouds, dark and moody, made the scene more dramatic and intimidating.

'Wow,' she said, as an involuntary reaction to the view. It was still impressive even with the jungle of a garden before them.

'Great isn't it?' Simon said, standing closely beside her. He gently touched her arm and pointed. 'These patio doors are coming out, and we're building an extension at an angle, so the doors can be opened even on the windier days.' A couple of men were already working on it, laying foundations, Maddy assumed.

'Oh, what a marvellous idea.' The wind would predominately come off the sea and would mean the current patio doors could really only be opened on the calmer days. And those didn't happen often. Not next to the Atlantic.

'I can see me finishing this project and Roy not wanting to sell it.'

Maddy looked at the garden again and thought of Harry. It was at least twice as wide and five times longer than her own garden, probably more, as it swept down to the footpath she knew was below. This would be a perfect job for Harry. 'Do you have someone in mind for the landscaping?'

'Yeah, I've hired a guy. Not that I see him much.' Simon sounded disgruntled. Maddy chose not to question why. 'He said he'll clear it, then landscape it.'

After standing, watching the sea for a moment, Simon showed her the rest of the house. The open plan lounge led to an in-progress kitchen-diner. This too had a fireplace, but a more modern wood burner had been installed rather than an open grate like in the lounge. They had a kettle plugged in on the worktop – *so the electrics must be working*. This kitchen was in a far better state than her own. It was pretty much complete with oak cupboards in keeping with the age and style of the property; it just needed the finishing touches like tiles. She noticed some sample tiles scattered on the solid wood work top with design photos of showroom kitchens.

As she picked one of the tiles up, to feel the rough texture, Simon asked, 'Which one do you think?'

'Oh, gosh, I don't know.' She put the tile back down.

'No, a kitchen needs a woman's touch. Roy told me to make the choices, but I'm stuck. Imagine if it were your kitchen?' He nudged her. 'Go on, you must have an eye for this sort of thing; you're an artist.'

Maddy studied the different coloured samples more closely. There were some larger tiles and some little square ones that looked more rustic. She liked the black slate ones. It would give the kitchen a mix of old with new, and slate was very Cornish. Then she saw some little square tiles, with different iridescent colours, which combined with the slightly larger square slate tiles would give a modern mosaic effect. Some of the tiles shimmered with blues and purples, making her think of the sea and sunsets. There was a design photo to give a better idea of how the tiles should look.

'These would be the safe option,' Maddy said, pointing to the grey slate, but then she gestured to the picture she was holding. 'However, these would give the kitchen its wow factor.' The more she stared at the mixed mosaic pattern of the tiles, the more she liked it. 'It's still neutral, and earthy, but different.'

Simon beamed at her. 'I agree. I'm just glad I'm not doing the tiling.'

They both chuckled.

'Come on, I'll show you the rest,' Simon offered.

Maddy spotted a scattering of floor tile samples by the back door, which also stood open.

'Stick with slate for the floor, though,' Maddy said.

'Yes, boss.' Simon led her back out to the hallway, gesturing up the stairs. The carpet was threadbare, and now dirty with decorating and builder dust. Would this really be better than living at Harry's?

Upstairs consisted of four good-sized bedrooms, all with great views. The largest of the four had a view of Tinners Bay, whereas the others looked out onto the surrounding fields and farmland. None of the rooms had carpet, only bare floorboards, and the walls were plastered but unpainted.

'This really is a cottage with a view,' Maddy said, finding herself staring out of the window again.

'It sure is.' Simon stood close by her. 'We're just giving the walls a few days to dry, then they'll get the mist coat on and they'll be ready for painting.'

Simon showed her down the landing. There was a decent sized family bathroom, with a large shower cubicle in the corner, and a double-ended roll top bath tub standing on gold feet. All traditional white with gold taps, and even though it was a new suite it was a mix of old-fashioned charm with modern style. This room looked finished. Maddy loved it. Especially the bath.

'Big enough for two, apparently,' Simon said, giving her a nudge and wink. She'd been admiring the bath far too long and blushed.

'My bathroom couldn't fit half of this in it.' A poor attempt at not confessing she'd been thinking the exact same thing as Simon. For some reason, she'd been picturing Harry in it and how well he'd fit. Who had Simon been thinking of? The way he looked at her, his eyes narrowing and the smirk in his smile, made Maddy blush, yet made her feel uneasy at the same time. She wasn't used to overt male attention. Now would probably not be a good time to tell him Roy wanted her in here to keep an eye on him and his men.

Although they appeared to be working.

'So when do you think you'll move in?'

'Oh, uh,' Maddy twisted a strand of hair through her fingers, 'I'm not sure yet . . . might not be for a couple of days.' *If ever.* Maddy didn't want to offend Harry, but at the same time, wondered if it would be better for the both of them if she put some distance between them. If she told Harry she was moving into this cottage in this state, he certainly would insist she stayed with him. *Then don't tell him.*

'Well, I'll work on fixing up the master bedroom first,' Simon said. He followed Maddy downstairs and to the front door. 'That way you'll have one room habitable as well as this bathroom.'

'I'll let Roy know soon.' Maddy decided to sleep on it before she made any decisions.

Chapter 15

'I'm on the sofa tonight. No argument.' Maddy had sneaked in and grabbed the bedding from the spare room and made up the sofa while Harry had done his workout at his gym. Harry stood freshly showered with his arms crossed and looking very much unimpressed. She hadn't told him about the cottage. She couldn't bring herself to. What if it made her look ungrateful for everything Harry had done for her this past week?

'I don't mind sleeping down here, Maddy——'

'Don't give me the 'I'm a guest' line.'

'But you——'

'This way Sookie will sleep down here with me, and you won't need to get up so early.'

'I don't mind her waking me up.' Harry made a move to get on the sofa, and Maddy barged him, meeting a solid force but throwing herself on the newly made up bed and hurrying under the covers, unable to hold in a giggle.

'And don't even think of dragging me off.' Because he was. She could see him contemplating it. She clutched the duvet, defiant.

He'd huffed, and had looked torn as to what to do, then, throwing up his arms had said, 'All right, I know better than to argue with you.'

She giggled and turned on to her side, closing her eyes as Harry turned out the lights.

Did she really want to move out? Harry was easy to live with. He wasn't untidy. So far, her only complaint was that he left the toilet seat up. But that was what most men did, and as it wasn't her house, she couldn't comment. They got on. *Maybe a little too well.*

Maddy awoke, her heart heavy and her head fuddled, having not slept as soundly as she'd hoped. There was a lot to be said for a comfortable bed. Harry's sofa wasn't one. She knew the sofa had little to do with it, though. All she'd thought about was the cottage, and whether to take up Roy's offer. Sookie rubbed her head against Maddy's chin, pawing at her chest and meowing. Maddy threw the duvet back, and slowly, with a stretch, made her way to the kitchen where she fed a purring Sookie.

She turned, and went to leave the kitchen but jumped and swore as she hit a wall of muscle.

'Christ, Harry, don't do that to me.' Eyes wide, she held her hand to her chest as if to stop her quickened heart from escaping. He was wearing a grey cotton T-shirt and matching pyjama bottoms which she knew he'd only thrown on to come downstairs.

'I'm sorry, but it is my house.' He chuckled, still rubbing the sleep from his eyes.

'About that. I think I'm going to move out.' *Where did that come from?*

'What!' Harry's tone changed. All of a sudden he wasn't laughing and his posture had stiffened. Maddy found it hard to look him in the eye.

'I've been offered a house to live in.' If Maddy didn't tell him of its unfinished state, he couldn't talk her out of it. 'I think I'll take it. Give you some space.'

'Maddy, you really don't have to.'

'I think I do.' Now it was out there, Maddy felt better about her decision. Living with Harry, albeit great, was also concerning her. Too many feelings jumbling around and setting off panic alarms in her head. She didn't want another Connor situation. Until last week they'd practically been strangers.

She liked Harry as a friend but was afraid of anything more happening between them right now.

'Where are you going? What brought this on?' he said.

'It's a house in Tinners Bay. Valerie organized it for me. Look, Harry, I'm really grateful for all you've done, but I don't wish to outstay my welcome.'

'You're not.'

'Come on, admit it, you had the best night's sleep ever, back in your own bed.'

Sookie chose this moment to purr around Harry's feet, tail pointed. Harry ran a hand through his tousled just-got-out-of-bed black hair, unaware how sexy he looked. Living with Harry was extremely hard on Maddy's hormones – *another good reason to leave.* 'What about Sookie?' he asked.

'Valerie's having her for me.'

'Don't be silly; she can stay here. You'll be back in your house before you know it.'

Maddy laughed. 'But you hate cats.'

'I don't hate cats. I just hate them crapping on my lawn.' As if to justify his words, Harry leaned down and scratched Sookie's head. The feline betrayed Maddy, purring more loudly at Harry and nudging him with affection. *Cats!*

'Okay, well that will take one worry off my mind.' Maddy went to squeeze past him in the small kitchen, but he gently grabbed her arm.

'Honestly, Maddy, I don't mind you being here.'

'I know.'

Harry hesitated then let go. 'When are you leaving?'

Maddy shrugged. 'I don't exactly know. I'll find out today when I can move in.'

From the gallery, Maddy made her phone calls. Delight spread through her veins when the insurance company informed her they'd received the reports from the police, and Maddy had been officially ruled out as a suspect – *phew!* – meaning work could commence soon. They set a date for the Loss Adjuster to visit. It was not soon enough in Maddy's eyes, but due to staff shortages, the date given was the earliest they could do. They also agreed to the payments of rent, so with that, she'd called Roy and he'd said she could move in when she liked.

'I'll get Geoff to take over the camp bed and wardrobe,' Valerie said, picking up her phone to call her husband. 'And our camping things, so you'll have cutlery and plates in the kitchen.' That morning Maddy had already given Valerie the rundown of her conversation with Harry. Maddy didn't want to get him involved with moving her into the cottage. He had already done enough for her, and besides, if he saw the place she was moving to he would insist she stayed with him. It was in his nature to help, and that made him protective towards her. She could already see that.

Another reason to leave.

So why did she feel guilty about being sneaky about this and not involving him? Surely he would see reason once he had his house back to himself.

'Look, if you and Harry have something going on, at least it won't get forced on too quickly as it would if you're under the same roof,' Valerie said, handing Maddy a mug of coffee once the phone calls had been made.

'Harry and I don't have anything going on.'

'Not yet.'

'Valerie, it's not like that.'

'Then stop feeling guilty about moving out. Harry will understand.'

But would he? She was moving to an unfinished house. There weren't even curtains hanging in the bedroom window. The kitchen was empty.

'After this, I'd better go home and pack some essentials I'm going to need at the cottage.'

'It's not like we're rushed off our feet.'

Another gloomy day had deterred visitors, other than the hardcore surfers, to the beach. Usually, Maddy used these days to get on with her paintings, but today she couldn't focus. It wasn't dissimilar to writer's block. Standing in front of a canvas, paintbrush poised, she still couldn't bring herself to paint.

In Annadale Close, Maddy packed a duffle bag of her essentials, taking towels from her house, and some clothes, and her toiletries from Harry's. She was just locking his front door when his truck pulled up.

'Hey,' she said, as he walked up the drive.

'Hey.' He frowned at the bag she was holding. 'You're going so soon?'

'I can move in today, so I might as well get comfortable.' Maddy was about to put Harry's door key in her handbag. 'Oh, do you want this back? I still have some stuff at yours, but I can collect it another day.'

'No, no, you keep it. Just in case you need something, or want to see Sookie.'

'Are you sure about looking after her?'

'Yes, it's fine. You'll confuse the poor girl if you move her again.'

'I'll drop some more food off for her in a couple of days.'

Harry nodded. 'Maddy . . .'

'Yes?'

'Nothing.' He shook his head again. 'Look, you know where I am if you need anything.'

'I know.' She smiled and kissed him on the cheek. 'Thank you. For everything.'

She'd already said her goodbyes to Sookie telling her to be good for Harry. Sitting in her car, she started the engine and wiped a tear off her cheek. Why was she crying?

It was only for a month, maybe two, if that . . .

By the time Maddy arrived at the cottage, it was early evening. She'd had some dinner with Valerie, and then headed over to the cottage. With her duffle bag full of spare clothes, towels and her wash things slung heavily over her shoulder, she found the peeling lilac front door unlocked. Maddy called out as she entered the hallway, but only silence greeted her. No radio blared, no hammering or drilling. In the kitchen on the new solid wood breakfast bar, separating kitchen from dining room, was a note with a key. The handwriting was spidery but legible.

'Roy told me to leave you a key. Welcome to your new home. Si x

P.S. we usually arrive around 8 am so switch the kettle on.☺'

Maddy rolled her eyes. She wondered how often she'd be supplying the tea and biscuits now she'd moved in. There was a box in the kitchen with Maddy's name on it. This would be from Valerie, kindly delivered by her husband, Geoffrey. It contained items like cutlery, plastic plates and bowls; all things Valerie kept for camping and barbeques. There was also a bottle of red wine – an Australian Shiraz – and a wine glass which put a smile on her face and erased some of her worries.

She put the key in the front door and locked it, then flicked on a switch to walk up the stairs. The lights worked, but there were no lampshades, only naked light bulbs. Maddy made her way to the master bedroom. The camp bed stood in the middle, made up with a violet floral duvet (very Valerie) and pillows, plus a bedside lamp beside it. Bless Val, she had thought of everything. Also, built and ready to use, was the fabric wardrobe. The room was still the colour of plaster, but there were some tins of magnolia paint in the corner, plus a curtain pole still in its packaging. Maybe it would only be for a couple of nights she'd have to live without curtains.

By the time Maddy had showered in the enormous bathroom and changed into her pyjamas, it didn't matter that there were no curtains, it was dark outside. She watched the moon on the sea for a moment, thinking it would make another great composition. The view was serene and calming. She hoped Harry would be okay with her moving out. She actually missed him. A ridiculous feeling, Maddy thought, only having known the man properly for a week. Would he miss her?

The camp bed wasn't as comfortable as Harry's king-size bed and was narrower than a single but Maddy, exhausted mentally and physically, fell straight to sleep.

Chapter 16

It took Maddy a few seconds to gather her thoughts and remember where she was. Early morning sunlight flooded the room, birds were singing and seagulls screeching. Maddy reached for her mobile to check the time. It was coming up to six-thirty a.m. The builders were due at eight. As she didn't want them to catch her still in her pyjamas and looking like she'd been dragged through a hedge backwards, she decided it was best to get up. Plus the camp bed wasn't comfortable enough to make her want to lie in.

It wasn't until she'd made a cup of coffee from the builders' stash that she realised she had nothing to eat for breakfast. Of course the cupboards would be bare. The fridge contained milk and some soft drinks which the guys obviously helped themselves to. Knowing the Spar shop in Tinners Bay would be open, Maddy walked down the coast path to fetch the basics. The red wine was a generous gesture from Val, but hardly breakfast material.

Maddy returned loaded with shopping and found the

house still empty of builders. She busied herself in the kitchen and ate her cereal perched at the breakfast bar on one of the high stools – they were the only seats she had in the house. She had a lovely view of the garden, even from the kitchen, because of the open-plan layout of the down-stairs. Walls must have been knocked through, creating a lovely light, airy feeling.

She was just about to take a mouthful of cereal when she noticed a man in the garden. An initial moment of anxiety soon calmed when she realised he must be the landscape gardener Simon had talked about. He was tall and broadly built with black hair, as far as she could make out. In fact, there was something familiar about him . . .

Harry.

He'd turned and looked at her through the window as if he had a sixth sense that he was being watched.

She left the bowl of cereal on the worktop and went out the back door, walked down the side of the cottage, and round into the garden.

'What are you doing here?' she said, placing her hands on her hips.

'I'm working.' Harry wiped his forehead with a gloved hand. He'd been cutting away at brambles. 'I could ask you the same thing?' He frowned at her. His blue eyes flashed with annoyance.

'This is where I'm staying.'

Harry removed his gloves and dropped them on the

ground and moved towards her. His expression said it all; his brow furrowed and his jaw tensed. This was the reaction Maddy had dreaded.

'If you'd told me you were moving here, I certainly wouldn't have let you go.' He gestured to the cottage behind him. He clearly knew what state it was in.

'You don't own me. I can live where I like.'

'Maddy, your own house is probably more habitable than this. This is a building site!'

'Slight exaggeration, don't you think? At least here I do have a kitchen.'

'And bare walls, plaster dust, the builders . . .'

'Look, I'm doing Roy a favour.'

'Roy?' Harry frowned, and the faint crow's feet around his eyes wrinkled.

'Yes, Roy Trewyn, the man who owns the restaurant, you know, where we dropped the paintings off in Padstow? Didn't you know that this house belongs to him?'

'No, I was hired by Simon, but that's good to know.'

'Why?'

'Because I'm not seeing a lot of cash.'

'Well, maybe if you were here more.' She now remembered why Roy had wanted her at the house, to keep an eye on the workmen . . . Was she actually here to keep an eye on Harry? Was he not pulling his weight?

'I told Simon I had other jobs I needed to keep on top of. It's the summer, grass grows, plants need attending to.'

Harry's voice rose with agitation. 'Besides, those customers are paying me regularly. Simon keeps giving me cash in dribs and drabs. I have a mortgage to pay; I need a regular income.'

'Okay, don't bark at me.'

Harry's intense gaze dropped. 'I'm sorry, but if I'd known you were moving here, I would have talked you out of it.'

'I know you would have. That's why I didn't tell you.' She hugged herself, rubbing her upper arms. The breeze was cool this time of the morning.

'Why Maddy? Why did you feel the need to move out?' He stepped closer. She couldn't bring herself to tell him the truth. Could she? How silly would it sound if she was reading too much into things? Living with Harry had been so easy . . . maybe too easy. She'd panicked, worried she was getting attached to someone she couldn't have.

Maddy shrugged. 'Like I said, I'm doing Roy a favour.' Harry shook his head as if he didn't believe her. 'And, I, uh, I didn't want to take advantage of your hospitality. I wasn't sure if you were really happy having me there.'

'I wouldn't have offered if it was a problem.'

Maddy was desperate to change the subject and go back inside to her breakfast. The sun hadn't spread its warmth yet. 'Do you want a coffee? Now I'm here, I can keep your caffeine levels topped up.'

'I could murder one. Thanks.'

***

204

Harry watched Maddy walk back into the cottage, then turned and kicked a wheelbarrow close by. He would have insisted she stayed with him if he'd known. It might be closer to her gallery, but there was no furniture, plus the builders were constantly coming and going throughout the day. What had been so bad about living at his?

He realised his anger was due more to the fact that he liked Maddy, much more than just as a neighbour. He cared about her. They'd become friends. It was ridiculous to feel this way in such a short space of time about someone – wasn't it? But he did.

Maybe the space would do them both good. But he still wanted to keep a look out for her.

He hadn't slept great last night, wondering where the hell she was staying. He'd risen early, and thought he'd get on with some work at the cottage before he went onto his other jobs. His regulars wouldn't be happy with him rolling up at seven a.m. to mow their lawns.

Harry walked into the house via the side door, straight into the kitchen. Maddy was at the counter pouring hot water from the kettle into two melamine mugs.

'Sorry about the cups, they're Val's.' Maddy handed him a cup of coffee.

'Thanks.' Harry looked around the room. The kitchen needed tiling but was all up together, i.e. the cupboards were fitted and the sink plumbed in. She even had hot water. The dining and lounge area needed flooring of some sort.

Wires poked out of the plaster where wall lights needed to be fitted. Harry dreaded what the upstairs looked like. 'Look, if you change your mind, I'll happily let you stay at mine again.'

Maddy didn't get a chance to answer him. The front door banged, and someone bellowed, 'Hello, are you decent?'

'We're in here,' Maddy called. She flicked the switch on the kettle once more.

Simon walked into the kitchen. A couple of other men carried on through to start work on the extension outside the lounge. Harry took an instant dislike to the smug grin all over Simon's face. He'd taken the job because a big contract would be good for business, but he didn't like the man he had to work for.

'Oh, I see you've met the gardener.'

'Landscaper,' Harry said, scowling at Simon.

'Yes, Harry and I are actually neighbours,' Maddy added.

Simon nodded his acknowledgement, then started spooning coffee into a couple of mugs he'd fetched off the draining board. Harry tensed. He didn't like the way Simon got close to Maddy, touching her arm as he reached for the sugar out of the cupboard.

'How did your first night go? Sleep okay?' Simon said, looking at Maddy and ignoring Harry as if he didn't exist.

'Yes, it was fine, actually.'

'I'll start on the bedroom today so that we can get the

curtain pole up and some curtains hung for you.' Simon rested his hand on Maddy's shoulder.

'Okay, thank you.'

'I've got some colour ideas I might run by you, too.'

'Oh, okay . . .' Maddy said. 'Would Roy want that?'

'Like I said, this place needs the woman's touch.'

'And I'll get a path cleared for you so that you can use the footpath below the garden,' Harry said. He shouldn't be jealous of Maddy's attention to Simon, but he was.

'Oh, that would be really great.' Maddy smiled at Harry. Simon's expression darkened.

'Going to be here all day today, then? Or just part-time?' Simon said, his eyes narrowing onto Harry.

'Yes.' He would be now. He would put off the other jobs he'd intended to do until tomorrow. 'I've told you, I can't do much until I get the mini-excavator, plus I need to keep on top of the other gardens I maintain. They actually pay me.' Harry glared back.

'Right, well, I'd better head off to the gallery.' Maddy placed her mug in the sink and eased out of the way of the two men. 'Catch you both later.'

Maddy grabbed her handbag, keys and hurried out the front door.

Simon exhaled loudly, then said, 'She's one hot chick.' He finished making the coffee.

'Don't even think about it.' Harry's fists clenched, so he shoved them into his pockets.

'Why, are you soft on her?'

'No, but she's a friend, and she doesn't deserve to be mucked about.'

'Who said I'd muck her about?' Simon shrugged. 'If she comes onto me, I'm hardly going to turn her down. Would you? Anyway, the girl probably needs some fun.'

Harry's jaw clenched, his teeth grinding. Would Maddy go for a guy like Simon? And why did that thought fill him with jealousy? Why did this guy rub him up the wrong way? Since taking this job on, Harry had felt a dislike for the man. It wasn't as if Simon had done anything wrong, except failing to stump up some cash up front, which Harry had said he'd need for the hire of the excavator. But Harry didn't like his cockiness and the arrogant way he carried himself. He would have to keep an eye on him.

As Harry worked cutting away at the brambles and weeds that had grown ferociously in the garden, he wondered if he should have said anything at all. He'd given too much away to Simon. He had shown his weakness for Maddy, his concern. Simon was the kind of guy who'd want to get one up on another man, one up on him . . . And would he use Maddy to do so?

Harry chided himself for his childish thoughts. Maddy would soon see through Simon's smooth facade.

***

Shattered and dying to try out the huge bath, Maddy returned to the cottage after six. It was nice to leave the car behind and walk to the gallery. She plonked her bag down on the kitchen worktop and her phone pinged to tell her she'd received a text message.

It was from Harry.

Have you eaten?

No, she texted back.

I'll meet you at the cottage in half an hour. I'll bring dinner. H x

She frowned but sent back, **OK**. To be honest, there was a brand new oven in the kitchen, but because it wasn't hers and the house was likely to be sold, she wasn't sure how much she wanted to use it – and get it dirty. *That would mean cleaning it.*

She hoped it wouldn't be long before she was back in her own house.

To busy herself, Maddy did the washing up. The builders weren't very good at cleaning. They clearly just swilled the mugs under the tap, because the insides still had tea stains. Maddy screwed up her face at the thought.

The kitchen had a space for a washing machine and a dishwasher, but those gaps were still empty.

She put the plates and cutlery on the counter and poured herself a glass of wine from the bottle Val had left. She only had one wine glass, though. Harry probably wouldn't want any if he were driving, she decided, taking a sip guilt free.

The knock at the door startled her. She opened it to find Harry holding two carrier bags, one smelling of fish and chips.

'Hey,' he said, grinning at her. It made her insides skip seeing him.

Stupid, stupid, stupid.

'Hey,' she replied, hoping her face wasn't giving her away. In the kitchen, she gathered the plates and cutlery.

'Don't worry about that; we'll eat outside.'

'Outside?' Although it was July, it still got chilly in the evening with the breeze coming off the sea.

'I thought I'd have a bonfire to get rid of some of the rubbish I cleared today, and we could sit by it.'

'I haven't got any garden chairs.'

'I have.' He handed Maddy the carrier bags and went back out the front door to his pickup. He was soon back carrying two folding chairs and took them out to the back garden where, unnoticed previously by Maddy, stood a pile of bramble and wood ready to be burnt. It was a fair way down, away from the cottage. Maddy donned her pink and grey Animal jumper that zipped up at the front and followed him out.

Harry appeared mesmerised by the flames, staring into the orange blaze that crackled and spat and smoked. He turned upon hearing Maddy's approach. For a moment she thought she'd glimpsed fear on his face, but he beamed his smile at her, and whatever he'd been thinking vanished from his expression.

'Everything okay?'

'Yes, yes . . . I forgot about the smell . . .' Harry shuddered. 'Not exactly environmentally friendly, but I used to love a good bonfire,' he said as the flames roared.

'Used to?'

'Yeah, it's a long story . . .'

'As an ex-firefighter, I'd have thought you'd frown upon garden fires.' She nudged him to show she was teasing and made her way forward towards the heat.

'Not too close, Maddy,' he said, blocking her with his arm to stop her from getting closer. 'As a fireman, I know to respect fire, like a surfer would respect the ocean.' He pointed out towards the tide, and the black dots of keen surfers still in the water. *A whole new level of bonkers those surfers were.* The area around the fire was clear and safely situated well away from the cottage. Yes, the safest person to start a fire was probably a fireman. Then Maddy thought of her mother's words as they'd driven to Truro. *A fireman would know how to start a fire too, and not make it look like arson.* Which her house clearly did look like, she chided herself. Harry was the last person to have set fire to her house.

Maddy and Harry huddled by the fire, eating fish and chips still in their paper. Once the fire had died down, Harry seemed more relaxed. He stuck two foil packages into the heat of the ashes at the edge of the fire.

'Today, I cleared a path, so you'll be able to come and go via the footpath more easily. And I fixed the gate.'

'Thanks, Harry, you didn't need to.'

He winked at her. 'Yes, I did.'

They watched the last of the surfers exit the water as the sun set, and the lights of the houses on the opposite side of the bay lit up as it got dark. Tinners Bay Hotel, looking as if ready for its maiden voyage, was the most prominent and brightest building. Maddy wondered if some candles out here would add to the ambience, then worried it might look too romantic, so ditched the idea – plus she remembered that she didn't actually have any candles at the cottage. Luckily, the fire gave off enough heat and light.

Harry added more wood and fetched the foil packages out of the fire with a gloved hand. He placed one on the pile of paper still in Maddy's lap and handed her a teaspoon.

She opened the package to find a cooked banana in its skin, with chocolate buttons pushed into it. All now melted and cooked. It was delicious.

Maddy let the banana and chocolate slide down her throat. 'So, why did you come tonight?'

'Thought you might like the company.' Harry tucked into his own banana.

The company was nice. Maddy couldn't argue with that. But was this Harry's way of making sure she was okay?

'How's Sookie? You fed her today?'

'Yes, of course, I fed her before I came here tonight,' Harry said. From a carrier bag by his chair, Harry brought out a flask, pouring its contents into two melamine mugs. He handed one to Maddy.

'What's this?' she said, which was a stupid question because the aroma gave it away.

'Hot chocolate.'

'You have come prepared.'

'I know. A proper boy scout.' Harry grinned. 'Now do you want your marshmallows on top or toasted?' He presented a skewer with a marshmallow on the end.

'Toasted!' Maddy hadn't toasted marshmallows over a fire in she didn't know how long. Probably the last time was one bonfire night when she and Ed were kids. She leant forward with her skewer, closer to the fire. 'Ah, thanks for this, Harry.'

Harry made to reply, but his smile dropped and he turned round. Maddy heard it too and looked over her shoulder. Someone was approaching them, but in the failing light, it was hard to make out who it was.

'Oh, it's you two. I saw the smoke and thought I'd better check it out.'

Simon.

'You were in the area, were you?' Harry spoke before Maddy could, and his tone was cold.

'Thought I'd call round, check on Maddy—'

'It's a little late to be checking on Maddy, don't you think?'

Maddy shivered. All of a sudden it was cold sitting by the fire, yet it was giving off plenty of heat. *You would have to be blind not to see the animosity between these two. It was so unlike Harry.* She zipped up her jumper.

'Well, you're here,' Simon said.

'I got here hours ago.'

Maddy didn't know the time, but the sun had fully disappeared and they were in complete darkness. The evening had flown by, relaxing with Harry. It had to be well past ten now.

'Anyway, I was going to ask Maddy if she fancied going for a drink down in the village,' Simon said, ignoring Harry and looking at Maddy.

Maddy had no make-up on and hadn't even showered yet – *and she'd been so looking forward to that bath.* Not showering wasn't a bad thing, considering she was sat by a fire and now stank of smoke. The last thing she wanted to do was go for a drink, especially with Simon. It was too late.

'Maddy?' Harry turned towards her now. The flames of the fire flickered in his eyes, his face an orange glow, probably like hers.

'Oh, um, thanks for thinking of me, Simon, but I'm happy here. Maybe another night?' *Oh, God, why did she say that? Now he'd try and drag her out another night.*

'Okay, well, I'll catch you in the morning, Maddy,' Simon said.

'Yes, bye.' Maddy waved, watching Simon retreat. 'You really don't like him, do you?' she said more quietly to Harry once Simon was out of earshot.

'There's just something off about him.' Harry started to put marshmallows onto a skewer and handed it to Maddy. He wouldn't look her in the eye.

'I'm glad you're here,' she said, smiling. 'Otherwise I may have got dragged out to a bar.'

'Yeah, that's what worries me. You sure you don't want to move back to mine?'

'Oh, Harry, this is only my second night here. It'll be fine.'

When finally Maddy couldn't eat any more marshmallows, and Harry had let the fire die right down so that he was happy it wouldn't be a hazard – *the fireman in him* – they retired from the garden into the kitchen. Maddy sniffed her clothes.

'I'd better jump in the shower before bed.'

'Yeah, I'd better leave you to it.' Harry gathered up his things. 'I'll leave the chairs here. You could do with some seats in the lounge by the looks of things.' For a moment, she saw his disapproval of her staying here flicker in his expression, then it was gone again.

'Okay, thank you.'

She showed him to the front door, where they stood awkwardly for a moment. Should she hug him, kiss him? She'd had such a lovely evening, she didn't know how to show her gratitude.

She rose on tiptoes and kissed Harry on the cheek. 'Thank you,' she said. 'Tonight was fun.'

Swiftly, he dipped his head, and kissed her back, his lips

lightly brushing hers, sending her heart racing for a second. 'Goodnight, Maddy.'

She wanted to ask him to text her when he got home so that she knew he'd arrived safely, knowing he had narrow country lanes to navigate but thought better of it. He'd think she was ridiculous. So she waved, closed the front door, locking it, and after switching all the downstairs lights off, headed upstairs to the bathroom, desperate for a shower. All the time, she tried deciphering her feelings for Harry.

Chapter 17

So much for escaping Harry – Maddy now saw him every day, usually in the morning, as she passed him in the garden on her way to the gallery. Or she would bring him out a cup of coffee. She always asked how Sookie was and felt bad she hadn't called home to check on her herself, but the schools were breaking up soon, and she needed to get as much painted as possible, in preparation for the busy period. She spent nearly all her waking hours in the gallery, only sleeping at the cottage.

She did wonder if Harry showed up more often at the cottage now she was here. She'd heard Simon mutter something along those lines.

As far as she could tell, the builders were working hard. Maddy wasn't sure what she would report to Roy if he asked. Maybe this had been Roy's intention: install a house sitter to get the builders working faster. Simon (or his men) had finished painting the main bedroom, and had hung a curtain pole, so now she had curtains, and didn't wake so early in the morning. She noticed the tiles on the roof had been fixed too. With each day, the cottage was coming back to life. Unfortunately, she couldn't say the same for the shrub climbing over the front porch. Yet, she still watered it.

'It's dead, Maddy,' Harry said, arriving armed with some garden tools. She knew this, of course, the fact it had no leaves on it was a bit of a giveaway. But still, she wanted to persevere. She emptied the old galvanised watering can complete with dents that she'd found abandoned in the back garden.

Simon followed behind him. 'And it's coming out, too, isn't it, Harry? It'll make it easier to paint the outside of the cottage.' Harry gave Simon a curt nod. Simon smiled at Maddy and entered the house. Harry lingered behind.

'What was it?' Maddy asked him. Harry rubbed a thick part of the trunk, twisted up the wall.

'Wisteria,' Harry said, then mumbled, 'It's going to be a bugger to dig out.'

'Oh!' Maddy found the broken nameplate hanging by the front door, near to the dead trunk of the shrub, with only the W remaining loosely fixed to the wall. 'I wonder if the W stood for Wisteria. Wisteria Cottage . . .'

Harry moved dead leaves and debris about. 'Can't see the rest of the plaque. It's a good name for a cottage.'

'Yes, if it were my cottage, I would call it that . . . and plant another wisteria,' Maddy said, pensively.

'I'll consider a wisteria plant in the garden design,' Harry said, giving her a wink.

Her heart lighter, Maddy headed towards the gallery, unable to get the cottage out of her head. She grabbed a sketchpad and started to draw a picture of it from memory, with the wisteria twisting up and over the porch and resting under the top windows. She knew what the flowers of wisteria looked like, as once she'd been commissioned to paint a house in Devon during late May when the creeper had been in flower. It looked beautiful with pendants of lilac-mauve flowers, heavily scenting the air.

'That's not your usual subject matter. I thought you were moving away from painting cottages.' Val stood next to Maddy watching her work.

'I know. It's Roy's cottage, the one I'm staying at. I'm imagining it finished and with wisteria climbing up the outside.'

'I'll have to come up and see how the work is coming along.'

'Yes, you must. It's a shame it'll probably be sold as a holiday home as it would make a great home for a family.'

'You don't know that. Someone might buy it to live in.'

'I doubt it in this area. They're usually second properties bought to let out. The locals can't afford to buy them.'

Maddy returned with Valerie that evening, to show her around. The builders had left, and so had Harry by the looks of things, as they strolled up the garden from the coastal path. It was a quicker route, and Harry had freed up the gate so that it opened with ease for her.

More brambles had been cleared and piled up, making Maddy wonder if Harry would be back to light another fire.

'Has Harry told you the plans he's got for the garden?'

'I haven't really asked. I think Roy just wants him to tidy it up for the sale.'

The small extension at the back of the house was starting to take shape.

'Apparently, the doors will be positioned so they can be open even on the windiest of days,' Maddy said, taking Valerie around to the front of the cottage to the shabby lilac front door.

'Oh,' Maddy said, as she slid the key into the lock, noticing the branches that had twisted up over the porch had now gone. 'Harry must have dug the wisteria out today.'

'You did say it was dead.'

'Yes . . . but . . .' *Oh, Maddy, be sensible, it was a dead shrub.*

Maddy showed Valerie around, leading her through the lounge, then into the kitchen-diner.

On the counter stood a couple of pink roses in a half-pint glass that had probably been pinched from a pub. There was a note tucked underneath.

'That's nice of Harry. I think he's sweet on you,' Val said, admiring the flowers.

Maddy read the note. 'It's not from Harry.'

'Then who's it from?'

'Simon.'

'The project manager?'

'Yes.'

The note read; *Let me know when you'd like that drink, Si x p.s. There's a surprise for you in the bedroom.*

'Doesn't hurt Harry to have a bit of competition,' Val said, nudging Maddy. 'Let's check out his surprise.'

Curious about Simon's note, Maddy climbed the stairs, Val following, heading straight to her bedroom. The camp bed had been stripped and packed away to make room for a double bed. It was a pine bed, which had a few knocks and chips, so clearly wasn't brand new. It had been made up with the bedding from the camp bed. Before Maddy could, Val checked the mattress, sitting on it and giving it a bounce.

'Not bad,' she said, raising her eyebrows. 'I wonder if Simon wants to share this with you.' She gave a little chuckle.

'Stop it! You're such a tease.' It was kind of Simon to do this, though. The camp bed was OK to sleep on, but this would be a lot comfier.

Val stood up. 'Now show me this bathroom you keep harping on about.'

***

Harry pulled up outside his house, reversing his pickup onto the drive. He wanted to think of another excuse to meet Maddy at Wisteria Cottage, but thought it best to leave her be. If he crowded her, she'd push him away. He'd hung around there long enough, hoping she'd come home from the gallery earlier, so he could see her. *What was he like? Maddy would think he was a stalker if he continued like this*. He'd thought of lighting another bonfire, but the other night had put his nerves on edge. He'd forgotten what the smell of smoke did to him. He'd buried his fears, and in the end, it had been such a good night, sitting there toasting marshmallows and laughing with Maddy, it felt worth it.

Across the road, he could see a man dressed in jeans and a baggy grey T-shirt on Maddy's driveway stroking Sookie's head. She was weaving around his legs in her feed-me-human way.

'Can I help you?' Harry said as he crossed the road to join the man outside Maddy's house. The man looked up at Harry. Knowing where her bread was truly buttered, Sookie trotted over to Harry, and he picked her up.

'I'm looking for Maddy,' the man said. He had a similar accent to Maddy, so Harry assumed he was from Bristol. Shorter than Harry, the man had dirty brown hair with a long fringe that he flicked across his face using an annoying movement of his head. He dropped a cigarette on the ground and stubbed it out with his trainer. 'Do you know where I can find her?'

'Are you a friend? What's your name?' Harry observed the scruffy man. He looked like he needed a bath, a shave and a good night's sleep. *The long drive from Bristol to Cornwall couldn't have been that bad.*

'Yes . . . yes, I am.'

'She's had a house fire and has had to move out.' *And should be staying with me.*

'Do you know where she's moved to?'

If this guy was a friend, wouldn't Maddy have told him where she was staying?

'Sorry, I didn't catch your name?' Harry said, still stroking Sookie's head, who was getting restless in his arms. She wanted feeding.

The man looked at Harry, narrowing his eyes. 'It's Connor.'

Harry's instincts confirmed, he replied, 'Sorry, Connor, she didn't say where she was staying, only asked me to look after Sookie. Next time she calls, I'll tell her you dropped by. Okay?'

Connor shrugged, hanging his head. 'Don't bother, I'll get hold of her.'

Harry watched Connor walk back off down Annadale Close. He'd parked his car further down, as if he'd not wanted Maddy to notice his car. *Strange.*

Inside his house, and after he'd fed an impatient Sookie, Harry dug out his phone and sent a text Maddy.

Hey, you've had a visitor. Connor. Don't worry, I didn't tell him where you're staying.

***

223

Maddy sank deeper into her bath and sighed. She loved this roll-top bath. One day she'd own one just like this, she promised herself. Valerie was long gone, and Maddy had run a bath and was soaking in bubbles up to her chin. She always forgot to use less bubble bath in Cornwall. The softer water made the bubbles go further. Unfortunately, she couldn't fully enjoy it and relax, though. She was churning over Harry's earlier text. *Why was Connor in Cornwall?* Harry had confirmed he hadn't told Connor where she was, but this didn't mean he wouldn't turn up at the gallery tomorrow. She toyed with the idea of texting Connor. Maybe she wouldn't have to meet him then.

She chickened out. Refreshed from her bath, and feeling tired, the last thing she wanted to do was contact Connor. Sitting in the lounge, on one of the folding garden chairs Harry had left, Maddy sipped a glass of red wine and read her book. Well, tried to; she was fascinated watching the sun set over the ocean in a dramatic cloudy sky. She took plenty of photos with her phone to use for another painting.

The double bed proved more comfortable, but it didn't aid her restless sleep.

The next day, Maddy's heart was filled with a dread every time the bell over the door chimed in the gallery. She was on edge expecting Connor to enter, regretting not texting him the night before. It was a windy day, coming straight off the sea, so the door had to remain closed, otherwise they'd have propped it open and the bell wouldn't have been ringing.

'Don't fret, I'll be here too, if he does show his face,' Valerie said, giving her a comforting rub on her back. Maddy wondered if it would be okay to open a bottle of wine to take the edge off her nerves. Living at Wisteria Cottage meant she didn't need to drive anywhere that day. But it probably wouldn't help her artistic productivity, so she thought better of it. Valerie supplied copious amounts of tea instead.

Maddy was out the back washing her brushes when the doorbell chimed again. Valerie had popped to the Spar; they'd run out of milk. *All that tea.*

'Be with you in a minute,' Maddy called as she shook out the brushes and then dried her hands.

'Okay,' a male voice called back. Maddy froze. She recognised the voice, but it wasn't Harry's. She realised she would truly welcome hearing Harry's voice right now. Taking a deep breath, she entered the gallery, still holding the towel she'd been using to wipe her hands on. She relaxed a little seeing the guy standing there admiring a painting.

Not Connor — Simon.

'Hey, what can I do for you?' Maddy said, plastering on a smile. She still felt suspicious. *Why was he here? Had something happened up at the cottage?*

'Thought I'd call in as I was passing.' He walked towards her, smiling in the cheeky way he carried off so well. He was dressed in his work clothes, his black T-shirt and khaki shorts covered in dust. What flesh was revealed, was tanned golden. 'How was the bed?'

'Great, thanks. You didn't need to do that,' Maddy replied. She hadn't seen Simon this morning to thank him as he hadn't arrived early like the other builders.

'Someone was giving it away. It was their spare bed, and they don't need it anymore,' Simon said, casually stuffing his hands into his pockets. 'Hey, while I'm here, would you fancy that drink tonight?'

'Tonight?' Maddy paused. *Think of an excuse.* 'Oh, I can't do tonight . . . Valerie invited me to dinner,' she said, as Valerie entered the gallery holding a two-pint poly bottle of milk.

'Did I?' Valerie said. Luckily, she quickly realised Maddy's glare was a cry for help, although her response was hesitant and unconvincing. 'Yes, I did. Sorry, I was forgetting what day it was. Yes, Maddy's coming for dinner tonight.' Valerie turned to Maddy. 'But you don't have to, dear. You know, I'll understand if you get a better offer.'

'No, I don't want to muck you about. You said you'd made something special.' Maddy glared at Valerie again. But their telepathic communication was suddenly interrupted by the sound of the doorbell chiming again — and Maddy's discomfort reached a whole new level as Connor walked through the door. She couldn't believe how scruffy he looked. Had he been sleeping rough in Cornwall?

'Maddy, I need to talk to you—'

'I have nothing to say to you. Get out. Go home, Connor.'

'Please, Maddy, you've made a mistake.'

'It's over, Connor. I'm sorry.' Maddy stepped back.

'Look, mate,' Simon stepped in front of Connor before he could come any closer, 'Maddy doesn't want to talk to you, so I suggest you make it easier on yourself and leave.'

Connor looked at Maddy pleadingly, but she shook her head. She had nothing to say to him. Her relationship with Connor was over. Anything she said would be going over old ground, scratching at old wounds. With a few more pleas, but Simon standing firm, Connor made hesitantly for the door.

Once Connor had left, Maddy let out her breath, realising she'd been holding it in. Her body was shaking, the adrenaline of confrontation and fear flowing through her. Valerie gave her a hug.

'You all right?' Simon asked, his hands on his hips and a worried frown on his face.

'Yes, thanks, I'm fine.'

'Who the hell was that?'

'No one important,' Maddy shook her head at Simon, 'look, thanks for doing that.' Maddy felt awful now for fobbing him off about the drink, but she still didn't want to commit to anything. 'Can we put the drink on hold? This time of year is really busy for me, I need to make this gallery work,' *or she would be returning to Bristol, or having to find*

227

a *'proper' job,* 'I need to put the hours in painting, I'm working late most evenings, so I just can't commit to anything at the moment.'

'Yes, sure, I understand, really I do. Let me know when you're free, yeah?' Simon smiled, and Maddy nodded, albeit hesitantly. 'Better get back to the cottage, otherwise the boys will be wondering where I've been. Only popped down to grab more milk,' he said, pointing to the milk Valerie was still holding. It sounded more like an excuse. As Simon left the gallery, Maddy watched which way he went, to see if he really was going to the Spar for milk. He turned right out of the gallery, which could mean he wasn't lying. But then he'd need to turn right to walk up the footpath to the cottage anyway.

Oh, why was she caring about this, whether Simon wanted milk or not? Connor had turned up, and she was grateful he'd been there to shoo him off.

'Why don't you want to go for a drink with Simon?' Valerie asked, wearing a puzzled expression. 'He's hardly unattractive . . . And he must be fairly well off if he runs his own business.'

Maddy rolled her eyes, and she laughed, glad to be distracted from the thought of Connor reappearing in her life. Would it sound odd if she said it felt like she'd be being disloyal to Harry?

'He's very charming, but I do get the impression he's a bit of a ladies' man.'

'And Harry?'

Maddy shrugged. 'What about Harry?'

'You don't think he's a ladies' man?'

'I think Harry would be loyal and trustworthy. One woman would be enough for him. Simon, I'm not so sure about.'

'You could just have a little bit of fun, and play him at his own game. He did provide a double bed.'

'Val! Even if I did, it would always backfire on me.' *She'd fall for the guy, and he wouldn't fall for her.* Maddy grew attached too quickly. 'Besides, I really am busy.' *And she already liked Harry too much.*

Again, proof that she grew attached too quickly.

Chapter 18

The days flew by and the school summer holidays were only around the corner, so Maddy needed to make the most of this busy period. She needed the gallery stocked with artwork and affordable pieces. She had lived at Wisteria Cottage (as she liked to call it) over a week now and had managed to avoid Simon most evenings. He hadn't suggested going for a drink again. Which suited Maddy, because working so hard in the gallery, she was returning late, eating late, and falling into her bed exhausted, after a long soak in the magnificent roll-top bath, with a good book. So she hadn't really been lying on that score.

She also hadn't heard from Connor again, much to her relief.

'Another cuppa?' Valerie said, waving a mug in front of Maddy, breaking her concentration and making her look up from the painting she was working on.

'Oh, yes, go on then,' Maddy said as her mobile started to ring. With a frantic rummage, she fetched it out of her bag and then frowned at the caller ID. 'Hello, Harry.' He never usually called Maddy, only texted her. He still kept in regular contact with her, even though she wasn't staying at his place any more.

'Hey, I've been into Padstow and bumped into the restaurant owner where we dropped your paintings off.'

'Oh, right. Roy Trewyn?'

'Yes, and he asked when we were going to visit his restaurant, so I've booked us a table for seven tonight.' Maddy glanced at her watch. It was half past four. Her *I-don't-like-to-be-late OCD'* wrangled with her nerves. 'Is that too early for you?'

'No, that's fine.'

'I thought I'd better call in case you stayed on late at the gallery, as it's a Sunday. It is okay, isn't it? Otherwise, I can cancel it.' Harry sounded doubtful.

'No, no, don't cancel,' Maddy said, trying to sound more positive. Dinner with Harry . . . in a restaurant . . . why did she feel nervous? 'Valerie won't mind locking up.' Valerie appeared with Maddy's cup of tea and raised an eyebrow upon hearing her name mentioned. She put the mug down on the small table beside Maddy's easel but didn't linger. She was good at not prying.

'Great,' Harry said. 'Shall I collect you from Wisteria Cottage? We can catch the ferry over to Padstow from Rock.'

'Yes, that would be great.' Maddy hung up and then realised she had nothing at Wisteria Cottage to wear, all her dressier outfits were at home or at Harry's. Did she have time to dash home?

'So who was that?' Valerie stood wearing a puzzled expression.

'Harry. He's booked us a table at Roy's restaurant in Padstow.'

'Has he now?' Valerie seemed pleased with this information judging by the mischievous twinkle in her eye. She rubbed her hands together gleefully.

'Don't jump to conclusions. He bumped into Roy earlier this afternoon. He asked Harry when were we going to pay him a visit, and so Harry booked a table for tonight.'

'So you've got a date with Harry? Finally!' Valerie beamed. 'Maybe Simon has helped give him the push he needed.'

'Well, push or no push, I don't have anything to wear at the cottage, so I need to go home first.' Maddy would want to shower, straighten her hair – plus it might take her twenty minutes to decide what to wear. She had a date with Harry.

Date?

Well, whatever it was, friends dining out together, she wanted to look nice. Roy Trewyn's restaurant wasn't some chippy in Padstow where you could buy a pasty. It was fine dining, up there with the other restaurants that gave Padstow its name – only a tiny bit more affordable. She'd want to wear a dress – which would probably need ironing.

'Why don't you treat yourself to something new out of the boutique next door?' Valerie said airily.

'I don't know . . .'

'Maddy, you deserve a treat. Spend a little of what you got in commission from Roy as a reward.'

Admittedly, Maddy hadn't bought anything new in ages.

'You're right, Val. Sorry, I've got no time for the tea then.' Maddy threw her phone into her handbag then gathered up her paint brushes to clean. 'I need to shop.'

'Yes, for a date with Harry.' Valerie sounded more excited than Maddy. She beamed from ear to ear.

Maddy shook her head, still busying herself with tidying away her paints. 'No, not a date . . .' The painting could stay on the easel for when she returned tomorrow. 'It's just dinner.'

'Yeah, yeah, well, don't worry about here. I can lock up. And Josie can stay on for an extra hour, can't you?' Josie, who was talking to a young couple about a painting, nodded. 'And leave those,' Valerie pointed to the paint brushes Maddy had dumped in the sink out back, 'I'll clean them.'

'Thank you.' Gathering everything she needed, Maddy gave Valerie a kiss on the cheek.

'But don't get too drunk, as you're opening up tomorrow, remember?' Valerie said. 'I've got an optician's appointment, it's been booked for weeks . . . but I can always cancel—'

'No need to cancel. I can open up.' Maddy headed for the door. 'And I'll tell you about my evening tomorrow.'

'Yes, I'll want to know *all* the details.'

'There won't be any details. This is just Harry. I'm talking about the restaurant, the food.'

'If you say so.' Valerie winked. 'Have fun. Oh, and remember – wear matching underwear!'

***

It didn't take Maddy long to choose a dress in the boutique. She'd been coveting one for a couple of weeks now. She even took Val's advice and bought underwear too. And of course, she needed shoes. She had nothing at the cottage except day to day wear. Back at the cottage, she jumped into the shower, shaving legs, underarms, and giving her body and scalp a good scrub.

It's not a date.

Maddy had the bedroom windows wide open to cool the bedroom down. No matter how cool the shower was, she'd still emerged feeling hot and flustered. She dried herself off and moisturised from top to toe. Her legs actually looked quite tanned – at least they weren't as white as they were during the winter months. Achieving this look took time, using high SPF sun cream and cheating with some self-tanning lotion – Maddy didn't go brown overnight, and could easily burn if not careful. But with some colour on her legs, she opted not to wear tights – *too hot*. Once the body lotion had been absorbed, she pulled the dress over her matching powder pink underwear. It didn't matter that no one would see the matching underwear, it was a girl thing – it had to be done for a night out.

Harry would not be seeing her underwear.

Looking in the mirror in the bathroom, Maddy dried her hair, then straightened it, giving it a sleek style enhancing the subtle layers she had cut through it, and applied her make-up. With a quick spray of her perfume, she heard a knock at the front door. Was that the time already?

Maddy answered the door.

Wow! He really shouldn't do that to her.

Harry looked the smartest she'd seen him, wearing a light blue shirt and a complementing tie that brought out the blue in his eyes, and stylish black trousers – which she just knew his bum would look fabulous in when he turned around. *Do not check out his bum!* He couldn't look more handsome if he tried.

'Wow.' Harry said, his eyes widening.

Did he read her mind?'

'What? Is the dress okay?' Maddy smoothed down her dress, giving herself a final once over. *Didn't the dress suit her? Was it too much?*

'More than OK. You look . . . great.'

***

Like the perfect gentleman, Harry opened the passenger door of his pickup for Maddy. His mother used to say chivalry went a long way. He'd watched Maddy's petite figure climb up into the seat in as ladylike a manner as she could and at that moment he wished he owned a car. Once in, she tucked the light-olive floral summer dress around her slim legs. The dress complemented her creamy skin tone and hair colouring. She looked stunning. But he had been too afraid to tell her this. All he could say was *great*. At least it wasn't as bad as *nice* or *fine*.

Harry walked around the other side of the vehicle and slid into the driver's seat. Maddy clutched her small handbag on her lap. He smiled at her hoping it would take away some of the anxiety between them. Why were they both nervous? Just two friends having dinner, wasn't it?

No, it's more than that.

It had been a long time since Harry had wined and dined a woman. Was he ready for this? Harry hadn't bumped into Roy Trewyn in Padstow – he'd deliberately called in at the restaurant after he'd finished a couple of regular jobs he had in the town. A couple of holiday homes needing their lawns mowed and flowerbeds tidied and watered weekly. He had wanted to talk money with regards to the cottage because he still wasn't seeing any from Simon.

'Ah, so you're my landscaper?' Roy had shaken Harry's hand warmly. Harry had expected some animosity, but Roy was very apologetic. Harry aired his grievances to the older man, who nodded and listened.

'It's my fault, I took on the house, but didn't realise I needed to pour so much money into the restaurant. We were retired, you see, we'd sold up and gone travelling, but my wife wanted to open another restaurant.' Roy had rolled his eyes, but the gesture was meant endearingly towards his wife. 'With our history, I was dubious about going with Simon's firm, but they came in with the best quote for the job.'

'You know him?'

'Yes, he was seeing my youngest daughter – a long time ago now, although he broke her heart. I thought we could keep this professional – which we have. But I still don't completely trust him. It's why I asked Maddy to live at the house.'

Harry had wanted to reply that Roy could have asked him to do that, rather than let Maddy live on a building site, but kept silent.

'I was unaware you were having problems with Simon and required more money up front, so from now on please deal directly with me.' Harry and Roy had shaken hands again as they parted and, feeling happier about his new client, Harry had been the one to ask about table availability – although he wasn't going to tell Maddy this piece of information. Roy had been only too happy to oblige and had made room for them as long as they could come early.

Harry enjoyed Maddy's company, and since she'd moved out to the cottage, he even missed it. He knew Simon was interested in Maddy as he would drop hints to Harry about how he felt about her, trying to get a rise out of him. He'd boasted about finding Maddy a proper bed, hinting that the mattress needed testing. He'd even bragged about saving Maddy from a guy called Connor in the gallery a few days ago. Something Maddy hadn't mentioned and he'd wait to see if she would. Going to see Roy had given him the perfect opportunity to take Maddy out for an evening, maybe get to know each other better, make his feelings known.

They caught the water taxi at Rock. Due to her heels, Harry offered to carry Maddy over the small bit of beach they had to walk on.

'No thank you, I know your kind of carry,' Maddy said, with a giggle, and slipped off her shoes, rubbing the sand off her feet once she was on the boat.

The short ferry crossing from Rock to Padstow was calm; the sun warm on their faces even with the breeze off the sea. They had a short walk from the harbour to the restaurant which was tucked away in one of the narrow backstreets.

Roy greeted them both as they entered the restaurant, and was cheerful and accommodating. Harry clasped his hand and shook it.

'I've had a word with Simon,' Roy said to Harry, as he showed them to their table. 'Told him I'll manage your payments from now on.' Harry nodded.

'I'd like to run through my plans for the garden with you one day.'

'Yes, we can arrange that. Maybe Maddy might have some design ideas, too?'

'Oh, I'm not so sure,' Maddy said, chuckling nervously. 'Harry's the expert when it comes to gardens.'

Harry tried to relax as he took his seat. The cottage's garden was the least of his worries at the moment. His thoughts were distracted by Maddy and how stunning she looked. They were seated near where one of Maddy's paintings hung – the reason they were here. Harry noticed Maddy's delight at seeing her canvas in its place.

'How is business going so far?' Maddy asked Roy as he held out her chair.

'Great, thanks, and it feels good to be doing it all over again. As I told Harry earlier, my wife, Anne, wanted to open another restaurant, even though we'd sold up a few years ago to go travelling.' Roy shrugged, but it was clear he'd do anything to make his wife happy. Wasn't that what love was about? All Harry wanted to do was make Maddy happy.

But he didn't love her.

Harry tried to focus back onto what Roy was saying. He mentioned his younger daughter, Sophie, who had visited last weekend with her husband and young family – two grandsons! – and how she had loved Maddy's paintings.

'I might have to commission you to paint another,' Roy said, chuckling as he handed each of them a menu. 'And then there's Tara, my other daughter, her restaurant is up the road – From Under The Sea. She would like one of your paintings, too.'

'Looks like I could be busy until Christmas,' Maddy said with a chuckle, catching Harry's eye.

Harry perused the wine list as Roy ran through the evening's menu. They agreed to share a bottle of Prosecco between them. Harry had already decided he'd leave his truck at Rock, and they could get a taxi home from there.

After a waiter had arrived with their Prosecco, pouring each of them a glass, then placing the bottle in an ice bucket beside the table, Harry raised his glass to Maddy. 'Cheers. We should celebrate.'

'Celebrate what?' Maddy frowned.

'That you're not guilty of arson.' Harry chuckled, then sipped the Prosecco.

'Yes, that's true. The worrying thing is, though, who did it?'

Maddy's grim expression made Harry realise he'd made a mistake mentioning the fire. 'Sorry, I was supposed to be cheering you up and giving us an excuse to celebrate.'

Maddy raised her glass towards him. 'How about . . . to Harry, and his incredible helpfulness?'

'Not so sure about the incredible.'

'You've been my hero. I'm not sure I'll ever be able to thank you enough.'

'To neighbours, then,' Harry said, clinking his glass against Maddy's.

'Yes, to neighbours.'

***

241

'No more Prosecco for me.' Maddy shook her head. She had a little left in her glass, but Harry had finished his.

'Yes, we've both got work in the morning.' Harry closed the drinks menu. However much she fancied a second bottle of Prosecco, after the other week's incident with the red wine, Maddy was determined to be on better behaviour and be able to remember the night's events. The food had been delicious. Sunday evening had been a set three-course dinner menu. Fine dining meant perfectly presented small portions, delicately served up on the plate, and eating all three delectable courses had left her full and content. She'd eaten more than enough but didn't feel bloated as if she'd eaten too much.

'Although you are a lightweight,' Harry said, teasing her.

'I think I'll save room for the coffee, thanks,' Maddy said. 'Plus, you're bigger than me. You can handle more alcohol. You have more body mass to soak it up.'

'Are you saying I'm fat?'

Maddy laughed at Harry's surprised expression. 'You are far from fat! But you're a good foot taller, and you do have a lot more muscle than me.' She pumped her arm to show her bicep and Harry leaned over and gave it a squeeze. 'See?'

'Okay, point taken.' Harry let her grip his bicep – hard and firm underneath his light blue shirt. He was even wearing a tie. *And she had checked out his bum earlier – it was hard not to.* Seriously, this man scrubbed up well.

Not that he didn't look hot in shorts and a T-shirt . . .
But it was good to know he wasn't afraid to wear a tie.
*Why was it good to know that? Stop looking at him as
future dating material.* Maddy knew what lay beneath his
shirt. Solid, honed flesh, and all tanned. She'd seen
enough of it when he'd returned home from work each
evening, or even when working at the cottage, stripping
off his T-shirt.

They had laughed, joked and teased the whole night,
slowly finding out more about one another. Well, Maddy
had done most of the talking, Harry seemed content to
listen and ask her questions, so that she couldn't ask him
anything. He'd divulged some childhood stories, and a few
anecdotes about firefighter antics, but he'd pretty much
kept the focus on Maddy throughout the evening. Men
weren't so open at the best of times, compared to most
women. But would Harry eventually open up to her? It
was too early to think these things. Why did she always
steamroller ahead in her mind? 'Take each day as it comes
and worry less,' Valerie's advice floated to the forefront of
her mind. Val would always say, 'You young-uns will look
back and realise your mistakes. I know I did.' Besides, it
wasn't as if she and Harry were an item . . . *Was this even
a date?*

'I tell you what, as the night is still young, shall we check
out the nightlife in Padstow?' Harry said.

'On a Sunday?' Maddy scoffed.

'Okay, so it may not be rocking . . .' Harry rolled his eyes. 'But we could take a look.'

'Coffee first, though. I need the caffeine to keep me awake.'

'The sea air will wake you up when you get outside.' But Harry summoned the waiter and ordered the coffees.

When the bill arrived, Maddy hadn't quite finished her coffee. Harry snatched away the little black wallet and inserted his credit card inside before Maddy could take a look. 'My treat,' he said to Maddy, who was about to argue.

She frowned. 'Are you sure? I was supposed to be treating you, as you drove me over here to drop off the paintings.'

'Yeah, but it was my idea to go out tonight.'

After saying brief goodbyes to Roy, who was rushed off his feet, and to his wife Anne, who'd come out of the kitchen to see them, Maddy and Harry took the short walk through the quaint narrow streets towards the harbour. Harry wanted to check out the night sky.

Harry turned and looked over the harbour, back towards the town. 'I love watching the sun set.'

Maddy loved this time of year with its long evenings. It was nearly nine o'clock, and the sky was suffused with a slight pinkish-red glow where the sun was setting. The rigging and sails of the boats in the harbour gently creaked in the breeze. The sound was soothing. As they leaned against the wall and looked across the Camel Estuary towards Rock, the sea breeze picked up and Maddy shivered, rubbing the goosebumps on her arms. 'I think I should have brought a thicker cardigan.' She hadn't even thought about later in the evening and how chilly it could get once the sun had lost its power. She'd brought nothing apart from a cream bolero, purchased with the dress, which was made of light cotton material and only covered the tops of her arms. It didn't quite do the job of keeping her warm.

Harry moved closer, and wrapped his arm around her shoulders, cocooning her. 'Better?'

'Thanks.' For a moment, she stiffened, then with the help of the wine in her veins, gradually relaxed into his body, savouring his warmth. He was like a radiator. *He smelled fantastic, too.*

'Come on, let's get inside a pub,' Harry said, giving her a hug. Then, and much to Maddy's surprise, he grabbed her hand. His hand, gently holding hers, was so much warmer than hers, sending a jolt of electric heat up her arm, and into her lungs, making her gasp.

He let go of her hand to open the pub door, and as they entered they were engulfed by the summer heat trapped inside. The pub was busy, busier than expected for a Sunday night, and as they eased through the crowd towards the bar, Maddy could feel contact with Harry again, the tender gesture of his hand at the small of her back. Protective, reassuring, sending a tingle up her spine. Maybe the Prosecco had gone to her head — should she be feeling like this? About Harry?

Once they'd got their drinks, they found a corner to

huddle in, forced to stand close to one another. There were no tables free to sit at, but Maddy didn't mind being this close to Harry. It didn't feel uncomfortable with him standing within her personal space. There was nothing invading about this man.

'So why's a good-looking guy like you single?' The vodka helped Maddy start this conversation. *Definitely the vodka.*

'I could ask the same about you.'

'You could, but I'm not a guy.' She raised her eyebrows.

'But you're good-looking.'

'You find me attractive, huh?' Maddy chewed her bottom lip.

'I do.' Harry lowered his head, his eyes not leaving hers.

Maddy placed her hand on his chest to stop him coming closer, which was hard as her heart pounded under her breastbone with the thrill of him being so close. 'But you're doing it again, avoiding the question. Come on, tell me, how long have you been single?'

'I haven't been with anyone since my last girlfriend, Karin. I've had a lot to work through.' Harry lifted his head and took a sip of his drink, not meeting Maddy's gaze.

'Did she end the relationship then?' Maddy still had her hand on his chest, toying with a button. He'd removed his tie upon entering the pub, and had the top couple of buttons undone, revealing a glimpse of his tanned skin.

'Yes, you could say that.' He closed his eyes and said, 'Maddy, please . . .'

Maddy knew to stop the questions. Cornering Harry on something he wasn't ready to tell her about was not going to work.

A couple of blokes entered the already busy pub, pushing past Maddy, and Harry reached a protective arm around her waist, pulling her in towards him, pressing her against his hard torso. So close, she could smell the hints of spice in his aftershave. As she met his gaze, Harry dipped his head and gently touched his lips to hers, kissing her.

Chapter 19

'Sorry, I've been wanting to do that all night,' Harry said, after he'd pulled out of the kiss. He hadn't deepened it, kept it light, but he had tasted the sweetness of the orange juice on her lips from her drink. The kiss had still sent blood rushing to his groin.

'Really?' Maddy's green eyes were fixed on his, her pupils large and dilated in the dim light of the pub. Her hand rested on his chest. Could she feel the rate his heart was beating? He hadn't had an intimate relationship since Karin. He'd missed it so much. His attraction to Maddy was unstoppable. Each day he'd wanted to get nearer to her, finding himself daydreaming about her even when he was busy at work. However hard he tried, he couldn't get her out of his head.

'Yes, in fact, I think I will do it again.'

This time Harry deepened the kiss, his tongue in search of hers, his hand gently supporting the back of her head as he turned her round to place his back to the room, his fingers entwined in her hair. And Maddy allowed it, now shielded from the eyes in the room, pressing her body against his, and curling her arms around his neck. He wrapped both arms around her. The problem Harry warred with was he didn't want to just kiss her, he wanted her whole body. While one hand caressed her upper back and neck, searching for her bare flesh, the other strayed down to curve around her bottom – and thankfully, there was no objection from her.

Harry let out a growl of longing into Maddy's ear.

'I think we should get the water taxi home.' He mouthed the words over her lips, not wanting to separate from her.

'I agree,' Maddy said, kissing him back.

'Did you want to go back to the cottage, or stay at mine tonight?'

'I do have a double bed at the cottage.' Maddy grabbed Harry's hand and pulled him towards the pub's front door.

And Simon did say something about it needing testing. But Harry kept that thought to himself.

Because the tide was low, they had to catch the ferry from a different point in Padstow, which meant going on the beach. This time, Harry lifted Maddy up into his arms, not in the fireman-carry, and carried her onto the boat, setting her down gently.

Once the water taxi started the crossing, Maddy got straight on her phone to call a taxi as Harry kept her close. 'Yes, a pick up from the ferry point in Rock, please.

We'll be arriving in ten minutes.' She ended the call and slipped the phone into her bag. With the sun down, the night air was much chillier on the short estuary crossing. She shivered, and Harry pulled her even closer, warming her up. She curled into his embrace.

It was dark now, and above them in the clear sky, stars brightened like tiny fairy lights. Harry stole another kiss, covering Maddy's arms with his own to keep her warm.

When the ferry docked, there was a taxi waiting for them. The car journey was laborious. Warming up, they both sat in the back, holding hands, Harry's thumb rubbing Maddy's palm while they made light conversation with the chatty taxi driver. He was only being polite, asking about their evening, intrigued to hear their opinion about the new restaurant in Padstow, but it didn't make the journey go any quicker for Harry, who wanted Maddy – all to himself.

At last, Harry closed the front door to the cottage and Maddy slung her bag at the bottom of the stairs and sighed as she removed her shoes. For a moment, there was an awkward silence. Did they continue what they'd started in the pub? He was out of practice at this. It had been two years since Karin. He hadn't felt like doing anything like this with anyone in all that time. It had seemed wrong, a betrayal of her memory.

He edged forward, and gently combed his fingers through her hair. He stroked her cheek, rounding her face, then finally his knuckles brushed under her chin, raising her head, her mouth to his.

The kiss deepened, her fingers fumbling with his shirt buttons, his hands lowering the zipper at the back of her dress. Fluidly, never breaking contact, they stood in the hallway, like love-struck teenagers, making out, kissing, caressing each other.

'Harry . . . I think,' Maddy said between passionate kisses and snatched breaths, 'we should . . . take this upstairs.'

'Hmm . . . yes, good idea,' Harry said, reluctant to remove his hands from her body. He ached for her, his trousers feeling tight around his groin. He hooked her, fireman's carry style, over his shoulder.

'Harry!' This time she squealed with delight and chuckled without a fight.

As he placed her on the bed, rosy-cheeked and hair tousled, but her expression mock-reproachful, he said, 'I thought this would be the quickest way to get you into bed.'

She sat up, leaning on her elbows. 'Did you now? There's me thinking you like it kinky.'

'I'll be anything you like.'

Eyeing him mischievously, she sat up fully, reaching around his bum and pulling him towards her. She undid the buckle of his belt, his flies, then pushed at his trousers, so they fell to his ankles. Slowly, she teased down his boxers, and he closed his eyes, concentrating on the warmth of her mouth, taking him into her. He groaned at the intense feeling as her lips and tongue ran along his hardness. Back and forth rhythmically, hardening him further than he thought possible.

'Stop.' Harry withdrew from her mouth. 'This is about you . . . not me.' And if she carried on like that he'd be good for no one.

Harry had to taste her. He craved her – had done all night. He removed the rest of his clothes and kicked them aside, then with urgency, slid Maddy's dress down, over her hips and free from her feet, revealing pastel pink underwear, the colour of spring blossom.

Fuck, she's gorgeous.

He wanted to kiss every inch of her.

Kneeling over her, he kissed her mouth, neck, collarbone, fumbling behind her back to unclasp her bra. He was definitely out of practice when it came to undoing bras.

Maddy chuckled. 'Shall I help you?'

'No, I've got it.' Finally, the bra released. Relieved, Harry smoothed the straps down her arms gently and pulled the garment free. He hadn't wanted to admit how long it had been since he'd done this kind of thing. Maddy might run a mile, thinking he was crap. He kissed her lips, plump and naturally red; they seemed to be compatible there. He could kiss her for eternity. Following his hands, he moved his mouth to her breast, then the other breast, toying with her nipples with his tongue. It was all coming back to him, just like how to swim – you never forget. She pulled her stomach in and arched her back, shifting in the bed, as he ran his tongue along her inner thigh.

She lifted her hips to aid the removal of her knickers and he threw them in the same direction as the bra, not caring where they landed. His own heart pounded with excitement – or was it nerves? – as he softly kissed and tasted her most intimate parts. A small voice inside his head nagged that maybe he shouldn't be doing this with Maddy . . . of all women . . . But he'd missed this intimacy, the foreplay, the thrill of pleasuring his woman. Right now, Maddy was his as her body gradually relaxed under his gentle caress. As his tongue licked, his finger, deep inside her stroked her soft spot. She gave her approval; her fingers combing through his hair as she whispered her enjoyment and gave little whimpers of pleasure.

'Harry,' her hand brushed his arm resting on her stomach, 'however fantastic that feels, I really want you inside me.' He looked up to meet her flushed gaze.

He wanted her too.

Condoms. 'Hang on!'

Leaning over Maddy on all fours, he rummaged for his wallet which was still in his trousers. He'd put condoms in there as a precaution, taking them from the stash in his bedside cabinet he'd never thought he'd use again. He tore open a foil packet and rolled the thing on. They were such passion killers, but it needed to be done.

His mouth found Maddy's as he entered her, and their

bodies connected at last. Harry held onto her for as long as he could. For the first time in over two years, he felt truly alive again.

***

Maddy awoke early to very pleasant memories of . . . she wanted to think lovemaking, but quite clearly last night had just been sex. Hot, incredible, sex. The first time hadn't quite rocked her world, but she'd put it down to the pair of them being a little nervous. The second and third times . . . Well, Harry'd had her in all sorts of positions, eager to find out what suited her best, which position gave her the most pleasure. She'd never known someone so considerate in the bedroom. Harry's strength, power, slowing it down, speeding it up, firm then gentle . . . the memory of these sensations alone sent flutters to her stomach. *She couldn't possibly still be horny?*

Fearing to move, she glanced at Harry, still sleeping; his arm draped over her. His chest rose and fell with his breathing and she could hear the air escaping. Surprisingly, she'd slept well last night, too – thanks to the alcohol, albeit not too much (she still had her memory) and the hot sex, and the fact the bed wasn't strange to her. Usually, when sleeping with someone new, she'd lie awake half the night.

But now the alcohol had worn off, would they both go back to being just neighbours or even friends? What had happened? The evening certainly hadn't ended how Maddy had planned.

Oh come on, who are you kidding? You'd worn your best dress, and matching underwear – just in case – and made sure you looked smoking hot.

Maddy's real fear was whether this would change the dynamic between them. Would it make things awkward? *At least she could stay at Wisteria Cottage . . .* And what if this didn't work out? *Probably jumping far too ahead now, Maddy – you had sex, he didn't ask for your hand in marriage.* But even once she moved back into her own house, the fact remained that they lived opposite one another. *Oh dear Lord, maybe this hadn't been wise.*

They were both adults. And sex wasn't a dirty word. It was healthy for two consenting adults. Commitment needn't be necessary. Maybe they could carry on as if it never happened, if needs be?

An alarm shattered the quiet in the room, jerking Harry awake and startling Maddy simultaneously.

'Shit, what time is it?' Harry glanced at his phone, silencing it. He rubbed his face and groaned, then focussed on Maddy lying naked beside him. He gave an approving smile, his black hair all ruffled. Gazing into his hard-to-resist blue eyes, Maddy realised she didn't want this to be just sex with Harry.

'I'm sorry,' he said kissing Maddy firmly on the lips, her own eyes widening at its suddenness. 'But I've got to go early this morning. I'm meeting someone to quote for a land-scaping job and need to collect my pickup from Rock first.'

'It's okay.' It wasn't: she was hoping to talk about last night, but the morning after was not the day to act like a demanding psycho bitch from hell. That was the number one rule in being the perfect girlfriend.

Girlfriend?

'Can I use your bathroom?' he asked, breaking her reverie.

'Of course. There's plenty of towels in there.'

Harry kissed her again and got out of bed, and Maddy bit her lip watching his tight bum as he walked naked out of the bedroom. She remembered her hands clasping hold of those firm pieces of flesh last night. *Heaven help her, he was gorgeous. A life sculpture of perfection.*

Maddy still hadn't moved when Harry re-entered the bedroom towelling himself dry. Last night's activities hadn't left him shy either. Before last night, Harry would have kept the towel firmly around his waist. Now he wasn't hiding anything. Unfortunately for Maddy – not that she was staring – Harry soon had himself covered up, donning his clothes from last night.

'Shall I give you a lift to your pickup? How were you going to get there?'

'If you've got time that would be great. But Maddy, didn't you say something last night about opening the gallery up this morning because Valerie had an appointment?' Harry said, frowning.

'Oh shit!' Maddy sat up in bed, pulling the duvet up to her chest. *Yes, she had.* She'd stood there last night, a tiny bit wobbly on her heels, telling Harry she couldn't get too drunk, and now he had to remind her she was opening the gallery up. It all came flooding back. 'What time is it now?' She looked about for her mobile phone.

Harry glanced at his watch he'd fastened on his wrist. 'Coming up for eight o'clock.'

Her mobile phone confirmed it too: 07:50 am.

She didn't have time to lie in bed. It was a Monday, not a Sunday, not that it made a difference running a gallery in the summer. It had to be open seven days a week. She had to be in work. Plus the builders would be arriving any minute. She needed to get dressed. Maddy bolted out of the bedroom, kissing Harry on the cheek, and dashed into the bathroom.

'I'll see you tonight,' Harry called through the bathroom door.

'Okay,' Maddy shouted over the noise of the shower as the water cascaded over her head. Had she avoided the awkwardness there? Had it been awkward or had she now made it worse? Should they have said more to one another?

Oh, hell, had sleeping with Harry been a mistake?

Chapter 20

In all his years, Harry had never been a guy for one night stands or flings. His first relationship had been with Nicole, his college sweetheart, although they'd known each other from school. But they'd been too young, and after five years they'd agreed they were more like friends than lovers. After Nicole, his relationships turned out not to last as long as he'd hoped, a month or two here, or a few weeks there . . .

And then he'd met Karin.

She had been his second serious relationship. He was in love with her. The head over heels kind, wanting to always please her, make her happy – which wasn't always easy –so when she was no longer in his life, and there was nothing he could do to get her back, it had hurt. Really hurt. Harry had never known agony like it. Something died inside him the day he'd lost Karin.

His relationship with Karin, albeit difficult at times, had been coming up to three years, with a baby on the way. Would they have been married by now, and adding to their family? After many months of darkness and pain, his doctor had diagnosed post-traumatic stress disorder – PTSD. Something he thought only soldiers suffered from, not fit and healthy firefighters.

But apparently, it could happen to anyone.

Okay, he needed to think happier thoughts as he mowed Mrs Gable's lawn. Maddy. Think about Maddy. Last night had reminded him how much he enjoyed getting intimate with the right woman.

Was she the right woman?

Right now, she was.

He killed the engine of the lawnmower when he'd got to the end of a line and looked back. Mrs Gable liked perfectly straight lines in her lawn as if it was a court at Wimbledon. He checked his phone. No text from Maddy. He knew he should really message her first . . . but what should he text? **Thanks for the fantastic sex last night, can we do it again soon?**

He'd had to focus on meeting a potentially new client for a landscaping job this morning, making notes so he could draw up a competitive quote for them. And from there he'd gone from job to job, garden to garden, and hadn't got around to messaging Maddy. The longer he left it, the harder it would get. He hadn't even managed to get back to the cottage, but after his conversations with Roy, he knew he could take his time there and concentrate on some of his more regular work. With the sun hidden behind the clouds, and the wind coming from the west, off the sea, Harry was grateful for a cooler day. It took a firm tug of the cord, even with the engine warm, to re-start the lawnmower, and Harry tried to concentrate on creating the perfectly straight lines in the rest of the lawn and what he should say to Maddy. They didn't usually text each other too regularly, so maybe she'd think this was normal.

No, if Karin had taught him one thing, it was that women could over-analyse.

***

Maddy had been unproductive all day, unable to even concentrate on her paintings. When the door opened and a customer walked in, Maddy was the first to greet them and strike up a conversation, anything to stop her thinking about Harry.

Maddy stared at her phone for the umpteenth time that day. Valerie had shown up later on after her appointment and plied her regularly with tea. Maddy stuffed her phone back into her pocket. Admittedly, down in Tinners Bay, the network could be hit and miss. A bit of cloud and there was no signal at all sometimes.

'He's probably busy, Maddy,' Valerie said. 'Gosh, in my day, you had to wait for a letter to arrive on your doorstep. This modern technology does nothing for your heart.'

'But what if it was just a fling, just sex? I never usually

do these things.' Except for a couple of one-nighters in her university days, it wasn't something she liked making a habit of. The next morning her heart always betrayed her, heavy inside her chest with an ache of rejection when the guy didn't ask for her telephone number or another date. Maddy fell too quickly for the wrong guy and would do everything she could to please, accommodate . . . This could be why she'd ended up with Connor.

'He doesn't seem the type to me.' Valerie frowned as she hooked a seascape painting in place on a wall, adjusting it so it hung straight.

'Oh, do one-night stands look a certain way? I didn't realise,' Maddy said, scowling. Then she softened her tone, 'Sorry, I shouldn't take it out on you. I just wish he'd text me.'

Valerie chuckled. 'You young girls today. Harry seems a gentleman, and I'm a pretty good judge of character. Plus, you both live on the same street, I'm sure he wouldn't want to do something to make things awkward between you. He's probably just busy.'

Maddy nodded, dipping her paintbrush into a mix of blue. Valerie was right, and older, so therefore much wiser.

'You know, you could text him,' Valerie said, raising her eyebrows in that all-knowing fashion. 'Modern women and all that.'

'No, he needs to text me first. How do I know if he's interested otherwise? And I don't want to be a pest. It's like a texting rule.' She didn't want to look needy.

Valerie shook her head, chuckling again. 'I'm sure he won't think you're a pest. I'm glad I don't know how to text, as I'd be breaking all the rules.' This was true. Valerie never sent Maddy texts. It was always phone calls. It was only in the past couple of years Valerie had apparently given in and purchased a mobile phone. Maddy believed Valerie's eldest son had actually insisted she entered the twenty-first century. Whether she had it switched on was another matter. 'But then again, in my day, I was a bit of a rule breaker.'

***

Maddy closed up the gallery and walked up to Wisteria Cottage via the public footpath. She found Simon still at the cottage. The tiling had been started in the kitchen, and he looked as if he was checking it. He grinned at Maddy as she entered.

'Hello, beautiful. How was your day? We still haven't had that drink,' Simon said. 'What about tonight?'

Damn, I thought I'd talked him out of that.

'Uhm . . . I better give the liver a rest tonight, Simon,' she said, unable to meet his eye. 'Had a bit to drink last night.'

'Did you now? Haven't seen your boyfriend have you?'

'Boyfriend?' Maddy blushed. Did he mean Harry? His tone had been sarcastic.

'Yeah, your neighbour, the gardener. I haven't seen him here today.'

Harry had agreed with Roy that Mondays would be his day to catch up with his regular customers so that he had a regular income coming in. Maybe he hadn't relayed this message to Simon.

'He said something about not working here on Mondays,' Maddy said, hesitant about what she should tell Simon.

'Right, well, I wish he'd communicate this stuff to me.' Simon gathered up his keys from the counter. 'Still a raincheck on that drink then, huh?'

'Yes. Sorry.' But she wasn't. Maddy toyed with her phone in her hand, her mind distracted, thinking of Harry.

'I'll be off then,' Simon said, and Maddy mumbled a goodbye. Simon closed the front door behind him and she heard his van start.

'Oh bugger it.' She had to see Harry. It was no use denying it.

Maddy caved in and sent him a text message.

I would like to see you, to talk. Shall I head over to yours? xxx

Maddy ran up the stairs two at a time. She jumped into the shower to freshen up and put some clean clothes on – ones not blotched with paint. And applied some light make-up – of course! *Seriously, she'd never worried about having make-up on for Harry before.*

For nearly twenty minutes Maddy paced the kitchen

waiting for a reply on her phone and her apprehension and anxiety rose. What was she to expect when she saw Harry? Would it be awkward between them? How was she to react? Kiss him . . . or keep her distance? Should she call him or had he not seen her text?

Maddy filled a glass with cold water from the tap, adding some ice and a slice of lemon. Maybe instead of water, she should have a glass of wine to calm her nerves? *No, lay off the wine. Keep your head clear.* What should she do? Should she start cooking some dinner and make enough for two and hope he came to the cottage? Or should she make her way to his? She had no idea what time Harry was due back. Usually, if it was good weather, with the evenings being light, he worked on into the evening. It was gone seven now. Should she carry on as if nothing had happened between them? What? How had she got herself into this mess?

Harry still hadn't replied to her text either.

Maddy stared at the contents of her fridge trying to think of something to create for dinner. Although her stomach rumbled for food, she'd lost her appetite, unable to stomach anything.

She really liked Harry, and thinking back to last night and how amazing he'd made her feel, she'd do it all over again in a flash. He was an incredible kisser . . . his body firm and strong, yet his touch soft and caressing. *Never, ever judge a book by its cover.*

There was a knock at the front door, making Maddy

jump and close the fridge door. She took a deep breath – in through her nose, out through her mouth, like she'd been taught in a yoga class once – before opening the door.

'Hey, there you are,' Harry said, beaming at Maddy.

'Did you get my text?'

'Sorry, my phone died on me.' He waved it at her. 'So I came straight to the cottage first.' His chest was bare, dirty and shimmering with sweat. All doubt about Harry whooshed right out of Maddy as she smiled back. Without hesitation, he approached her and reached for her, placing his hand behind her neck. He planted a firm kiss on her lips, knocking the breath out of her. His other hand swept up her thigh and under her cotton dress, to squeeze her bum.

'You need a shower, you stink.' She screwed up her nose as she pulled away from him.

'That'll be the horse manure.'

'*Nice.*'

'I'm thinking you should come shower with me.' He tugged her closer.

'But I'm not dirty, and I've just had one.' She drew back.

'That's not a problem; I can get you all dirty.' Harry pulled her into his arms, as she tried recoiling while laughing at him. Again his hands wandered, and the sensation on her skin was thrilling, sending heat between her thighs. 'See you are dirty now.' He sniffed her hair, while his arms enveloped her. His groan was of approval as his hold tightened. 'You definitely need to shower with me.'

'Need someone to scrub your back, do you?'

'Something like that.' His expression was mischievous. How could Maddy resist someone so bloody sexy? 'I've got some tension in my muscles.'

She rolled her eyes, then sensibly, Maddy gestured towards the kitchen. 'But I could start making dinner while you're—'

'No. I want you.' *He was seriously sexy when he got all authoritative.* He tugged her into another kiss, wrapping his arms around her shoulders as if to make sure she got fully dirty and couldn't escape him.

Maddy followed Harry up the stairs, holding his hand. 'These were clean clothes.'

'You can wash them.'

'As if I haven't done enough washing.'

'Shhh . . . and get in the shower.' He had the audacity to pat her bum. Harry turned the shower on, then stripped off, pleasantly surprising Maddy to see how turned on he was already. Maddy found a stray hair band on the window-sill and tied her hair up in a messy knot – she didn't need to get all her hair wet again. Harry assisted Maddy in the removal of her clothes as if she wasn't getting them off quick enough.

Harry stepped into the shower, then holding Maddy's hand as if escorting her, he helped her in, too.

Water ran over his tanned torso. He had a brown tan line around his waist, his skin white to halfway down his thighs. His darkness was a contrast against Maddy's paler skin tone. Harry had squirted some shower gel over his body and lathered it up quickly, clearly not fussed about its citrus scent. Maddy slid her hand up over his chest, massaging the bubbles over his skin. Then she slid them around his neck, pressing her body against his as she kissed him, the bubbles finding their way between them. The water fell around them, as their passion built, his hardness against her softness, his arousal solid against her flesh, making her ache for him, pooling low in her belly.

'You know, the bath also fits two . . .' she said between kisses. In this shower, they were probably using enough water to fill the bath.

'We'll have to test it,' Harry replied, his lips still pressed to her neck.

As one hand stroked his neck holding his head to hers, her other found his erection and pumped, the rain of water adding to the sensation. With this, one of his hands grabbed her buttock and squeezed, pulling her closer, while the other delved between her thighs, urgent to return the same pleasure.

Between the kisses, she said slowly, 'This isn't getting you very clean.'

'I don't care.' Harry rumbled the words slowly in her ear. The assertiveness and sexiness of his voice made her crave him more, her kisses no longer soft, but urgent, nipping his tongue, his lip, making him growl with excitement.

'To hell with this.' Harry let go of Maddy, quickly rinsed off any soap then turned off the shower. With both hands he ruffled his hair to get rid of the excess water and scooped Maddy up into his arms, making her squeal – she held on for dear life, and gave a silent prayer he wouldn't slip or drop her in the shower. But with ease, he carried her from the bathroom to the bedroom.

'You'll get the bed wet,' Maddy said as Harry carefully lowered her onto the pine bed.

'I don't care. This weather, it'll dry quickly enough.'

Maddy buried the practical side of her and relaxed onto the duvet, her worries soon forgotten when Harry gently stroked her legs, running his tongue along her inner thigh, then kissing her intimately. Maddy closed her eyes and allowed her whole body to sink into the covers, grasping the bedding into her fists. The man knew how to paralyse her with pleasure. Slowly, the pressure built in her lower abdomen, the butterfly sensation increasing until she could hold on no more and her body gently pulsed with the electricity only an orgasm could provide.

Harry appeared on all fours, kneeling over her, with a smile of satisfaction, 'Would you like to do that again, but this time with me inside you?'

'What are you like?' Her eyes widened.

'But you enjoy it.'

'Hell, yes, I do.' Maddy grinned, then held her hand up

against Harry's chest. 'Did we just get clean so we could get dirty all over again?'

'Oh, yes.'

***

'I'm a mess, thanks to you,' Maddy said, finally getting out of bed.

Harry watched with admiration as she slipped on her underwear and chose a fresh summer dress out of the fabric IKEA wardrobe and pulled it over her head. Her cheeks glowed from their lovemaking. 'You look absolutely beautiful to me.'

'You're going to say that after what we've just done. It would only be polite.' Maddy tugged at her hair with a comb. The sex had been fantastic, and Harry had done everything with his willpower to keep it going for as long as possible. There had been a couple of times he'd come close to losing it, letting go, but he'd changed the position, decreased the intensity for him, so he'd had longer buried inside her with their bodies entwined. He didn't know what he felt for Maddy – *far too early days for that* – but he definitely knew he fancied the pants off her. The sooner he had her naked, the better he felt. Whether it was sex induced, or not, his head had cleared too as if a great big cloud had been swept away; the pain of losing Karin finally lifted. When he wasn't with Maddy, she was in his thoughts. He treasured every minute he could spend with her.

'I am not saying it because I've fucked you senseless,' Harry said, dropping a kiss on Maddy's bare upper arm, then nuzzling into her neck, noticing the goosebumps rise along her arms. He smiled knowing he clearly did have an effect on her. 'Okay, if you think you look a mess, I'll agree with you. But I know how you came to look so dishevelled.'

'Yes, and you were the cause of it.'

'And so, I find it bloody sexy.' He kissed her again.

She turned in his arms. 'By the way, have you got any clean clothes with you?' Maddy looked him up and down. He was still naked except for the towel he had just wrapped around his waist.

'Luckily, I carry clean clothes on me in the pickup. Just in case I have to meet a client, and I'm covered in mud.'

'Or manure.'

'Take your time, I'll go fetch my clothes . . .' he smoothed his hand from her waist to her hip, 'before I lose it again, and have to get you all dirty.'

He made his way to the bedroom door.

'Harry, are you going out like that?' Maddy frowned at him.

He shrugged his shoulders. 'Nobody will see. And besides, they're not your neighbours, are they?'

She chuckled, shaking her head.

***

271

'Shall we go out for dinner?' Harry shut the fridge door.

'Oh, um . . . I don't really feel dressed for it.'

'You look great. I look like a tramp in comparison.' He gestured to the clean jeans and dark blue polo shirt he was now wearing. 'Come on.' He grabbed his wallet and Maddy's hand, escorting her out of the back door and along the garden path. Once he'd shut the gate behind them, he took her hand back, and they headed out towards Tinners Bay. 'I'm so hungry.'

'It's your fault we're eating late. You dragged me into the shower.'

'I wouldn't have had it any other way. Much more fun.'

There were only a few places to dine in Tinners Bay. They chose a pub that overlooked the beach on the opposite side to the cottage. They found a table and Harry placed their food order at the bar, returning with a bottle of white wine and two glasses.

'I'd better have only the one glass. Driving, remember?' Henry said, pouring only a small glass for himself.

'Nonsense. You can stay at mine.'

Harry liked that Maddy had invited him to stay at the cottage. He didn't like the idea of sleeping without Maddy. He would much prefer sleeping with her. He didn't care if he had broken sleep with her beside him, he'd still prefer her to be next to him.

They finished their food, and still had some wine left, which Harry emptied into their glasses.

'After this, shall we go for a walk?' Harry said. It was getting dark, but there was enough light for an evening stroll.

'Yes, all right.'

Harry finished his wine before Maddy. She grabbed her cardigan off the back of her chair, took her last sip, then they set off for a walk through the town and onto the soft sand of the beach. Harry held her hand as they strolled, fingers linked, palms touching. When they stopped to look out at the ocean, he stood behind her, and Maddy snuggled into him. Encouraged by this closeness, he wrapped his arms around her to stop Maddy feeling the chill in the wind. There was the constant roar of the waves crashing, and occasionally the breeze would bring the scent of the fish and chip shop to them over the otherwise salty sea air, but all the seagull cries had disappeared with the approach of dusk.

'Red sky at night . . .' Harry said, looking at the sky on the horizon.

'Does that mean it will be a good day, the next day? Shepherd's delight . . . Or it's been a good day? I'm never sure.'

'We'll see tomorrow won't we?' He hugged her tighter.

She turned in his arms, to look up at him, and he dropped a kiss on her lips, which she deepened. He could taste the wine on her tongue. Standing on the beach, oblivious to other late evening strollers, the sun sinking beneath the horizon, they kissed.

Harry withdrew, the intensity of the kiss moving south in his body. 'At this rate, I'll be wanting you all over again.' He needed to let go of Maddy, except her hand, to allow the breeze to cool his thoughts, and reduce the tightness in his jeans.

'We'd better keep walking then; we wouldn't want you being done for indecency.'

Chapter 21

Harry awoke with Maddy curled into him, his skin a little clammy from their body heat. His hardening groin had awoken him. Nothing to do with the light mornings, the sound of the ocean and the birdsong outside – if that's what you could call seagulls squabbling.

Last night, they'd drifted off to sleep, cuddling. Their post-shower sex had left them exhausted and satisfied, mutually agreeing they needed to sleep. But sometimes that intimacy alone was better than sex. However, this morning was a different matter altogether. He wanted Maddy. Now.

He started kissing her, nudging her belly with his hardness. 'Good morning, gorgeous.'

'What time is it?' She rubbed her eyes.

He'd already checked the time on his phone charging by the bed. 'It's just gone five thirty.' He nuzzled her again, stroking her hair off her face to find her lips.

'Oh, Harry, it's far too early. Go back to sleep,' Maddy grumbled, her eyes still closed. She rolled over, her back towards him, her warmth leaving his side but her naked form now revealed to him. In the short time they had lived under the same roof, Harry had learnt Maddy was not a morning person. But he was sure he could persuade her.

'I can't help it. You make me like this.' He traced a finger down her spine, kissing her shoulder blade.

'I haven't done anything . . . I've been asleep.'

'But I'm in your bed, and you're wonderful.' Harry ran his hands gently over her body, stroking and caressing, from thigh, to buttocks, along the side of her back, and down, brushing the side of her breast, loving the feeling of her body at his fingertips.' Naturally, I'm going to wake up horny.' He snuggled in, kissing her neck and along her shoulder, and she gave a whimper of appreciation. She was responding, waking slowly, her mood lifting. He slid his free hand between her parting thighs and inserted a finger up into her moist warmth. Finding the soft, smooth internal spot, he massaged it with gentle strokes. Her body reacted, relaxing into his touch.

Then, surprising Harry, her hand reached behind her back and grasped his erection firmly.

'Well, it would be a shame to waste it,' she said, still sleepy.

Wide-awake, Harry quickly found a condom and tore at the foil wrapper. Once protected, he gently eased himself in from behind, becoming one with Maddy. Spooning her, slowly, rhythmically, in and out, the intensity grew. He reached around with his free hand to gently rub where it would please her most.

The more-awake-Maddy soon wanted the position changed, and Harry was happy to oblige. They moved into the good old missionary position, where he got to kiss Maddy, and hold onto her. He loved how her nails would scratch along his back. Not too deep, breaking the skin, but enough to tantalise and excite him.

They played, toyed and experimented, until Maddy, now straddled on top of Harry, began to breathe more heavily, her skin pink with heat and excitement, and gave a humming moan, letting Harry know she'd climaxed.

She relaxed onto him in a heap, with him still inside her. He stroked her back. 'Feel better?'

Her breathing slowed. 'Hmmmm.'

'Not so grumpy now, huh?'

She lifted herself up onto her hands, moving, rocking her hips slowly. Her core tightened around him. *Fuck, that felt good.* Harry gripped her hips more firmly, and exhaled a breath as his body tensed. It wouldn't take him long if she continued this rhythm.

'Me? Grumpy?' she said, then nipped his lip.

'You know you are . . . Moody.'

'Well, before I change my mind, and jump off—'

'Not a chance!' Harry grabbed her hips, holding her on him.

'You better take me then.'

'Take you?'

'Yes, however you like.' Maddy lowered her head to his ear, kissing near his earlobe, then whispered, 'Fuck me hard, soft, however the hell you like.'

***

Maddy wasn't sure where the naughty side had come from, but maybe with Harry she needed to keep things sexy, spicy. Men liked being talked dirty to. Connor always insisted on it, but it never felt right with him. Maybe that had been one of the early signs she should have read, that she wasn't totally comfortable being intimate with Connor. But being playful with Harry seemed natural. He responded too. Even when he played it a little rough, he never hurt her, always wanting to make sure she enjoyed the experience as much as he did. A thoughtful lover. Had Connor been a thoughtful lover? Maddy was finding it hard to remember. Maybe in the beginning, but then he started to become more controlling, even down to the sex: he'd tell her how *she* liked it . . . whether he was right or wrong.

Although her body ached from the morning's sexual antics, Maddy was alert and in a fantastic mood, her morning blues dispersed. She was positively glowing – at least that's what Valerie's comment would be if she could see her. Which she couldn't, because Maddy had to wait at her house for the Loss Adjuster to arrive, so Valerie would be at the gallery opening up for her today.

Harry's early wake-up call had been necessary after all. He'd needed to leave early to go home and load his truck ready for today's work, and Maddy was meeting the Loss Adjuster. Thankfully they'd both left the cottage before Simon and his builders arrived.

While Maddy waited she checked her Facebook updates on her phone. Did she put on her status what a terrific mood she was in? Update all her friends back in Bristol? *No, early days.* Maddy didn't want to jinx anything. *Plus the Loss Adjuster might ruin this good mood.* Although it would be brilliant to finally get things moving on her house. Maddy sent a tweet instead. She'd been neglecting her social media accounts lately – Instagram and Pinterest she used for advertising her paintings. It was a free marketing tool. Twitter was a good way to share news too.

'Loss Adjuster coming today. Can't wait to get my house back. Can't believe how long it's been since the #fire #FedUpOfSmellOfSmoke'

In the silence of her home, she pondered on Harry again. *Was this normal? Did this happen? What was this with Harry?* They had gone from living together – as a favour – to sleeping together, and it seemed to be propelling into a full on relationship. Not really dating first, apart from dinner on Sunday evening. Although Harry made her feel amazing, Maddy couldn't help listening to the alarm bells going off inside her head. She needed to take this slower, she never wanted to go through another Connor scenario again. Moving to the cottage hadn't even helped slow it down. It was too tempting to move back into Harry's — she hated being apart from him. It would be better to live separately and just date — like normal people — wouldn't it?

No, she would use Wisteria Cottage as a haven, a place to distance herself from Harry, so things didn't get too intense, too quickly.

On the dot of nine a.m. her doorbell rang.

'Hello,' Maddy said, answering the door.

On the doorstep stood a tall brunette in her mid-thirties, wearing a black trouser suit. 'Hi, I'm Carol Campbell,' she said, showing her ID badge, which confirmed her job title and the company she worked for. 'Are you Maddison Hart?' She checked her notes.

'Yes, that's me.' Maddy smiled. 'Come in.'

'Oh, yes, I never get used to that charred, burnt smell,' Carol said, entering. The stench was mild by the front door and in the lounge, but when they walked into the dining room, it really hit them.

'I'll be glad when that smell's gone.'

'We'll try to be as quick as we can. Are you living here?'

'No, no . . . I'm staying in a cottage in Tinners Bay now, but I was staying across the road for a bit. My neighbour took me in on the night it happened — well, actually he slung me over his shoulder in a fireman's carry, and locked me in his house.' Carol's eyes widened. 'I *was* being rather hysterical.' Maddy could feel her cheeks burning, probably turning pink as she spoke.

'Sounds very Neanderthal.' Carol chuckled.

Maddy shrugged her shoulders. 'Yes, but at the time, he did me a huge favour. I needed to calm down. And he's been so good to me since.' He was being good in so many ways. Maybe Carol didn't quite need to know they were now having fabulous sex with one another, though. The thought of how Harry turned her on set off butterflies low in her belly and she feared her cheeks were reddening again.

Stop thinking of Harry and concentrate.

As Maddy showed her around the house, Carol, as efficient as her appearance suggested, made notes about everything.

Carol was methodical and meticulous with her notes, nodding to herself at times. As she went through the house, she explained to Maddy what she could claim for and what she couldn't.

The insurance company would allow up to a certain amount of money for the kitchen. Basically, they would pay to replace everything to its original standard. She wouldn't be able to replace it with an all singing and all dancing one from an expensive range with those fancy soft-closing drawers – not that Maddy would want that. What's the point if you can't slam a drawer in anger?

'This is my direct line, but if I'm busy you'll get

redirected, so ask for me, Carol Campbell.' As Carol handed over her business card, Maddy noticed her wedding and engagement rings. All sparkly and shiny. 'I know – the soup jokes I've had from friends.' Carol chuckled. 'But when you fall in love, you can't be choosy about their surname, and Campbell is more interesting than my maiden name, which was Smith.'

Maddison Tudor.

Dear Lord, why was she even thinking that?

Stop it! If past relationships were anything to go by, this could end as fast as it started with Harry.

Maddy hoped not. She and Harry were neighbours after all.

How awkward is that going to be?

If it wouldn't look unusually stupid in front of Carol, Maddy would have slapped her forehead with the palm of her hand right then. What had she been thinking, sleeping with Harry? *That's just it, you hadn't been thinking. You get horny, and thinking goes out the window.*

He'd swept her, quite literally, off her feet.

Once Maddy had shown Carol out, she called Valerie to tell her she'd be late arriving at the gallery, so she could look at kitchens and organize a quote.

'Take your time, love,' said the ever-accommodating Valerie. 'It's very quiet today as the sun isn't out.' Maddy looked out of her front window. Cloud had come in off the sea and had made the day much cooler and gloomier. It even looked like it might rain. You could tell the school summer holidays were about to start. Rain was coming.

No wonder people chose to holiday in Spain.

Maddy drove to Bodmin, where she knew there were a couple of retail outlets that supplied and fitted kitchens. She started to get excited about the prospect of shopping for a new kitchen. Maddy's heart sank with disappointment when she saw the kitchen fitted in Wisteria Cottage that she loved so much. It was out of her price range.

'Fancy seeing you here.' Maddy recognised the voice and turned, in the middle of opening a cupboard with an 'open me' sticker.

'Oh, hello, Simon,' she said. 'What are you doing here?'

'Getting some supplies.' He waved a couple of small bags which contained nails or screws, she couldn't make out which. 'Didn't see you this morning.'

'We . . . I mean, I had to leave early,' Maddy said. She couldn't meet his gaze.

'We, huh?' He raised an eyebrow.

What was this? The third degree? Why was Simon so interested in her whereabouts? He was worse than her mother.

'Harry stayed over.' Maybe honesty was the best way to rid herself of Simon's interest. She certainly only had eyes for Harry. Maddy continued looking at the kitchen displays. Simon still followed her.

'So you two are an item now?'

Harry and Maddy hadn't exactly sat down and discussed

whether they were in a relationship, as such, but the regular sex – these past few days – said something, didn't it?

'I suppose we are. Yes.'

Simon's expression betrayed a brief hint of disappointment. 'Shame, we never had that drink.' A young man came to Maddy's rescue, noticing she was opening cupboard doors where it said 'open me' or 'look inside'.

'Can I help you both?' he said, addressing them as if they were a couple. Maddy felt the need to make it clear she wasn't *with* Simon.

'Yes, actually, you can help *me*,' she said. 'I'm looking for a new kitchen – obviously.' Clearly, she wasn't looking for a bathroom in the kitchen department. She focussed her attention fully on the young assistant. 'I had a fire in mine, and need to get quotes off to my insurance company.'

Fortunately for Maddy, Simon took the hint and waved at her, 'I'll catch you later.'

She nodded then returned her attention to the shop assistant.

'Shall we book you in for a quotation? It's the easiest way. We send someone to come along and measure up and create a design?'

'Yes, that would be perfect.'

Twenty minutes later, with Simon long gone, Maddy had a date with a kitchen designer.

When she arrived in Tinners Bay, she parked in her usual spot behind her gallery. Wanting to share her news, albeit not that exciting, she quickly sent a text to Harry as she walked – slowly. She had a habit of bumping into lampposts or people. Texting on the move was dangerous. How people sent texts while driving she would never know.

'Hey, how'd it go?' Valerie said as Maddy walked through the door.

'Oh, great, I got an appointment in a couple of days.' Maddy nodded and gave a thumbs up to Valerie who was standing out the back in their tiny kitchen area waving the kettle at her and pointing. 'Come and have a look at these brochures then.'

'Hang on, hang on, kettle's boiling.'

Valerie perched herself next to Maddy, who was setting up at her easel in her corner, carrying two mugs of tea. They thumbed through the brochures, Maddy showing Valerie her favourite designs. Valerie's taste was a little different to Maddy's, favouring the more old-fashioned pine styles or plain white surfaces. Maddy saw those as a pain in the arse to keep clean.

'I'll reserve judgement until I see the designs. Apparently, the software will be able to show me my kitchen in my choice. I like the shiny modern styles, but I do love the oak effect look too.' Shutting the brochures, Maddy said, 'Right, best get to work. Time is running out.'

An hour into her painting, Maddy looked up as the gallery door opened. It was Harry.

Her heart lifted like an excited teenager. She really did need to get a handle on this reaction to him.

'Fancy a late lunch and a stroll across the beach?' he said. 'I was at the cottage and thought I'd call in.'

Maddy looked at Valerie guiltily: she'd not been in the gallery long. 'I don't know; I've only really just got here. Valerie's been slaving away for me.'

'Don't be daft. You two go out for a bit. I'm fine here,' Valerie said, with a mischievous expression. Maddy thought Val was jumping the gun slightly: she wanted to buy a new hat and dress, clearly. 'Declan said he'd pop in soon, too. So he can help me out if we get busy.'

'Okay, if you don't mind.' Maddy left her brushes in water, it wouldn't harm them for a bit, washed her hands and grabbed her bag.

Harry took her free hand into his, and even though he'd held her hand last night, at first it felt alien, not used to the show of public affection a relationship involved, but she enjoyed the sensation of touching him in its simplest form. She soon became at ease with his touch, actually hating it when he wasn't touching her in some way. They reached the cafe at the top of the beach where they made freshly prepared sandwiches right in front of you.

'What sandwich do you want?' Harry asked, eagerly looking up at the board. 'I think I'll have a chicken salad with plenty of mayonnaise,' he said to the member of staff behind the counter, keen to take his order.

'I've already eaten in Bodmin. I'll have a smoothie.'

Another member of staff threw the fruit into the blender

while the other made Harry's doorstop sandwich. Harry paid, and then they walked along the beach, Maddy slipping off her flip-flops to stop flicking sand up. They wandered along the warm sand, Maddy enjoying the dry sand between her toes. A seagull cry made her wonder if it would be mad enough to attack Harry for his sandwich, but they managed to walk along without being harassed.

'I work in a couple of those houses, too,' Harry said, pointing up above the beach to a line of houses with seafront views on the cliff. 'That's how I found out about the cottage.' He balled up the paper bag that had contained his sandwich and put it in his pocket.

'I would adore one of those houses,' Maddy said, thinking how much she loved Wisteria Cottage. Its location was perfect. She would love to work from there, but the noise from the builders would not be a good working environment for her to paint in. She needed peace and calm, not banging and hammering, and men singing along badly to songs on the radio. 'I would be able to work from home and not have to paint from memory.'

'Yeah, it would be lovely to live in Tinners Bay. Look at the size of their gardens. The couple of places I maintain have fantastic grounds, but they're holiday homes. Sadly half the places get bought up to be just that – only lived in during the summer. Wisteria Cottage will probably end up as a holiday home too.'

'We can dream,' she said, looping her arm through his.

They walked to the water's edge – the tide was only half way up the beach, so they hadn't as far to walk as if it had been low tide. Maddy paddled as she had bare feet, but Harry stayed back. The shock from hot sand to cold water caught her breath. Gradually, she got used to the freezing temperature, but she didn't let the water go past her ankles. Quickly, when he wasn't looking, she flicked up some of the salty water with her foot at Harry.

'Hey!' He laughed, arching his body to avoid any more splashes. 'Careful, or I'll have to put you over my knee.'

'Well, you've already put me over your shoulder.' She laughed. 'Right, I'd better be getting back. It's not fair on Valerie. I've been out most of the day.'

'I'll walk you back – before you get me any wetter.'

Outside the gallery, Maddy gave Harry a kiss on the lips, but not too lingering. 'See you later,' she said. 'Thanks for the smoothie.'

'It was good to have company for lunch.' He gave her a wink and walked back down the small high street. She watched, wanting to pinch herself. Harry was a catch, and she'd caught him.

For the rest of the day she remained engrossed in her painting – although Harry appeared in her head quite a lot. Valerie left early, leaving Maddy to lock up, as she'd opened. Valerie had done her so many favours, she deserved a break from the gallery.

Maddy was in the mood to continue, every brush stroke

she made feeling therapeutic. The painting was going effort-lessly today. Sometimes, she couldn't get what she wanted right, and it would frustrate her, but today it flowed and thinking about Harry helped. She locked herself in the gallery at seven o'clock, turning the 'open' sign round to 'closed', deciding she could do another hour undisturbed. If she didn't think what she was painting would be any good, or her mood wasn't in it, she'd have packed up and gone home. But she was in the mood to stay and paint. She sent Harry a text to tell him she was staying on, made another cup of tea and found a couple of chocolate digestive biscuits to tide her hunger pangs over, then settled to work on her seascape. Her earlier anger meant she had painted the waves crashing fiercely on to the rocks. Her intention had been to paint a much calmer piece, but this actually worked. She enjoyed creating the foam of the surf, the way the water moved around the rocks. She had so much freedom in painting the ocean.

Half an hour in, her phone beeped. She put her paint brush down and reached for her phone. It would be Harry, probably. Anxiety nestled into her chest when she saw the sender ID. Connor.

Your mum needs you. You need to come home, Maddy.

Chapter 22

'Is everything okay, Mum?' Maddy asked, when her mum answered the phone. She hadn't texted Connor back but immediately called her mother. She wasn't stupid.

'Yes, of course, why?' Sandra trilled down the phone. Maddy was sure Hyacinth Bucket (pronounced 'bouquet' obviously) from *Keeping Up Appearances* had been based on her mother, only a lot frumpier.

'Oh, well,' *God, how did she put this?* 'This is going to sound weird, Mum, but Connor texted me to tell me I needed to come home, that you needed me.'

'Did he? Are you sure? Why on earth would he do that?'

'I don't know, but I've got the text on the phone.'

'Maybe he sent it to you by mistake and it was meant for someone else. Does he have a sister or brother?'

'Yes he does, but no, the message had my name in it. It was for me,' Maddy said, frowning. Was this Connor trying to scare her into returning to Bristol?

'Oh, well, I don't know why he texted you, I haven't even

seen him,' Sandra said. 'And anyway, you know your father and I would contact Edward if we needed help. He lives closer, and we wouldn't worry you unless absolutely necessary.'

This was true. Ed was very good at supporting their parents. 'So everything's okay? Nothing for me to worry about?'

'Absolutely not, I've had a fabulous day with your nephew and niece as it happens.' Alfie and Izzy were Ed and Clare's children. *Next minute she'll be going on about how they need cousins.* 'However, if you wish to come home and stay with us, rather than with your neighbour . . .' Sandra's tone sounded disapproving, 'then you're more than welcome. It wouldn't take me long to make up the spare room.'

If only her mother knew the half of it where Harry was concerned.

They'd at least been practising for making cousins . . .

'I'm not living with Harry, I'm staying at a cottage in Tinners Bay.' *That ought to keep her quiet.*

'What? When? You never said.'

'Sorry, I've just been so busy. Val organized it for me, so thanks for the offer, Mum, but I am fine.' Maddy tried to sound grateful, rather than lick her finger and tally an imaginary score sheet against her mother. 'I saw the loss adjuster today, too, and work should start on my kitchen soon.' Maddy then filled her mother in about all the details and lost another good twenty minutes – omitting the information about her and Harry having shared the same bed. By the time she'd got off the phone, her mother catching her up on Ed and Clare, and how adorable their kids were – which they were – all her creative energy to work on her painting had drained away. While she was on the phone, Harry had also sent her a message which implied he wanted her to come over – he was cooking dinner.

'Shit! Is that the time?' Maddy said, glancing at her watch. It was getting late. The sun was low over the sea, a pink sunset forming with the clouds scattered in the sky. Her stomach rumbled, reminding her she was hungry, too. Maddy hated eating late. It made it more difficult for her to sleep.

Harry will make it difficult for you to sleep.

No, no, no, come back to the cottage after dinner.

She washed out her brushes quickly, and headed 'home' – she seemed to have three at the moment. Throughout the whole journey, her thoughts rattled around in her head caused by the annoyance of Connor's text. But she knew better than to reply to him. It was best to ignore him.

***

'There you are,' Harry said, tucking the oven gloves under his arm to greet Maddy. He kissed her. This afternoon when he'd last seen her felt like weeks ago.

'Something smells good,' she said, but he watched her

smile fade and her shoulders slouch as she threw her handbag over the bannister at the foot of the stairs. He frowned, anxiety creeping into his thoughts, but mentally shook it off and squeezed the top of her arm reassuringly. He hoped this wasn't about him . . . that she'd had second thoughts . . .

'Everything okay?'

Maddy shrugged. 'I didn't get to do half of what I wanted to with my commission. I spent half an hour needlessly on the phone to my mother.'

'Oh. Why needlessly?' He went to the hob and turned down a saucepan bubbling with their vegetables for dinner, easing the lid to stop it rattling. At least it wasn't about him . . . or had he been the topic of conversation?

She shifted her weight, and wouldn't look at him.

'You can tell me, Maddy.'

'Can I?'

'Yes, we're friends . . .' Now he was worried.

'We're a bit more than friends now.' Her determined green eyes narrowed on his.

'Exactly. So tell me what's wrong. You look like someone's died.' Harry drew her into an embrace, tucked her head under his chin and massaged her back. She relaxed into his arms, reciprocating the hug.

'Connor texted me,' she mumbled, her head still pressed against his chest. 'It was vague, but he said I needed to go home because my mum needed me.' She sighed and pulled out of Harry's hold. 'He gave me such a shock, I felt sick, but when I called, she and dad were absolutely fine. What's he playing at?'

Harry didn't know much about Connor. All he could see was Maddy's reactions towards just the mention of his name, which meant Harry didn't like him. But then would he ever really like any ex-lover of the woman he was sleeping with?

'Did you call him?'

'No!' Maddy's eyes widened as if horrified by the thought.

'Well, I don't know then, but maybe the police might catch up with him eventually, and ask him where he was on the day of your fire.'

'Who, Connor? I don't think he did it . . .'

'Well who did then? He'd be number one on my hit list.'

'Why?'

'You haven't really disclosed the circumstances of your relationship ending, but if you ended it, then he might be trying to get you to run back to him. He might not be accepting the rejection.'

'Nah, he was a controlling shit, but arson . . .?' Maddy paused as if considering it. She would be the only one to know what Connor was capable of. But in Harry's experience in the fire service, he knew what lengths some jealous exes would go to. It wasn't a regular occurrence, but it did happen. He'd seen plenty of horrific things, but none of them had affected him until Karin.

Karin . . . trapped . . . car unrecognisable . . . smoke . . . flames . . . explosion . . .

295

'Are you okay? Harry . . . Harry?'

'Oh, sorry.' Harry shook his head. He couldn't change the past. He had to look to the future. But it didn't take away the guilt. Time would never take away the guilt.

'I lost you for a moment. It was as if you were in another time zone.'

'Yeah, yeah, shall we have dinner? I'm starving.' Harry moved towards the oven, grabbing the oven gloves on the way. He buried his feelings, locking them back up deep inside. He needed to be strong for Maddy. 'Take a seat. I'll bring it out.' Opening the oven took away the chill that had swept through his body.

He dished up the cottage pie. He'd planned to tease Maddy that he'd slaved away in the kitchen to make it, but it was really a shop bought ready meal he'd picked up on the way home. Like the carrots and green beans, already prepared. All he'd had to do was throw them into boiling water. But he wasn't sure he was in the mood to joke now. Memories of Karin would always haunt him, but Connor worried him.

He couldn't undo what happened to Karin. But Connor had the ability to change everything.

'How was Connor controlling?' Harry said after some time. The food filled a gap being so late in the evening, but it wasn't anywhere near as good as what they'd had on Sunday evening, or even when Maddy made a dinner from scratch.

Maddy was pushing food around her plate clearly lost

in her thoughts; she hadn't spoken much during dinner. 'At first I didn't realise it was controlling behaviour, but he used to get funny about me going out with friends, and would want me in by a certain time.'

Harry snorted, trying not to choke on his food. He sipped his water. 'Sounds worse than living with your parents.'

'It was. And the sulks. He always thought he knew what was best for me. But I think when I found the strength to move to Cornwall and open a gallery, he realised he didn't have much of a hold on me after all. When I received my grandfather's inheritance – my parents felt they didn't need it all so gave me and my brother a good lump sum each to help us set ourselves up – Valerie convinced me to move. She knew it was something I'd always wanted to do. I spent a great deal of time to-ing and fro-ing from Cornwall – usually staying with her – because of the landscapes and seascapes I enjoyed painting, and the commissions I was getting – cute cottages just like Wisteria. Valerie never liked Connor.' Maddy pushed the remains of her food to the back of her plate, placing her knife and fork together. 'Sorry, it was very nice, but I don't feel hungry. I think it's a mixture of worry, heat and it being so late.'

'It's okay, I was going to make out I slogged over it, but when I saw your expression when you came in, I left it.'

'The box on the side also gave it away.' Maddy pointed through to the kitchen where the packaging stood on the counter.

'Oh, yeah, I should have disposed of the evidence.' Harry rolled his eyes. 'I thought this was easy to cook but slightly healthier than a pizza.' He gathered the plates. 'So, how long were you with him . . . if you don't mind me asking?'

'We were together about three years I think.'

'Wow, how did you stick it for so long?'

Maddy's face reddened, and again she wouldn't meet his eye.

'Maddy?' Harry's instinct to protect her uncoiled, spreading down into his limbs. He refrained from reaching out to her, though. He waited for her answer.

'He threatened to kill himself if I ever left him.'

Briefly, she looked at him, and he could see the sheen glossing her eyes, where she was holding back tears.

'Shit.' Instinctively, he grasped her hand and clutched it between both of his.

'Yes, it was rather, but I moved here, and said he could come with me, but I soon realised it was nonsense. Being closer to Valerie gave me the impetus to kick him out of my life for good.'

'But the bastard keeps pulling little tricks. Shit, Maddy, after hearing all this, I'm sure now that he caused the fire.'

'But there is no proof. And he handed me back the key.'

'He could have got another cut beforehand.'

'We can't prove that.' She sighed, finding a tissue in her short pocket and wiping her nose.

'I'll clear the plates, you go shower, or take a bath, and come down when you're ready.'

'I should go back to the cottage.'

'Nonsense.'

***

It was too hot for a bath, so Maddy stood under the shower for ages, probably using as much water as filling the bath. She let the pressure of the water massage her shoulders and back.

Could Harry be right about Connor? Was he playing his usual mind games?

When she had ended their relationship four months ago, he'd left for Bristol almost immediately. He'd made a scene, begged her to take him back, and when he'd realised his pleas were futile, he'd finally gone. She'd receive the odd text message to ask how she was, that he missed her, but that was it. Until the house fire.

Noticing her fingers were prune-like, a sure sign she'd been in the water too long, she turned off the shower and towelled herself down. After moisturising her body and her face, she slipped into a clean pair of pyjamas which she took from a bag of ironing she hadn't cleared from Harry's house. It was driving her nuts not knowing where all her belongings were. Some were now at the cottage, some still here, some at home – although not many as she'd avoided taking stuff back while the house still stank of smoke.

She headed downstairs with her wide-toothed comb, combing it through her towel-dried hair.

Harry had poured them each a small glass of red wine.

'Thought this might help relax you further,' he said, handing her a glass.

'You definitely don't want me to go back to the cottage.'

'Looks like you've already made the decision unless you're driving back to the cottage in your pyjamas?' Harry pointed at her, eyebrows raised.

She chuckled. 'Good point.' She sipped the wine. The taste of the smooth, deep red liquid clung to her mouth, and with a swallow, it took some of her anxiety with it. Harry made her feel safe, like a lion protecting his lioness.

Would he be her protector? Against the crap life liked to throw at her from time to time . . . against Connor . . .

The way she felt about Harry, she would do the same for him.

He guided her to the sofa and, taking the comb, started to gently comb through her hair. Having someone comb her hair was something she found very relaxing. She loved visiting the hairdressers for that reason. Unfortunately, she couldn't afford to go as often as she'd like.

Eventually, her head started to weigh heavy on her shoulders so she lay back, resting on Harry's solid warm chest and cuddled into him. He still continued to play with her hair, brushing his fingers gently through it, stroking her scalp, his other hand trailing slowly up and down the top of her arm. They barely spoke, only whispers, making sure the other was comfortable. Her eyes got heavier and heavier, until she was unable to fight to keep them open. She gave in and closed them, concentrating on Harry's sensual touch.

Maddy could feel his arousal, yet he didn't act on it as if knowing she needed something much more than sex tonight. Comfort, security, *love* . . . No man had ever made her feel like this – whatever *this* was. Did she even know? She was too scared to think too deeply about this moment. She concentrated instead on Harry's caresses, the physically relaxing feelings he engendered in her . . . She didn't want to give into her other feelings; she wanted to keep them locked away for a bit longer. She'd given so much over to Connor; he'd drained her . . . She needed to learn to love again.

At some point, Maddy stirred. Vaguely conscious she was being lifted, carried, a creak on a floorboard, then laid onto a soft surface, cool sheets.

Chapter 23

Harry sat bolt upright, sweat plastered over his body, the bed sheets damp. A recurring nightmare. A woman trapped, slumped, broken and bleeding, cold dead eyes staring at him, images replaying over and over, but different from the reality. *In the dream, he's so close to the car, he's wrenching open the door, dragging out the body, but the explosion always wakes him as it throws him off his feet.*

But the woman in the nightmare hadn't been Karin this time; it had been Maddy.

It took Harry a couple of minutes to shake off the night-mare, letting his heart rate slow as he told himself over and over it was only a dream. He turned on the bedside lamp to reassure himself that Maddy was sleeping safely beside him. A tangle of blonde and copper curls framing her delicate face, he watched the rise and fall of her chest as she peacefully breathed. A few weeks ago, if someone had told him he'd be sleeping with the woman from across the road he'd have told them hell would have to freeze over first, but here he was – and he didn't want to change it.

The last couple of nights he'd forgotten to take his medication: blissfully happy with Maddy, he'd felt better, whole again. He also knew it tended to knock him out, so much so that a bulldozer could drive through his bedroom and he'd not hear it. And although Maddy knew he took medication, she didn't know why. He didn't feel confident enough to tell her yet . . . he didn't want to scare her off before they'd even got started. But he'd need to tell her . . . soon.

Or was this nightmare a wake-up call? Should he risk getting close to another woman? Could he live with losing another . . .? The chill of fear swept over him, turning him from hot to cold instantly, goosebumps rising over his chest and arms. He shivered and checked the time on his phone; it was three a.m. Too late to take the medication now as he had an early start and didn't want risk feeling groggy, or worse not hear his alarm in the morning.

Turning off the lamp, he slid back underneath the covers and curled into Maddy, giving her a hug and a kiss. Her warmth and unique scent gave Harry some comfort. But deep down, an ache in his chest questioned whether he should get any closer to this woman. Should he keep his distance? *Probably too late for that now.* But was he ready to love so deeply again?

He never wanted to experience what he went through with Karin ever again. He feared he'd never survive it.

***

Still spooning into Maddy, Harry's alarm woke him with a start. She groaned sleepily too and rubbed her eyes. He ran a hand up her thigh, then reached behind him and turned off the alarm, aware of his arousal.

He needed to get up, but his alarm was set deliberately early to allow him to hit the snooze button . . . so fifteen minutes wouldn't hurt . . . or twenty . . . probably a good half hour if he was lucky.

Harry pulled Maddy closer into him so she could feel his hardness. He kissed her neck, and she turned to face him, so he could kiss her thoroughly, pressing his groin against her leg.

'Good morning,' she said, smiling. 'Sleep well?'

'Not really,' Harry said, realising he should have withheld his honesty.

'Oh, why?'

'Dreaming about fucking you.'

'Think we should make it a reality.' Maddy positioned herself under him, wrapping her arms around his neck. Her eyes sparkled, sleep replaced with lust.

They kissed, fumbled, throwing the duvet back and drove

each other mad to the point where he urgently needed to claim her.

Harry straddled Maddy, his powerful thighs tensed, holding his full weight off her – he was so much bigger he feared crushing her – and reached into the top drawer of his bedside cabinet to grab a condom.

He ripped the foil, rolled on the condom, and looked at Maddy, stunningly beautiful and biting her lip sexily.

Then, out of nowhere, came a sudden flashback of his nightmare — Maddy or Karin, he couldn't tell which, lying eyes open, vacant, dead . . . It drained the blood from his face . . . and elsewhere.

He'd drooped. And it didn't matter how much he tried to get it back, running his hand firmly over his cock, it wasn't coming back.

'Shit, I'm sorry.' Harry wanted to die. 'It's not you . . . it's me.'

'Hey, hey, it's okay, these things happen . . .' Maddy reached for him, but he backed off the bed, pulled the condom off and chucked it in the bin, swearing under his breath.

He stormed into the bathroom, slamming the door harder than intended. He took a good hard look at himself in the mirror. 'Fuck, what just happened?'

***

Maddy scrambled to the bottom of the bed and gathered the twisted bed sheets up around her. What had just happened? Why'd Harry reacted so badly? Sometimes these things happened, but right before, Harry had gone white as a sheet and she'd lost him for a split second to another world.

It wasn't as if she'd laughed at him . . . God, did he think she would?

And then Maddy's own anxiety crept in. Was it her? Did he not really fancy her? Was she not so pretty first thing in the morning? She always felt self-conscious first thing in the morning. Hair a mess, teeth not cleaned, sleep in her eyes, not quite 'fresh' down there . . . even the possibility of a dribble mark down her mouth – not that she dribbled . . . or at least she didn't think she did . . . but it might have happened. Subconsciously she wiped around her mouth with her fingers, then gave a sniff under her arms. No, she was okay.

Harry emerged from the bathroom, almost catching her smelling her armpits – *God he didn't see that, did he?*

'Hey, I'm so sorry, I had a rough night, and it all came flooding back.' Harry sat beside her, cupping her face. He leaned in and gently kissed her.

'What do you mean rough? I didn't realise.' She'd slept so well. 'Do you want to talk about it?' She copied his own action by stroking his face, looking into those blue eyes that appeared darker this morning, matching his solemn expression. Was it too soon to care so deeply for someone?

He stood, shaking his head. 'No, it's fine. Something I need to deal with.' The moment between them vanished.

'Harry, you can talk to me. I'm a good listener. I don't overreact . . .' *Really?* The reason they'd ended up in this situation – living together, sleeping together! – was due to her overreacting. Her being hysterical at the firemen had resulted in Harry carrying her over his shoulder quite literally kicking and screaming. But her house had been on fire. She would always stick to that line of defence. *It was a perfectly plausible excuse to overreact.*

'I know, Maddy. But I'll confide in you when I'm ready.' *Confide? What did he need to confide in her about?*

'Okay.' Maddy thought it best to leave it there. Men often liked to keep themselves to themselves. It had to come from them, the opening up side of things. She knew Harry was holding back on something – the medication for a start – but by pushing it, she would only make him withdraw further. She'd wait until he was ready. *Men were from Mars after all* . . . 'You know where I am when you want to talk about it.'

***

In the gallery, Maddy didn't have time to dwell on Harry. She busied herself, cleaning, hanging paintings, making sure the price tags on the pictures were clear. All of a sudden, the school holidays were approaching – this Friday most of the schools would break up – and Tinners Bay was about to get a whole lot busier for the next six weeks. She needed to make sure she had enough paintings hung, and backups to fill the spaces, in the hope of huge sales. These six weeks were crucial to her business. The rest of her year she would fill with commissions, hoping to gain some in these important weeks.

'Is everything all right, you seem very focussed today?' Valerie said, dusting pictures and shelves, carefully manoeuvring around some sculptures on display.

Maddy hadn't told Valerie about Connor's text. Or that she'd spoken to her mother. And certainly not about this morning with Harry. 'I think I'm just stressed. Tomorrow I've got the appointment with the kitchen designer, and as of this weekend we're going to be doing a lot more hours in this gallery.'

'Josie can do more hours, remember, and Declan has offered his services, too,' Valerie said. 'Oh, I know what I was going to say to you, your mum called me last night. She's worried about you.'

'Did she tell you I called her last night?'

'Yes. Because of Connor, right?'

Maddy nodded.

'Sandra hasn't even seen Connor, not since the last time she called you. Anyway, she was concerned about you,'

Valerie said and Maddy huffed. 'She wanted to know about the cottage you were staying in.'

'Oh, God, you didn't say it was full of builders did you?'

Valerie laughed. 'Of course not. I did say I'd keep an eye on you, though, like I always do. That seemed to appease your mother.' Valerie smiled, giving Maddy a hug.

'Thanks, Val.'

'Well, I never liked Connor. Shame nothing ever happened between you and one of my three boys. Then you really would have been my daughter.'

Nothing had happened with any of Valerie's sons – maybe the distance between Bristol and Cornwall had done it, as Valerie and her husband had moved when Maddy was only eight. But, clearly, growing up, they'd seen Maddy as a sister, and she had seen them as three brothers, or cousins. Two older and one younger than her. James was the same age as Edward, thirty-one now, George was a year older than Maddy and Jacob a year younger. Jacob had been Valerie's last hope of having a girl.

'Although, how's it going with Harry? You've gone quiet on me about him.'

'Yeah . . . it's all right,' Maddy said, hesitantly, which Valerie instantly picked up on.

'Oh, you don't sound so enthusiastic.'

Did she confess? Admittedly, Valerie might be able to put some perspective on it. 'I feel like he's hiding something. Without going into details, this morning, something happened, and when I asked if he wanted to talk about it, he said he would when he's ready. What could be so bad?'

Valerie frowned. 'Men often aren't as open as us women, and you haven't known each other long.'

'Don't remind me. I'm fully aware of how fast this relationship has spiralled.' *Was it spiralling out of control, though?* 'I thought moving into the cottage would have slowed it down, but it hasn't.'

'Maybe give him time, but if it continues to bother you, then raise it again.'

'Yes, I will.'

'Good, because a relationship will never work if you hide things from one another.'

Chapter 24

Maddy didn't get to raise anything with Harry. The next few weeks passed in a blur. From an appointment with the kitchen designer to them commencing work sooner than expected because they'd had a cancellation, she was either at the gallery, or overseeing the work done at her house, or sleeping at Wisteria Cottage – trying to keep her distance from Harry and slow down whatever their relationship was. She was busy choosing handles for the kitchen cabinets, looking at new fridge freezers and ovens, and selecting carpet and paint samples for the dining room and the hall, stairs and landing. Harry was busy with his gardens, including that of Wisteria Cottage. This time of year the grass grew quickly, and plants needed a lot of watering. She and Harry were like ships passing in the night, or to be more precise in the morning, as at the same time she left Wisteria Cottage, he arrived to start work. The garden was taking shape slowly. They saw each other some evenings. Some were quiet, cosy affairs, a glass of wine cuddled up in front of the television, and other times he had her pinned to the kitchen counter, hitching up her dress, gripping her, fingers digging into her buttocks, claiming her mouth with his, seducing her. The incident in the bedroom seemed long forgotten.

Maddy had never had sex like it. It drove her crazy – in a good way. Harry could be rough but sensual, his hands entwined in her hair. He knew how to touch her, ignite her, his tongue licking her intimately while his fingers built a pleasure inside her to a point she feared she'd surely explode. His size compared to hers meant he could lift her up and place her wherever he wanted her. Usually, if they were at Harry's place, they would start in the kitchen, move to the dining room table and end in the bedroom. At Wisteria Cottage, Harry would wait for the builders to leave, then haul her upstairs, seducing her into the shower.

'Are we just fucking, or making love?' Maddy realised this probably wasn't the right time to be asking. Clearly, right now, he was fucking her. The evening was warm and Maddy, perched on Harry's dining room table, had her legs wrapped around his waist while he drove into her. But it had started to bug her that she wasn't sure where she stood. Would they return to being neighbours when she moved back into her house, which she could technically do soon? She'd even warned Roy she might not need to stay at Wisteria Cottage for much longer. Was their relationship just sex?

He never shared how he felt about her, so Maddy would hold her tongue, too, not wanting to look foolish.

'Right now, I'm fucking you,' Harry said, gleaming with sweat. She'd been stripped of all clothes except her bra. He was naked with his boxers and shorts at his ankles. This evening, as soon as she'd arrived at his house, he'd come to her with an urgency. All the curtains were drawn, Harry had learnt to do that early on, for Maddy to be comfortable and relax. However much she enjoyed pleasing him, she wasn't an exhibitionist. 'And in a minute,' he kissed her between words, 'I'm going to take you upstairs and make love to you.'

And he did just that. He had to disconnect from Maddy briefly, to remove his clothes, otherwise he'd have tripped – yes, they'd giggled about that – then he picked her up off the dining room table, hooking his arms under her legs and she wrapped an arm around his neck. He carried her up the stairs, where he started pleasing her all over again, but this time with slower, sensual kisses and touches.

He hadn't told her he loved her. But then this hadn't been going on that long, in relationship terms. How soon did you tell someone you love them? Did she love Harry? Or was this really only sex?

Snuggled into his chest, sated by their passion, Maddy braved the question, 'We're on the same page here, aren't we?' she said. Her stomach fluttered with anxiety. Would she like his answer?

'How'd you mean?'

'Well,' she hesitated, forming the words in her head before she spoke, 'I'm not wanting you to announce your undying love or anything so serious . . . it's far too early.' she gave a little chuckle, hoping it would keep the conversation light, 'but I, um, well, you like me, don't you? Like I like you?' She slapped her hand to her forehead. 'God, listen to me. I sound like a teenager.'

Harry raised himself up onto an elbow, his hand supporting his head, the other stroking her body. 'Yes, we're on the same page, if that's what you mean.' Harry gave a reassuring smile, and then kissed her. 'I really like you, and want to see where this goes. My feelings for you are strong, Maddy. Stronger than I've felt for anyone in a very long time.'

Wow. She wasn't quite expecting that.

'Good, good, because I really like you too.' It sounded a lamer response than she'd intended, but it was the best she could muster. Harry addled her brain. A month ago she'd never imagined she'd be telling her neighbour she *liked* him. Wasn't it funny how things could change with time? She pulled herself up to his mouth and kissed him, and it deepened, his hold tighter on her, yet his kiss was still so gentle, loving. It sent a tingle of delight through her body to her very nerve endings.

'God, I could have you all over again, but I think we need to have some dinner,' Harry said after pulling out of the kiss, his hardness pressing against her stomach.

He was about to get out of the bed. Maddy swallowed again. Something else was bugging her. 'Harry,' she reached for his arm, 'I can move back to my house soon.' In fact, she could move back right away, if she wanted to cope with decorators and kitchen fitters. Considering what she'd been used to at Wisteria Cottage, with Simon and his men, dealing with the workmen at her house would be a breeze.

She stroked his muscular arms with tender caresses. 'I'm just worried our relationship may change. We'll live in close proximity to one another again. The cottage has helped to keep a distance between us, forcing us to make dates . . . because this relationship has probably moved on faster than both of us would have intended.'

'I'm not worried about it at all. Me and you. It feels so right.'

And right then, in that moment, Maddy knew she loved him.

***

It had been a couple of days since Maddy had discussed with Harry moving back into her house. He'd insisted she had the locks to her front door changed, too. The more he thought about it, the arsonist had obviously used a key to get into Maddy's house. His money was on Connor. When the guy had come to fit the new uPVC back door and kitchen window, organized through the insurance company,

Harry got Maddy to ask him to change the locks on the front door too, and Harry agreed to pay what the insurance wouldn't cover.

Harry could feel his anxiety weighing him down. The stronger his feelings for Maddy became, the worse his unease got. He badly wanted to love her, but he was so scared of losing her like he'd lost Karin.

He wasn't sure he could go through that level of devastation again.

Whether he'd been right to do so, he'd been burying his fears and losing himself in the sex with Maddy. He knew he needed to be more open and honest with her.

Harry felt happier, once he knew the locks had been changed, lifting some of the weight off his anxious shoulders. He needed to know Maddy was safe. If she moved back in across the road, Harry would feel more at ease knowing whoever had entered her house wouldn't be able to do it again.

Anxiety was creeping back into Harry's life, he wasn't sleeping too well, but he didn't want to pay the doctor another visit, as he wanted to wean himself off the pills, not increase the dose. He put it down to being busy with the gardening; he'd taken on more jobs to start once the holidays ended, and he still had a lot to do at Wisteria Cottage. He couldn't bring himself to discuss his illness with Maddy either. What if she rejected him as some fruit loop? People tried to be sympathetic about PTSD, but they didn't get it. They visualised damaged war veterans usually. Like depression, you couldn't snap out of Post-Traumatic Stress Disorder. Harry did everything possible to keep himself fit and healthy, to keep the darkness at bay . . . Maybe he needed to take a run along the Camel Trail, to help fight his demons.

He hated explaining that he had watched his girlfriend die in a car wreck. Helpless, useless and devastated. He hadn't got there in time. He'd failed Karin. What had been the point of being a firefighter if he couldn't save the woman he loved? She'd been carrying their baby, only four months pregnant, just entering the second trimester, but they'd had their twenty weeks scan booked at the hospital . . . Harry hadn't known anger like it before, and the grief had exhausted him. He'd felt he wanted to die right alongside them. Apparently, she'd been dead before the car caught fire, but if he'd dragged her out in time they might have been able to save her. He'd seen people brought back to life with CPR. It was the what-ifs that haunted him the most.

The pain inside his chest, back then, had been debilitating, the overwhelming grief consuming him to the point that he didn't want to get out of bed. He couldn't even be bothered to eat. His mother had nursed him in some sense of the word back to reasonable health, and the pain had numbed very gradually over time.

When he'd thought he was well enough to return to work, it had been obvious he still wasn't ready. That's when he'd been diagnosed with the PTSD. He'd accepted a transfer from Exeter to Bodmin fire station, hoping this might rectify the situation. A change was supposed to be as good as a rest. A change of scene to help ease the terrible memories. He was on medication to help, too. His medication had been milder then, and he couldn't take it when he was working night shifts when he'd need to be awake and alert quickly.

I'm still not taking my medication regularly now.

But a sickness down in his gut would hit him every time a road traffic collision was radioed in. Back then, the smell of fire itself sent him into a place Harry couldn't explain. Lost, dark, inescapable – his nightmares would return. He lasted six months at Bodmin, then decided to concentrate on his gardening full time, which his doctor even recommended. Gardening was therapeutic, relaxing, and eased stress. He wasn't any use in the fire service any more. He couldn't help people like he used to, the buzz from it was gone. He was a hindrance, and as such could get another killed, a colleague or a member of the public, and Harry could never live with himself if that happened.

Shaking himself out of his dark thoughts, Harry wandered over to Maddy's house. The front door was open because there were men working inside. Harry hesitated. He hadn't set foot inside Maddy's house before for fear of what the stench would trigger. He'd kept her garden tidy, fixed the gate, and only looked through the kitchen window to see the devastation. Even then he hadn't lingered over it. He breathed deeply, taking in the fresh air and then stepped over the threshold.

A decorator stood on the upstairs landing applying a light olive green paint Maddy had chosen to the walls, while a couple of kitchen fitters hammered and banged and swore away in the shell of a kitchen. Maddy's brand new back door was wide open and the radio was blaring. Paint fumes and the smell of freshly sawn and sanded wood, plus the air blowing in covered any lingering odour of smoke. The carpet in the dining room had been thrown in the skip a week ago. Harry relaxed.

'Hey, guys, did you get given a key to the house?'

The older kitchen fitter of the two reached into his pocket and pulled out a key. 'Yeah, she did give us one, explaining she wasn't always around some mornings, as she's living in Tinners Bay.'

Harry nodded, wishing Maddy would move back in with him. Recently, she'd been insistent on staying at the cottage and keeping some space between them. She'd call him and say she was finishing late at the gallery and would go straight to the cottage. Those evenings he really missed her. 'Maddy's had the lock changed on the front door, so I'll give you the new key.' Harry took the old key off the man, un-looping it from the key ring and threading the new key on it. 'Here you go.'

Harry checked his watch and said his goodbyes to the workmen. He needed to get a move on; he had work to do himself. Like Maddy, at this time of year it was important to make as much money as possible because business was slower in the winter months. He had already loaded his pickup while the guy changed the lock. He thought about texting Maddy to confirm the lock had been changed, but left it. He'd probably catch her later at the cottage. He needed to be left to his own thoughts today, Karin's death playing on his mind. Sometimes he worried that lifting Maddy over his shoulder and carrying her into his house that night had been a very bad idea . . .

Chapter 25

The gallery had been crazy with people all day. Maddy hadn't stopped. A sunny day brought plenty of people to the beach, and it was mainly women – mothers and grandmothers, girlfriends and daughters – tired of beach games and surfing and wanting some respite from the sun, who strolled up to the little high street for some retail therapy, if you could call it that in Tinners Bay. With the beach on its doorstep, there was only a small row of shops either side of the road that ran through Tinners Bay, ranging from a mini-supermarket, a gift shop, a couple of surf shops, a trendy boutique, an ice cream parlour and coffee shop, and a couple of cafes/restaurants as well as Maddy's gallery. She'd had a bumper trading day today.

As she checked her phone, before slipping it into her handbag, she realised there had been no texts from Harry. He did go quiet on her some days, even if she left him a couple of texts. Why didn't he reply sometimes? Even in her busiest periods, she'd always found time to send him a text, and reply to other friends. Maybe she was imagining it, but he went hot and cold on her. Yet, when she was with him, she couldn't doubt how he felt about her, being so attentive with kisses and cuddles.

Wearily, but grateful because the tiredness meant a successful day, she turned the sign on the door from 'open' to 'closed' and locked up the gallery. Valerie gave her a friendly goodbye kiss on the cheek.

'Catch you tomorrow, darling,' Valerie said with a wave, then wandered up the hill, towards her seafront home.

Maddy headed in the opposite direction, calling in to the Spar to pick up some food for dinner, then continued up the other coastal path towards Wisteria Cottage, listening to the odd but calming noise her flip-flops made as she walked. Her legs ached from standing all day, and she decided she would soak one last time in the cottage's beautiful roll-top bath. In some ways, she wished it was winter, so she could make the bath hotter and stay in it longer. Maybe if Harry was still working up at the cottage, she could convince him to join her.

Maddy was pleased to see Harry in the garden as she strolled up the path. He was shirtless with the evening sun still warm on his golden tanned back and his skin glistened with sweat due to hard work. As he dug and turned the soil over, she watched his muscles flex. Her excitement soon dropped to disappointment upon seeing Simon and his men still working at the cottage, too. *That would delay her bath.*

Most of the work inside had been completed. But they were still finishing the extension. She wouldn't want to run the bath until they'd gone. It would hardly be relaxing with strangers walking around yelling and hammering, even with the door locked.

'Hey, you,' she called out as she approached Harry, fearing she'd scare him half to death if he hadn't heard her come up the path. Busy working, he had his back to her and hadn't seen her.

He stopped and turned, and grinned when he realised who'd been calling him.

They kissed briefly, greeting one another. *A very couple thing to do.* Maddy liked it.

'You're working late,' Maddy commented. She'd closed the gallery at seven tonight.

'I wanted to catch you.'

'Did you now?' she said, smiling and wiggling her eyebrows. 'And on the way up here, I was fantasizing about sharing a bath with you in the huge bath this delightful cottage has.'

Harry glanced at Simon and his men working. 'I like the sound of this fantasy, however, don't you think they'll ruin it?'

'They should bugger off soon.'

'I have a present for you,' he said, delving his hand into his shorts' pocket.

'Really, what brought this on?' She beamed. Maddy wasn't

used to receiving gifts. And buying her something meant Harry had been thinking about her.

'Don't get too excited.' He raised a key in front of her face. She frowned, her anticipation vanishing. 'It's the new key to your front door.'

'Oh, yes,' she said, remembering the fitters had come this morning to install a new back door and kitchen window. 'But I still think you're overreacting about changing the lock on the front door too.'

'Maddy, how many times do we have to go over this? Your house fire was arson,' Harry said with a stern expression. 'And if you move back into your house, I want to know you're safe.'

'Oh.' She scratched her head, ruffling her hair.

'When you move back in, I want to be able to sleep at night, and not worry you're in danger.'

'I'm not in danger.' Maddy scoffed a laugh.

Harry's expression remained serious. 'Maddy, whoever set fire to your house, I believe they used a key. I saw a man on your driveway as if he'd suddenly appeared. He'd come out your front door. I'm sure of it. I just didn't see it.'

'Okay,' Maddy said, more soberly. 'I suppose it's better to be safe than sorry.'

'You'll sleep easier too.'

'I'll sleep easier, and safer, with you in my bed.' She reached out, her fingertips brushing his back, relishing his hot flesh.

Harry dropped his shovel and pulled Maddy in for a

fierce kiss. 'I'm not sure you're safe with me in your bed.'

She chuckled. 'But I don't like the thought of sleeping alone.' Maddy swept her hands over his bare skin, toying with some of his chest hair. 'Maybe you'll have to share my bed with me, the first night I move back in.'

'Great minds think alike.' He dropped his head, so his mouth found hers again, and their kiss deepened. Closing her eyes, Maddy was lost to his touch, his tongue, the pooling sensation low in her abdomen. Her knees softened, relaxing into his hold. This man weakened her.

A wolf whistle startled them both.

They both looked in the direction from where it had come. Simon and his workmen were watching them. They had an audience.

Maddy disentangled herself from Harry. 'I'll let you get on. I'll get some dinner on, then we can have that bath.'

'I like your thinking.' Harry winked. 'And later, I want to run some ideas by you for the garden.'

'Which garden?'

'This garden.'

'But you're the landscaper.' Harry had cleared the garden now and had slowly been digging it over with a mini excavator to clear the weeds and bramble roots and maintain a path for Maddy to use. It looked so much larger now it had been cleared and would look fantastic once completed.

'Yeah, I know, but if this was your garden, how would you like it to look?'

'Oh, I haven't really thought about it,' Maddy said, glancing around the bare garden. Which was a tiny white lie. In her head, she'd pictured creating all sorts of nooks and crannies within the garden. She just didn't want to get too attached to it as she was leaving soon.

Maddy left Harry to continue working and approached the cottage. The extension was taking shape but was still not quite finished.

'You're working late,' she said to Simon as she drew nearer. His men had resumed whatever they were doing, but it did look like they were packing up, so Maddy hoped she would soon have the cottage to herself. She knew time was running out and she would need to move back to her house, which she would be glad about, especially being back in her own bed, but she had a soft spot for Wisteria Cottage. The views, the location, the layout of the cottage . . .

'Just making the most of the sunshine,' Simon said. 'You never know when the weather can turn. Rain is forecast this weekend.'

'Oh, is it?' Rain was never good for business. It meant instead of visiting the beach, the tourists took trips out to all-weather attractions. She wondered if Simon had been at the cottage all day, or had sloped off. She'd been asked to live there to keep an eye on things, but what things she wasn't exactly sure. Each day there looked as if there was progress made on the property. 'When did Roy want the work finished?'

'We're aiming for mid-September, but you never know.'

Maybe Simon was dragging it out so he could charge more money? Either way, Maddy would have to move out soon. Her house would be habitable again, and the insurance company wouldn't pay for rent they didn't need to. Harry had insisted after their night out in Padstow that he had it all under control with Roy, and she didn't need to get involved.

'Right, well, I'll probably catch you tomorrow morning,' Maddy said, giving a little wave as she walked around to the side door which led into the kitchen. She turned the oven on, to cook the salmon fillets she'd bought. This time of year she never fancied cooking much. She planned on having a mixed salad with the salmon and there was enough if Harry wanted some too. She put a bottle of white wine in the fridge to chill.

Half an hour later, Harry was still busy in the garden, but the builders had gone. Salmon cooked and cooling, Maddy ran the bath, pouring in the bubble bath, remembering just in time about the softer Cornish water. She didn't want soapsuds overflowing the edge of the bath.

Maddy stripped off, tying her hair up into a messy bun, and sank into the warm bath. She rested her head back and closed her eyes.

'Maddy!' She heard Harry call up the stairs.

'In here.' She'd left the door open so that he could join her.

Harry entered the bathroom barefoot, wearing only his khaki shorts, his T-shirt slung over his shoulder.

'Want to join me?' she asked with a waggle of her eyebrows.

To answer Maddy's question, Harry was already removing his shorts and boxers. He climbed into the bath, slowly sinking in, making the water rise even further. He pulled Maddy into his arms, kissing her. Water splashed over the side. Once they'd exhausted themselves kissing, Harry leaned back at one end, resting his head, and Maddy copied him at her end of the bath. She loved how they both fitted comfortably, the plug and the taps in the middle, so no one got the duff end. Harry found her foot under the water, resting on his thigh, and with his thumbs, massaged her foot. She sank deeper and sighed, letting the heat of the water relax her, enjoying her much-needed foot massage.

'This is nice,' he said, his hand travelling up her calf, then back down to her heel. His thumbs then worked along the arch of her foot. 'After a hard day's work, to come home to a bubble bath with a beautiful woman in it.'

'I hope you're not expecting too much for dinner,' she said as she laughed. 'Because it's salad.'

'Sounds perfect to me.'

Maddy closed her eyes again.

After a moment, Harry spoke again, 'So tell me what you'd like to see in the garden.'

'But it's not my garden. Maybe you should ask Roy.'

'He told me he'd leave it up to me.' Harry changed over and started rubbing Maddy's other foot.

'Well, it if was my cottage, I'd have another wisteria growing up the front.' Maddy thought more. 'And I suppose, because of the length of the garden, there could be different areas where you catch the sun at different times of day. You could have a path snaking down through the lawn to the bottom, and at the end there could be a patio area, facing east, to catch the sun in the morning.'

Maddy reeled off her ideas, and Harry nodded dutifully. 'Might not be able to incorporate all of these ideas, Roy has a budget, you know.'

'You did ask.' Maddy chuckled, splashing Harry with some water.

There was mischief in Harry's eyes. 'Right!' He shifted forward in the bath, so he was lying on her. She wrapped her legs around him as he leaned in, kissing her passionately.

'Harry, you're going to get water everywhere!'

***

That night, as much as it pained him to do it, Harry drove home. The image of Maddy stayed vividly in Harry's mind as he drove down the dark country lanes, coming across a badger and then a fox. Maddy had been wearing fresh cotton pyjamas as she'd stood on the doorstep of Wisteria Cottage, kissing him goodbye, smelling of bubble bath.

'Thanks for organising a new key for the door,' she'd said, her lips pressed to his.

'I need to know you're safe, Maddy,' he'd replied.

He could feel a darkness coming, trying to shroud him. He needed to make Maddy his light.

Chapter 26

Work had slowed at Maddy's house. There had been a delay with some of the parts for the kitchen, which had meant Maddy staying at Wisteria Cottage a little longer. *Or she'd used it as an excuse to stay longer.* Harry knew she loved that cottage.

He regularly called in on the workmen at Maddy's and checked on the progress. He admired the new kitchen that was going in. Maddy had opted for a change of style – oak effect instead of the white that had been there. It was a mix of a contemporary design with a hint of country cottage. In fact, it was a similar style to the kitchen at Wisteria Cottage. She'd even picked out similar tiles. She'd told him she loved the kitchen there so much she'd picked as close as she could within her budget to match.

But there were no excuses now that Maddy's back door had been replaced last week. The house was secure, and she could move back in.

Harry started to prepare dinner. They'd agreed to eat at his, and sleep at hers.

'Hello!' Harry heard Maddy call out.

'I'm in the kitchen,' he said, and waited for her to appear at the doorway.

He felt her lips on his neck as she slipped her hands around his waist. 'Oh, I've missed you today,' she said.

He turned, brushing loose tendrils of hair off her face as he kissed her back. 'I've missed you, too.'

They deepened the kiss, pressing their bodies against each other, he tightening his hold on Maddy as he kissed her, and she lacing her arms around his neck.

There was a sizzle, and the smell of burning brought him back to reality as it hit the back of his throat.

'Oh, shit,' Harry said, detangling himself from Maddy and returning to the pot on the stove. He turned the gas off. He froze, his face paling, the stench triggering buried images . . . Karin, trapped, burning . . .

'Harry? You okay?' Maddy frowned at him. 'Is the food ruined?'

'Sorry,' Harry said, shaking his head. 'It's only something simple; I was making a cheese sauce for a macaroni cheese. It'll survive.'

'Oh, comfort food.' With a seductive grumble, she tucked her hand into the waistband of his shorts, unable to stop touching him. He shifted so that she wouldn't feel he wasn't aroused. He was trying to shake off the bad memories. *Focus on Maddy*. He kissed her nose.

'I figured I could put it in the oven in case you were late home. How was the gallery?' He wanted to change the subject, think of the everyday things.

'Mad.'

'Yeah, it's been crazy with the gardens too. The bit of rain we had the other night, then all the sunshine, makes the grass grow ridiculously.'

'How long till dinner?'

'It'll need to be in the oven twenty minutes to brown. Go put your feet up in the lounge. I'll join you in a minute.'

She kissed his lips. 'Okay.'

Harry returned to making the dinner, but he couldn't concentrate properly. The smell of burning from the saucepan had made him want to retch. Had Maddy noticed?

Of course she had. She'd questioned his sudden silence.

Harry didn't want to let Maddy down. He needed to start taking his medication regularly again. His moods were changing, his sleep was disturbed, and that debilitating darkness in the corner of his mind . . . was growing . . . It didn't matter how many times he shut himself in his gym and worked his body hard, it wasn't working. His illness was returning . . .

He needed to come clean with Maddy, tell her everything . . . but he was afraid. Afraid she might reject him. Did he even deserve her love?

He wasn't a coward. But he couldn't think straight . . . Karin haunted him.

Think about Maddy, not Karin. Think about Maddy.

***

At first, it felt strange waking in her own bed, and it took her a moment to let it sink in. Not long ago it had seemed impossible to ever be here, at this time and moment, as if she'd never return. Although she hadn't been out of the house that long, not quite two months, so no more than an extended holiday really. People holidayed in Australia for longer. Maddy could smell the fresh, cotton sheets mingled with the scent of fresh paint wafting from the hallway, but still there was the underlying smell of smoke. Only very faint, but it was still there, a reminder of her worst night ever. Maybe if she went around and bleached everything? The windows, cupboards, everything that could be wiped down. And sling the windows open. Let the air circulate throughout the whole of the house. Maybe it was more of a stuffy smell, a the-windows-haven't-been-opened-in-weeks type smell, and once she moved back in properly the house would lose the staleness in the air.

Feeling Harry's warmth beside her, she wondered if the night of the fire really had been her worst night ever. She spooned in behind him, kissing his back. At the time it had been horrendous, but now, knowing how close she'd become to this man, how he continued to be her rock, would they be together like this if the fire hadn't happened? Or would they still be arguing about her cat and where he parked his pickup, blind to the underlying attraction between them?

Sookie was clearly glad to be back home. She'd slept on the end of the bed happily. Would the poor cat get confused? The kitchen fitters and the decorators hadn't finished yet, but it did feel comforting to be back in her house, her bed . . . with Harry beside her.

Last night, she and Harry had both felt tired, so had cuddled until they fell asleep. She'd noticed Harry had been off-ish, a little grumpy. *And he had the cheek to call her moody at times.* Maddy had put it down to being exhausted. It reassured her that the relationship wasn't just about sex either.

Her kissing and touches awoke Harry, he turned and kissed her back. 'Good morning,' he said, pulling her in close so she could feel his arousal.

'Harry, the kitchen fitters will be here soon.'

'So, we'll be quick.' He kissed and nuzzled, his mouth finding her breast, making her gasp at the pleasure of it. Their limbs tangled, their bodies responding to each other.

'Harry . . .' She kissed him back, feeling more and more turned on, and barely able to concentrate. 'I don't know if I have any condoms here.' He made her so horny, though, a part of her didn't care, she'd risk it . . . she wanted to feel him inside her . . . But as if she'd thrown a bucket of cold water over him, he sat bolt upright, fully awake now.

'I can't get you pregnant,' he said, pulling away frostily, his blue eyes darkened by sadness. She noticed as he sat up his arousal had once again disappeared. As if ashamed, he covered himself up.

'Harry?'

But like the previous time, he shot out of bed and escaped to the bathroom. Within seconds, she heard the shower running.

Was it her? Was it something she'd done? Okay, it might be too early in their relationship to be discussing children. But his reaction to the thought of her being pregnant . . . it had looked like it repulsed him. Did he not want a family some day? It wasn't something Maddy thought about obsessively, and maybe she should speak to a doctor about some birth control alternatives, but she hoped, eventually, she'd meet someone who she could start a family with. She wasn't averse to the idea of children. She adored her brother's children, her niece and nephew. If Harry didn't want children – ever – then they really were on the wrong page, and their paths in life were very different.

Should she end this before she got seriously hurt? Before she fell any deeper in love with him?

Because that's what was happening. She was falling in love – *too late, she was in love*. She hadn't learnt to harden her heart and protect it – *obviously*. However hard she tried not to, Maddy gave her heart over willingly, every bloody time, and it usually ended in tears – her tears.

That's why after Connor, she was meant to concentrate on herself; her life, her gallery, her home . . . until the fire . . . until Harry.

Well, Maddy needed to know, and she needed to know now. They needed to talk about this. He couldn't keep running out on her, leaving her to feel this shit. Like a volcano about to erupt, she could feel her anger rising. She knew she wasn't likely to face this as calmly as she needed to. But the longer Harry hid in the bathroom, the hotter Maddy's temper got.

***

Harry let the hot water pound the back of his head and run down his body. He needed to get out and face Maddy. And apologise. She didn't know he had this fear; she didn't know Karin had been pregnant when she died. Hell, she didn't even know Karin had died! He carried this almighty ghost around with him, with the fear that history would repeat itself.

He switched off the shower, grabbed a towel, and dried himself before stepping out of the bath.

'Harry, open up this door,' Maddy shouted from the other side of the door, banging on it hard.

He opened it, and there stood Maddy, a dressing gown wrapped around her, her arms folded across her chest.

'Can you please tell me what the fuck is wrong with you?'

Maddy said, clearly enraged. Cheeks flushed crimson, green eyes narrowed on him.

'Maddy, I'm sorry, I want to tell you, but I can't. Not now.' Harry still couldn't open up, especially in this fraught emotional atmosphere. Only the ones closest to him, his family, knew the full extent of what had happened and his subsequent illness. He knew he really should talk to Maddy about it, but she was already so angry.

'No! I need to know where *this* is going?'

'How do you mean?'

'This has happened a couple of times now. Is it me?'

'Oh, God, Maddy, no, it's not you.'

'Please don't give me the 'it's not you, it's me' bullshit. I know we haven't been seeing each other long, and I know it kind of happened suddenly, but one day – ONE DAY – I would like children. So if this is something you don't see in your future, then I need to know – now.' The last time he'd seen Maddy this upset her house was on fire. He just couldn't cope.

'I'm not talking about this now, not when you're in such a rage. I'm sorry, okay.' Harry barged past Maddy, into the bedroom, throwing yesterday's T-shirt over his head.

'You said we were on the same page. Are we? Maybe we should have discussed where we were actually going with this,' Maddy said sadly. Tears streamed down her face as he scrambled around for his underwear and his shorts, grabbed his phone and house keys, and ran down the stairs. He couldn't get out of the house fast enough. His heart pounded, ringing in his ears, his lungs tightening as if he couldn't breathe. He panicked. Like a stag caught in oncoming headlights, he didn't know which way to run.

Maddy screamed behind him. 'Where are you going? Harry . . . Harry!'

Inside his own house, he grabbed essentials mindlessly, his medication and his toothbrush, but he couldn't think what else he needed beyond that. He wasn't even sure what he was doing. But he had to get out of here. He had to leave.

He slammed his pickup door, and started the engine. Maddy ran across the street, her face wet with tears, and although she'd looked angry earlier, her face had paled as she banged on his window.

'What are you doing? Where are you going? Talk to me, Harry!'

'I love you, Maddy. That's what I'm afraid of.' But he knew she couldn't hear him. He'd mumbled it under his breath as he'd wrenched his truck into gear, reversing off his drive. His wheels spun as he pulled away.

His chest ached, his body shook. *She'd be safe. He'd changed the locks.* He knew he had to get away. The suffocating darkness was closing in again, and he couldn't cope. He'd realised he wasn't ready to love again.

***

Maddy watched Harry's black pickup disappear out of Annadale Close, and then collapsed sobbing. She didn't care that she was in the middle of the street. Her body doubled over, as she expelled the air in her lungs, and released the tears that fell onto the tarmac. She rested her hands on her knees, and cried, the pain in her chest unrelenting. Love really did hurt. How could this morning have gone so wrong? One minute they were kissing and cuddling, the next minute Harry had gone. And something told her he wasn't coming back. He hadn't even looked at her.

As per usual, she'd handled the situation in the wrong way. Why hadn't she remained calm? Maddy was angry with Harry, but she was even more furious at herself.

When she was ready, she pulled herself up and walked back into her house. The kitchen fitters would be here any minute, and they didn't need to see her in a mess. This thought alone stopped her in her tracks, and the tears welled in her eyes once more, her throat tightening. Unable to hold in her tears, she broke down again. Luckily, by this time she was behind her front door, not making a spectacle of herself in the road. Why had she got angry with him? If only she could go back, just before he'd frozen, and say something different, anything else but what she'd said.

If she had stayed in bed . . . let him come out of the bathroom . . . approached it more calmly . . .

He would still be here.

Gathering all the strength she could muster and wiping

away her tears, she climbed the stairs, showered, and got ready to face the day, although all she wanted to do was climb back into bed. Every time she looked in the mirror, tears would well up. Even as she tried to apply some make-up in the hope of hiding her red, puffy face, her eyes glistened with tears.

How could she feel like this about someone after such a short space of time? Her life already felt emptier at the thought that Harry would no longer be in it.

Maddy hid her upset well when the decorators and kitchen fitters arrived. Maybe Harry would come to his senses, and return later, tail between his legs, apologetically bearing a huge bunch of flowers and announcing how much he cared for her. Maddy dared to romanticize that he loved her. Then, she soon realised it was best not to think those kinds of thoughts because they brought on the tears.

He couldn't love her; he'd left her.

Valerie was Maddy's pillar of strength in the gallery. She fetched the box of tissues, gave her a mug of tea, and sat her down out the back. 'Tell me all about it.'

So, through moments of welling up and unable to hold in her tears – she'd dehydrate at this rate – Maddy told Valerie what had happened, even down to the lack of arousal – something she would never share with her mother.

'Well, he could be embarrassed, and there could be other things going on we do not know about. But I didn't really have him down as a complicated soul,' Valerie said, rubbing Maddy's back.

'He's on medication for something.'

'It could be depression.'

'But why hasn't he talked to me about it?'

'Maddy, you've not really been seeing him that long. You were both forced together, rightly or wrongly, by your house fire. Maybe it's too much for him, and he's had to escape to his cave.'

'Cave?'

'Yes, and he'll come out when he's good and ready. You'll make matters worse if you try to coax him out before he is ready.'

'So should I text him?'

'Yes, I suppose so. It can't do any harm. Tell him you're here to talk when he wants to. Or something along those lines.'

Valerie went back out into the gallery to talk to some customers who were browsing while Maddy fetched her phone from her handbag. Seeing no messages from Harry gave a lurch of further disappointment to her gut.

Hey you, not sure what happened this morning. I'm sorry for getting angry. I'm here if you want to talk about it. I really like you, Harry. M Xxx

She hovered before clicking the little envelope that would send her text message. Should she say she loved him? Did she love him? Was it too soon to admit it? Would she look

stupid if he didn't love her? It could scare him off further . . .
She left the message as it was, deciding to keep it simple so
it couldn't be misconstrued. If he replied, then she could go
from there.

Chapter 27

Not even sure where he wanted to go or what he wanted to do, Harry just drove, his thoughts dark and his heart heavy.

After half an hour he stopped for fuel, alerted by the light on the dash that his fuel tank was empty. While in the petrol station, he grabbed a bacon sandwich too. Although he didn't really fancy eating, he knew he should because he'd skipped breakfast. The dry bread and the over salty bacon didn't do anything for his appetite. Feeling full after one half, he threw the rest in the bin.

Harry followed his nose along the A38, driving through Plymouth, and around the south-easterly edge of Dartmoor National Park until he reached his parents' home in a village on the outskirts of Exeter. If he'd realised that was where he was heading, he'd have taken the A30 which was more direct. The hour and forty minute route had taken him over two hours with the rush hour traffic he'd hit in Plymouth in the morning, but he didn't care.

As if to add to his torture, he'd driven along the stretch of road that had taken Karin's life. Before he'd realised it was that particular bit of road, he'd been unable to change his route. No evidence of a wreckage now, clearly, after two years, only his memory remained of the fateful day. Although the stretch of road was set at the national speed limit of sixty miles per hour, it was straight and clear; accidents happened rarely on this part of the road. So why had it happened to Karin? Even to this day, he couldn't make sense of her accident.

'Harry! How lovely!' His mother, April, answered the door. Her expression changed from trepidation about who on earth could be ringing her doorbell to joy and surprise upon seeing it was Harry.

'Hey, Mum.' He tried to smile.

'Why didn't you call and let me know you were coming? You're lucky you've caught me in,' she said. Her expression sobered quickly, seeing his grim, cheerless appearance and she ushered him through the front door. She glanced up at the clock in the hallway. 'Go through to the kitchen; I need to make a call first.'

Sitting at the solid oak kitchen table, he took in the familiar surroundings of his old home; the various old plates his mother had collected over the years hung on one wall, a welsh-dresser displaying her best crockery, the kitchen always immaculate. Leaning on his elbows, chin resting in his hands, he could hear his mother making a call to a friend. 'Hi, Sue, it's April, I'm so sorry to do this to you, but can we reschedule lunch? My son's surprised me with a visit . . . yes, yes, that'll be perfect . . . thanks. Bye, love.'

'Right then, that's sorted,' April said, entering the kitchen. 'Shall I put the kettle on?'

He shrugged and didn't say much. His mother made conversation while the kettle boiled, telling him what they'd been up to, that his father was at work and had a number of gardening jobs on at the moment, what his sister, Cathy, was up to. Cathy preferred to be called Cat, but he hadn't the energy to correct his mother. April had never liked the nickname Cat.

'So, how are things with you?' He could hear the hesitation in his mother's voice, not sure if she wanted to know or not.

'Work's good.' He wasn't lying there.

'Aren't you seeing a new woman? Maddy . . . is that her name? So how's that coming along or don't I dare ask?' His mother's caring, loving face looked at him, as she placed her hand over his. Her blue eyes were a little darker than his own, and she wore her mousy blonde hair bobbed, framing her attractive face.

He rubbed his face with his big hands, exhaustion washing over him. He hated himself. Replaying the incident over and over again, if he'd done things differently, would Karin still be here? But if she were, he wouldn't have met Maddy.

Harry was afraid of how he felt about Maddy. These feelings were what had made him bolt. He hadn't felt like this in a long time . . . not since Karin. He wanted to love Maddy . . . but there was this fear, an internal struggle, that if he got close, if he opened up and truly loved her, the same thing could happen. He couldn't bear losing another woman.

And then there was the guilt. Was it right to love another woman again, perhaps even more than he'd loved Karin?

However, regardless of how he felt, Maddy probably deserved better than him, someone who could love her without fear, without the depression.

Did his mum deserve to go through all this again? But he had nowhere else to turn . . .

With this mixture of guilt and self-loathing roiling around inside him, he suddenly needed to be on his own. He wanted to go to bed.

'Mum, do you mind if I go to my room for a bit?'

'Yes, yes, of course, darling.' She ruffled his hair as if he were still ten years old. 'I'm here when you want to talk about it.'

She knew how to deal with him. She'd helped him when this had really taken a savage hold of him, and they hadn't been quite sure what it was. At first, they'd thought it was the grief of losing a loved one, but then they'd realised it was so much more.

Harry slipped off his shoes and lay on the bed, on top

of the duvet, too warm to actually get into bed. He still called it his room, yet it looked nothing like it had when he was a child growing up. His mother had put a double bed in with a bedside cabinet placed either side, and there was a chest of drawers squeezed in opposite the bed. It was now the guest room, tastefully decorated in creams and reds, with one wall – the headboard end – papered with big printed red and silver floral wallpaper. A feature wall, as Maddy had suggested to him in fact. Much more fashionable than the chintzy wallpaper in his house.

For the first time that day, Harry looked at his phone and saw there was a text message from Maddy. Should he reply? Then his phone battery beeped and died. In frustration, he threw the phone across the room. The splitting, cracking sound of it hitting the wall didn't bode well for his phone's life. He certainly wasn't making things better for himself, only worse.

Did he really care?

Harry stared at the ceiling, his heart weighing him down so he didn't want to move. The tension in his chest knotted, growing larger and larger, tightening his throat, forming tears, the only way the pressure would release. He didn't know what to do for the best. This is where a crystal ball would come in handy. He wanted someone to tell him that his future would be okay, he'd survive, and he'd live happily with someone . . . have children, grow old, that sort of thing.

But would it be with Maddy?

Chapter 28

Harry never replied to her text. Maddy would look at her phone every five minutes, then every half an hour, before finally burying it in her bag. She couldn't concentrate on painting, so she updated the gallery's social media pages – from its Facebook page, displaying images of new paintings and photographs for sale, to its website with similar updates.

Val was very concerned. 'You poor thing, you really have had your emotions put through the mill these past couple of months. First the fire, now Harry. Why don't you go home?'

Maddy had thought that too. Today the gallery was the last place she wanted to be. She hated feeling this way because the gallery was her passion. Maybe Harry had come home, and she'd find him there and would be able to talk to him.

Rain had come in off the sea, as if mirroring Maddy's bleak, grey mood, so the gallery had quietened, with only the hardened surfers clad in wetsuits left on the beach. Even though it was mid-August, without the sun it was a miserable, almost autumnal, day, the warmth gone, and all the holiday-makers had taken cover from the wind and drizzle in the refuge of a pub or cafe, or back in their caravans, chalets or tents, leaving the high street of Tinners Bay deserted.

'Do you mind?' Maddy said and wiped her eyes again. She'd nearly emptied the tissue box, blowing her nose and drying her face. She feared she had no trace of make-up left. She would need to see to Sookie, and certainly couldn't face Simon and his builders at Wisteria Cottage.

'You're no good here. Go home. Drive carefully, in fact, text me when you're home.'

'Are you sure?'

'Of course I'm sure.'

'I mean about texting you.'

Valerie rolled her eyes. 'I'm okay reading them, but not very good at replying. Now go.'

Maddy didn't need telling again. She hugged Valerie and left the gallery. This was not the right time of year to be distracted. She needed to concentrate on her work, but she really was useless today. Carefully, she drove home along the narrow country lanes, gloomy with the rain, not needing a car accident added to the rest of her problems.

At home, there was no sign of Harry's pickup as she came round the corner of Annadale Close. The workmen were still in her house, so she poked her nose in to see how well the kitchen and decorating was coming along.

'Be ready for the tiling tomorrow,' one of the men wearing dusty black overalls in the kitchen said. Maddy had the chosen tiles stacked in the dining room ready. 'Not long now, and you'll have your kitchen back.'

'That's wonderful,' Maddy said, not feeling as happy as she sounded. She flicked through the post she'd picked up by the front door. Mostly junk mail and leaflets, but there was one envelope from her insurance company, containing a voucher to be spent on buying a new fridge freezer. She couldn't fault their efficiency really at getting her house back to normal.

'I'll be over the road if you need me,' Maddy said, deciding to get out from under the men's feet. She knew she worked better without someone hovering over her, so they probably would too.

Inside Harry's house, Sookie joined her, meowing for food. Despite it being earlier than normal, Maddy fed her, and became mildly comforted by her purring, before setting about making her own dinner. Not that she felt hungry. Should she make enough for two? There still hadn't been a reply to her text from Harry, which worried her further. What if something had happened to him? What if he'd been involved in a car accident, and was lying in some hospital bed unbeknown to her?

Maddy made a simple cheese and ham omelette, throwing in some mushrooms that were also in the fridge, because she actually couldn't face cooking. She washed everything up afterwards and plonked herself on the sofa with a glass of red wine, the television on in the background for noise. Sookie jumped on her lap, making herself comfortable.

Without Harry there, Maddy couldn't stay in his house. It made her uncomfortable, and last night had proved she was safe to sleep in her own home. Taking her wine with her, with Sookie following her as if she'd picked up something was wrong and she needed company, Maddy climbed the stairs.

In Harry's bedroom, she went around to his side of the bed and lay down. She gathered the sheets into her arms, burying her face into them and breathed deeply. It gave her a flash of him smiling at her, his blue eyes, bright and cheerful, his arms strong as he held her and made love to her.

Finally, she straightened the bed and started packing all she could into a couple of carrier bags. She would move her things out of Harry's house. Tomorrow she would collect what belongings she had at Wisteria Cottage too. She was moving back home. Her kitchen wasn't finished yet, but Maddy was determined to survive this, to stand on her own two feet. *Seriously, if she had to bring home a takeaway for a couple of nights, it wouldn't be the end of the world.* She checked the bathroom although she'd taken most of her toiletries when she'd moved to the cottage. Her thoughts darkened; Harry had cleared out his toiletries from the bathroom too, and his toothbrush was gone. It looked like he wasn't planning on coming back any time soon.

Her worst fears were confirmed.

Immobile, the pain in her chest swelled, moving up into her throat, and before she could stop herself, she choked and tears streamed from her eyes. For a moment, all she could do was cry and concentrate on breathing. She took deep breaths, blowing out through her mouth to calm herself, to gather her thoughts, to try and stop the tears.

She grabbed some tissue off the loo roll, blew her nose, wiped her face and threw it down the toilet, angrily pushing down on the flush. She went from feeling hurt to rage.

Men!

After Connor, she'd sworn she wouldn't let this happen again. It just went to show she had no control over it.

Why did it hurt so badly?

Because she'd let Harry in. Without realising, she'd let him into her heart.

She'd tried keeping him at bay, but it wasn't until you lost someone that you realised how much they meant. She'd become reliant on Harry, he'd helped her through the fire, he was always there of an evening, and now he was gone, and she needed to find the strength to do this on her own.

The grey clouds were making the evening darker than normal, so Maddy trudged between the two houses while it was still light, clearing her belongings out of Harry's place and placing them back in her own.

Then, still unable to contemplate going to bed – on her own – she cleaned her bathroom. She did what she'd thought about this morning, she cleaned, wiped, dusted. She brought over Harry's bleach and cleaning products, as she had none – everything in her kitchen had been emptied into a skip, not that any of it had really been salvageable. The heat had distorted or destroyed most things. She would replace anything she used, so it didn't feel like stealing. Which was ridiculous, because if Harry had been there, he would have insisted she used his stuff. Turning her thoughts to Harry was really bad. She became saddened, and as if paralysed, the tears and grief would start up again.

Things had to get easier, right?

Eventually exhausted, but satisfied the stench of smoke, however mild, was now gone, Maddy climbed into bed. As she'd done in Harry's bed earlier, she hugged the pillow he had used the night before. It had his scent on it. She breathed it in like a child would use a comfort blanket, and fell asleep holding onto it.

***

'Did you hear from him?' Valerie asked as Maddy walked into the gallery the next morning, later than she'd intended. Her sleep had been broken, and when she was due to get up, she hadn't the energy.

Maddy shook her head at Valerie.

'The man may have his reasons,' Valerie said, frowning. 'Later on, if you get to speak to him – which you will, he lives opposite you for Christ's sake! – he may have some legitimate excuse. And then you can decide how to react to it, to forgive him, or not.'

'True.' Maddy had thought of this last night. Maybe Harry just needed some time. Maybe this had all gone too fast too soon for him as well. But then he'd instigated most of it . . .

Men, they never knew what they wanted.

Valerie shrugged her shoulders, huffed and said, 'But it could have been worse. This could have been eight months or two years down the line when he disappeared on you. At least it's only been two months. You'll survive, my darling. Whatever happens, you will survive.'

Gloria Gaynor singing *I Will Survive* popped instantly into Maddy's head. How many times had she sung it with girlfriends at a karaoke night? But she'd always thought those song lyrics had been poignant every time a boy had dumped her through school and college. And when things ended with Connor, when he'd belittled her, telling her she wouldn't cope without him. But she had coped, and was coping, and would continue to do so. And the same would apply in Harry's case, too.

Maddy straightened up, holding her head higher, Gloria Gaynor inspiring her. 'You're right, Val, this could have been so much worse if he'd done this later on. And even so, although it hurts, we women always survive. Right?'

'Yes, we do. Cup of tea?'

'Coffee, please. I think I need the caffeine.'

'That's my girl.' Valerie put her arm around Maddy's shoulder, giving her a reassuring hug.

'Shame we haven't got any Baileys to go in it.'

'I can always get some.'

Chapter 29

As long as she was surrounded by people, Maddy was fine, absolutely fine. When she was kept busy in the gallery, with customers and Valerie chatting, her mind remained focussed on her work, her paintings, her passion for art. But the minute she got home, the loneliness crept in and she felt lost and empty. A blackness would creep inside her, consuming her, and tears would form out of nowhere. She would stand in her bedroom or in her kitchen and shout to herself in frustration, 'I don't even know why I'm crying,' while her tears would fall.

But she did know. She feared loneliness.

She'd managed to overcome this feeling after Connor had gone, because although the ending of their relationship had brought some relief, there had still been that fear of loneliness. In fact, her life had been getting back on track, and the feeling of missing someone and the need to be loved had diminished — and then the fire had happened. And so now, here she was, having to get used to it all over again.

She needed to find the strength to be a single woman again, relying on no one but herself. From past experience, she knew time would heal her, but she also knew it was like riding a wave, up until the point when time had done its healing. *If only there were a fast forward button to ease this awful, depressing mood.*

Luckily, she tried to reassure herself, her relationship with Harry had been shorter, so getting over him would be easier and quicker. But cooking for one was no fun, and her motivation would go as soon as she set foot in her house and wondered what to eat. She'd either have a couple of slices of toast or a bowl of cereal, rather than cook herself something. These were the hardest moments when she realised how much she missed him. No one to go for an evening stroll with, or share a bottle of wine.

A part of her wished she was still staying at Wisteria Cottage, so she didn't have to step out of her front door and see Harry's empty house, with no pickup truck parked up, getting in her way.

Sookie sensed her sadness, or so Maddy presumed, because her cat was being very attentive and loving. Maybe she missed Harry too?

The end of the school holidays approached. It would be September in a few days, and Harry had been gone a couple of weeks now, with not a murmur from him. No texts, calls, absolutely no sign of him. One minute Maddy would feel sad, then the next minute she'd get angry, because if he could treat her like this, and feel it was acceptable behaviour, then he was not worth it. She deserved better than a man who gave her no thought at all.

On the days when she wasn't feeling so angry, Maddy would let herself into Harry's house and check his mail, and pile it neatly on his dining room table. She would water the plants in his garden, but she didn't know what else to do. She didn't know if she should do these things anymore, either. Maybe he wouldn't want her meddling help. But what about his business? Should she call his customers? She didn't have the first idea where to start, so decided to leave it. Harry was a grown man and responsible for his own actions.

With her kitchen almost completed, she was able to live perfectly comfortably in her own house again, and was getting back into her old routine. Bits and pieces still needed tidying up, and she would sometimes find basic utensils and pieces of kitchen equipment missing when she went to use them. On the way home from the gallery one afternoon she had to make a detour to the kitchen shop to purchase a cheese grater and a salad spinner. She restocked her new cupboards with food supplies and tried to keep her brand new oven clean. (How long it would last was another thing.) Her new fridge freezer had been delivered a few days ago, so she could now store fresh food.

All of this meant that she had no need for Harry's house anymore. And eventually, she'd learn to live without him in her life, if that was what he wanted.

The worry remained, though - when he did return they would have to face one another every day as neighbours. How would that make her feel?

Chapter 30

Harry virtually lived in his old bedroom at his parents' house for the next few weeks. In fact, he actually wasn't sure how long he'd been there. An itchy beard had grown, but he couldn't even be bothered to shave. And he hated facial hair. Years in the fire service, where he had to be clean-shaven so the masks fitted securely, had made him that way. His mother would bring him food and cups of tea, and occasionally he would go downstairs for dinner, but he found it hard to make conversation with his parents. His father had picked up the remains of his phone, rescuing the SIM card, and contacted his clients, and yet Harry had ceased to care about the business he'd worked so hard to build. He missed Maddy, but believed this was for the best. If he stayed away, she'd get over him and move on, and his feelings for her would lessen too. They had to, eventually.

Time was a good healer. He'd been told this frequently after Karin's death, and in part, he knew it was true. But in part, it wasn't. Because here he was, more than two years later, still traumatized by memories of the day she died.

And he couldn't get Maddy out of his head.

But she deserved better than him.

Lying on his bed, hands behind his head with his eyes closed, and wearing an old grey T-shirt and a pair of jogging bottoms, Harry tried not to think about what Maddy would be doing at this time of day, or if her house was finished and she'd moved back in . . .

He hoped she no longer went to Wisteria Cottage, so Simon couldn't wheedle his way into her heart.

'He's back to how he was two years ago.' He could hear his mother talking to his father outside the bedroom on the landing. 'I really don't know what to do. Maybe I should call the doctor. I was hoping he'd come through it in his own time . . .' She was speaking softly, an edge of worry in her voice, probably assuming Harry was asleep.

'You should tell him what you know, April,' his father replied more loudly, probably hoping Harry would hear. And he had.

Harry sighed, rubbed his face and got out of bed. He opened the bedroom door and stood, leaning against the doorframe for support, catching his mother and father in the hallway where they were not exactly being very discreet. 'Tell me what?'

His father, Arthur, was similar in height to Harry, although Harry was half an inch taller and they'd always teased each other about it. It was obvious where Harry had inherited his genes from – with bright blue eyes and wavy black hair, showing flecks of grey now, his father, like an older model of Harry, was standing arms folded, facing his mother. He gave Harry a look as if to say, 'I'll let your mother deal with this'. Arthur, much like Harry, kept his emotions tucked away.

'Go and sit down in the kitchen, let me make some tea first,' April said, shooing Harry with her hands. Barefoot, with heavy steps, he went down the stairs. He needed to shower and shave, he thought as he rubbed his hairy chin. But not wanting to leave the house, it hadn't felt necessary. He'd lost the motivation to care about his appearance and doubted he smelt pleasant either.

April made the tea and placed a plate of biscuits in front of him. He'd not been eating much, he'd lost weight, and his muscle bulk had reduced. His Dad would soon be teasing him that he was the bigger of the two.

'So what was Dad talking about? What is it that you should tell me?'

'I bumped into Karin's mother a couple of months ago.'

'And?'

'They've had a terrible time of it, you know. Karin's father has never been quite the same since, and poor Elsa has had to deal with both the grief of losing her daughter and her husband's illness, which was probably brought on by grief too. It's so sad.'

'I didn't realise Jim had got sick.'

'Well, you wouldn't have, would you?' April frowned lovingly at Harry, reaching across the table for his forearm and squeezing it. 'You weren't much better yourself. But yes, apparently he went downhill with one thing or another. He's now in a home. She couldn't cope.'

'Maybe I should go and see her?'

'Elsa would like that. She feels she lost a son-in-law as well the day Karin died.'

'God, I didn't even think about them.' Harry rubbed his face and itched his chin, disliking the feel of the prickly hair growth.

'Harry, you can't blame yourself. What you witnessed, well, it wasn't fair, but I need to tell you something, about the accident.'

'What about it? Because I know what happened, Mum. I was there!' Harry said, clenching his fists. His heart raced, and he tried to shake off the image of the accident, of finding Karin trapped in her car. He needed to calm down too because he could see his mother's apprehension. She loved and cared about him so much; he knew that. She wasn't trying to hurt him. And getting angry at her wouldn't help matters.

'Look, after the funeral, and once she felt ready, Elsa went through Karin's things, the things I'd taken over from yours, and she found a diary . . . did you read the diary?'

Harry shook his head. 'To be honest, Mum, I can't

remember. You sorted most of the stuff. I couldn't bring myself to look at anything.' And the rest was now in boxes at his house in Cornwall.

'No, you're right,' April said, with a gentle rub of his back, as if recalling the events. 'One of the diaries was recent. She was depressed, Harry.' His mother stared at him, meeting his gaze. 'Suicidal.'

Harry shook his head again, but could feel a growing ache in his sternum and his eyes stinging with tears. 'No. Karin was happy. She had mood swings and was sometimes withdrawn, but she always told me it was the time of the month.'

'She hid it from us all, Harry. Elsa said she'd suffered with depression when she was a teenager, but even they thought it had been a phase and she'd got over it. It was just her A-Levels getting her down . . . It was no one's fault. You can't blame yourself for what happened, Harry, because Karin caused the accident deliberately.'

'No!' The police had said Karin had been to blame for the accident. But Harry couldn't believe she'd caused it deliberately. *It had to have been an accident.*

'Harry, she wanted to die.'

'But she was carrying my baby! Our baby!' He physically hurt now, as if someone was punching him from the inside out.

'I know, love, I know.' Harry could see his mother's eyes welling, too.

'I should have saved her!' His throat tightened, his own pain ready to spill out, remembering talking to Karin, promising he'd get her out of the car, but it had been futile.

'Harry, you did all you could, sweetheart. You can't go on blaming yourself. And you can't stop yourself being happy with someone else. Karin wouldn't have wanted that. Maybe we all failed her for not spotting the warning signs and saving her, but whatever was going through that poor girl's mind, you must carry on and live your life, Harry. Please . . .' His mother had tears streaming down her face, as she sobbed into the back of her hand. Maybe she feared the same fate for Harry, worried that Karin's depression had somehow transferred to him after the accident. Which in some ways it had: he'd been prescribed drugs to suppress the anxiety and depression, to ease the nightmares and the insomnia, the guilt. It had been working until lately. He had always promised himself that he'd get help if things ever got to a stage he couldn't deal with. That's why he'd returned to his parents in the first place because now the nightmares featured not Karin's face, but Maddy's. Being frightened of loving someone and losing them engulfed him like a cloud of thick, choking smoke, not allowing him to be happy again.

'Why didn't Elsa say something sooner?'

The chair scraped the tiled floor as April got up from the table and grabbed some kitchen roll. She blew her nose, dabbed her eyes and took a deep breath. 'She was very apologetic that she hadn't been in touch sooner. She hadn't realised you'd suffered like you had, and by the time she'd found the strength to look at the diary, Jim had started his downhill struggle. I don't know where the woman has found the strength, to be honest.'

'Why didn't you tell me as soon as you'd seen her?'

'Harry, when I met Elsa, as far as I was aware you were happy with your life in Cornwall. You were happy in your new home and your business was keeping you busy. I wasn't sure you'd want all this trauma about Karin to resurface, so I left it. Then suddenly, you showed up, holed yourself up in your old room and I've been waiting for you to . . . I don't know, show some sign you'd be ready to digest this information. I wasn't sure whether it was something you needed to hear or not. But your father is right, you do need to hear it so you can move on.' April's voice trembled, and she held her hand to her mouth to compose herself. 'What happened to Karin is deeply sad, and we'll never forget her, but you only have one life, Harry, one life. So make the most of it, don't waste it, for goodness sake. You're still young.'

Harry rose to his feet and hugged his mother, and she sobbed into his shoulder. He let his tears fall, too. As if suddenly granted permission, he cried in his mother's arms. They held each other. Harry felt like the small child he once was, running to his mum for comfort after grazing his knee, or trapping his fingers in a door. She smelt the same, and

371

felt the same, only he was so much larger and stronger now, his head resting on her shoulder rather than in the softness of her bosom.

At the time, he was not aware Karin was so ill. But looking back, seeing how others behaved in certain circumstances, to how Karin reacted to the same situations, it was clear to him now that she had shown signs of depression, only he hadn't recognised it at the time when it mattered. He would have to live with that. And live with the fact he couldn't save her from the injuries she suffered in the accident. He would always carry a burden of guilt for that.

However, his mother was right; he couldn't waste this opportunity to start afresh. He had moved on. Cornwall was treating him well, and Maddy was amazing. He wasn't sure if he believed in all that soppy crap about everything happening for a reason, but Maddy had been placed in his path and he was going to snatch the chance. Who knew what the future held, but he was certain Maddy was a very different woman from Karin. She had a much happier disposition – even with the house fire, she took each day as it came, soldiering on. She was a strong positive force who would envelop him, and carry him along with her.

And he missed her so much. Staying away from her wasn't making him feel better. Hell, he felt so much worse.

He couldn't change what had happened to Karin, but he could change his own life around and make a real go of things with Maddy.

But after disappearing without a trace and ignoring her messages – if she'd sent any more he wouldn't know as his phone was in bits – would she be prepared to take him back?

***

Maddy was busy getting the gallery ready for another day. With a soft broom, she swept the sand that came in off people's shoes into a pile on the stone tiled floor, then grabbed a dustpan and brush. She was about to empty it outside when Valerie walked in, cheerful as ever.

'Good morning, darling,' Valerie said, holding a hessian carrier bag. 'How are you doing today?'

'I'm not too bad.' Maddy sighed. She wanted to put her feelings for Harry behind her, but it was difficult. She heard a clink of glasses and frowned curiously at the bag. 'You're early; I wasn't expecting you until later.'

'I couldn't wait. I have a surprise for you.'

'A surprise?'

'Yes, I thought this would cheer us up!' Valerie pulled a bottle of Taittinger from the bag and revealed two champagne glasses to go with it.

'What's the occasion?'

'What's the occasion!' Valerie said, shaking her head with incredulity as if Maddy should know. 'It's the anniversary of the day you signed the lease on this place.' She gestured towards the gallery. 'You've been here a whole year.'

'By God, it is, isn't it? Thirty-first of August.' The weekend just gone had been the bank holiday, and manic. Maddy hadn't had time to dwell on Harry then.

'It was lucky for you the old leaseholders sold up because their business wasn't doing so well, not surprising really with their overpriced tat.'

'I can't believe the schools will go back next week. Tinners Bay will be a ghost town again. These six weeks have flown.'

'And the gallery has done marvellously, so I thought we should celebrate what you've achieved in the past year.'

'With your help, Val. I couldn't have done it without you.'

'Nonsense. But you need cheering up,' Valerie said. 'I've brought in homemade scones – I didn't make them, my neighbour did, before you start thinking I've turned into Mary Berry—'

'You've got twenty years on her.' Maddy laughed.

'Just under! Anyway, we can have champagne and a cream tea.'

'Lovely, but a cup of coffee to start, I think.' Maddy put the dustpan and brush away, and flicked the switch on the kettle. 'It's a bit early for champagne.'

'Maddy, darling, it is never too early for champagne. I've brought orange juice, so the first could be a Buck's Fizz.' Valerie popped the cork and started pouring.

'Wow, you have come prepared.'

'I like to spoil my surrogate daughter.'

The day went exceptionally fast, helped along by the

bottle of champagne. Valerie had said it would put her in a great mood all day, and she'd been right. Nothing could upset Maddy either, not even some miserable old man complaining about the prices of some of the artwork. She had politely explained that the price tags represented the time spent on the pictures, not just the materials used. She couldn't believe how un-rattled she'd felt by this exchange. It must have been the champagne.

'Oh, no more for me,' Maddy said, placing her hand over her glass as Valerie attempted to top it up with the last of the champagne. 'I can't walk to Wisteria Cottage any more, I'll have to drive home.'

'Stay at mine tonight,' Valerie said. 'Then we can have another bottle later. I've rather got the taste for it.'

'Yes, why not.' Without hesitation, Maddy clinked her glass with Valerie's and let her top up her glass.

All in all, one year on, through rough and smooth, love and fire, Maddy had to be proud of her achievements. It just showed that so much could happen in one year.

Where would she be this time next year?

Chapter 31

Harry certainly wasn't ready to just up and leave his parents' house. He thought he could, but with his pickup's keys in his hand, stepping outside the house actually took a lot more effort than he realised. He'd paused on the front step and started shaking. He looked a mess, a shadow of his former self. He still wasn't ready to return to Annadale Close. Kicking the brick wall of the house, back hunched, he walked back inside.

'What's the matter?' his mother asked, startled by Harry's sudden return.

'I can't do it. Not yet. I'm not ready.'

'I did worry you might be running before you could walk. Take it slowly, Harry.' She smiled. It was so reassuring it eased his soul, the tension in his shoulders ebbing away. He nodded assertively. He needed to take baby steps.

Harry built himself up day by day, getting out of bed, showering, shaving, eating with his parents at the correct time, trying to be more sociable. He started taking his prescribed drugs regularly too. However much he hated taking the medication, he realised he still needed it to recover fully. He pottered in his dad's garden, started to make calls to his customers, including Roy, and then, borrowing his dad's trainers and sports shorts, started running.

Even when he'd bought a new phone, he still couldn't bring himself to contact Maddy. What would he say? And wouldn't it be better said to her face? His mother seemed to think so.

Every day he ran, alternating a short distance one day, a long distance the next. Then he'd do exercises to build his muscles, using logs in the garden, anything he could lay his hands on, until his father pointed into the back of the garage where some gym weights were gathering dust.

'Why don't you use them anymore?' Harry said.

'I joined a gym – more free time now I'm semi-retired.' Arthur patted his son's back proudly. 'Besides your mother wanted to turn the box room into a study. And when you've been married as long as I have, Harry, you know not to argue.' They both chuckled, and his father helped him move the equipment.

Harry started training, building up his muscle bulk again, getting himself fitter. Lying in bed had done him no favours, mentally as well as physically, and now, running and exercising, the fog in his head was clearing and he was able to focus on the happier, brighter things in his life.

Like Maddy.

***

Considering it was mid-September, the sun was relentless. It was another hot day in the gallery, albeit quiet.

'Your phone's ringing, Maddy!' Valerie called from the kitchen area at the back of the gallery, where Maddy had left her handbag.

A few weeks ago, she would have dropped everything and made a dash for her phone, praying it would be Harry. She'd lost all hope now that she would ever see him again. Instinct told her it wasn't Harry. It was probably some damn company going on about PPI, or trying to sell her a new gas boiler or solar panelling. These people didn't just leave messages on your landline now, they called your mobile too.

Annoyed by the disturbance, and toying with the idea of letting the phone go to voicemail, she placed her paintbrush down, and wiped her hands on an old cloth she kept to hand by the canvas. Declan – the handsome and fit artist who had exactly the right amount of tattoos on his upper arms in Maddy's opinion, and who Valerie and Josie couldn't stop swooning over although he was openly gay – was helping out in the gallery today. He swiftly took the bag from Valerie, holding it out to Maddy. She rummaged inside it for her phone, Bruno Mars singing to her. Her handbag wasn't big, but at this moment it felt more like Mary Poppins' carpet bag – she could never find her damn phone or car keys for that matter. However, if she bought a smaller bag, she'd never be able to fit her essentials in it. As Maddy's hand grasped her phone, Bruno Mars stopped singing *Uptown Funk* at her. Entering her four-digit pin, she unlocked her phone's screen and looked at the caller ID. It was her mum and dad's landline number. She frowned and checked the time on her phone. It was ten past three. What could they want? She redialled their number.

'Hello?' Maddy's father picked up after three rings.

'Dad, it's me, Maddy. Did you just call me?' Of course he did, but it might have been by mistake . . . then even that was silly, only mobiles called numbers randomly while in the back of your jeans pocket, or thrown around inside your bag.

'Yes, sorry, Maddy, I don't want to worry you,' her father's tone alone worried her, 'but there's been an accident.'

'Oh my God, Dad, are you all right? Where's mum? The car is only a bit of metal; it can be replaced. Are you two okay?'

'It wasn't a car accident,' Dennis said. Maddy could hear the shaky tone in her father's voice.

'Dad, tell me.' Maddy started to tremble, fearing the worst.

'Your mother had a fall outside her gallery. They think she's broken her leg.'

Relief washed over Maddy momentarily - *bones could mend* - then her panic returned. 'Is she all right? Nothing caused her to fall?' Maddy feared a heart attack or a stroke, but her mother, albeit plump, carried her curves voluptuously in her sixties keeping herself pretty fit. She regularly attended aqua aerobics – as she often reminded Maddy – and took long walks with Dad.

'Other than her leg, she's got some cuts and bruises.'

'I mean, what caused her to fall, Dad? She didn't have a . . .' Maddy couldn't bring herself to ask.

'No, no, nothing like that,' Dennis said, pre-empting his daughter. 'But she's in a terrible state. To be honest, Maddison, I don't know what to do . . . I think I'm in shock.' Her father wasn't a weak man, he always stood his ground, and as children, Edward and Maddy had always avoided angering him, but Dennis did let Sandra think she wore the trousers in their relationship. Possibly for an easier life, but Maddy knew without a doubt that her father loved her mother. She'd always seen how much he cared about her. After all these years, he still held her bags, or her hand, kissed her cheeks and came home with flowers. He always did the little things some took for granted. Love wasn't about grand gestures, it was about the small acts of affection. He showed her, rather than told her. And her father did it every day for her mother.

'Where are you?'

'I'm still at the hospital; they've taken her down for x-rays . . . tests . . . Oh, Maddy . . .'

'Dad, have you rung Edward?'

'I was just about to.'

'Right well, give him a call, but I'm on my way, okay. I'll be with you as soon as I can.'

'Maddy, it's a long way for you to come.'

'It doesn't matter. I'll only worry more here. I need to go home first, grab some things, then I'm coming, okay?'

'You don't have to. I'll be all right.'

'No, I'm coming,' Maddy said. *Try and stop me.* Her mother might drive her mad at times, but she loved her. *And even if her mother didn't need her, her dad did.*

'I didn't want to ask, as I know you're busy.'

'It's fine, the summer holidays are over and I've caught up with a lot of commissions.' Maddy could take a sketchpad and some pencils to draft out future pieces in the quiet moments, if she got any.

After some more reassurance, and her father reiterating she shouldn't rush, and to drive carefully, Maddy put her phone back in her bag. Her mother was safe and well in the hospital; they were keeping her in as a precaution in case she'd incurred any head injuries.

'What's wrong?' Valerie looked aghast having heard half of the conversation. 'You've gone very pale.'

Declan stood beside Valerie frowning, equally concerned. With his arms crossed, his biceps bulged and the Salt Rock vest-top he wore stretched across his pectoral muscles.

Maddy repeated the conversation she'd had with her father to them.

'Well, of course you should go,' Valerie said. 'I'll hold the fort here. I can get Josie in to help more on our busier spells at the weekends.'

'I can help Valerie, too, so don't you worry,' Declan said, giving Maddy a squeeze. He was a wall of muscle, like Harry, only not as tall, and for a brief moment, Maddy missed Harry terribly. The sinewy muscle, his strength, wrapping around her and making her feel safe. 'Oh, you poor thing, of course you should visit your mother.'

Maddy started fussing with the paintbrushes she'd been using.

'Leave them, I'll clean those, you get yourself off,' Valerie said, taking the brushes from Maddy's grasp. Declan moved Maddy's easel so the painting could dry and not be touched by visitors.

'Yes, yes.' Maddy was in a world of her own, thinking about packing, and what time she'd get to Bristol as she gathered up her belongings.

'Maddy, please drive carefully. I'm sure your father said the same.' Valerie looked at her sternly, still holding the brushes.

'Yes, better to get there late, than not at all,' Declan added with a nod.

Valerie gave a chuckle. 'If I know Sandra, she's bossing those poor nurses and doctors about.'

'God help any of them who call her Sandy.' Maddy laughed briefly, Valerie's humour being infectious.

'Yes, that's more like it. Your mother won't want you worrying.' Holding the wet paintbrushes away from Maddy, Valerie leaned in and gave her a kiss. 'Give your mum my love.' She winked. 'Let me know when you've got there, though. Or I'll worry.'

At home, Maddy threw clothes and travel essentials into a suitcase. Anything she'd forgotten she could buy when she was in Bristol, and she knew her mum's bathroom was always stocked with plenty of toiletries. She squeezed a week's worth of clothes and underwear into her case and hurtled down the stairs to be met by a mewing Sookie.

Maddy gave her a whole heap of food, then after putting her luggage in the car, knocked on the door of the house adjoining hers.

'Hi, Mrs Delphine,' Maddy said as the older woman opened the door, her expression softening from wariness to recognition. Mrs Delphine wrapped her cream cardigan around her. 'I'm terribly sorry to bother you, but my mother has had a nasty fall, and I need to go to Bristol for a few days, would you mind feeding my cat, Sookie?'

'Of course, dear. Do you want to come in for a bit?'

'No, no, thank you, I really must get on the road.' Maddy knew she was rambling but couldn't stop herself, anxiety and worry about her mother on her mind. 'I'd have asked Harry, but unfortunately he's AWOL.' *Why did she say that?* She hadn't thought about Harry in weeks, well actually who was she kidding, more like days . . . Had the neighbours noticed they'd been together briefly as a couple? Of course they had. Did they really need to know Harry had disappeared and Maddy didn't have a clue where or why?

Maddy gave herself a mental shake. *Calm down.* She handed the old lady her spare key to the back door and explained where everything was in the kitchen.

'There's a cat flap so she can come and go as she pleases,' Maddy said, waving, walking backwards up the short path – she didn't think it felt right to cut across the lawn. 'I've fed her now, so she'll be all right until the morning. Thank you so much.'

'It's not a problem. I hope your mum recovers quickly.'

'Oh, I'll give you my number, though, in case there is one.' Maddy ran back, rummaging in her bag. She used an old receipt she hadn't cleared out of her purse, found a pen and scribbled her mobile number. Mrs Delphine gave Maddy hers, too. 'Call me if there are any problems.'

After fussing further over Sookie and making sure the bedroom doors were closed, Maddy stood in her kitchen. *Have I got everything?*

'Now be a good girl,' Maddy said to Sookie. *As if she understands.*

As Maddy locked her front door, another fear entered her head. She did not like the idea of leaving her house for long periods of time. It was bad enough each day going off to the gallery. What if it caught fire again?

Could lightning strike twice? And if Harry believed it was arson, could whoever was responsible do it again?

He'd changed the locks on the front door, and the back door was new. It would be much more difficult to break in again. *Stop worrying.*

Maddy threw her bag onto the passenger seat, started the engine, and reversed out of her drive carefully. Not that she needed to worry about Harry's truck parked in the road. He wasn't there. Hadn't been for a month.

Where the hell was he?

Chapter 32

Due to hitting rush-hour traffic on both the A30 and the M5, Maddy's journey to Bristol took over three and a half hours. She hadn't stopped, she'd just kept on driving, intent on getting to her destination, her anxiety keeping her alert and determined. She wouldn't relax until she got to Bristol. *Home.*

She arrived at her parent's house as the sun was setting, although it was obscured behind the Bristol cityscape. She imagined how it would be looking back in Tinners Bay, hovering on the horizon above the ocean, making the sky pink and the water reflecting it. She'd never tire of looking at that view or painting it. The image helped calm her.

Maddy parked her car on the quiet street and looked up at her parent's Edwardian house with its sash windows. This was not Maddy's childhood home. Her mother liked to move every now and then, especially once Maddy and her brother had left school. Sandra would get bored and need a new project. *Poor Dad.* The move to Cornwall for Maddy was stressful. She couldn't understand why her mother would put herself through so much hassle every couple of years. They'd been in this current house for three years, which had been the longest so far. Maybe her mother had found somewhere to settle at last. The house was in Clifton, not far from Sandra's gallery, and she liked to walk to work – it kept her fit. The house was a mid-terrace, with five bedrooms – Lord only knew why her mother needed so many bedrooms at her age, Maddy found it hard enough to clean her small, modern semi-detached house. Admittedly, one of those five bedrooms was Sandra's art studio, something Maddy would love to have in her house. Maybe the low maintenance back garden and the courtyard front garden allowed her mother more time to clean. Although the garden was more her dad's domain.

Maddy's sister-in-law, Clare, answered her parents' door. 'Hello!' she said, pulling Maddy into a hug. 'You made good time then.' Clare was always enthusiastic, wore her heart on her sleeve. They usually had good fun together, like sisters. Maddy didn't need the 'in-law' bit.

'Not really, got stuck in rush-hour traffic.' Maddy dumped her bags on the tessellated tiled floor next to the antique mahogany writing bureau in the hallway and hung up her light denim jacket on the coat hooks above her. Her mother had furnished the house with a mix of modern and antique pieces, in keeping with the era of the house, and it worked. Modern art and classics decorated the walls – her mother had a thing for the human form, especially ballerinas. Some were her own work, some by other artists and some were prints by the likes of Degas. Maybe it explained why Maddy had been forced to attend ballet classes at an early age. She would like to think she had fond memories of ballet, but she didn't – all she could remember was standing still in a ballerina pose in a pink tutu at the age of seven, and her mother getting cross as she tried to capture her daughter on canvas.

'You're here safe, that's what matters.'

'Where are the kids?'

'Both in bed.' Clare gave a massive grin and two thumbs up. This was probably the reason mum had five bedrooms. It allowed her to have her grandchildren over to stay. 'Would you like tea or something stronger?'

'I'd better go and see Mum.'

Clare waggled a finger, like telling off a naughty puppy. 'No, you're on strict instructions not to see her tonight. When Dennis said you were travelling up from Cornwall, she said, in her painkiller-drugged state, she didn't want to see you until the morning – and that was an order!'

'Wow, she knows how to make me feel wanted.'

'It's not that she doesn't want to see you. Apparently, she got quite choked up, but she fears you've travelled so far today already, and will be tired. She'd rather see you tomorrow when she feels better, too.'

'Is she sure?'

'Yes, and to be honest, visiting time will soon be up,' Clare glanced at her watch, 'so you'll be making a mad dash to the hospital to only see her for ten minutes. She's fine, Maddy. She's broken her leg, and we'll help Dennis. I think he was shocked, and panicked.' Clare's last statement made Maddy feel like there was more to the incident, something they weren't telling her. Clare helped herself to things in Sandra's kitchen, knowing her way around it as if it was her own. Maddy watched as she pulled two wine glasses out, and a bottle of rosé from the fridge, the glass frosted with condensation.

'He does love Mum very much.'

'It's beautiful to see. I hope Edward and I are like that twenty years on.' Clare handed Maddy a much-needed glass of White Zinfandel – the name always baffled Maddy considering it was clearly pink.

'I'm not sure you want to turn into my mother.'

Clare chuckled. 'No, silly, I hope Ed and I are as happy as your parents are.'

'I'm sure you will be.' This was Maddy's dream too, but it seemed highly unlikely in her current single state.

'Anyway, your mum isn't so bad. She spoils her grand-children rotten.' Grabbing the baby monitor from the kitchen counter, Clare said, 'Come on, let's move to somewhere more comfortable.'

They made their way up to the first floor and into the lounge – the drawing room as her mother referred to it –

which had two Chesterfield reddish-brown studded leather sofas, with their arms rolling out regally, and a matching armchair. Maddy arranged the scatter cushions behind her back, to give her support on the couch. She always thought the couches looked harder than they actually were, and tended to sink.

This light, airy room with cream walls was filled with more ornaments and pictures hanging from the picture rail. A large patterned rug lay between the sofas covering the wood flooring. Maddy admired the original Edwardian fireplace, with its slate hearth and cast iron grate and surround, and the ornately carved mantelpiece, which was something you didn't get in modern houses anymore. Her own house didn't even have a chimney – the television had become the focal point instead. This was Maddy's favourite room at Christmas with the fire lit and a huge, beautifully-decorated Christmas tree. In the warmer months, her mother placed a tall vase of fresh flowers in front of the grate. Currently, a mix of lilies, gerberas and roses in an array of oranges and yellows perfumed the room.

Although it was now getting dark outside, the room had two large sash windows allowing plenty of light into the room and enabling them to have a fantastic view of parts of Clifton. Maddy relaxed, sinking further into her seat. She'd feel happier once she'd seen her mother, but at least she was close at hand to help her family, and find out what happened.

'Clare, do you know how Mum fell? Where was she?'

'She'd popped out of the gallery for something, and she fell down the small flight of steps leading up to her shop.' Clare sipped her wine, sitting opposite Maddy in the armchair, baby monitor placed on the coffee table beside her. Clare hesitated, then continued, 'She says someone barged past her, or even pushed her, but it was all a blur.'

'Someone pushed her? A mugger?' *In Clifton. The posh part of Bristol.* She knew it wasn't exempt from crime, but even so . . .

'I don't know; she keeps changing her story, almost as if she's protecting someone. She doesn't want the police involved.'

Maddy frowned. She would only get the answers from her mother. She alone knew the actual details of the incident.

Clare and Maddy talked more, changing the subject to Maddy's niece and nephew.

'Izzy will be so thrilled to see her favourite aunty,' Clare said, excitedly.

'Yes, it feels like it's been a while since I last saw them. I've been so busy with the gallery.'

'And a new man, I hear.'

'Um, no . . .' Maddy swallowed. 'That's ended.'

'Oh,' Clare said. 'I am sorry.'

'Don't be. It's nothing. Tell me more about Izzy.' Maddy desperately wanted to change the subject away from Harry.

392

'Oh, yes, she's growing up fast and is at pre-school now. Which allows me more time to spend with Alfie.' As the two women caught up, the time flew, and before they knew it Maddy's father and brother arrived.

'So this is where the party is,' Dennis said, entering the room, followed by his taller and slimmer son. Edward had been blessed with blond hair, less red than Maddy's. Clare got up and kissed her husband, while Maddy hugged and kissed her dad.

'How is she?' Maddy asked.

'Battered and bruised, but the doctors assure us it's nothing to worry about.' Her father dragged a hand through his thinning grey hair. He looked pale and tired but appeared to be putting on a brave face, hiding his worry.

'She'll be back to normal before you know it, Dad.' Maddy squeezed his upper arm. 'Maybe make the most of the peace and quiet for now.' To her relief, her dad chuckled. As they say laugh or cry, and none of them wanted to cry.

After some more small talk, and polishing off a bottle of wine or two between them, Maddy found herself yawning. It always amazed her how driving a long distance could be so tiring. *She'd only been sitting down for over three hours.*

'Let's show you to your room,' Clare said. Edward carried Maddy's bags down to her room. She was in the fifth bedroom-slash-study, on the lower ground floor. 'We thought it made sense to have the room next to the kids and this way you get an en-suite. And the kids can't wake you up too early.'

There were so many levels to this house. How would her mother cope with the stairs with a leg in plaster? Tomorrow they might have to reorganize the sleeping arrangements because there was no way her mother would make it to the top floor of the house where the master bedroom was situated.

'We'll leave you to it. Night, Maddy,' Clare said, closing the door behind her and Edward as they left.

'Good night.'

This room had another large patterned rug over the tiled flooring and an original fireplace. There was a desk in the corner and bookshelves in the recesses either side of the chimney breast, filled with books, as well as a large lipstick-red sofa bed. It had already been pulled out and made up for Maddy. Clare must have been busy while she'd been travelling down.

The room, however, did bring back memories. In the interim period between moving out of their rented accommodation, and buying the house in Cornwall, Maddy and Connor had stayed in this room for a couple of months.

She looked back at those times and gave a shudder. She couldn't imagine Connor being in her life any more. That he was ever in her life felt like a distant dream. Looking back, she could see his faults more clearly and wondered how she'd ever put up with him. He'd been so controlling Maddy was surprised how she'd ever managed to convince him to move to Cornwall. And that he'd let her.

***

Maddy placed the flowers on the cabinet by her mother's hospital bed and sat in the high-backed chair beside her bed. Her father grabbed a plastic chair from the ward and joined them.

Her mother looked worse than Maddy had imagined. She had bruising down one side of her face, where she'd hit the pavement. Now Maddy understood why the doctors had kept her in to monitor if she had a concussion. Her left leg was in a plaster cast and was elevated. Could she even be comfortable like that?

'Hi, Mum, I think I've seen you look better.' Maddy smiled and leaned over to kiss her mum's cheek – the side without the bruising.

Her mother chuckled. 'Well, there was another time when I went skiing – but you hadn't been born then.'

'Is this why I've never had a skiing holiday?' She looked up at her dad, who nodded.

'Absolutely. I told your Dad I was never going again.'

'Yes, that was the worst surprise holiday I arranged. Never again.'

They all laughed, but Maddy was trying not to get upset. *It could have been much worse.*

'So what happened, Mum?' She frowned, her expression sobering.

Sandra gently turned her head from side to side on the pillow. 'I don't know, darling. One minute I was on the top step, then the next I'd fallen.'

'Clare said someone pushed you.'

'Nonsense.'

'Mum, I can tell you're not telling me everything.' She hadn't looked Maddy in the eye once.

'Dennis, dear, could you grab me a cup of coffee, please? Maddy, would you like one?' Sandra looked at her husband earnestly. Maddy knew Sandra wanted to speak to her daughter in private. Even with her bruised face, she could tell.

'Yes please, white no sugar, and see if the nurses have some biscuits. I should have brought some,' Maddy said to her father. Once he was out of earshot, she turned to her mother. 'So?'

'Okay, I was pushed, but he warned me if I said anything he'd hurt you.'

'Me?' Maddy's eyes widened. She couldn't hide her shocked expression. 'I thought it was some mugger. Did you know who did this? Who are you protecting?'

A tear trickled down her mother's bruised cheek. 'I'm not sure I want to get him into trouble, it was probably an accident; he sounded desperate.'

'Who was it?' But Maddy already feared she knew exactly who it was.

Hesitantly, her mother mumbled something inaudible, and when Maddy continued to stare at her, she said quietly, 'Connor.'

'The bastard. I knew it—'

'Shhh . . . Keep your voice down.'

Fuelled by anger, Maddy ignored her mother. 'I had this really horrible feeling. God, maybe Harry was right, maybe he did torch my house.' Rage bubbled inside of her. When she got out of this hospital and she found Connor . . . *God help him*. 'We should tell the police.'

'No!' Sandra tried to sit up but winced. Maddy placed a hand on her arm and eased her back onto the pillow. 'I don't want to make trouble.'

'Mum, he can't do this. I don't want him in my life anymore, and he certainly can't attack my family. Can you identify him? Are you absolutely sure it was him?'

'Who?' Dennis reappeared around the curtain, holding two cups of coffee. He placed them on the table at the end of Sandra's bed. 'What are you two shouting about? We can hear you down the other end of the ward.'

'Nothing, Dennis, love,' Sandra said soothingly.

She wanted to hide this from him. Maddy's dad was a placid man. He wouldn't hunt Connor down – would he? Or did Sandra want to keep things simple, and less stressful for Dennis? But even such an easy-going man might not react well to his wife being pushed down some steps and his daughter being threatened. He might be

Sandra's calming influence, but he certainly wasn't a push-over.

Before Maddy could say anything further, the doctor arrived, pulling the chart up from the end of the bed.

'We'll talk about this later, Mum.'

Chapter 33

'The gallery is fine, you stay with your mum,' Valerie said, on the other end of Maddy's mobile, 'Declan is a dream to work with.'

'I hope you and Josie aren't still lusting over the poor man,' Maddy said with a chuckle.

'Of course not, I'm old enough to be his mother.'

'His nan more like!'

'Cheeky cow, I'm way too young to be a nan.' Valerie scolded, but laughed at Maddy. Her boys hadn't provided her with grandchildren yet. 'Good job you didn't say that to my face.'

'I knew I could get away with saying it because you're over a hundred miles away.'

'In fact, I'll have you know I've become Declan's surrogate mum – he doesn't know it yet, of course.'

Maddy laughed more. 'Well, if you're sure everything is all right, then I'll stay a week or two more. I'm helping mum out at her gallery, and I am doing some painting, too – so I am working.'

'Send my love to your mum, and I'll try to see her soon – probably will have to be after you return.'

'I will. And thanks, Valerie, for everything.'

Maddy was spending the day working in her mother's gallery. A couple of weeks had passed since the accident and by now it was nearly the end of September. She had stayed on in Bristol to help her mother and father. Edward and Clare did what they could, but Ed had to work, and Clare had two young children to contend with, so Maddy was more than happy to pitch in. Ed and Clare had gone back to their home, but they only lived on the outskirts of Bristol in Westbury-on-Trym, so they called in when they could. During the day Maddy would help her mother at the gallery and would stay on if her mother got tired. In the evenings, she would help her father with dinner, and then they would sit in the lounge, nursing a glass of wine, and talking and laughing about the good old days, reliving stories of Maddy and Ed as children, or playing a game of cards, as if it were Christmas. She was enjoying this quality time with her family.

She had been moved out of the fifth bedroom, and into where Clare and Ed had been staying, to allow Sandra to sleep downstairs – because as predicted she was not able to make it up and down the stairs in the house, and this way she did have easy access to a bathroom too. Sandra was getting around rather swiftly on her crutches now. She'd wobbled initially, but her stubbornness and unwillingness to fail had her up and mobile in no time at all. The one time when Maddy had reached to help her, Sandra had snapped, 'I can do it!' And from then on, she had known to let her mother get on with it.

The thing that most annoyed Sandra was that nothing she wore went with her cast and so she wanted to shop for a new wardrobe of clothes. And the fuss she made about shoes! Dennis had talked her out of buying loads of clothes, but today had offered to treat her to a trip to Cabot Circus shopping centre. Maddy had quickly excused herself by saying she'd watch the gallery. She wasn't patient enough to walk round the shops with her mum at the best of times, let alone with her on crutches. Although, her dad did say something about a wheelchair being available.

As she made herself a cup of tea, Maddy reflected that she hadn't managed to tackle her mother about Connor. The police had taken a statement, Maddy and Dennis had wanted the incident noted, but Sandra had insisted she didn't know who her 'attacker' had been. That made it sound even more frightening. But whoever it had been – and Maddy knew full well it was Connor – they hadn't been after her purse or possessions, because they hadn't been taken, making the whole thing sound suspicious.

Maddy made another quick call, this time to Mrs Delphine to check on Sookie, then concentrated her efforts in her mother's gallery. This morning was already busy.

Unlike her gallery, there were no quiet days. Clifton was busy all year round.

***

Harry had driven home yesterday evening, eager to speak with Maddy. He hadn't expected her car not to be on her driveway, yet Sookie had trotted over to welcome him, purring profusely. Now it was the morning, anxiety was creeping in because Maddy still wasn't home. *She can't be still living at the cottage.* He'd waited up until late, too. He dressed, shoved some breakfast down his throat, and rung her doorbell just in case, only to be greeted by a mewing Sookie again. With this, Harry jumped into his pickup and drove straight to Tinners Bay. Surely, she'd be at the gallery? Maybe she'd stayed at Valerie's or a friend's or at the cottage? These thoughts had whirled around his brain most of the night, keeping him from sleeping soundly.

What if she'd moved on and found someone else? It sickened Harry to think this.

As it was still early morning, he drove to Wisteria Cottage first in case Maddy had stayed there. Instead of her car parked outside, he found Simon and Roy standing in the front garden in deep discussion, with the cottage – freshly-painted white and a new lilac front door, no longer looking sorry for itself – standing proudly behind them. *It needs something growing up over the door, to finish it off.*

The two men stopped and stared at Harry as he walked towards them.

'Look who it is, speak of the devil. The wanderer returns,' Simon said, as he scowled and placed his hands on his hips. 'Where the hell have you been?'

'I had urgent matters to attend to. Family business,' Harry said, hoping his excuse would be good enough. He didn't meet Simon's gaze.

'No phone calls, nothing.' Simon looked Harry up and down disdainfully. 'It's not a good way to do business, mate.'

'I know, but to make matters worse I broke my phone.'

Simon muttered under his breath. Harry knew it all sounded like poor excuses.

He turned to Roy, as he couldn't care less about Simon's displeasure. Roy paid him; Simon did not. 'Look, I'm sorry, Roy. I'll get straight back to work, but I need to find Maddy first. Have either of you seen her?' He hated to ask Simon this and even feared the answer.

Roy shook his head, and Simon shrugged his shoulders. 'She moved out a few weeks ago now,' Roy said. He grimaced, looking first at Simon, then gestured to Harry to follow him, so that they walked out of earshot of Simon. His voice was firm but low when he spoke to Harry 'I'm not happy about this, Harry. I nearly had to find another landscaper. Are you back for good?'

'I'm sorry, Roy. I promise I won't let you down. I'll finish the job; I just need to find Maddy first.'

Roy nodded after giving it some thought, and they walked back towards Simon.

'Have you seen Maddy, Simon, or heard from her?' Roy asked this question before Harry could but it sounded better coming from Roy. Simon was likely to give Roy a more honest reply. 'Nah, I haven't seen her for a while actually.' Relief washed over Harry as Simon said these words: at least Maddy hadn't got involved with the builder. 'But then I haven't been down to the gallery,' Simon said.

'Ok, thank you,' Harry said nodding. 'I'll call you tomorrow, Roy.' *I probably have a lot of customers to call tomorrow.*

'OK, Harry.' Roy shook his hand.

With anxiety inching its way up his spine, Harry drove down along the high street, parking his pickup in the beach car park in Tinners Bay. The tide was out, leaving a huge expanse of sandy beach in front of him. He could feel there was a chill in the air, being late September, and October rapidly approaching . . . He'd been away about six weeks, or had it been longer? He'd lost track of time. He could feel that October was around the corner, the sun wasn't getting so high, and he'd have shorter days to work in. He'd have his work cut out, too, raking leaves and clearing dead bedding plants to make room for winter flowers and planting bulbs – that's if he had a business to come back to.

His hands started trembling on the steering wheel. What was he going to say to Maddy? *Other than sorry.*

He knew it wasn't probably the greatest idea to approach Maddy in her gallery, but he didn't want to wait another moment. He had left it too long as it was.

He couldn't bear the thought of losing her, but he had to face facts – he might have lost her already. He would do everything in his power to win her back, though. He wasn't going to give up without a fight. At the very least, he'd rebuild their relationship so they could be friends. He'd explain everything to her. *Everything*. Maddy had a good heart, but did she have a forgiving one?

Taking a deep breath, Harry locked up his truck and headed towards the gallery. There were a scattering of people walking on the beach, some wearing wellies and coats, one holding the hand of a small child, carrying a fishing net and a bucket for a spot of early morning rock pooling, and one family already set up behind a windbreak. Late holiday-makers with very young children, who could take holidays out of term times were Tinners Bay's clientele now. Harry could also make out some surfers, mad enough to brave the waves. There were considerably fewer people about than when he'd last been to Tinners Bay. Then it had been August and the height of the summer holidays, and the village had been bustling from early morning until late evening.

Harry's nerves jangled as he entered the gallery. He was trembling, as if he'd not eaten enough food and his blood sugar levels had dipped. Without having a chance to scan the gallery for Maddy, he was approached by a young man with dark gelled hair and muscular, tattooed arms. A flash of jealousy shot through him, as he feared Maddy had a new boyfriend, but when the guy approached, clearly eyeing him up, his fears vanished.

'Hi, I'm Declan, one of the artists exhibiting here, how can I help you today?'

Yeah, he's definitely looking me up and down! Although Harry wasn't back to his usual level of fitness, he had worked out and got his body back into shape. He stood taller than Declan, too.

'Oh, um, I'm looking for Maddy.' Harry hated sounding so hesitant. But he was thrown, never having met this man before. Then Valerie appeared from the back of the shop, paint brushes and paints in her hand.

'Harry?' she said, her mouth gaping open. Harry froze, waiting for Valerie to say something. She looked like she was trying to find the right words, not the first words that entered her head. She nodded briefly at Declan who immediately grabbed the paints and brushes from Valerie and made himself busy. 'Where have you been?'

Harry ran a hand through his hair and sighed. 'It's a long story, but I've not been well. I'm looking for Maddy.'

'She's not here.' Valerie's stony response took Harry by surprise. She had always been warm and bubbly. *She's protecting Maddy, you fool.*

'I'll explain everything to her, I promise, but I need to see her in order to do that. Where is she?'

406

'Maybe you should have *explained* to Maddy that you weren't well, rather than disappearing off the face of the earth. No messages or phone calls – there's no excuses in this day and age, my boy.' Valerie scowled.

That's me told.

'I wasn't in my right mind . . . Look, I don't want to talk about this here,' Harry said hurriedly, glancing towards Declan. However much he needed to be more open, there were some people who simply didn't need to know his business. Valerie took the hint and gestured to him to walk out the back with her.

She flicked the switch on the kettle. 'Do you want tea?'

'Yes, go on. Thank you.' Not sure if he had a choice, because Valerie was already pulling mugs off the mug tree, and throwing a teabag into each of them, before glaring at him, as if to say, *well go on, I'm listening*.

Harry sucked in a deep breath. Then, breathing out, he told Valerie about Karin's accident, the baby, his PTSD . . . everything. It would be a practice run for when he got the opportunity to talk to Maddy. Harry was grateful that Valerie didn't interrupt him as he spoke. She just nodded and listened.

'I know I should have told Maddy about it all, but it was early days in our relationship, and I was afraid of losing her. Then everything got on top of me, and I thought she was better off without me, so I ran,' Harry said, sipping his tea, now at perfect temperature.

407

Valerie placed a soothing hand on his upper arm. 'Oh, you poor man, this does explain the odd way you just disappeared,' she said, her expression much softer and like the old familiar Valerie now, her earlier hardness gone. 'Doesn't make it excusable, mind, but depression makes people behave in different ways. You should have told her, Harry.'

'I know that now. Where is she? Please, Valerie, I need to see her. She's okay isn't she?' Harry feared the worst — what if something had happened to her, and he'd not been here to help her, to protect her? He'd never forgive himself then.

'Maddy is absolutely fine. She has been in Bristol the past couple of weeks.'

'Why?'

Valerie frowned. 'Her mother had an accident — broke her leg — and Maddy returned to help her family. She's staying there to give them a hand with her mother's gallery. I've told her to take as long as she likes, as it's quieter here and we can manage.'

'Valerie, can you tell me where she's staying. Please . . .? I need to see her.'

'She might not have time for this, Harry.' She remained stern.

'I promise if she tells me to leave, I will. But I need to set things straight. I need to tell her how I feel about her. I can't leave it any longer.'

Valerie crossed her arms, grimacing.

'Please, Valerie, please . . .' *Should he get on his knees? How did he convince her?*

'Okay, okay, I'll write down her parents' address, and the name of the gallery in Clifton, but if she asks you to leave her alone, you do it, OK? Otherwise you'll have me to deal with.'

Valerie grabbed a bit of scrap paper and wrote a Bristol address on it. 'Luckily for you, I know Sandra's address off by heart. And the gallery is Hart Designs, in Clifton. But I don't have the address.' Valerie went to hand Harry the piece of paper, but hesitated. 'Don't make me regret giving you this.'

'You won't!' Harry hugged and squeezed her, giving her a kiss on the cheek. 'Thanks, Valerie, you're a star.'

'Stop it, you're making me blush. And remember, Maddy is like a daughter to me.' She wagged a finger and narrowed her eyes, but her manner was more playful and a lot less cold than when he'd first entered the gallery.

'Thanks for the tea, and for listening.' Harry placed his empty mug in the sink.

'Good luck.'

Back in his pickup, catching his breath, Harry plugged in his sat nav, securing the screen to the windscreen, and programmed it with the postcode Valerie had given him. It told him he had a long journey ahead of him of over two and a half hours.

He knew he should really do the rounds with his customers and make his apologies, but Maddy came first. Harry wouldn't rest until he'd spoken to her.

Chapter 34

Maddy had been rushed off her feet since putting the phone down to Valerie that morning. Her mother ran an art class from her studio. Sandra had trained as a teacher in her day, and when she'd finally had enough of snotty kids, she'd followed her passion and her dream of owning a gallery. The class allowed adults to come along and work on pieces of their own, or Sandra would set up a still life subject, which they could draw, paint, or use any medium they liked to recreate it. Out the back of her gallery, she had a small studio equipped with easels, which comfortably accommodated ten people. Maddy thought it was a good way of generating a regular income and wondered if she could do the same in Tinners Bay during the quieter winter months.

Broken leg or not, Sandra had insisted these classes go ahead as usual. One was on a Wednesday evening, for those who worked full-time, and there were two held during the day, one on a Tuesday afternoon and one on a Thursday morning – which was today – aimed more at retired folk or shift workers, enabling them to continue an interest, mix with like-minded fellow artists, and encourage one another with their art.

'A lot of them only make time in this two-hour session a week to paint. They'd be devastated if I cancelled it, darling. I can hobble around for two hours, with your help.'

Maddy had been in charge of setting the room up. She was getting to know some of the attendees better, and they helped with the set up if they arrived early enough. She had been obliged to bite her tongue a few times at her mother, though.

'Maddison, move the terracotta pot a bit further to the right. That's it, perfect. And that yellow vase, yes, just over a bit.' Her mother had been lucky she hadn't thrown it on the floor and smashed it. She closed her eyes, taking a deep breath, and counted to three. *Why couldn't she not interfere?* OK, it was her mum's class, but as she was on crutches, Maddy had hoped Sandra would let her use her own initiative. She was an artist too, after all.

Maddy enjoyed the silence and focus of these sessions, broken only by the occasional bit of chatter between the class members, encouraging each other, or her mother advising a student about how to improve their picture. But otherwise, all you could hear was the sound of the brushes against the paper, the application of paint. It was so quiet you could almost hear the concentration. No music played in the background. Maddy had suggested tuning the radio to a classical music station, but Sandra had said she'd once asked her students if they wanted any background music, and they all preferred silence.

Now the class was over, her dad had collected her mum from the gallery, leaving Maddy in peace to tidy up. With no energy in her limbs and her brain in a fog, she felt emotionally and physically tired today, and it wasn't even one o'clock. Her mother, unintentionally, was draining at the best of times, let alone with her leg in plaster. Maddy was reminded why she'd moved to Cornwall. Even though the class was over, the gallery remained open until five-thirty – closing time. She refilled the coffee pot to make a fresh brew. Another idea she'd steal off her mum. There was room in her little kitchen area back in her own gallery for a coffee machine by the kettle. Sandra liked to offer coffee to her regular customers, however today, Maddy intended to drink the whole pot by herself – she needed the caffeine. She yearned to sit in a corner and read a book, or sketch out her next idea for a painting, but no such luck. Maddy wondered how her mother even found the time to paint. The shop had been busy all day with people, passers-by calling in to peruse the art. In between customers, she took bites of the tuna sandwich her dad had made her, washing it down with coffee, hoping she wouldn't get indigestion.

***

Sitting outside Maddy's parents' home in his pickup, Harry wondered if he'd been in too much of a rush to get here. He was over two and a half hours from home and was woefully unprepared. He hadn't brought anything with him. A change of clothes and a toothbrush might have been a good idea. Not that he expected to be put up by Maddy's family, but he might not be travelling back to Cornwall today. His stomach was starting to growl with hunger. He should have picked up more than a bottle of water and a flapjack from the motorway services. He'd knocked on the door earlier, but no one was home. Harry snoozed in the front seat, the long journey having taken its toll. He could murder a cup of coffee, but like a stakeout, he didn't want to leave his post in case he missed Maddy.

A car pulled up outside the house, waking Harry from his nap. The silver BMW faced him so that the passenger door opened onto the pavement. The driver, a man in his sixties, helped his passenger out of the car. It had to be Maddy's mother – she had her lower leg in plaster and was being helped up on to the crutches. Harry could see her resemblance to Maddy; she had the same blonde hair with hints of coppers and reds — although at her age it was probably coloured now, rather than natural — twisted up into some chignon. (*If that's what you called it.*) Considering the cast, the woman was smartly dressed.

Harry stepped out of his truck and came to the aid of

the man, who seemed to be struggling. He assumed he was Maddy's father.

'Dennis, stop fussing, I can do it,' the woman said, batting her husband's hands away.

'Here, let me help,' Harry said, holding out his hand to the woman.

He could see the woman hesitate, about to insist she didn't need any help, but with one look at Harry she took his hand and said, 'Oh, thank you, dear.' The man trying to help the woman definitely rolled his eyes and mumbled something inaudible under his breath.

Once the woman was stable on her feet, Harry let go of her.

'Dennis, can you fetch my handbag, please?' she said, and the man obliged, leaning into the passenger foot-well, retrieving the bag. He closed the door, pressed a button on his key fob and the car beeped and locked.

'Well, thank you for your help,' the woman said, and started to head up to her house on her crutches.

'Um.' Harry paused, and the two people turned and frowned at him. 'Are you Mr and Mrs Hart?'

'Yes, we are,' Mrs Hart replied, her plastered leg hovering. Harry thought he had better be quick before the poor woman got tired or lost her balance.

'I'm looking for Maddy.' Both looked at him suspiciously now, obviously trying to work out whether they knew him or not.

'Why?' It was Mr Hart who asked.

Because I'm in love with her.

'I'm Harry, her next door neighbour.'

'Oh, God, please don't tell me something else has happened to her house.' Mrs Hart leaned on to her husband for support.

'No, no, no, nothing's happened to her house,' Harry said, also moving to aid Maddy's mother. 'It was perfectly fine when I left this morning. No . . . I'm not sure how much she's told you.' *Oh, God what had she told them?* 'But, well, we had a thing going on—'

'You were romantically involved,' Maddy's father said, raising his eyebrows.

'Yes, and then I did something so stupid.'

'Like disappeared.' Mrs Hart scowled. 'Yes, she's mentioned some of it, but not much. Enough, though.'

Harry heaved a sigh, clearly Maddy's mother disapproved of him. He'd hurt Maddy; he knew that. And lost her trust, possibly for good. 'Yes, and I need to see her to tell her the truth.'

'And to apologise, I hope.'

'Sandra, let the man speak. You can see he's having a difficult time here,' Maddy's father said, tapping the arm he supported with his other hand.

'Yes, and to apologise. I explained to Valerie this morning, and she gave me your address. I need to see Maddy to explain everything to her. Please, Mr and Mrs

Hart, if she wants nothing to do with me, I promise to leave.'

'What do you think, Sandra?' Mr Hart turned to his wife. 'He did help Maddy after her house fire, so I don't think he's a completely bad egg.'

Sandra huffed. 'All right, but if you hurt my little girl again, you'll pay. She's working at my gallery, Hart Design . . .' Sandra gave Harry directions and an idea of the best places to park. Clifton could be incredibly busy, she warned.

After they'd introduced themselves properly, Harry said, 'Thank you, so much.' He kissed Sandra on the cheek and shook Dennis' hand. He had so far convinced Valerie and Maddy's parents. But could he convince Maddy to trust him again?

Chapter 35

Harry found the gallery in Clifton, and as he drove by he caught a glimpse of Maddy, which sent his heart racing inside his chest. The swish of a strawberry blonde ponytail and a petite figure. It had to be her.

He wasn't sure if he was trembling due to the fear of facing Maddy or the fact he was hungry. Once he'd parked his truck, which took longer than anticipated, he decided to grab something to eat from a nearby bakery. They had high stools and a counter in the front window, so he sat inside, eating his freshly prepared chicken and salad sandwich with a generous helping of mayonnaise, and a cup of coffee for energy. However impatient he was to face Maddy, and the consequences of his actions, he needed to eat first. When he stopped shaking and his sugar levels had returned to normal, he made his way to the gallery on foot. Having never been to Bristol before, he tried to take in landmarks and notable shops, so he'd be able to retrace his steps back to the truck.

Unfortunately, as he got closer to the gallery and could see the overhanging sign saying 'Hart Design', his nerves started up again. The trembling had been nothing to do with a lack of food after all.

***

Maddy heard the bell on the shop door jingle. 'I'll be there in a minute.' She finished washing the soap off her hands, wiped them dry then entered the main gallery to greet her customer. She'd sent Angel, the member of staff helping today, off for a break.

'Hello, can I help . . .'

Maddy stood stock still, frozen on the spot. Her body reacted very differently to how she thought it would upon seeing this man. She'd been filled with anger, and wanting to say some choice words. But all she felt now was fear.

Connor.

'What do you want?' Maddy said, scowling. She wiped her hands on the back of her skinny jeans, to check the back pocket. *Phew, her phone was there.*

'I need to talk to you, Maddy.' Connor hadn't looked great when he'd turned up at her gallery in the summer, but today he looked even worse. His face looked a little bloated, and his eyes were bloodshot as though he hadn't slept. His hair needed a cut, too, his brown fringe being flicked out of his eyes as if he had a twitch. In fact he looked, quite frankly, a mess with his unshaven jawline and baggy clothes. What had she seen in this man? Of course, those were the days when he'd had a good job, and rolled up suited and booted. He'd dressed to impress; Maddy realised now. It hadn't lasted long, though. Connor had found it difficult to keep up the pretence that he was a successful, hardworking guy.

Connor made to take a step towards her, but she stepped back, holding up her hands. 'You stay where you are!'

'I'm not going to hurt you.' His eyes widened. 'I love you; I'd never hurt *you*.'

'Really? Am I safe? Or were your threats to my mother true?' She brushed her hand over her phone in her pocket again for reassurance. Just in case she needed it.

'What threats? I would never hurt you, Maddy.' Connor dashed towards her, and fear froze her to the spot. 'I love you.' Connor placed his hand to her cheek. She jerked away, slapping his hand aside.

'Don't touch me! Connor, you pushed my mother down those very steps.' She pointed out the front door. Through the glass, the concrete steps could be seen. Sadly, no one stood on them wanting to enter. She really needed someone to walk into the empty gallery right now.

Connor sniggered, shaking his head. 'Did she say that? She has no proof. She just tripped, she's an old woman.'

'Oh, you saw it happen, did you? And that's why you made threats about hurting me?'

Connor's face hardened. He actually looked menacing, a

cold expression on his face. 'I said that so she wouldn't call the police on me.'

'So you did push her?'

'No!' Connor shouted. With a shaking hand, she pulled out her phone. 'What are you doing?'

'I'm calling the police.' Her hand was still shaking, and her ears were buzzing. She needed to concentrate. Even with the phone locked she could still dial 999. *Calm down.*

Connor leapt forward, making a grab for the phone. Maddy turned, and he shoved her roughly into a painting on an easel. It crashed to the floor.

'Hey!' Maddy heard a male voice. In all the commotion, she hadn't heard the front doorbell ring. She turned, heart pounding, ears ringing, phone still in her hand ready to dial, to see the back of a much larger man, a man with short black, wavy hair easily restraining Connor.

***

Five minutes earlier, Harry strolled up the street, gallery in sight, heart quickening, with still no idea as to what his first words to Maddy should be. Would she even listen to him? His stomach flipped as he watched a man climb the steps and enter the gallery. He wasn't sure, but it looked like the guy had peered through the window first. *Maybe he was checking if it was open.* But Harry thought the guy's demeanour looked suspicious, so quickened his step, then slowed as he rationalized his thoughts. He was probably being over anxious about everything, and if the guy was in there to look at the art, it meant Maddy would be busy, and wouldn't need him entering right now. And he still hadn't figured out what he was going to say to her.

Listen to what I've got to say, and if you still don't want me around, I'll go.

Or words to that effect.

For fear of Maddy spotting him before he wanted her to, Harry kept to one side but was able to peer into the gallery window to see if it was busy. It had white, curved sash windows, either side of the front door, allowing him to stand at the edge and watch. Some paintings on easels obscured his view so he couldn't see the man so well, but he could see Maddy. The sight of her filled Harry with hope. He had missed her so much.

Maddy's whole body language wasn't right. She seemed hesitant, even scared of the man. Was he a new boyfriend, had they had a row? Harry's heart sank, and his fears worsened when he saw the man tenderly reach out and touch Maddy's cheek. But when she slapped the hand away, her face reddening with anger, Harry battled with himself whether to step in.

Great, he wants to talk calmly with her, and this is happening. Would she appreciate the interference? Only get involved if he tries to hurt her.

'Shit!' As soon as the man made his lunge, Harry flew

up the steps, through the door, and seized the man, shouting, 'Hey!' Harry easily towered over him, but then he towered over most men. Harry was stronger too.

'Leave the lady alone, okay?' He gripped the guy by his T-shirt, his fist underneath his chin. He recognised him; his face was familiar, but he couldn't place where he had seen it before. His back was to Maddy; he could sense she was staring at him, her eyes burning into his back.

This was not how he'd planned to apologise.

'Harry? Is that you?'

Harry turned, and tried to smile. 'This isn't exactly the entrance I intended to make. What did this guy want?'

The man struggled to get free. Maddy's eyes widened and she screamed. Harry certainly didn't want this turning into a fight.

Then it dawned on Harry – he'd seen the guy before outside Maddy's house. It was Connor.

'I'll let you go when I know you're not going to hurt anyone, especially Maddy,' he said, narrowing his eyes at the man, who seemed to be going redder by the minute. Harry wasn't sure if it was anger or whether he was pressing on the guy's windpipe. Fortunately for Connor, Harry's medication kept him composed, otherwise it would have been like being in the grip of the Incredible Hulk. Harry thought it best not to quote, '*you wouldn't like me when I'm angry.*' He didn't want to enrage this weasel any further.

'Don't break anything in this gallery. My mum will go spare. Take him outside.'

Maddy opened the door and Harry shoved Connor out onto the pavement. He cursed, trying to turn and square up to Harry, but Harry stood outside the door, on the top step, towering even more over the little prick, arms on his hips, blocking his way.

Just try it, mate.

'Let me talk to Maddy,' Connor said, fists clenched and his breathing heavy.

Maddy squeezed past Harry and stood in front of him. 'You've said enough, Connor.'

Harry scrutinised Connor's face. 'Maddy,' Harry looked her in the eye, 'I'm sure this is the guy who was outside your house the day someone started the fire.'

Maddy glared at Connor. 'Was it you? Did you do it?'

'I'm sorry, Maddy, I was desperate. I wanted you to come home to Bristol, to me,' Connor said. Harry clenched his fists; he didn't trust this guy. Did he really believe burning her house down would have made her want him back? He hoped Maddy wouldn't fall for this shit, but now Connor was making a confession, Harry wanted him to keep talking. 'It was only supposed to scare you when you came home. I didn't mean it to destroy your kitchen.'

'Scare me?' Before Harry could hold her back, Maddy was running down the steps towards Connor, red with anger, her whole body tense, screaming into Connor's face.

'Oh, it scared me all right. I thought I was going to lose my home. You bastard!' She slapped Connor hard. If there hadn't been passing traffic, the sound would have echoed off the buildings. After the initial moment of shock, Connor removed his hand from his face, where a red mark scorched.

'You bitch.' He lunged at Maddy, and Harry launched himself in between them.

'Leave her alone.' Harry managed to control his anger – he wanted to pummel the man's face and let all his own frustrations out – but instead tried to get him to the ground, but the weasel was quicker, fuelled with a new hatred and anger.

'Who the fuck are you anyway? Mind your own business,' Connor targeted his anger at Harry now.

'I'm Maddy's neighbour,' Harry said, standing firm, determined to remain in between this man and Maddy. 'I'm the one who spotted your pyromaniac antics.'

'Why are you here now?'

Harry's eyes narrowed and brought his face level with Connor's. 'It's none of your business.'

Harry should have known better, but he couldn't resist prodding Connor on his breastbone. Connor growled then lunged at Harry, his fist catching him in the mouth.

This brought Harry's own loathing and rage hurtling to the surface, the medication no longer keeping him calm. He wanted to get angry and take it out on this arsehole. He could hear Maddy, but her words were dream-like and went over his head.

'Break it up, you two.' Harry could feel arms around him, restraining him, and as if giving him the mental shake he needed to bring him back to the here and now, this planet. Everything refocused. Two police officers were separating him and Connor. Maddy was trying to tell them Connor was at fault.

'He's an ex-boyfriend, but he pushed my mother down those steps . . . and he tried to burn my house down.' Tears streamed down her flushed face, frantically using the back of her hands to wipe them away. 'I hate you,' she spat at Connor.

'I'm cool. I was protecting the lady.' Harry shrugged off the officer, holding his arms up, all the fight leaving him. He touched his lip, and blood was on his fingertips.

The officer who'd seized him held out a tissue. 'Sounds like you were in the right place at the right time, Sir.'

While the two police officers restrained Connor and read him his rights, on the other side of the street, they'd gained an audience.

'Who called the police?' Harry said, quietly, more to himself.

'I did. In the gallery,' Maddy answered, keeping her gaze on Connor. 'That bastard hurt my mother. He is going to pay for it.'

'He's the reason her leg is broken?'

'Yes.' Maddy finally looked at him, her eyes bloodshot from crying and her face puffy. He wanted to reach out and touch her, hold her, but didn't know if he had the right. 'How do you know about my mother?'

'I went to your parents' house first, and they told me you were here.'

'They never should have sent you here, but in some way . . .' She looked back at Connor, and they both watched him being pushed inside the back of a police car. 'I'm glad they did.'

'Maddy, I'm so sorry . . .'

'No, Harry. Not now. I can't do this now.'

'But we need to talk.' He reached for her hand, but she pulled it away. Tears welled in her eyes once more, and he watched her swallow them back.

'Do we? Thank you for your help today, but I can't let you hurt me again.'

A police officer approached Maddy and started talking to her about making a statement. Harry watched, cold fear creeping into his heart and spreading through his body. Pain rose in his throat, tightening his windpipe, as if he couldn't breathe.

He'd lost her.

Chapter 36

Maddy shut the gallery door behind her and turned the sign to 'closed'. Her mother would understand the need for an early closure. She'd left Harry on the pavement dejected. She tidied the gallery, moving a couple of display easels back into place, standing up the one that had been knocked over, her hands still shaking with the shock and adrenaline coursing through her. The police would be in touch. Connor would be charged and pay the penalty for his actions. This reassured Maddy — he would no longer be able to hurt her or her family. She would phone her parents once she had gathered her thoughts to let them know what had happened today. But why did she still feel so terrible?

Harry.

Had she sounded ungrateful? She hoped not. He'd saved her, been a true hero – yet again.

Seeing him again — his dark wavy hair, the dimple in his chin, his towering build and those sincere blue eyes

— had all come as such a shock. Her memories were distorted. He was even more gorgeous in the flesh than she'd remembered, during all those weeks she'd clung to his memory. The heat and scent that radiated from him she'd totally forgotten, being so busy with her family. During the incident with Connor, she hadn't really had the time to process her surprise at seeing Harry again. Connor's actions had spun all rational thoughts out of her mind.

Maddy couldn't stop the tears from falling. Like all her feelings — hate, love, disappointment, trust, fear — her anger could be held in no more. *It's just shock.* She didn't know what to do for the best. If she pushed Harry away now, would she regret it? But could she trust him not to hurt her again?

She should at least listen to what he'd got to say. She might regret never knowing his side of the story, why he'd disappeared. They would eventually have to live opposite one another again, be neighbours. She liked answers, the truth. It had been eating away at her the past few weeks why he'd left, where had he gone . . . the not knowing. Only the past couple of weeks with her mother had stopped these thoughts. But they still crept in occasionally, when she was left on her own, when it was quiet . . . or when she went to bed. She would lie there, churning over her thoughts, speculating about what had caused their separation. If she didn't speak to him, she would continue to dwell on it for months to come.

'Why has the door got the 'closed' sign on it?' Angel walked into the gallery, returning from her lunch break, confusion on her face. 'Oh, what's happened? You look terrible!' Maddy tried to wipe her face with some tissues she'd grabbed out of a box by the till, and blew her nose.

'There's been an incident. If you don't mind, I'm going to go home. I need to see my parents. We've caught the man who pushed my mother down the steps.'

'Oh, God, I've missed all the action. Look, you go, I can lock up. Sandra sometimes leaves me to it on quieter days.'

'Are you sure?' Maddy's earlier tiredness was nothing compared to how she felt now – physically and mentally exhausted, all energy drained from her. One way or other, the gallery was closing. Maddy didn't have the strength to stand on her feet for much longer. She needed to go home, to bed, but not before she had filled her parents in about today, though.

'Yes, go. I'll even open up tomorrow.'

'Thank you.' Out of habit, Maddy checked her mobile. She'd got used to it being quiet since Harry had left, so was surprised to see a text. It was from Harry.

Maddy, please let me tell you my story. Afterwards, if you want nothing more to do with me, I will just be your neighbour and friend. Love H x

***

431

In the cab of his truck, Harry sat and stared at his phone on the dash, willing it to message him back, drumming his fingers on the steering wheel. He'd even turned it off and on again, in case it had lost signal. Sometimes phones did that. No message from Maddy arrived, but then she could be busy in the gallery. He'd moved the truck out of Clifton to near the Clifton Downs where it was free to park.

Should he drive back to Cornwall or find a hotel here in Bristol? Would he need to give her more time? He could drive to her parents and wait for her there . . . but would that make her angrier? Hell, he didn't want to turn into Connor, becoming obsessive and a stalker. But he wanted Maddy to know how he felt about her – without looking like a weirdo. If he chased too much, she could run away for good, but if he didn't do enough, then would she think he wasn't really interested?

Had he put enough in the text message? Should he have told her he loved her?

Harry thumped the steering wheel, yanked open the truck door, then slammed it and kicked the tyre, yelling out in frustration. It echoed down across the green open space. He startled an older woman, walking past the houses on the other side of the road, who put her head down and quickened her step, pulling her coat around her tighter.

'Sorry!' Harry called out to the woman. But she ignored him and carried on, still faster.

Harry didn't know what to do. He knew this was like a

giant fork in his life. Would his actions take him in the right direction?

Whatever's meant to be is meant to be.

Right?

He so badly wanted Maddy to be *meant to be.*

He hated his PTSD; he hated that he'd fled and not faced Maddy. What if he'd irretrievably fucked this up? Harry wanted to punch something, anything . . . anger and frustration building back up inside of him. But he'd learnt a long time ago – the hard way – that punching immovable objects like brick walls or trees (as he was surrounded by some) hurt, and adding a broken hand to his problems would not help his current situation in the slightest. Especially as, if everything else failed, he needed to get back to his landscaping business.

His phone started ringing. He couldn't hear it from outside of the truck, but he could see it flashing in its phone cradle on the dashboard. The caller ID said Maddy. In his frantic movement to get to it, pulling open the door, he clumsily dropped the phone as he snatched at it. Harry let out another yell of frustration as he fumbled for the phone in the foot-well. *Nothing was going right. Nothing.* By the time he answered, it had rung off; she'd gone to voicemail. He didn't want to know if she'd left a message or not, he just dialled the number back. To his relief, it rang. She answered quickly.

'Harry?'

'Yes, sorry, didn't get to the phone in time. You called me?' Harry winced. He couldn't string his words together. What did he say? Fear gripped him: he mustn't say the wrong thing.

'Yes, yes . . . where are you?'

'In my truck, parked on Clifton Down.' He sat back down behind the steering wheel. 'I don't know whether to drive home or not. I don't know what to do for the best, Maddy.'

'Neither do I. Look, stay where you are, I'll come find you.'

'Okay.' Harry nodded, not that Maddy could see it. Some relief rippled through him that he hadn't left for Cornwall. Maddy wanted to talk.

'See you in ten minutes.'

Harry slipped his phone into his pocket, and stood outside his truck, watching the traffic, waiting for her. His body tensed. Thoughts went round and round in his mind. What to say, how to say it . . . This was it; this was the crucial fork in the road of his life. Would Maddy be going with him, or going the other way, alone?

***

Maddy hoped the police wouldn't contact her parents before she got home, but however tired and terrible she felt, she needed to speak to Harry. Since she'd walked back into the gallery and left him on the pavement, he was all she could think about. The sadness in his expression, when she'd brushed him aside, haunted her. He'd come all this way too, to find her, to speak to her. He had saved her from Connor. She should give him this time. She'd be lying to herself if she said she didn't want to know why he'd disappeared. Of course she wanted answers.

As she drove, the Downs were on her left, so she kept an eye out for Harry's truck. She spotted it not that far along, and she saw Harry standing outside, waving at her. Unfortunately, she couldn't park next to him and had to drive a couple of hundred yards until she found a parking space. A quick check in the vanity mirror in her overhead sun visor showed her she didn't look like she'd been crying anymore. Ideally, she would have liked to have put some more make-up on because she was conscious she did look a mess. Rummaging in her handbag, she found her hair-brush, and gave her hair a quick brush through, tidying her ponytail. Surely, she should have done this at the gallery? As she put the brush back, she spied a lip-gloss, so hastily applied some.

After a deep breath, and a check in her wing mirror, Maddy hurried out of her car and shut the door, locking it. She stepped across the grass verge and onto the path and headed towards Harry, who was walking towards her.

'Hey,' she said as she met him.

'Hey.'

'Let's walk this way.' Maddy pointed to where the path

forked through some trees. 'There's a bench around the corner.'

'Okay, I'll follow you.' He gestured with his hand.

They walked silently for a while. It was awkward. *What should they say, where did they begin?* Then Maddy remembered earlier events and how Harry had come to her rescue.

'Look, I'm sorry about earlier. I don't know if I conveyed it to you properly, but I was very grateful for you stepping in with Connor.'

'I wasn't going to stand by and let him hurt you, Maddy.'

'I know.' She'd never felt unsafe with Harry. From the day he'd thrown her over his shoulder, he'd done everything in his power to make her feel safe, protected.

It seemed odd walking side by side and not holding Harry's hand, or even linking an arm through his. She missed the closeness too, longing to touch him. But would it be a show of weakness? She hadn't decided yet what she would do. Maybe he knew not to impose on her boundaries, as he had his hands tucked into his jeans pockets, looking awkward and tense as he walked. Maddy held the strap of her handbag slung over her shoulder. Yes, he was an attractive man, yes she fancied him like crazy, but he'd hurt her, and was capable of doing it again. She would listen to what he had to say before she made any decisions. It wasn't as if she hadn't had enough practice listening to bullshit. Connor had given her a qualification in it. NVQ level 3 in bullshit detecting.

The trees cleared and they came out onto a small green, the path continuing around, with a spectacular view of the Clifton Suspension Bridge. To Maddy's relief, the bench on the corner was empty, and she gestured for Harry to head towards it. With the blue sky and a scatter of clouds like white candyfloss, it really was a spectacular sight.

'Wow,' Harry said. 'Impressive view.'

'Yes, Bristol's landmark,' Maddy said. 'Paris has the Eiffel Tower; Bristol has the Clifton Suspension Bridge. Not sure if anyone actually proposes here, though.'

Harry chuckled. Maddy sat down on the bench while Harry walked over to survey the view. Up by the fence, you could look down into the Avon Gorge and across to the city. She let him take his time, sensing he had something big to tell her. He had been quite closed off to her about some areas of his past. When she came to think about it, she realised she knew relatively little about him.

Harry finally strolled towards her, his lips pursed together, a determined expression on his face. Then her mobile phone rang.

'Shit.' Unzipping her bag, she grabbed her phone and saw it was her mother. 'Sorry, I'd better take this, it's Mum,' she said to Harry. He showed no disappointment in his expression, only concern. 'Hi, Mum.'

'Where are you, darling? I called the gallery and Angel said you'd come home. But you're not back, so now I'm worried. What happened at the gallery? Angel said some

437

man attacked you. Was it Harry? I feel wretched because I told him where the gallery was—'

'No, it wasn't Harry. It was Connor, Mum. Look, I'm with Harry now. I was coming home, I'm so exhausted, but I needed to talk to Harry first. Then I will come home and tell you all about it. Connor is with the police.'

'That scoundrel.' Sandra started off on one of her rants. Maddy pulled the phone away from her ear, rolling her eyes at Harry, who smiled, trying to make light of what was really a serious situation.

'Mum! Mum, we'll talk when I get home. But I can assure you I am safe, okay?'

'Okay, dear. Maybe you should have called your mother first, though?'

'Yes, yes, sorry.' Maddy felt fifteen again. Did her mother not realise she was twenty-seven?

Maddy switched off her mobile to prevent any more disturbances and placed it in her handbag. Harry took a seat beside her, but there was still distance between them. She sat on one end of the bench, and he on the other. How had they drifted so far apart?

Chapter 37

Harry took a deep breath, Maddy looking patiently at him. How did he tell her this without sounding bonkers?

'I suppose I'll start from the beginning, or maybe with the tablets in my bathroom cabinet.'

Maddy shifted her body towards him, placing her handbag on her lap. 'Go on.'

'I suffer from PTSD – Post-Traumatic Stress Disorder.' He always assumed he needed to explain the abbreviation.

'I thought only soldiers got that?' She frowned.

'No, apparently anyone can – anyone who is subjected to a deeply shocking or life-threatening incident can be affected. My PTSD is due to an accident that happened a couple of years ago when I was still in the fire service – although I wasn't on duty at the time. God, this is so hard to tell you – I don't want you thinking I'm some nut job.'

'I don't. Tell me, Harry.'

'Okay, okay . . .' Harry rubbed his palms along his jeans,

439

already starting to feel the perspiration. 'Karin, my girlfriend, was involved in a traffic incident. I was first on the scene. I'd worked a late shift, but we'd been on a job and couldn't leave until the day crew turned up to take over, and then by the time I'd chatted with my colleagues and left the yard, it was nearly ten a.m. I'd been in no rush to get home; I thought Karin would be at work. We worked four days on and four days off, and so that had been my last shift.' Maddy nodded, looking intently at Harry.

'Anyway . . .' Harry's hands shook. Reliving this memory again, and retelling it always made him tremble. For a moment he feared he wouldn't get the words out, or he'd freeze up. But he had to tell Maddy the truth. All of it. 'The road wasn't busy – rush hour was over – and Karin had hit an oncoming articulated lorry—'

'Oh, shit.'

'She was trapped inside the car. I was travelling the same way as the lorry on a straight road heading out of Exeter – we lived a few miles from Exeter – so I saw it happen.' Harry remembered as if it were yesterday the crash unfolding a few hundred yards in front of him. The lorry's break lights, smoke from the tyres, a car – metal and glass spraying – spinning and jamming up against the lorry. 'I didn't realise it was her car until I stopped and ran to the scene of the crash. I'm a fireman, that's what I do. I help people.'

'That's what you did the time we were coming back from Truro.'

Harry nodded, remembering his fear that it could be an accident, and his relief the car had only broken down.

'Anyway, she was conscious, apologising, and I promised I'd get her out. I was talking to her the whole time making sure she stayed awake. But she was trapped by the dashboard. The impact had crushed everything down, trapping her. Her driver's door was wedged up against the side of the lorry's trailer, and I couldn't get to her from the passenger side. I had nothing to cut her out with. Nothing. The airbags had deployed, there was a toxic smoke emitting from the vents – it was choking me and her. I had already dialled 999 – someone else may have in the traffic too – but I knew the response time. I checked on the lorry driver; he kept saying she came out of nowhere.' Tears welled in Harry's eyes. Although the events of that day were usually blurred, he could remember them now as clear as day. 'A couple of other people helped with him – because of the smoke emitting from Karin's car, I told them to get the driver out if they could but with minimal movement. He only suffered cuts and bruises in the end.' Harry looked Maddy in the eye. 'I couldn't save her, Maddy, I couldn't save her.' Tears fell, wetting his cheeks. 'I failed. She died, carrying our baby, she was four months pregnant.' On that day his whole future had been wiped out in a split second.

'Harry, it's not your fault.' Maddy placed her hand on his knee. Her eyes glistened.

'I promised her. I promised her I would look after her

and our baby. The crew turned up, ambulances, but the car burst into flames. They told me she was already dead before the fire started.' Harry remembered the fire crew dragging him away from the car, two crew members holding him back, restraining him as he screamed Karin's name, as he watched his future burn in front of him. For a moment, he gathered his thoughts, aware Maddy had taken his hand and squeezed it.

'I'm so sorry, Harry.'

Harry breathed deeply, filling his chest with air, and wiped his face as he looked out at the beautiful view ahead of him. Blue sky and sunshine, a mild autumnal day, some of the leaves on the trees were beginning to turn from their lush green to their yellows, golds and reds.

'Once deemed fit to return to work, I realised every incident, the smell of fire, was a trigger. I got flashbacks, nightmares. I transferred from Exeter to sleepy, quieter Cornwall in the hope a change of scenery was maybe all I needed. But again, although big incidents happened less frequently I'd arrive at RTC's—'

'RTC's?'

'Road traffic collisions – I'd arrive and freeze. I was no good to anyone, in fact, I was more likely to get someone killed than save someone. So I left the fire service and concentrated on landscape gardening which I'd been doing on the side anyway – you need something to do on those four days off.' It had started with him helping his dad in the early days, but when he moved to Cornwall he decided to set up his own landscape gardening firm. 'I could build up the business, increase my customer base, and commit to bigger jobs. And that's when I moved to Annadale Close.'

'And so what happened between us was a result of your PTSD?'

'Maddy, I try to manage it as healthily as I can. I stay active, exercising regularly, and the gardening is a great stress reliever, too. My doctor actually encouraged this route for me. I'm on medication too, to help me sleep, keep me happier, but then your house caught fire . . . which I handled . . .'

'I kind of wish it hadn't,' Maddy said.

'Well, no, but we started getting close because of it, and I was afraid to fall in love again because I feared I would lose you like I lost Karin, and when you joked about getting pregnant, it was like pushing me over the edge. I panicked. I'd never thought I'd meet someone else and feel like I did again. I'm sorry. It's not your fault. And if anything, I've learnt these past weeks I can't bear to be without you. Leaving you didn't make me happier, it made me more miserable. I thought you'd be better off without me . . . and maybe you are?' He glanced across to her, realising he'd been staring out across the Gorge.

'Why didn't you call me?'

'When I left I was in a very dark place. You have to remember I wasn't thinking straight either – I'd decided you were better off without me. And in my frustration, I broke my phone.' Throwing it across a room hadn't been one of his brightest moves. 'When I realised my mistake, I had left it too long. What I had to say couldn't be said over the phone or in a text message. I needed to face you. So I built myself back up, got my thoughts straight, then came to find you.'

'Where did you go? Where have you been staying?'

'With my parents back in Exeter. While there, I learnt that Karin apparently committed suicide because she was clinically depressed. Which I didn't want to believe, but now my head is clearer I remember the lorry driver saying there was nothing else on the road to explain what had happened. At the time I thought maybe she'd swerved because of a rabbit, a fox or a deer – anything. I mean why would a healthy human being just move to the wrong side of the road and hit a lorry?'

'She wasn't overtaking another vehicle?'

Harry shook his head. To this day, the accident had never made sense.

'I'd sent Karin a message to say I was running late. She never told me she'd phoned in sick at work. All I got in a text was 'I'm sorry', which I never saw until after the accident, because I'd been driving.'

Harry brushed his hand along Maddy's cheek, looking from her slightly parted lips to her eyes. How did he convince her he'd made a mistake? How did he regain her trust? 'Maddy, I love you. I am so sorry, and I really regret running like I did. Tell me what I have to do to fix this, and I'll do it.'

***

Maddy hung on Harry's words. His hand still held her chin, and she thought he was going to kiss her. Would she stop him if he did try? The distance between them on the bench had reduced, their knees touching, his heat radiating up her thigh. The buzz of electricity between them reminded her of the first days they had shared together in the summer. Her gaze flickered between his gently parted lips, and then his blue eyes; from their colour, you'd think he was a man of ice, but he was the warmest person she'd ever known. She longed to be intimate with him again, but it could not be out of pity. Should she give him one last chance? Her heart pounded as their heads edged hesitantly closer, tilting to touch lips. *Be brave . . . kiss him . . .*

A dog barked, Maddy jumped, and exhaling, she pulled away. A man and his collie strolled past on the path, silently apologising for the dog's sudden outburst with a wave and a nod. The dog wagged his tail, then sank to all fours, eager for his owner to hurl a ball.

She looked at Harry, who'd rested an arm on the back of the bench, looking more relaxed and casual, as if talking about the past had helped relieve the tension and stress he'd been carrying. His hand brushed her upper arm.

'If you need time to take all this on board, Maddy, I understand. I know I've hurt you.'

'I . . .' she hesitated. 'I've got so much going on in my head. Mum, Connor, then you turning up.'

'I know, it's unfair of me to pressure you,' he rubbed his hands down his jeans, 'I'll give you some time to think about it. I'm not going anywhere. Well, except back home, to Cornwall, as I haven't really come prepared today. No hotel, fresh clothes, nothing.' He chuckled. His expression sobered, and he leaned in, kissing her cheek, the gentle warmth of his breath sending a tingle down her neck. 'You know where I am if you need me. This time I will answer my phone. I promise,' he said, then hesitated. 'I love you.' His last three words were exhaled with his breath as if spoken from the depths of his heart, the effects rippling into her own heart.

Maddy watched him stand up, stretching out his long legs, as he looked at her thoughtfully, his blue eyes hopeful but sad. He took another look at the Suspension Bridge then started walking back the way they'd come. She hated the feeling of watching him go even though he'd promised he wasn't going for good. He was giving her time, but she felt empty, hollow and alone. An ache in her chest swelled, rising to her throat. She feared she would lose him. She'd only just got him back.

The wrench of him parting from her, even momentarily, and not necessarily even forever spurred Maddy into action.

'Harry, wait!' She ran after him. He stopped and turned,

and she thrust herself into his arms, unbalancing him a little. 'I don't need to think about this. I know what I want – you!'

Harry's hold tightened around her back, pulling her closer, lifting her off her feet to kiss him. As their kiss deepened, her feet gently found the ground, but her arms wove around his neck, pressing their bodies together as close as their clothes would allow. The buckle from his belt dug into her stomach, but she didn't care. How long they stood, embracing, Maddy didn't know. The kiss sealed the weeks they'd spent apart, a promise to do things better. His touch was gentle and loving and she reciprocated. This one pure, whole heart-stopping kiss, would stay with Maddy for the rest of her life.

'Shall we both tell my parents what happened today?' she said, finally tearing away from Harry's lips but unable to let go of him. 'This way you can meet them under better circumstances, my mother will love you for being the hero, and you'll be forgiven for making me miserable these past few weeks.'

'If you think that's the best way forward, then I'm happy to go with it. I won't let you down again, Maddy – not intentionally. I promise.'

'I know you won't.'

Epilogue

'H mmm . . . How many nights have I stayed at yours now?' Harry nuzzled into Maddy, trailing kisses from her neck, down her naked back.

'Harry, you've not slept in your bed for a couple of months now.' Maddy laughed and sighed, his kisses sending a pleasurable sensation through her body, better than a warm bath. 'We said we'd take it in turns, remember?'

'But your bed is so much more comfortable than mine.'

Maddy doubted it. His bed was bigger.

'You know, I've been thinking about this.' He propped himself up on his elbow. He was fully dressed and ready for work. Maddy didn't need to get to the gallery so early in the winter months. Harry had a landscape project thirty minutes' drive away so was leaving the house while it was still dark to miss the traffic. 'It's a waste to have two houses; maybe we should live in one bigger house.'

Maddy sat up, scratching her head. 'What . . . buy a place together?'

'There's a place up for sale in Tinners Bay. Come and see it with me today.'

The gallery would be quiet. Valerie and Maddy were basically painting as much as they could, fulfilling commissions and using the gallery more as a studio than anything else. She'd easily be able to get away for an hour, and she'd already be in Tinners Bay. 'Yes, okay.'

'Great.' He kissed her. 'Meet me at Wisteria Cottage.'

Maddy frowned. 'But that place sold weeks ago.' She'd felt sad upon hearing the news, although she wasn't sure it was actually called Wisteria Cottage, it was the name Harry and Maddy had always used for it, and it had stuck.

Harry shrugged. 'There's a cottage for sale near it. But it's easier if you meet me there.'

***

Around two in the afternoon, Maddy made her way up the familiar footpath, which ran along the right side of the beach, hugging herself for warmth. The December wind off the sea was freezing. She reminisced about the summer months, about walking along this path in her flip-flops. Now she was wearing leather boots, her thick winter coat, scarf, gloves . . . She could hear the sea roaring angrily as its waves broke and crashed. It would be cheeky to take the short cut through the back garden of Wisteria Cottage, so she continued past while having a nose over the low fence to see if she could catch sight of the new owners. How she envied them owning such a beautiful cottage. She could see the extension had been finished, and the garden, albeit dreary in these winter months, would be fantastic in spring. Harry had landscaped the areas she'd suggested, putting in a little patio and then a decked area further up to capture the sun at different times of the day. She hadn't been able to find out if it was going to be let as a holiday home, or be lived in. Even Valerie had been unable to find out about the new owners from Roy.

Harry was standing outside Wisteria Cottage when she arrived, actually on the doorstep, under the small porch. The new front door, freshly-painted lilac, contrasted nicely with the white-washed walls and grey slate tiles. Even on a dreary day, Wisteria Cottage looked pretty.

Harry plastered on a massive grin as he saw her. She remained at the gate.

'Harry, should you be in there? Which house are we looking at?'

Instead of mud, there was a recently laid crazy-paved path cutting through a new lawn, and to the right a driveway, also paved. Then, she noticed a small vine had been planted on the right side of the door, to train up the cottage. It was small and looked as dead as the bush that had been taken out in the summer, as it had no leaves, but the earth was dug over fresh.

'It's a Wisteria,' Harry said, watching her take it all in. 'I planted it – for you.'

'For me?'

He stepped aside revealing a slate wall plaque the other side of the door. It read in beautiful curly writing, 'Wisteria Cottage'.

'Oh, so the new owners called it Wisteria Cottage.' Maddy clapped her hands and walked towards Harry, although she felt like she was trespassing. Why she was excited, she didn't know. It wasn't her cottage.

'Yes, they did.'

He pulled his hand out of his pocket, and in his palm lay a key.

'What's this?'

'It's a key.'

She rolled her eyes. 'I know that, but aren't we supposed to be meeting an estate agent at another place?' She looked around, to see if there was anyone about. She hoped whoever did live at the cottage were not in.

Harry pulled a face. 'I told you that to surprise you.' He handed her the key. 'Open the door to your new home, Maddy.'

'You're kidding. How? When?' Maddy fumbled with the key, but it opened the front door. Harry was far from joking.

'I had a word with Roy. We agreed on a private sale, so I put my house on the market—'

'You've sold your house?'

'Yes . . . That's why I've been living at yours.' He winked. Maddy rushed through to the lounge. She knew the layout, but she had to check out the extension, see the place again. She'd dreamed of living here, never believing it would become a reality.

'Look at that view, Maddy. All your inspiration right on your doorstep.' Harry gestured out of the large window in the lounge. 'I was thinking you could have the bedroom above as your studio if needs be.'

'I don't know, I really liked it as the master bedroom.' Maddy couldn't believe it. 'Have you really bought this cottage?'

'Yes.'

'How?' Maddy blushed with her outburst. But even selling his own house, this cottage would surely have been out of his price range.

'I had savings from my house with Karin. When she died, her life insurances paid out, but I didn't like the idea of using the money. Until now.' He kissed her gently on the lips. 'Will you move in with me?'

Maddy's eyes widened with disbelief.

'Yes.' She didn't need to think about it. She kissed him.

'I know it was completely rash of me, and normally I would want to make the decisions with you as a partnership, but when Roy told me he intended to sell the cottage earlier than originally planned, I had to act fast – you know how places like this sell at lightning speed,' Harry said, reaching for her. 'I wanted to surprise you in a good way, Maddy, not take control.'

She nodded. Everything they'd done together so far had been a joint decision, a partnership. And admittedly, a girl liked the odd surprise. However, this was a pretty big one.

'And, as there are enough bedrooms, maybe we could think about filling them with a family.' Harry held her around her waist, his gaze never leaving hers. Then, taking Maddy completely by surprise, he dropped to one knee and produced a small, light blue box from the inside pocket of his jacket. Maddy swallowed, trying to calm her breathing, knowing full well it was a ring box. He opened it, and sparkling back at her was a solitaire diamond ring.

'Maddison Hart, will you marry me?'

Maddy looked at the ring, then at Harry, his blue eyes more sparkling and precious to her than any diamonds. Could she be any more surprised?

Her hands trembled as she reached for the ring. As she slipped it onto her ring finger, she smiled, and said, 'Yes.'

The End

Acknowledgements

Acknowledgements and huge thanks to:

Steve Miles for his firefighter expertise and showing me a horrifying DVD of how fast fire can truly spread.

Lisa Simpson for all her help on Crime Scene Investigation and answering my random texts swiftly.

Nick Blocksidge for his help with all the insurance questions I had.

And last but not least, Fay Jessop who has helped and encouraged me with the development of this novel. May our coffee meetings continue for many writing years to come!

Author's notes:
Padstow, Truro and Wadebridge are real places in Cornwall, however I may have tweaked their geography slightly to suit this book, so not all things mentioned may exist in these places.